Praise for
CAN I GET AN AMEN?

"A sparkling debut novel about dealing with family and finding love. An absolute treat!"
—Janet Evanovich, *New York Times* bestselling author of the Stephanie Plum series

"An emotional and satisfying novel that's as tender as it is funny—a fabulous debut that's fresh, honest, and addictive. Don't miss it!"
—Emily Giffin, *New York Times* bestselling author of *Something Borrowed* and *Where We Belong*

"Sarah Healy's *Can I Get An Amen?*'s wonderfully flawed heroine suffers like Job at the book's opening. Infertility, unemployment, divorce. At thirty-one, Ellen is forced to move back home to New Jersey, and in with born-again parents she can't relate to. Former enemies surface, as do old hurts and bad memories. . . . Funny, smart, wise, and refreshing, *Can I Get an Amen?* is the work of a great new talent and an obviously gifted writer. [This book] doesn't need my blessing to be a huge success!"
—Valerie Frankel, author of *Thin Is the New Happy* and *Four of a Kind*

"A soaring debut! Sarah Healy examines divorce, parental relationships, sibling relationships, religion, and love with humor, poignancy, and a compelling tension. *Can I Get an Amen?* is a beautiful story that will leave readers waiting breathlessly for her next book."
—Beth Harbison, *New York Times* bestselling author of *Shoe Addicts Anonymous* and *When in Doubt, Add Butter*

"*Can I Get an Amen?* is touching, funny, and full of heart. A highly entertaining novel about love and family, secrets and forgiveness. Don't miss it!"
—Lisa Scottoline, *New York Times* bestselling author of *Come Home* and *Save Me*

Can I Get an Amen?

. . .

SARAH HEALY

NEW AMERICAN LIBRARY

NEW AMERICAN LIBRARY
Published by New American Library,
a division of Penguin Group (USA) Inc.,
375 Hudson Street, New York, New York 10014, USA
Penguin Group (Canada), 90 Eglinton Avenue East, Suite 700, Toronto,
Ontario M4P 2Y3, Canada (a division of Pearson Penguin Canada Inc.)
Penguin Books Ltd., 80 Strand, London WC2R 0RL, England
Penguin Ireland, 25 St. Stephen's Green, Dublin 2,
Ireland (a division of Penguin Books Ltd.)
Penguin Group (Australia), 250 Camberwell Road, Camberwell,
Victoria 3124, Australia (a division of Pearson Australia Group Pty. Ltd.)
Penguin Books India Pvt. Ltd., 11 Community Centre,
Panchsheel Park, New Delhi - 110 017, India
Penguin Group (NZ), 67 Apollo Drive, Rosedale, Auckland 0632,
New Zealand (a division of Pearson New Zealand Ltd.)
Penguin Books (South Africa) (Pty.) Ltd., 24 Sturdee Avenue,
Rosebank, Johannesburg 2196, South Africa

Penguin Books Ltd., Registered Offices:
80 Strand, London WC2R 0RL, England

First published by New American Library,
a division of Penguin Group (USA) Inc.

First Printing, June 2012
1   3   5   7   9   10   8   6   4   2

REGISTERED TRADEMARK—MARCA REGISTRADA

LIBRARY OF CONGRESS CATALOGING-IN-PUBLICATION DATA:

Healy, Sarah, 1977–
Can I get an amen? / Sarah Healy.
p. cm
ISBN 978-0-451-23677-7
1. Life change events—Fiction.   2. Adult children living with parents—
Fiction.   3. Mothers and daughers—Fiction.   I. Title.
PS3608.E2495C36 2012
813'.6—dc23   2011048197

Set in Stempel Garamond Pro
Designed by Elke Sigal

Printed in the United States of America

For my parents, Peter and Maureen

ACKNOWLEDGMENTS

My sincerest thanks . . .

To my editor, Ellen Edwards, for her skill and patience in shepherding this book through the publishing process. And to my agent, Stephanie Kip Rostan, whose keen instincts and insights have been invaluable.

To my parents, Peter and Maureen Enderlin, for believing in me before I did.

To my siblings: Matthew Enderlin, for occasionally returning my calls; Jonathan Enderlin, for all of those delicious nuts; and Erin Enderlin Bloys, for loving this story despite the fact that I wrote it.

To my husband, Dennis Healy, whose kindness, optimism, and love have sustained me. And to our three beautiful boys, Noah, Max, and Oliver.

And finally, my deepest gratitude to my remarkable sister, Jennifer Enderlin Blougouras, without whose generosity of expertise, encouragement, and time this book would simply not exist.

Can I Get an Amen?

. . .

CHAPTER ONE

We loved Jesus. We loved Jesus and Jesus loved us. This was what we were told. This was the message that accompanied the lukewarm apple juice and stale Nilla Wafers we had every week in Sunday school. We were Christians, and that meant that an omnipotent and benevolent deity had our backs. He bestowed upon us his love in the form of blessings, which we preferred in lump sums, as *blessing* was often just another way of saying *tropical vacation* or *new car.* We had blessings. And we prayed for more.

We went to Christian camps where fresh-faced counselors with bangs and friendship bracelets coached us on accepting Christ into our lives. We said our prayers, we read Bible stories, and we never, ever played with Ouija boards. "Amy Jenkins used to play with Ouija boards," warned our mother with crossed arms and wide eyes. Yes, *Amy Jenkins.* She was once a sweet little blond girl whose well-respected family belonged to our country club. Now she lay foaming at the mouth and strapped to a bed in a mental institution. My mother's head began a subtle and rhythmic nod as we connected the dots; terrible things can happen if you allow Parker Brothers to patch you through to Satan.

Oh, Satan. He was a nasty one. Any ill that befell us could be attributed directly to the work of Satan and his minions. We understood that this was the primary reason for being a Christian, to avoid Satan and his black realm of fire, torture, and agony. It seemed pretty simple and really quite reasonable: just accept and worship God in the earthly realm and you could spend the afterlife lounging on fluffy white clouds. You could hear the clear, bell-like voices of angels rather than the eye-piercing shrieks of the damned. Those were the rules and we followed them. We didn't ask why.

But like a political party changing its platform to attract the next generation of voters, the God that we were presented with slowly evolved as we grew. The tit-for-tat God that slammed the pearly gates and shooed you away with a broom was replaced by more of a Match.com type of deity. "The Lord wants a relationship with *you*, Ellen!" my mother would plead. "Your heavenly father wants you to know him!" This was after I stopped referring to my parents, brother, and sister as *we*. This was when they were no longer able to force me to get into the car and attend a two-hour service where palm fronds were waved and demons were cast out. This was when I was supposed to be forming a new *we*.

I still selected "Christian" on hospital registration forms; it was as much a part of my makeup as other check boxes such as "female" and "Caucasian." I always cottoned to the concept of a God and was quite keen on the idea of his unconditional love. My mother claimed that she loved us all unconditionally, but we knew better. There was always a loophole.

"Would you still love me if I had a dead, milky eye?"

"I'd love you more."

"What if I was a porn star?"

"Ellen!"

There is a limit to human love.

I found this out when Gary came solemnly into the house one breezy summer evening in July. He set his briefcase on the floor and placed his keys quietly on the countertop. "Ellen, we need to talk." I could see how he had steeled himself for this conversation. How his shoulder muscles were tensed, how his face held that determined set. It was early, too. At least for Gary, who had been putting in twelve-hour days at the firm for as long as I could remember. It was eight o'clock and I was just finishing up the dishes from the dinner that now sat neatly organized in square glass containers in the fridge.

It turned out he wasn't, as he had said, "okay" with the fact that we might never have children. And since the problem seemed to be mine and not his, the solution was simple. I wrapped my arms around myself as I fought, with clenched jaw and scarlet face, not to cry.

"But the doctor said that we could try in vitro again," I managed.

He sighed, and only then did I see pain in his eyes. He pulled me to his chest and held my head against him, then spoke in quiet, sympathetic words. "Elle . . . we've tried that," was all he said as he silently tabulated the bill for his ideal family of four children.

"Maybe my parents could help this time," came my desperate, muffled words.

But there was the cost, and then there was the likelihood of success. And besides, blessings were few and far between these days, for both my current and my former *we*.

Gary left that night with a bag he had taken the time to pack that morning. A bag that had been sitting in the trunk of his car all day, a bag that knew before I did that my husband was leaving me. I wondered who else knew.

I stayed up until three a.m., sitting in a dark room in front of my laptop, poring over the same familiar Web sites and confessional posts in which sad, childless women talked about their feelings of failure, both as women and as wives. But rather than camaraderie, I felt nothing but animosity and resentment that I shared their emotions. *Fuck you,* I thought. *I am nothing like you.* I pictured a group of middle-aged women with faces like balls of rising dough sitting on folding chairs in some dank church basement, wads of tissues stuffed into the pockets of their terry-cloth sweat suits. *I* had done everything right. We had started trying three years ago, when I was twenty-eight. I was healthy and educated and I was *supposed* to have children. I fell asleep that night just knowing Gary would come back. That we would somehow conceive. Or that he would change his mind about adoption.

The next day, when I heard the clatter of dishes echo through the vacant house as I emptied the dishwasher, I began to understand what had really transpired the night before. I drove to work with no recollection of how I got there; I simply found myself at my desk, clicking through e-mails and drinking a cup of cold coffee. Throughout the day, I waited and prayed and pleaded that my cell phone would ring, that I would hear Gary's voice. And when I had to leave my office and face our home again, I held my breath as I turned onto our street, waiting to see him weeping on the porch with flowers in his hand. He would fall onto his knees and beg me to forgive him. It was only when I slipped my key into the lock and shoved open the front door, swollen from the summer humidity, that it all began to seem real. It was then that I decided to call my mother.

Her heart broke for me in a way that only a mother's can. It was a brief conversation. I told her that Gary was leaving, or rather that he had left, and I told her why. She wept and moaned and offered to drive up from New Jersey to stay with me. "No," I said. "Please don't, Mom." I know that when I hung up, she got down on her hands and knees and begged God for his mercy. During those first few nights, when I felt the gash of loss most acutely, I crawled down from my bed, clasped my shaking hands together, and did the same.

"Did you feel at peace last night?" she asked, desperate to think that her prayers were answered, silently saying another that my response would be yes.

I took a deep, relief-less breath. "Yeah, Mom. I did." It was a lie, but at least I was capable of showing mercy even if God was not.

"Oh, thank you, Jesus! I know how hard this is, Ellen. But this is just an opportunity to trust him. The Lord wants you to *trust* him."

While my mother turned to God, my sister, Katherine, turned to her wellspring of anger and hostility, formed when she was young and wild and believed what boys told her. By the time I was ready to talk to her, I welcomed it.

"That motherfucker," spat Kat. "That Gary-named, visor-wearing motherfucker."

"I hated that visor."

"I hope he marries some fat sow named Linda, and they spew out dozens of ADHD little freaks. I hope her vagina rips open during childbirth and for the rest of his life it feels like he is fucking a bowl of soup."

I hoped for worse. I hoped for unspeakable things. But it was all directed at my faceless replacement, a woman with a farm-fresh reproductive system that churned out healthy, fertile eggs by the dozens. Because Gary would move on and move on quickly; *that* I knew. He was single-minded when he wanted something, a trait I used to find admirable but now saw as borderline ruthless. And he wanted to be a father, more than anything. More than me.

Fatherhood was part of the idealized future he had concocted for himself as he spent his adolescence behind his brother's wheelchair, taking care of the two of them while his mother tried desperately to eke out a living. Gary had grown up in a working-class neighborhood outside of Boston, and his father had died suddenly of a heart attack when he was eleven, leaving the family, including his brother, whose body was captive to cerebral palsy, without life insurance or any real savings. Gary wheeled that chair through slushy streets during New England winters. He patched its tires and thwarted holes in the seat with duct tape.

We heard stories about families like this in church, and we prayed for them. We prayed that God would change their lives and that money and good health and comfort would flow to them in torrents. And then we went home and sat surrounded by our blessings. But Gary wanted to be the one to change their lives. He wasn't waiting for prayers to be answered, and he wasn't going to rely on the generosity of strangers. Gary was unfailingly devoted to his small, sad family, and *he* was going to be the one to pull them out of their shitty, gray little existence, with its chain-linked fences and one-bedroom apartments. His vision for the Reilly clan was straight out of Camelot. They were going to live like the Kennedys. His mother and brother would sit in comfortable, shaded chairs as he and his sons played touch football on the lawn of their well-appointed home. His wife would bring out a tray of iced teas for everyone after the game, and he would regale them with stories from the courtroom, where he was a living legend. I had been cast in the role of the lovely wife. And I am sure he appraised me like a Thoroughbred horse breeder. He noted my thick, shiny brown hair, my good bones, and the blue eyes that I had inherited from my mother. My tall, slender frame would marry nicely with his thicker, mesomorphic body. It was a good match, despite one quiet little detail that was lying in wait.

To his credit, Gary was well on his way to achieving his idealized future. He had gone to a well-respected Boston-area college, thanks to a combination of financial aid and scholarships. And after taking a few years off to save and work and save, he entered law school. He took out student loans and lived like a pauper, and because he didn't have a gray-haired father in a leather chair writing checks on his behalf, he had a ferocious ambition to succeed. But though he graduated near the top of his class and won a position with a well-known Boston firm, law school had left him with a hefty pile of debt, making more than two rounds of in vitro impossible, at least at present.

But he would soon find someone who would render that unnecessary. They would conceive without the aid of hospitals and drugs and procedures. Gary was a handsome, charming lawyer who wanted to find a woman to marry and have his children. He was a devoted son and brother and, to the right woman, I'm sure, husband. He wouldn't be single for long.

When Gary finally did call, three days later, he was all business. He gave me cursory apologies and told me that he did love me, that he always would, but then he changed the subject to the delicate matter of our divorce. I nodded and mumbled and was too dazed and wounded to take an active role in my fate.

Within two weeks, we had put our house on the market, the house that we had purchased when we planned on starting a family. It was a sweet little cape within walking distance of the local elementary school in an affluent Boston suburb. We had planted blueberry bushes, picturing barefoot children running out in the summer to fill their fists and mouths. There was an oak tree in the front yard that had the sort of low, horizontal branches that little arms and legs could scramble right up. And it had four beautifully dormered bedrooms that we planned to fill. It became my secret, masochistic indulgence to give myself unfettered access to those memories. To close my office door or drive aimlessly, draining tanks of gas, and let myself live entirely in a future that never had a chance of existing. To imagine the life of a mother.

"You need to get yourself to church," my mother urged, her faded southern accent always becoming more pronounced when imbued with emotion.

"I'm not going to church, Mom." I was tired of this conversation, of her easy answer to everything.

"Church is where you go when facing these things, Ellen. That's what churches are for." I could imagine her emphatic gestures as she spoke, her gray bob bouncing with every exaggerated shake of the head. "They are there to help you get your eyes on the Lord when you're broken."

"So I sing songs and shake hands and tell my neighbor that God loves them; that's going to help me in some way?"

My mother paused. "Don't let this make you bitter, Ellen. Your creator has a plan for you. He knows your future."

I rolled my eyes. "Church isn't where I need to be right now, Mom." Work was. Work was where I should be. It suddenly seemed so clear.

During those first few weeks, I threw myself into my job more ferociously than I had in years. There had been too many late arrivals due to doctors' appointments, too many hours spent perusing fertility Web sites that all offered the same advice and encouragement. I was newly rededicated to my job and the timing was perfect. The small advertising agency where I worked was facing tough times as clients' wallets tightened and the unemployment rate continued to climb. The recession had been the media's singular focus for months, but it had been almost background noise to me, as I was on a relentless quest to conceive. Month after month I thought that this was the time it was going to take; this time I would get pregnant. Then I would ride out my three trimesters and have the baby, and my career would go on an extended hiatus.

I hadn't told anyone at work that Gary and I had split up, so you really can't blame them for the timing. When they laid me off, I took the news with absolutely no fluctuation of expression. I didn't cry; I didn't frown or smile. I sat stone-faced as my humorless boss ran through her boilerplate speech, about the economy and budgets and how it was all business, nothing personal. I nodded along, as if to hurry her up. Then I told her that I understood, got up, and left. I had simply run out of devastation. *Good decision,* she surely thought. *Less deadweight around here.*

My relative composure was quickly replaced with monumental fits of self-pity. Oh, it was biblical, my plight! It was something straight out of the Old Testament. Left by my husband and relieved of my duties at work in the matter of a month. Surely no one had faced such tragedy! To ensure my cocoon of misery was impenetrable, I studiously avoided stories sadder than my own. I didn't want to hear about the six-year-old boy who was about to begin treatment, yet again, to rid his body of cancer. Or the single father of three who recently became a paraplegic. Perspective, whether delivered by my mother or by *People* magazine, was entirely unwelcome.

But our tragedies, no matter on which end of the spectrum they fall, often have a will of their own. And while I was myopically focused on my own recent blows to the gut, I had no idea that what I really needed to do was brace for the aftermath. Because it's after you think the dust has settled that life really gets to have its way with you.

CHAPTER TWO

"Just look at it this way." Luke grinned as he slammed shut the tailgate of my car. "At least you don't ever have to worry about your thirty-one-year-old daughter moving back in with you." I punched him in the stomach, which had a comforting layer of pudge despite his status as "single gay male." Only my brother, Luke, could get away with making a joke about both my infertility and my imminent move to my parents' house. Because only Luke would take three days off from work to help me pack up my things and make the drive back to New Jersey.

Of course it felt like another failure; I was joining the ranks of adult children living at home. Maybe if I had had more fight in me, I would have stayed. I would have found a new job, carved out a new life, joined a support group or two. But I have always favored flight. Even as a child, when mean-girl politics or shifting allegiances left me in the rotating role of outcast, I would run. I would fake sick or avoid recess or skip the party, because exile that was at least quasi-self-imposed allowed me the illusion of being in control.

I had my excuses, too. Thanks to the sluggish real estate market, the house hadn't sold, and the prospect of continuing to live there through the showings and open houses, with no job to escape to, seemed unbearable. Besides, "Vacated houses tend to move much faster," said our real estate agent through her cloud of suffocating perfume. I didn't know whether this was true or she just didn't want the stench of divorce hanging in the air, with our walls of missing photos and half-empty closets. And with every visit from Gary, always made during the day when I was at work, our house had begun to look more and more like the carcass of a marriage.

I wasn't bringing much with me just yet, mostly clothes, toiletries, those kinds of things. I had taken the time to pack some boxes with other personal effects but had stowed those away in the basement for now. So everything fit, though snugly, in my Volvo wagon. Luke, who had arrived by train, took on the role of driver and was kind enough not to delve too deeply into questions regarding my meeting with Gary the night before. In truth, there wasn't much to tell. An encounter that had taken on momentous importance in my mind had turned out to be a depressingly quiet and uneventful affair, like a funeral with a poor turnout.

We met at a Starbucks, where he sat reading the *Boston Globe* and sipping a coffee with Splenda and milk. I paused at the door, smoothed my sleeveless black wrap dress, and tucked my hair behind my ear. He stood when he saw me approach and gave me a long, tight hug. I hoped he could feel my pounding heart, my shaking body. I hoped that he understood what he was doing to me. I never thought I would feel so uncomfortable in the presence of my husband. I told him that I was going to stay with my parents for a while, that I had been laid off.

"God," he said, shaking his head, as if losing my job was what had just sent my life into a tailspin and his leaving me was nothing more than a bit of turbulence. Then he moved on to the business at hand, delicately reaching for the forms that needed my signature. "Formalities, as we discussed," he mumbled. I signed blindly, reading nothing. When it was finished, he told me again that he loved me and that he would be in touch soon.

Luke came with me to the group home where Gary's brother, Daniel, lived. I had wanted to say good-bye and drop off a few gifts, including a new Celtics T-shirt, the Celtics being the only entity that Daniel adored almost as much as he did Gary. While I sat chatting with Daniel, Luke stood on the sidelines, feeling the discomfort and pity felt by all first-time visitors. I could tell what Luke was thinking as he watched the palsied movements and heard the slurred voices. We grew up being told that God created each of us, handpicked our pieces and parts, both physical and otherwise. *What, then,* Luke thought, *had happened here?*

I told Daniel that I probably wouldn't be by for a while. *Ask your brother why,* I thought. *Ask him.* But from Daniel's behavior, I could tell that he had already been given the gist of it. As I got back in the car, I obsessed over what Daniel would tell Gary about our visit. When would Gary realize that he was making a mistake? His next wife wouldn't care this much about Daniel. She wouldn't bring him home every Sunday; she wouldn't take him to basketball games and movies. With a brood of children to look after, she would soon become too busy. He would become a nuisance, then a burden, before he was forgotten entirely. And what would happen to Daniel then? *Are you willing to sacrifice him, too, Gary?*

Though neither of us was a smoker, Luke and I bought a pack of Marlboro Lights and kept one burning for almost the entire car ride. We stopped only once, at a dismal little rest stop where a tiny Hispanic woman stood in front of a bucket of filthy water, absentmindedly pushing a mop across the brown-tiled floor. Once we hit the New Jersey Turnpike, the highway rose above the sort of postapocalyptic industrial wasteland that often defines the state, with heat rising in waves off the acres devoted to stacks of empty cargo containers and oil tanks. But soon the blinding late-August sun was tamed by the lush green of the sub-urbs, where the men who sat in window-filled corner offices in Manhattan skyscrapers kept their homes.

Luke asked me if Mom had told me the latest about our father's newest project, Channing Crossing, and the financial issues it was going through. "Yeah," I said, "she mentioned it." Due to my mother's almost biological need to prophesy doom, she had been *mentioning it* for months. My father, a real estate developer, had rolled the dice big-time on an enormous new mixed-use development in Pennsylvania that offered both hous-ing and commercial space. Then the real estate bubble burst and what had seemed like a potential gold mine turned into a major financial liability.

"I think it might be worse than she wants to admit," said Luke as he turned into the long paved driveway of my parents' very beautiful home.

I felt my shoulders tense. Things were supposed to be *better* than my mother indicated, never *worse*. "Like, how much worse?"

"I don't know, Elle. I just think it's weird that they didn't rejoin Rook National this year."

I thought back to the conversation in which my mother had

said that they didn't plan to renew their membership at the club. "But Mom said that Dad's shoulder has been bothering him too much for golf."

"I know," said Luke hesitantly. "But I think they are just temporarily in a tight spot. I'm sure it'll pass, though." And we both settled into that ambiguous but comfortable thought.

· · ·

"Oh, praise you, Jesus!" came my mother's elated voice as she saw Luke and me walk safely into the kitchen. She abandoned the bowl of pasta that she was tossing and, wiping her hands on a dish towel, bustled toward us. "I was so worried about y'all driving on that terrible I-95. Just last week someone from our church nearly had an accident with a tractor-trailer just outside Stamford." I was first on the list for a hug and she reached her thin little arms up around my neck. At five feet six inches, she was the shortest member of my family by three inches. "My little Ellen. My poor little baby girl! I am so sorry, Ellen." I hadn't seen her in person since before Gary left. "I know that you can't see it yet, but this is all part of God's plan for you."

"Mom . . . ," I started by way of a warning, but she had already moved on.

"Luke, thank you so much for going up there to help your sister." She held him long and tight and I knew what she was doing. She was doing what she had done each and every time she'd seen him since he came out of the closet: she was trying to pray the gay out of him. She was trying to save his soul. While my mother adored Luke, she didn't adore, as she put it, "his lifestyle." His being gay was incredibly hard for my parents to accept, so she adopted a bifurcated view of her son: there was the gay part and then there was the rest of him, the part that God had made. When my mother came up for air she eyed us suspiciously. "Have y'all been smoking?"

"Just crack, Mom," answered Luke. "Some blacks were selling it by the side of the highway."

She swatted him with a dish towel and dropped that line of questioning. "Daddy's going to be home later," she said as she pulled pasta bowls out of the cabinet. "He had some meeting at the bank." Luke shot me a meaningful look. "So, tell me," she went on. "How was the drive? Y'all have any close calls?" My mother viewed the perils of the American interstate system as a constant and relentless menace. She was always astounded when we managed to travel them unscathed and viewed our safe journey as nothing short of a miracle. Luke and I just shook our heads. "No?" she asked, sounding a touch disappointed. "Well, that was God's mercy."

She began ferrying pasta over to the table. "Lukie, grab some forks," she said, plucking a mushroom from the top of one of the bowls and popping it in her mouth. "I made that tagliatelle with the white wine–mushroom sauce that Aunt Kathy told me about. Wait till y'all taste it."

As she scampered back to the fridge to grab some Parmesan cheese, I noticed how her narrow hips seemed to swim in her white linen pants. "You look like you've lost weight, Mom." She was always on the slender side, but she was beginning to look fashion-editor thin.

"Everything gets harder when you get old, honey," she said as she flitted back to the table like a hummingbird. "Even eating." She plopped into her chair and I heard the clang of her heavy gold watch hit the table. It rested above the same hand that held her small, humble engagement ring, a relic from an earlier time.

Taking off her headband, she readjusted it on her head, pulling her silvery gray hair away from her face. "But I'll make up for it tonight. I'm starving." I stared at her for a moment. My mom was still beautiful, even without makeup. Her well-moisturized skin bagged beneath her eyes a bit but still clung nicely to her enviable bone structure.

Luke complimented the dinner, and my mother launched into detailed but characteristically frenetic instructions on its preparation. Her recitation of the recipe faded into background noise as I took in the room. My parents had built the house eight years ago, after I was already out of the house and living on my own, so I had never really spent much time there. The odd weekend here or there, maybe a week between Christmas and New Year's; that was it. The kitchen looked like it was lifted from one of my father's model homes. It was nice, very nice, in a ubiquitous granite-countertops-and-stainless-steel-appliances kind of way. It flowed into a living area that had cathedral ceilings with enormous windows flanking the massive stone fireplace. All the furniture was big. Big leather couches, big armoires, big oriental carpets. We sat at an enormous farm table that seated twelve, above which hung two big drum-shade chandeliers. Luke took a sip of water from a big goblet. I instantly missed my little cape.

Snapping me back to the present was my mother's voice. "So you saw Gary before you left?" Her thumb rubbed at her index finger, a nervous tick.

"Yeah," I said, twisting the stem of my water glass. "We met for a cup of coffee last night."

"And how'd that go? Do you think he's going to come to his senses?"

I slumped back in my chair. "I don't know, Mom. I kind of doubt it."

Her gaze darted up to a framed family photo that hung on the wall. Luke was fifteen, I was thirteen, and Kat was twelve. Her eyes lingered on Kat. "I don't know why God chooses to give children to some women and not others." Her expression was distant, as if she was trying to make sense of events from the past in the context of the present, as if it was all part of some complex equation that had to add up. Then she quickly shifted gears, telling us about Aunt Kathy's recent trip to Ireland. Aunt Kathy, for whom Kat was named, was my mother's only sister, and they were bonded in a way that none of us entirely understood. As siblings, we were all close, but Aunt Kathy and Mom were like veterans of the same war; they knew each other on a level that no one else could.

After dinner Luke offered to help bring my things upstairs. "Which room?" he called from the foyer, a bag in each hand.

"The blue room!" replied my mother. Gary and I had slept in that room before, with its calming mist-colored walls and big white bed. I liked the blue room.

By the time my father came home, Luke and I had brought up all my things and I was beginning to unpack. Somehow the physical act of unzipping suitcases with the intent of putting things in drawers—drawers that were not my own—summoned an unexpected and unwelcome sense of panic.

When I heard the echo of my father's heavy footsteps on the stairs, I quickly fought to regain my composure. "Where's my girl?" he called as he headed down the hallway.

Though I knew that he knew exactly where I was, I played along. "In here!" I said cheerfully as I blotted the wet streaks on my face with the backs of my hands.

The door cracked open and he stuck his head in. "Hey, Dad," I said, forcing a smile as I sat on the bed in front of an open suitcase, the bedside lamp giving off a soft, yellow glow. Somehow it was harder to see my father than it had been to see my mom. Gary was exactly the type of man my father had wanted me to end up with, his hardscrabble roots appealing to my father's up-at-dawn, midwestern sensibilities. "He's a self-made man," my father would declare proudly when describing Gary to his friends. These were churchgoing men, pillars of the community who admired ambition, perseverance, and a strong work ethic. "Put himself through college *and* law school. And you should see how wonderful he is with his brother."

"Oh, Ellie," he said sadly as he stepped inside and saw my red-rimmed eyes. He looked tanned and vigorous, his thinning white hair appealingly wind whipped. He sat down next to me and tousled my head gently. "Everything is going to be fine, kiddo. Just fine." He flashed the soft, comforting smile of a primetime network television father. "All this with Gary is going to work itself out." I sniffed and nodded. I hated to disappoint my dad. We all did. But one by one, each of us in our own way had let him down. Luke was gay, I was getting a divorce, and Kat . . . Well, Kat was Kat.

He gave me a kiss on the forehead and told me again that everything was going to be okay; then he went downstairs to begin an evening routine that involved a glass of Scotch, a leather chair, and Fox News. As soon as he closed the door, I lay down on the bed and wept, gripping a pillow against my face to muffle the sobs. It was an angry, indignant cry. But when I was fully purged, I clenched my jaw and balled my fists and vowed that that was it. I wasn't going to become some sad, barren spinster, puttering around my parents' house like an invalid. I was going to put one foot in front of the other and move on from this shit. I would get over Gary; I would accept our divorce. *God, she's so healthy,* people would think. *She's really pulled herself through all this.* And if I couldn't do it, then I would pretend to. I was good at pretending.

I ran a dry hand towel over my face and then marched downstairs to join my parents. I expected to find them in their typical posts, my father sitting back in his chair with his feet resting on an ottoman and my mother reclining on the couch, with her reading glasses on and a magazine splayed open and lying on her chest. But tonight they sat next to each other, their heads inclined in intense discussion. Over the relentlessly raised voices of their news show, I couldn't make out a single word of their conversation, but as soon as they saw me, they both adopted bright, easy smiles. Instantly, the concern and anxiety vanished from their faces so convincingly that I smiled, too. Turns out we were all good at pretending.

CHAPTER THREE

It was eight thirty a.m. and I was having a cup of coffee when the phone rang. My mother answered. "Oh, hey, Jill honey," she said with a smile. "She's right here." Jill and I had been friends for so long that she still knew my parents' home phone number by heart. There was something nostalgic about my mother handing me the phone to speak with Jill.

"Jillie, hi," I said, warmed by the very existence of my old friend.

"Elle, I know it's under terrible circumstances, but I am so glad you are back home."

"Thanks, Jill." Jill and I didn't need to go through the rote so-sorry exchange, as she was the one friend I had kept in touch with over these past few weeks.

"Listen, I'm going to pick you up in an hour. We're going to the mall. Kat's meeting us."

Jill was married to a successful businessman, Greg Wadinowski, whose family owned a chain of convenience stores. She had long ago given up the charade of her thirty-five-thousand-dollars-a-year PR gig, despite the fact that they hadn't yet started a family, and was now content to lunch and shop and worship the gods of retail. But Jill was so forthcoming and ironically without pretension that you couldn't hate her for it. Kat was a hairdresser with an irregular schedule who often had chunks of midweek time available for Jill's adventures, and the two had become very close over the years.

Jill picked me up in her late-model Range Rover and handed me a whole-milk latte from one of the few remaining locally owned coffee shops in our area. "I still can't believe you waste the fat grams on these milk shakes," she said, adjusting her large designer sunglasses. Her own skinny cappuccino, which was certain to contain at least a quarter inch of Splenda sediment, sat in the console cup holder.

I smiled. The Great Milk Debate had long been an issue between Jill and me. "I don't like skim," I said simply.

"Nobody *likes* skim," she said with disgust. "But to not drink it . . . that's like, that's like . . ." Jill was never very gifted with simile. While she spun her wheels, I took a gratifying first sip. Giving up, she shook her head and threw the car into reverse. "You don't deserve to be thin."

Jill and I had met when she was a pudgy seventh grader whose type A mother had her doing Weight Watchers at twelve years old. We both came of age during the days of the T-Factor diet, and Jill was still paralyzingly frightened of fat, the charter member of an increasingly large club whose ranks now included carbs, sodium, and alcohol.

On the ride to the mall, Jill caught me up on the gossip from our prep school, Horton Academy, a tony institution where Jill and I had bonded over our feelings of inadequacy. "You heard about Duncan Vose, right? And his movie that got all those awards at Sundance?" I had. "I never saw it," she continued, then added grudgingly, "But I heard it's actually pretty good." She went down the list of usual suspects—the boys we had crushes on, the outcasts who were now doing interesting and meaningful work, and the popular girls into whose ranks we were intermittently accepted. "And of course Parker Collins is still an evil bitch."

"You still see her?"

"Unfortunately. She's always decked out in some cotton-candy Lilly Pulitzer number. And she's in the Junior League. Who joins the Junior League these days?"

Parker Collins was our mutual high school nemesis, and our loathing of her always seemed to be rekindled when we were in each other's company. In twelfth grade, after circulating a very unflattering photo of Jill in her underwear with "Jillie Jelly" scrawled across the top in her bubbly, loopy writing, she started a rumor that I had given Mr. Ridley, our doofy twentysomething history teacher, a blow job, even going so far as to plant a pair of my underwear in his classroom. Parker's rumor mill was so well-oiled that both Mr. Ridley and I were called into the headmaster's office for separate but I'm sure equally humiliating rounds of questioning.

. . .

We walked in silence up to the mall, Jill staring into the mirror-like exterior windows and checking her reflection in the glass, always sucking in her stomach just a bit and holding her shoulders back. Jill was not fat, but she was also never going to be rail thin, no matter how many hours she logged at the gym. She just wasn't built that way. But she *was* beautiful, with a mass of blond curls, a heart-shaped face, and a smattering of freckles over her delicate nose.

Kat was at the makeup counter at Neiman Marcus when we arrived. When she saw me, she flashed her signature half smile and sauntered over to give me a hug. "So, when do we get to boil some bunnies?" she asked, rubbing her hands together. Then she threw an arm around my neck and leaned back to look at me. "You look good, Elle. I thought that maybe you'd have drowned your sorrows in spinach dip, but it looks like misery is agreeing with you."

Gee, thanks, Kat.

"Seriously. When Ali from the salon got divorced, she gained twenty-eight pounds in three weeks. Apparently it was all Subway."

"Subway?" asked Jill, horrified.

"Yeah. She was the anti-Jared."

"Kat," began Jill, switching gears, "your hair looks *amazing.* Who did it?"

"Jim," she said, giving her new do a little stroke. "If you're going chin length or shorter, you really need a gay."

Kat was constantly rotating through hairstyles, and at present her already naturally dark hair was dyed a shiny jet-black and cut into an Anna Wintour bob. I could see Jill trying to determine whether she could flatiron her blond corkscrew curls into submission to achieve the same look. But Kat preempted her. "Don't you dare cut your hair, Jill," she commanded. "It's beautiful. It's Botticelli hair."

Even though Kat was younger, Jill and I gave her total jurisdiction over matters of taste. She was always so effortlessly stylish, the type of woman you'd want to mimic, imitate.

"All right," Kat said, getting down to business. "I have a date on Friday. I need to find something to wear." Kat was always dating but never had a boyfriend, which she claimed was exactly how she liked it. Linking her arm through mine, my little sister led me into what was her prescribed course of treatment for what ailed me: shoes, salads, and sarcasm.

And that was how I spent the next couple of weeks, cosseted in the calming, sedative womb of marble-swathed department stores. It wasn't a bad little sojourn. Everything was so beautiful, so easy. If you wanted something, you just laid down your credit card and smiling salespeople would hand you a thick bag with a braided rope handle. "Have a great day," they'd say with a smile.

My mother eyed every new shopping bag with disapproval. "Ellen, you can't buy happiness," began her cliché lecture. "Only the Lord can bring you that." *Oh, really?* I wanted to ask. *You're not happy living in your six thousand square feet of hardwood floors and imported stone?* But that sort of confrontation was more Kat's milieu.

With Jill and Kat as my constant companions, it was as if I was able to hit rewind on my life, to a time before Gary. Before Boston and our house and three soul-destroying years of trying to have a child. I could pretend that none of it had ever happened, and I found that living in the past was a fantastic way to avoid the present.

I knew that reality would need to be dealt with at some point. And I waited with dread for my cue to come. So I'm not sure why I felt so utterly blindsided when it happened, when reality rudely and abruptly shook me awake.

We were sitting at a café in the mall having lunch. Kat was grilling me on how I was able to live so relatively contentedly with our parents. "Honestly, Elle. I don't know how you can deal with it, with all their James Dobson, Tea Party bullshit." I was about to tell her that Luke and I just didn't pick fights the way she did, but the instant I heard my phone ring, I was frozen. It was Gary's ring.

"What is it?" asked Jill.

I reached into my bag and stared at the screen. "It's Gary." My heart was racing.

Jill and Kat exchanged glances. "Pick it up!" urged Kat.

I stood and hit the ANSWER button. "Hi," I said cautiously as I made my way out of the restaurant.

"Hi, Elle. It's me."

"I know." *You don't have the right to identify yourself as "me" anymore*, I thought.

He cleared his throat. "Listen, I have some good news. Or at least I think it's good news."

And I totally fell for it. I thought he had reconsidered, that he wanted to work things out. The past eight weeks had been a nightmare, but our relationship was going to be even stronger now! I could go home and pack up my things and drive back to my little house and my husband's open arms. We could just forget about all of this. My father had been right: everything was going to be okay!

"Oh?" I asked eagerly, sweetly. Practically hyperventilating with anticipation, I paced outside the café, waiting for whatever form his apology would take.

"Yeah, so I've been doing some thinking. We don't need to find a buyer for the house." Oh, here it was! "If you'll agree to it, I'd actually like to purchase your half from you." And for a moment, my heart stopped beating. I turned to the wall next to me and leaned my forehead against the cool stone surface.

"Elle?"

I didn't answer.

"Elle, are you there?"

I couldn't formulate words; I was lost and spinning. I was too stunned to cry, too stunned to speak. And then I heard her voice. It was a seconds-long sound bite before the unmistakable rustle of a hand covering the mouthpiece of a phone. I couldn't even make out what she said, but I knew exactly what had happened. Just a little misunderstanding. She hadn't known Gary was making *the call* and came into the room to ask him where he wanted to go for dinner or if he'd seen her sunglasses. As soon as she saw he was on the phone she clamped her hand over her mouth and Gary's hand darted to the receiver.

"Who was that?" I asked, suddenly fortified with fury.

"What? That was nobody," said Gary quickly. "It was just a friend."

I felt venom creep into my voice. "You know, we're still married, Gary. Did you forget that little detail? The divorce isn't final yet."

"Ellen, please don't be like this."

I hated the reasonable, calm tone he was using. "Be like what, Gary? Be like any other woman who just found out her husband is cheating on her?"

"It's pretty clear that our circumstances are a little different from that," he said, bristling at his morals being called into question.

My mind was working quickly now and I suddenly understood how divorces became hateful and bitter and cruel. "Well, I guess some funds that weren't available for in vitro have suddenly been freed up for a real estate opportunity."

"Ellen, stop. It's not like I have an offshore account. I'll take out another mortgage. This really isn't at all uncommon in situations like ours."

"You want the house, Gary? You can have the fucking house."

I hung up the phone, but I didn't cry.

CHAPTER FOUR

I went out that very night. I put on my sexiest underwear and lowest-cut top and went out to meet men. "What bar should I go to?" I asked Kat, determined and furious, leaning into the mirror as I smeared charcoal gray shadow onto my eyelid.

"Elle, why don't you just give it a little bit. Maybe it's not a good idea tonight."

We sat in my bathroom at my parents' house, Kat's very presence there an indication of how concerned she was. Although she lived only twenty minutes away, she tended to make only obligatory visits on holidays and birthdays. "Kat, I need to go get a drink."

"Fine," she said. "I'll come with you."

Kat drove us to a bar near the train station where commuters into New York often stopped for a drink before heading back to their waiting wives and sleeping children. I ordered a Manhattan and immediately tried to adopt the persona of a fun, carefree girl out for a night on the town. I was all hair flips and smiles. Kat regarded me warily as I tried to engage her in meaningless small talk, as I batted my eyes at attractive older men with loosened ties, silently pleading that they return my attention. We both knew that I was holding on by a very thin thread. Soon, a decent-looking guy offered to buy Kat and me a drink. Kat turned it down—she was still nursing her glass of white wine—but I happily accepted and proceeded to flirt desperately and shamelessly. He eventually moved on and I ordered myself another drink. Then another.

"Elle, I think we better get going."

"Come on, Kat. Please. Just stay." My words were starting to slur and I was rapidly approaching the kind of sad, sloppy drunk that's no longer fun. That's too revealing to be fun. I was a wounded, pathetic divorcée who wanted, who *needed*, to believe that she was still beautiful, that she still had a chance, that she was still—despite all evidence to the contrary—a woman.

. . .

I started going out a lot, with Kat or Jill when they could be convinced to come, and often by myself. I never really wanted anything more than a bit of male attention. But sometimes a hand would run up my thigh or a fingertip would brush against my lips, and I would find myself pressed against a cold brick wall, the cool fall air mixing with alcohol-heavy breath as a stranger and I kissed in that frenzied, wild way of two people who have no illusions of love or a relationship. It was cheap and fast, but I never let myself sleep with any of them. When the suggestion was eventually made that we move on—to a car, a hotel, my place—I'd back away, wipe my mouth, and say that I had to get going. Maybe it was that I still considered myself a married woman, but I think it was more likely some dim, fledgling sense of self-preservation; on some level I knew that once I slept with a man, I wouldn't be able to pretend anymore. He'd leave me weeping and shaking in a hotel room as he hurried down the hall, wondering how he had managed to pick up such a basket case. Psychiatrists would say that I wanted to be the one to leave, and I'm sure they'd be right. Once, I let a man go down on me in the bathroom of a bar. I leaned right up against the door, closed my eyes, and tangled my hands into his thick, dark hair. But that was the furthest it ever went.

If they asked for my number, I'd give it to them. Sometimes they'd call. I had no trouble attracting men, but a few minutes into a conversation they'd sense that I wasn't good for more than an evening of entertainment. I wasn't, as the cliché goes, the type of girl they'd take home to Mother. I'd let the intervals between flirtatious smiles get a little too long or cast my eyes about the bar distractedly, looking for something that wasn't there.

The lectures from Kat and Jill eventually stopped, though my mother stubbornly continued to attempt her version of talking some sense into me.

"You aren't dealing with your pain, Ellen. I know a wonderful Christian counselor that you should just *talk* to."

"Good-bye, Mom," I would say as I slung my purse over my arm and headed defiantly out the door.

"God loves you too much to let you continue down this path!" she'd call after me as I stomped toward my car, feeling a heady rush from the rebellion, feeling like Kat always must have felt.

Though my mother was an expert at melding dime-store psychology with religious dogma, in time even she bit her lip. Instead, she scurried around the house having hushed conversations with the women from her prayer group, conversations that I myopically thought were limited to me. I sensed that my father was avoiding me. Everyone treated me like I was one step away from the deep end, and like any false move could send me plunging into true blackness. In time, I preferred to go out alone.

. . .

Luke led a busy life in New York, so his information regarding my behavior came by way of regular updates from my mom and Kat, both of whom tended toward hyperbole. Luke was initially skeptical that things were actually as bad as they claimed. He said as much over dinner one night at a trendy noodle bar in the city. We sat across from each other on wooden benches in the austere but bustling dining room.

"So," he began, with an expression that was meant to put me at ease. "I hear you've been auditioning for *Girls Gone Wild*."

I fished around in a steaming-hot bowl of brothy noodles with a pair of chopsticks. "Did Kat tell you that?"

"Well, I took a little poetic license, but yeah, she and Mom both said that you've been going out, like, a lot. Like a-Lindsay-Lohan lot."

Shaking my head, I gave an exasperated little chuckle. *Oh, those two!* "I mean, I've definitely been going out, but I was married for four years and with Gary for two years before that. I'd say that I'm just cutting loose a little."

"That's kind of what I told them, but even Kat thinks it's gotten . . ."

"What?"

He looked me right in the eyes. "A little out of control."

"Lukie, come on! You know how Kat and Mom completely blow things out of proportion. It's the one thing they have in common."

"All right, but you should probably chill out a little. You need to start figuring shit out, you know?"

"What do you mean?" I was on the defensive now. "What do I need to *figure out*?"

"Like, what you're going to do for money?" he began, astounded that I needed him to recite what should have been my ever-present concerns. "When you're going to go up to Boston to deal with stuff? Where you're going to live?"

I took a sip of wine, angry that Luke had managed to sour what was hitherto a perfectly enjoyable evening. "Well, thank you, Luke, for accurately framing for me what a train wreck my life is right now."

Luke sat back and eyed me with that same look of serious yet tentative concern that I had seen on the faces of my parents, my sister, my childhood friend, even the occasional bartender. It was clear that the sudden change in my mood confirmed in Luke's mind everything that Kat and my mother had been telling him. Breaking eye contact, he searched about the room for something, anything else to discuss with me. We spent the rest of the evening making the kind of meaningless chitchat that you might hear between two acquaintances who happened to sit next to each other on the bus, when they would really rather have ridden in silence.

I had driven to Hoboken and taken the PATH train—New Jersey's version of a subway—into the city. After the de facto interminable wait during the non–rush hour time period, I finally boarded a car and made the trip back to my side of the Hudson. Hoboken was a busy town on a Friday night, chock-full of the sort of fresh-to-the-workforce college grads who slipped out of their Brooks Brothers suits and into baseball caps before heading out for drinks. I made my way past the bars, their flashing flat-screens eternally tuned to ESPN, to the parking lot where I had left my car. It was an unseasonably warm evening, so I walked slowly, catching snippets of sidewalk conversations between friends, lovers, and those who fell somewhere in between. On the drive home, I was beginning to feel the nagging call for self-reflection that always followed sobriety, so before heading back to my parents', I pulled off the interstate and headed to the bar that I had gone to with Kat on that very first night—and many nights since.

The bar masqueraded as a restaurant, so there were a few tables of customers finishing a late meal of pretentious but unre-markable fare. The bar was large and U-shaped, and the decor tried to approximate what the owners must have viewed as a New York look, but it was sadly a miss. Above the bar's shiny, galva-nized steel surface hung sleek, modern-looking pendant lights, which fought to illuminate the charcoal gray walls. It looked as though the renovation was a couple of years old, and all the clean lines and sleek surfaces had started to show some dings and dents, making the place look cheap and prematurely past its prime. The crowd was the usual, traders who should be home by now but were looking for a balm for the wounds they suffered daily in the floundering market; older men on dates with blond, manicured women who were hoping to achieve the enviable title of second wife.

I sat down and ordered a scotch on the rocks, which had become my go-to drink, as I imagined that men found it sexy to see a woman with her hand curled around a lowball full of the rich amber liquid. So much more sophisticated than any sort of idiotic 'tini. When ordering, I pretended to care about the liquor's age and provenance, but all that mattered was that it would be soothingly numbing. As I watched the bartender add one, two, three cubes of ice, I noticed a man sitting across the way who seemed utterly out of place. He looked like he belonged in a hip New York boîte, not in this slick Jersified imposter. He had honey brown hair that was just long enough to look slightly disheveled as it brushed the frames of his thick black glasses, the sort that could be worn well only by a man with his sharp, chiseled features and strong jaw. His fitted, faded gray T-shirt looked like it was tailored explicitly to showcase his long, well-defined muscles. He was a man at whom everyone in the bar, female and male alike, found themselves involuntarily sneaking glances. But no one approached him. Something about him was too uncomfortably authentic. In a bar that was full of pretense and posturing, he sat sipping a bottle of Budweiser and quietly laughing with two of his friends.

I had to will myself not to stare at him, at all three of them. But he, in particular, looked so comfortable in his skin, so engrossed in conversation with his companions, that I found myself involuntarily drawn to him. After a few minutes, one of his friends, the tall, thin one, picked up a skateboard that was leaning against his stool, stood, gave his buddies a combo high-five/handshake, and left, still smiling as he slipped past frowning men and Botoxed, expressionless women on his way to the door. My eyes followed him out, and then I turned back to look for the man with the glasses, only to see that he had been watching me. His expression was not arrogant or mocking, but kind. I blushed and immediately turned away to see that someone had taken up the seat next to me, a man who looked about my age with a quick smile and well-cut suit.

He extended his hand. "Hi. I'm Ted."

I smiled and shook it. "Ellen." He launched into chitchat and

I was not at all surprised to learn that he was in sales. He was attractive enough, in a sort of frat-boy way, and had the kind of thick, dense body that looked strong and solid, but without much definition. He was easy to talk to, though, and provided a distraction from the man across the bar.

"So, where are you from?" he asked as he reached for the Asian snack mix in a small black bowl in front of us, pushing away the pieces that he didn't care for and digging around for the sesame sticks.

"Well, originally here, but I just moved back from Boston."

"Boston! Nice!" he said, happy to find a connection. "I went to school in Boston."

We went through the Boston thing. Where precisely I had lived, restaurants I liked, all of that. I steered clear of any reference to my marriage.

"So, Ellen from Boston, Sox or Yankees?"

I hated this question. Baseball didn't mean a thing to me, but to the type of person who asked this question, it definitely did. And ambivalence was unacceptable. I tried anyway. "Oh, I don't know . . . Baseball's not really my thing."

"Come on," he said, playfully pressing on. "You're from Jersey but you lived in Boston; you have to be either Sox or Yankees."

I could tell he was not going to give up. "Fine," I said, lifting my hands as if weighing my options. "Sox." It would be my final act of loyalty to Gary.

He lifted his glass in a toast to my apparently correct answer. "I knew I liked you, Ellen." And he bought me a drink. But unlike on dozens of evenings past, I found myself unwilling to overtly flirt, as I was constantly aware of the man across the bar. Ted was clearly interested, and he continued to try to make conversation, turning the topic first to real estate and then back to sports.

"I have a few trips planned to Boston this winter." He was staring straight ahead now, but I could see that he was gauging my every reaction, hoping to find my sweet spot. "My buddy works in management for the Celtics, so I go up there for some home games. I get amazing seats."

· "Oh, I love the Celtics!"

Bingo. His eyes brightened and something flashed there that I didn't quite recognize. I would later describe it as victory. He turned his whole body to face me. "Really?" he asked, clearly pleased. "You like hoops?"

I nodded, thinking back fondly to a very different time and place. A very different me. "Yeah, I do."

"You know, I've met a lot of those guys," he said, referring to the Celtics. "I have a basketball signed by last year's starting five."

I paused, remembering Daniel's face, ecstatic and engrossed, as we sat in the thundering Fleet Center, watching agile, superhuman bodies rocket themselves off the ground. "I know someone who would love to see that."

He jerked his thumb over his shoulder at the door. "It's in my car right now. I just brought it for an appraisal. Want to check it out?" He saw my hesitation. "My car's *literally* right outside."

I didn't really want to leave the bar to check out a basketball, even one signed by the Celtics, but Ted looked so eager, so proud. It would have been like disappointing a child. "Sure. Why not?" I said with a shrug.

I walked next to him with my arms crossed over my chest. Ted's hand hovered behind my back to guide me in the direction of his car, which was on the ground floor in a nearby parking garage. I started to feel inconvenienced by walking even the block and a half, which by definition was *not* literally right outside. Ted seemed like a nice enough guy, but I found myself wishing I'd found a way to politely decline.

It was late and the parking garage was all but empty, illuminated only by the streetlights outside. Ted hit a button on his keys and a huge black SUV gave an alert double-beep, beckoning us in its direction.

We were a few feet away from his car when I heard him stop. I reflexively tensed, some long-dormant, primal, preylike sense awakened. Glancing nervously back, I saw him gesture forward toward the car. "It's right in the backseat," he said with a smile that under the shadowy light no longer looked so innocent. "Just open up the door."

Only then did it occur to me how strange it was that he happened to have a signed basketball in his car. Frame by frame, I played out what was about to happen. I would open the car door, leaning in to look for the basketball, with a 225-pound man behind me in a dark, barren parking garage.

The car's interior light was on, but by now I didn't expect to see the ball. "Actually, Ted, I really need to get going." I started to step back, but he was right there. Spinning around to face him, I was now backed up against the cold, black metal.

"Come on, Ellen," he said, reaching for the handle and effectively wedging me tight between him and the car. "I thought you loved the Celtics." He was still playful, but this no longer felt like a game. None of it did.

"No, Ted, I really have to go." My heart started to race and I tried to push past him, but he caught me around the waist and pulled me into him from behind. Laughing and swaying, he held me tight, his arms reaching up around my chest to restrain me.

From a boyfriend or lover, it would have been an affectionate hold. "Whoa, where you going, huh?" he whispered in my ear, his breath thick with alcohol.

"Let me go!" I yelled, trying to twist free, but his hand darted up and clamped down over my mouth.

"Shhhh," he said, chuckling. "Relax, baby. I know you're the type of girl that likes to have a little fun." I could feel now how hard he was. He wanted me to feel it as he pressed himself against me. His damp mouth was again at my ear. "I've seen you before." And finally the tears came. They rolled down my cheeks in frantic, crisscrossing lines, forming tiny pools where they met his hand. I wondered if this was how it always happened, if all the aggregate mistakes of a lifetime suddenly crystallize the very second it becomes too late.

I didn't hear any footsteps and neither did he, but I felt him startle when we heard a man's voice from behind us say, "Let her go. Now." Strong and clear, the words overtook the empty garage.

Ted's body reluctantly relaxed; his grip loosened. An onlooker definitely put a crimp in his plans. I immediately broke away and reeled back to see the man with the glasses standing with his arms crossed, staring—almost menacingly—at Ted.

"Hey, man, listen," started Ted casually—he had slipped right back into his charming salesman mode—"I can totally see what this must have looked like, but I was just joking around. I wasn't going to do anything." He was so convincing, so totally believable, that I almost wondered if I had been imagining the danger, wondered if I was some hysterical girl who constantly had her finger on the trigger of a can of pepper spray, certain that every man was a potential rapist.

Without taking his eyes off Ted, the man with the glasses pointed in my direction. I was trying to steady my breath and control my tears, halting gasps ineffectively filling my lungs. "Does it look like she thinks it was a *joke*?"

Ted made a face, a petulant little puckering of his mouth that made clear it didn't matter what I thought. It was probably the same face he had been making since middle school: at teachers, at his parents, and at women he just happened to meet at bars. "Dude, whatever," he said, scratching the back of his head. "That chick is nuts. I was just trying to calm her down when you came."

The man with the glasses moved immediately, grabbing Ted by his shirt and slamming him hard into his shiny black car. Their faces were now inches apart. What the man said, I couldn't hear; I wasn't meant to hear. He spoke in low, whispered words, and from my vantage point all that I saw was Ted's face change. After a few breaths the man with the glasses slowly let go, then tentatively turned to me, as if not to alarm me.

"Are you all right?" he asked me softly. I only nodded, as I was still fighting the hysterical breaths escaping my mouth. "Come on," he said, his head tilted toward the street. "Let's get you out of here." And not for one moment did I hesitate.

We walked quickly and without speaking. I kept turning back nervously, expecting to see Ted following us, expecting to see him rush the man with the glasses from behind. "Don't worry; he won't come anywhere near you," he said, suddenly stopping. "My name is Mark, by the way."

I managed to speak, though my words came out in jagged, halted spurts. I sounded like a hysterical child. "My car . . . is on Summit . . . Street."

He shook his head. "No, you're in no shape to drive," he said definitively. "I can take you home."

"No, wait . . ." I squeezed my eyes shut to think. Though I felt an instinctive and almost reflexive trust in Mark, I knew that the sensible thing to do would be to call a cab, call Kat, anything but get into a car with another strange man. "I should just call my sister."

Mark nodded, seeming to follow my train of thought, and stood a respectful distance away while I pressed my cell against my ear. I expected to hear Kat's sleep-laden voice, reproachful and annoyed, but instead without so much as a ring I was sent to her cool, brief voice-mail greeting.

After I was hung up on by one cab company and never actually reached a human being at the other, Mark looked at me hesitantly, his hands in his back pockets. "Sometimes they just let it ring and ring at this time of night." I nodded and looked around, as if expecting some other solution to suddenly materialize. "Listen," he said, "why don't you just let me take you?" I looked at him, searching his face for something that would give me pause. "I promise I'll get you home safe."

"Okay." Tears began to well up in my eyes again. "Thank you. Thank you so much."

He smiled a small, sympathetic smile. "My car's this way," he said, leading us on. It wasn't until much later that I realized his car was in the opposite direction of the parking garage from the bar. He didn't just happen upon Ted and me on his way home. He wouldn't have. How and why he found me there would become one of the many questions that I longed to ask him.

We approached a nondescript blue Subaru and he opened the passenger door. The seat held a scattering of papers and books, and he quickly gathered them up and tossed them into the backseat, muttering an apology about the mess before gesturing for me to sit and closing the door behind me.

I took a deep breath and rested my head against the headrest, letting it all hit me. The gratitude, embarrassment, humiliation, and fear. I had been so stupid. Fresh tears began to spring from my eyes and I quickly brushed them away as Mark opened the driver's side door. He sat down and pulled an iPod from his pocket, plugging it into a tangle of wires and adaptors hanging from the dashboard. Bob Dylan blasted unexpectedly loudly from the speakers before Mark quickly adjusted the volume. Afraid to look at him, I stared toward the ceiling, hoping to maintain some control. I felt his hand hover lightly above my forearm, and I let my eyes focus first there, then on his long arms strapped with sinewy muscles, before meeting his eyes. He had the most sincere, intelligent, dark brown eyes.

"Are you sure you're all right?" he asked. In the dim light of the car, I took in his face. He was also older than I had thought, probably a few years older than me, with a smattering of crow's-feet and long fine lines running across the width of his forehead, which added an element of depth to his otherwise surreally handsome face.

"I'm okay," I said, even though I knew it wasn't entirely true.

He sighed and ran his fingers through his hair before sticking his key in the ignition and coaxing the engine to life. The wagon was a standard, and he stepped onto the clutch and grabbed for the gearshift. He was about to move it into reverse when he stopped, as if deliberating, and turned to look at me. He opened his mouth to speak, then closed it again before finally saying, "You shouldn't punish yourself."

I didn't know if he meant for tonight, for what had happened with Ted, but it seemed that his meaning went deeper than that, that though I had never laid eyes on him before, he had somehow seen what I had been doing, and he knew why.

CHAPTER FIVE

He waited while I wept into my hands. Like any man, he tried for a while to calm me down, saying how sorry he was for upsetting me, that he only meant I hadn't done anything wrong, not to blame myself. But then he just sat wordlessly. When I finally stopped, I apologized. "I'm so, so sorry," I whimpered. "I didn't mean to ruin your night."

He smiled kindly. "You didn't ruin my night. But maybe now you could tell me your name?"

I blushed, realizing that this man who didn't even know my name was witness to so much. "Ellen."

"Ellen," he said, trying the name out in his mouth. "So, where do you live?"

I launched into another round of apologies, saying how I couldn't believe that I had just let him sit there, how inconsiderate I was. But he chuckled good-naturedly. "Please don't worry about it." Glancing at the clock on his stereo, I saw that it was two thirty in the morning.

I directed him to Kat's condo, reaching deep into my bag to confirm the presence of the spare key that I had figured I would never have occasion to use. Kat's was closer than my parents' and for some reason I didn't want him to see their large, handsome home.

The ride to Kat's took ten minutes, during which I tried to think of topics of conversation that wouldn't seem either silly and inconsequential or heavy and intimate. I asked him about his friends, making sure that they weren't stranded without a ride home. "Don't worry about those guys. O'Brien had already left and Jay can take care of himself," he said.

My stomach lurched when we turned into Kat's complex and I realized that I had to leave him, that I had to stand up and open the door and get out of his car. I felt immobilized. It was so much more than a physical attraction; I just couldn't imagine him driving away, and never seeing him again. I told myself that it was because he had saved me. There had to be a name for what was happening to me, that some doctor had given an eponymous title to the condition of being attracted to your rescuer.

"So," he said, eyeing the white buildings, the car creeping forward, "which one is yours?"

I pointed toward Kat's. "Number seventy-eight."

He pulled right up front and double-parked, the emergency brake creaking compliantly.

He turned to face me, then smiled again kindly. "Ellen, you take care of yourself, okay?"

"Thank you for everything, Mark." I hesitated, not wanting to leave. As we stared at each other, I sensed that we both had more to say, but neither one of us spoke. Finally, I reached for the door. "Well, good night."

"Good night."

He didn't leave until I was up the stairs and had opened Kat's door. Dead bolting it behind me, I slipped off my shoes. I pulled out my cell phone and scrolled to my mother's name, sending her a text to let her know that I was sleeping at Kat's, a fact that I was sure she would check in the morning.

Kat's condo was beautiful but surprisingly traditional. Most people expected her to live among clean modern furniture arranged with a minimalist's eye, but Kat's place was all about comfort. Thick, cable-knit cashmere throws were draped over big white slipcovered couches. The hardwood floor was partially covered with a nubby wool area rug, and her old TV was hidden away inside an imported Balinese armoire. Everything was serenely soft and neutral.

I tiptoed up the stairs and creaked open the door to Kat's room. She immediately jolted up in bed, squinting toward the door.

"Kat, it's me."

"Ellen?" she asked. Her usually sleek hair was in disarray and she was wearing a hideous V-necked nightshirt that had slipped off one shoulder. My mother gave us nightshirts each Christmas, and, surprisingly, Kat actually wore hers. "They're comfortable," she'd claim when Luke and I would tease her. This one had a frolicking dolphin pattern, as they all tended toward the juvenile and girlie. My mother usually had better taste, but I imagined that she still liked to picture us sleeping in a pastel pink bedroom with a crucifix above the bed and white cotton underwear in the drawers.

I walked over to Kat's bed and slipped off my cardigan, tossing it on the chair in the corner.

"Ellen, what's wrong?" she asked, more alert now.

She reflexively made room in her bed and I slid in next to her under the fluffy white down comforter. We nestled into each other like we had done as children, when one of us was scared or in trouble. It used to be Kat who came red eyed and sniffling into my room.

Again I found myself fighting tears. "I have been so fucking stupid, Kat."

I felt her chest rise and fall. "At least you know it now, Elle," she said. Her voice was laden with a fatigue that came from more than sleep.

· · ·

I told Kat everything that had happened, with Ted and then Mark. She listened, and I could feel her rage building. "You need to go to the police. You have to have that asshole arrested."

"Go to the police and tell them what, Kat? That some guy lied about a basketball and put his hand over my mouth?"

"That's not what happened."

"But that's how he would make it sound. Believe me." And even Kat couldn't argue with that.

I could tell that she was suspicious of Mark, and heard her disapproval when she learned that he had driven me there. "You shouldn't have gotten in the car with him, Elle."

I let my head cock to one side. "Check your voice mail, Kat. What was I supposed to do?" I waited for her to become visibly chastened before continuing. "Anyway, I promise that it was totally safe. He wasn't going to do anything."

"Elle," she said, "frankly, you don't have much credibility as a judge of character right now." And it was my turn to be silenced.

All my concerns and regrets competed for attention, keeping

me awake long after Kat had fallen back asleep. I thought about Gary and the divorce, how stupid and reckless and selfish I had been. I saw Ted's face and felt his heavy hand over my mouth, feeling a shame that was so unbearable, I had to relieve myself with thoughts of Mark. Thinking about him was like a respite from the rest of it.

The phone gave a jolting ring at exactly 6:03 a.m., and we both knew exactly who it was.

"You talk to her," commanded Kat, facedown next to me, her voice muffled by a pillow.

I reached over and grabbed the portable, waiting for the caller ID to confirm what I already knew. Again the phone rang loudly, frantically, demanding to be answered, as if it understood the urgency felt by the caller.

"Hi, Mom," I said, feeling like a guilty child.

"Ellen! I can't believe you think you can stay out all night long. Your father and I—"

"Mom, I texted you. I wasn't out all night," I said, weakly defending myself. "I slept at Kat's."

My mother was fiercely intuitive and sensed from my softer, almost contrite tone that something was wrong. "Oh my Lord . . . What happened, Ellen?"

"Nothing, Mom." I felt my face redden, and my voice cracked. "I just woke up." *So to speak.*

. . .

"You need to give me another couple of hours," muttered Kat. But my mind was already spinning, so I went downstairs and made a pot of coffee. Kat had recently redone her kitchen, and like the rest of the condo, it was understated and elegant, with white cabinets and soapstone counters.

We had all shaken our heads and clucked our objections when Kat had decided to become a hairdresser. *What a shame,* everyone thought. She was always the most athletic of the three of us and seemed to cruise by academically with very little effort. She may have been the one for whom our prep school education paid out its dividends, until, as it was whispered, *she threw it all away.*

But being a hairdresser had worked out nicely for Kat. She worked in one of the best salons in New Jersey, cutting and coloring the hair of the women who would normally go into New York for that sort of thing. Her schedule was fairly flexible and she never tried to make any inane conversation with her clients, garnering her big tips for the peaceful hour and great blow out. She *heard* a lot, though, often calling with bits of gossip about people we knew. "Remember Ashley Morrow?" she would say. "Two years ahead of me, one ahead of you? Anyway, her mother is leaving her father *for a woman.*" Kat was no prude, but she knew how scandalized the Morrows' circle would be; anything having to do with homosexuality always sent the WASPs lunging for their vodka tonics.

Finally Kat padded downstairs and poured a cup of coffee, joining me at the breakfast bar.

"The kitchen looks nice, Kat."

She ignored me and took a sip. "Thank God you made the French roast. I have some hazelnut shit that my neighbor gave me. I was afraid I'd come down to my house smelling like a Yankee Candle shop."

"Why don't you throw it away?" I asked, knowing Kat's distaste for flavored coffee.

"Because Mrs. Martin is a sweet little old lady, and if she comes over I'll have to make her some." Kat really was so much kinder than she wanted anyone to know.

. . .

It was Friday, Kat's busiest day at the salon, so she dropped me off at my car on the way to work. As we turned onto Summit Street, I craned my neck to spot it, half expecting it to be gone, a penalty exacted in lieu of the danger I had escaped. But my car stood exactly where I had left it, looking conspicuously static. It felt like everything had changed, but here was my silver Volvo wagon, with not so much as a parking ticket to show for the events of the previous night.

"I'll check on you later," said Kat as we hugged good-bye.

When I got home, my mother was primed to take advantage of my vulnerability. Even though she didn't know what had happened, she *knew*. She always knew. Of course she could have no idea of the specifics, but in her mind the Lord had finally stepped aside, allowing me to see the inevitable and natural consequences of my behavior. That there were no phone calls from the police or hospital, no irreparable and devastating damage, was just further evidence of his goodness and mercy.

My mother realized that she had a window of opportunity to bend me to her will, and she intended to maximize it. She sat at the kitchen table, reading from *Evangeline*, one of her magazines that focused on the issues affecting the Modern Christian Woman. On the cover was a man staring lewdly at a computer screen, with a dreamlike bubble floating above his head featuring an amateurish montage of a marijuana leaf, a few lines of cocaine, and a stack of money. The cover line read, THE PRINCE COMPLEX. It was hopelessly goofy and out of touch.

"Hi, Ellen," she said, almost formally, when I walked in the door. "How is your sister?" It was unnatural, her speech, forced.

"Good . . . ," I said tentatively, placing my keys on the

counter. I knew what was coming, and I stood waiting for my mother's lecture like it was a flagellation.

She purposefully closed her magazine. "Ellen, I have kept my mouth shut over these past few weeks, but I've seen what you've been doing."

"I know, Mom. I'm really, *really* sorry."

She assertively raised one finger, her eyes flashing. "I'm not finished, Ellen. You are going to listen to me." She had been waiting weeks to give this speech and was not about to let me rush her through it. "You have been running away from your pain, trying to pretend that everything with Gary never happened. Instead of pressing into the Lord, you've been looking for escape in all the wrong places." She paused for effect. "You thought you could find comfort in *men*." It must have been with a heroic effort that she maintained eye contact, for any reference to sex, no matter how oblique, never failed to embarrass her.

"Mom . . ." I felt my face flush in humiliation.

"Not to mention how you've been hanging out at the *mall* all day." She said *mall* as if the word had a particularly offensive flavor. "You need to get your priorities straight. I know how much you have been through, but it's time to face reality."

"I know, Mom," I said as I stared at the shiny granite counter. "I'm going to look for a job. I'll start looking online today."

"I don't mean *start looking* for a job. I mean *get* a job. I don't care if it's at the supermarket." My mother sat up straight as she went in for the kill. "Your father and I also want you to start coming to church with us."

I sighed deeply and let my head flop back, but that was my only protest.

"I mean it, Ellen. That is our condition," she continued, primed for more of a fight. "If you want to live in this house and come and go as you please, all we ask is that you attend church and bring in an income. Your father and I can't support you indefinitely." There was an edge to her voice, a slightly hysterical twinge. Accurately interpreting my silence as acquiescence, she continued. "And the Arnolds are coming over for dinner tonight. We'd like you to join us."

"The Arnolds?" I said weakly. I knew I was beaten but had to make my displeasure known.

"Yes, the Arnolds," she said, daring me to push the matter further.

The Arnolds were the reigning monarchs of my parents' church. Edward Arnold had started a company that several years ago rode the wave of the technology boom and sold for hundreds of millions of dollars. He was now content to invest and donate, both of which he did with equal acuity. Christ Church now had an enormous new wing for its, ahem, *contemporary* services, the funds for which came from an anonymous donor who was anything but anonymous. Lynn Arnold was on the board of every conservative charity in the state and ran a weekly gathering for well-heeled young women at her house, at which she provided tutelage on how to be a "fine Christian wife." It was, she figured, the least she could do.

Only after my mother saw that her demands would be met with little resistance did she soften. "Come here, my baby girl," she said, standing and wrapping her arms around me. "With all that's happened, you've been trying to go it alone rather than relying on your *savior*, your heavenly *father*." Her hand stroked my hair. "We live in a fallen world, Ellen. Terrible things happen all around us. They happen to everyone, whether we see it or not. But it's Jesus who sees us through. He is the only thing that we can rely on always, for eternity." Slumping, I buried my face into her shoulder and, squeezing my eyelids together, felt tears escape from the corners.

I told my mother that I loved her and went upstairs. Turning the shower on hot, I let the bathroom fill with steam before I got in. Sitting on the floor, I watched great beads of condensation form on the mirror, growing heavy and fat before rolling down the glass, leaving thin lines of clarity. When I finally stepped underneath the soft, steady stream of water, I stood there motionless for a long time. It began without warning, as it always did. The words reflexively slipped from my lips as barely articulated whispers. *Thank you, thank you, thank you, thank you. Thank you, God. Thank you.* It was a prayer of fleeting thanks in a moment when I felt grateful for everything I still had. I was home. I was safe. I was alive.

. . .

My mother spent the day preparing for the Arnolds' visit, flitting nervously about the kitchen, cleaning, then cooking, then cleaning again. She declined my offer to help, insisting that the best thing I could do was stay out of her hair. She had never been the you-chop-while-I-slice type, so I made good on my promise to begin the job search. It was another vehicle for procrastination, as there was another, more grim task in front of me: calling Gary. I had been avoiding his calls, ignoring his messages, sending noncommittal e-mails about moving forward with the sale of the house, the divorce. But I was too emotionally drained to speak with him, so I sat in my father's study and pored over the meager job listings.

Prospects were slim and my mother may not have been far off when she suggested a job at the supermarket. When I realized just how little demand there was for my vague skill set, I toyed with the idea of taking a nap. I told myself that I didn't deserve a nap, but I felt useless and weak and thought that maybe it was the best thing for me. I expected to see Ted when I closed my eyes, to smell his vodka-heavy breath and feel his thick slab of a body. But it was Mark who filled my mind.

My father knocked on my door at five o'clock.

"Come in," I called with a sleep-heavy voice, hopping out of bed.

He poked his head in. "Have you been sleeping?" he asked reproachfully, surveying my disaster of a room. There were shopping bags scattered about and dirty laundry on the floor, and my suitcases still lay open and shoved into a corner.

"Just for an hour or so," I lied. "I spent most of the day online looking for a job."

He eyed me skeptically. "Why don't you get ready and see if your mom needs some help." It wasn't just a suggestion, but an order. Dinner with the Arnolds would be the beginning of my penance.

.   .   .

"Well," said my father, who was studying the label of a bottle of wine when I walked into the kitchen, "don't you look nice." He was always pleased when his daughters looked and behaved like ladies. My parents were both wearing their most flattering colors, and I knew that my mother had orchestrated their outfits, she in a nicely tailored navy blue shirtdress, while my father wore a salmon-colored button-down. I had selected a pencil skirt and a Lynn Arnold–friendly ivory twinset. The house looked beautiful, too, with the kitchen island already housing a spread of

plump shrimp, a board with several small and interesting arti-
sanal cheeses, and a platter of charcuterie. At the wet bar sat a
good bottle of scotch; a few different wines, including a nice
Sancerre; and several bottles of San Pellegrino so that Lynn
Arnold could make herself a spritzer. From what I understood,
Lynn did not approve of women becoming inebriated. My
mother saw me eyeing the bar. "Ellen," she said, looking at me
from beneath her brows as she pulled Saran wrap off a bowl of
olives, "I want you to take it easy on the alcohol tonight, okay?"

"Yeah, I was planning on it, Mom." My mother always got
worked up before company came, but she seemed particularly on
edge tonight and was clearly pulling out all the stops for the
Arnolds.

"Good girl," she said, sticking a spoon in a simmering pot of
lobster bisque. "Your father and I really want tonight to go well."

My parents seemed to have attached an inordinate amount of
importance to tonight's dinner and I wondered why. Aside from
the occasional church gathering or event, I had never known
them to do much socially with the Arnolds and was aware that
my mother had her secret misgivings about them, as she had
about many members of their church. "They may go through the
motions every Sunday, but that doesn't mean that they have a
relationship with Jesus," she'd say. It was no secret in my family
that my mother preferred the flamboyant, charismatic Christian
church that we had attended as children to the more staid, conservative Christ Church, where my parents were currently members. My father had convinced her to switch, and Luke, Kat, and
I all gratefully echoed his wishes, hoping that my mother would
learn to tone it down, to blend in. While both of my parents iden-
tified themselves as "born again," my mother was unapologetically outspoken about it. She had never really fit in at Christ

Church, as her brand of faith tended to make everyone a little uncomfortable. While the rest of the congregation went to church each week and attended the occasional Bible study or prayer meeting, my mother rarely went more than ten minutes without mentioning Jesus. It wasn't just about tradition or community for her; Christianity was the lens through which she viewed everything. And Jesus was as real to her as I was.

The front doorbell chimed and my mother's eyes widened. It was showtime. "Roger, the door," she commanded, though my father had already sprung into action.

I heard the greetings from the kitchen. From their tones, I could visualize the scene as easily as if I were standing right there. My father and Ed would engage in a robust, who-has-the-firmer-grip handshake, while Lynn waited, smiling, her scarlet lips never parting. Then my father would politely turn to Lynn and kiss her chivalrously on the cheek, helping her off with her jacket before hanging it in the foyer closet, which my mother had just straightened. I stood as they entered the room but let my mother rush to greet them first. After she complimented Lynn on her shoes, classic Ferragamo flats, she turned to me. "And you remember our daughter, Ellen," she said in her most exaggerated southern drawl, cueing me to follow suit and charm the Arnolds.

"Mrs. Arnold," I said, extending my hand. "So lovely to see you again."

"Hello, Ellen dear," replied Mrs. Arnold with practiced warmth. "What a pleasant surprise." She was plumper than my mother, with full breasts and overly coiffed anchorwoman hair.

Mr. Arnold then turned on his campaign-trail smile and, like a politician, attempted to put the single fact he knew about me to good use. "How's Boston?"

I saw my father shift uncomfortably, but I flashed a winning, easy smile. "Well, I actually returned to the New Jersey area a couple of months ago, so I may need to get back to you on that." Recognition clicked on Mrs. Arnold's face and she shot her husband a discreet look, wordlessly instructing him to drop all talk of Boston.

"Can I get you a drink?" my mother offered.

"Thank you, Patty. I'd just love a glass of ice water," answered Lynn.

My father and Ed immediately stepped off to the sidelines and stood shoulder to shoulder holding their scotches, easing in with talk of football. I stood with my mother, while Lynn regaled her with the trials and tribulations of planning the various charity events that were coming up during the busy holiday season.

"Every year, it just seems to start earlier and earlier," sighed Lynn.

"Isn't that the truth?" agreed my mother. "Why, half the stores in town already have their Christmas decorations up and it isn't even Halloween!" Both women shook their heads as if the four horsemen of the apocalypse were going to arrive just after Labor Day, pulling a tinsel-festooned sleigh.

After studiously ignoring the spread of food for a polite interval, my father and Ed finally began slicing off great hunks of oozy cheese and dunking fat shrimp into horseradish-flecked cocktail sauce. They sipped their drinks a little more heartily, their voices got a bit louder, and Lynn finally made herself a spritzer. Fearful of being stranded with Lynn while my mother attended to dinner, I graciously offered to plate the soup. "Why, thank you, darlin'," gushed my mother, playing up the happy family for the Arnolds.

"Ed," began my father, when we were finally seated around the table, "would you lead us in prayer?" We formally held hands and bowed our heads. Though we always said grace before a meal, I thought this was a bit much.

Ed said a perfectly nice prayer and Lynn looked adoringly at her husband. She took a dainty slurp of her soup. "Patty, this is absolutely delicious; you *must* give me the recipe."

"I'll write it down for you, Lynn," said my mother. "It really is so simple." This was a lie. I had seen her painstakingly remove the meat from the lobster and boil the shells to make the stock.

We had just finished clearing the soup plates and getting ready for the second course when I heard Kat's voice call from the foyer, "Elle? You up there?"

Fleeting panic washed over my mother's face. Kat never dropped by unexpectedly, and though she had mentioned that she would check up on me later, I never imagined that it would be in person. My parents had no choice but to pretend that theirs and Kat's relationship was placid and unstrained, that the long-standing issues and decades-long grudges had vaporized. Kat, on the other hand, was under no such obligation. The Arnolds were exactly the type of people whose hypocrisy Kat loved to flout.

"Katherine, sweetie," called my mother, trying to disguise her unease, "we are in the dining room." She glanced nervously at Lynn and Ed as she fiddled with a strand of her silver hair and forced her face into a look of pleasure. "We have company. Come and say hello."

Kat walked tentatively into the dining room and, upon seeing Lynn and Ed, broke into a beaming smile. "Oh, it's the Arnolds! How wonderful!" I was sure that everyone could identify her sarcasm. Kat, like me, knew the Arnolds only nominally, so her overexuberant greeting was deliberately out of place. I shot her a pleading look, begging her to fall in line, but I could tell that she was feeling sadistic.

"Why don't you join us for dinner, dear?" asked my mother, hoping to defuse the situation with camaraderie. "We're just digesting a bit before the main course."

Kat cocked her head and stared at my mother with that same obnoxious, plastic smile. "Oh, the main course! Why, thank you, Mother. I would love to." Kat seemed to have zeroed right in on the sad, desperate way in which my parents were courting the Arnolds. But in Kat, rather than uneasiness, it spurred only rage.

"Oh good, honey," replied Mom, trying to figure out Kat's angle. "Why don't you go get yourself a plate?"

Kat ignored my mother's suggestion and walked purposefully over to the bar and poured herself a hearty glass of red wine, while my mother tried to get the conversation back on track, immediately taking refuge in the safe and familiar.

"So, Ed, Roger tells me that you've arranged for Eugene White to come and speak at church." Eugene White was a rockstar preacher who presided over the enormous New Light Church in California. He had a bestselling book, a television show, and household-name status throughout much of the country. His coming to Christ Church was a very big deal and would have been unthinkable were it not for Mr. Arnold's connections and, I suspected, deep pockets.

"Yes, sometime in December. We've had some difficulty finalizing the date," replied Edward.

"Well, I can imagine, as busy as he is. But won't that be wonderful?"

Kat returned to the table and dramatically sat, leaning back and taking a long sip of her wine, while Lynn picked up the thread of conversation. "Well, after I read *Journey Eternity*, I told Ed that we just had to get him to come."

"You know, Roger hasn't read that book yet," said my mother.

"Oh, Roger, it's fabulous," chimed Lynn. "It really provides a road map for putting Jesus's teachings into practice in your life."

Lynn would have probably launched into a book report had Kat not abruptly and impatiently interrupted. "So," she began, "did you all hear the latest about Richard Farrington?" Here it came. I shot Kat another desperate look. Richard Farrington was a right-wing member of the Senate who had built his career on his socially conservative agenda, preaching family values and calling for an end to the "homosexual hold" on our country. A few days ago, he had been caught in a car with a male prostitute, and yesterday he had announced that he would be stepping down from his seat.

Though Lynn thought she was being gracious and diplomatic, she took the bait. "Unfortunately," she said, keeping her gaze on the rim of her plate, "there are terrible people on both sides of the political spectrum."

"Tell me, Lynn," said Kat, leaning in for the kill. "What makes him terrible—the fact that he got his dick sucked by a prostitute or the fact that it was a man?" Lynn winced at the vulgarity and averted her eyes. Ed looked down at the table and shook his head.

"Katherine," my father said, indignant and stern, "that is terrible language." My mother knew that any comment she made would only incite Kat further, but my father made an attempt to placate everyone. "Besides, I think we can all agree that what is most unfortunate is the impact on his family."

Lynn was still too shocked and offended to speak, but she rolled her head around in tight-lipped agreement.

"That's right, Roger," offered Ed.

But Kat was not finished. Looking directly at the Arnolds, she asked with mock innocence, "Speaking of family, tell me, how is Christian?"

My father was furious; he shot Kat the look that used to curl my toes when I was younger. His nostrils flared slightly and his eyes narrowed and he exhaled through his nose like a bull. Christian was the Arnolds' beloved youngest child and only son. Though I never really knew him, he was in Kat's year at school and was the subject of a good deal of gossip. He had married a pretty British girl when he was in his mid-twenties but proceeded to cheat shamelessly and unapologetically. There were rumors that he sometimes used a high-end escort service and would disappear for days at a time with no explanation, but it was still shocking news when it was learned that his wife had left one night without warning for England, taking their two children with her. From what I understood, Lynn and Ed were quite sensitive about it.

After that, the evening was unsalvageable. My mother pushed the food around on her plate but didn't take another bite, as she made desperate attempts to regain the evening's prior momentum. The Arnolds sat quietly and stiffly in their seats before making an excuse to retire early. My parents walked them to the door, leaving me alone with Kat as I cleaned up the dinner dishes. I simply shook my head.

"What?" she asked defiantly.

"Why would you do that to Mom and Dad?"

"I didn't do anything to Mom and Dad," retorted Kat dismissively. "All I did was say the word *dick* and ask the Arnolds about their son. If they felt uncomfortable with that, well, then, maybe that's their issue." Kat had an irrational compulsion to make people see what they didn't want to see. Watching it was like seeing the Ludovico technique performed. And though tonight's victims were the Arnolds, the real target was always, *always* my mother.

We heard the front door close and immediately my mother's angry footsteps came charging into the room. She was shaking with fury.

"Katherine Susan Carlisle!" she shouted with a punctuating stomp of her foot. "How could you? How could you behave that way?"

Kat made no attempt to answer, continuing to lean casually against the refrigerator.

My father, who had not rushed into the room, but walked slowly and purposefully, was now behind my mother. While Mom turned angry, Dad turned ice cold. "I have never, *never* been so disappointed in anyone," he said in a low voice filled with rage.

Kat rolled her eyes. She was her seventeen-year-old self all over again. "I don't see why you're so upset. So I made an off-color comment. Aren't the Arnolds supposed to be Christians? *Judge not lest ye be judged* and all that shit."

"Oh, don't you dare. Don't you *dare* pretend that all you did was 'make a little comment,'" hissed my mother, taking a breath before the tears came. "You have no idea what you just did."

"I want you out of this house right now, Katherine," commanded my father.

Kat's chin lifted, almost regally, before she turned and walked silently toward the door.

"I will never forgive you for this," whimpered my mother after her, her hand cupped over her mouth to stifle the sobs.

Kat stopped in her tracks and wheeled around. "Well, then, now we've both done something unforgivable."

CHAPTER SIX

I got in my car and drove. After everything that had just happened, I needed to get out of the house. It had been less than twenty-four hours since I found myself in a dark parking lot with Ted, and over the course of a single dinner, the cease-fire between my parents and Kat had ended explosively. I told myself that I had no premeditated destination, but I knew exactly where I was going. I slowed to a crawl, peering into the enormous front windows of the bar as I passed, trying to make out the faces of the figures around the bar and looking for one in particular. I never planned on going in.

Though I had known before I got in the car that Mark wouldn't be there, I circled the block and drove by again. I looked for Ted, too, expecting to see him with a woman perched next to him. The bar was packed tonight with the Friday night crowd, and it was hard to see through the thicket of people, so I double-parked and cautiously opened my car door. I had neglected to bring a jacket with me, so I crossed my arms to ward off the chilly air. Standing a few feet from the glass, I watched the scene, the din of which was dulled and muted by the thick windows. I studied the casual glances, given over the shoulder or across the room, under the guise of looking for the restroom or at a painting, but all the while surveying who was deserving of attention, whether as competition or as prey. Mark could not have been at the bar, as those glances would all have found their way toward him. He had that kind of pull.

I dared Ted to be there, dared him to walk out onto the brightly lit street. The speech that had failed me the night before would come this time. Then Mark would appear, suddenly and clearly like he had before, and then Ted would be gone, a lure that had served its purpose. Mark and I would walk together back inside and I would ask him what books he was reading and if he liked to travel and whether he was close to his family. These were the questions that I wondered if I would ever ask another man, because I couldn't allow myself to be in a position to have to answer any in return. *So why did your first marriage end? Do you want a family?* They were the questions that haunted me. As if I was waking from a trance, my head snapped up and I walked abruptly back across the empty sidewalk to my car. I got in and drove home. Tomorrow I would call Gary.

. . .

"Ellen," he said, answering on the second ring. I had waited all day to call, hoping that at seven o'clock he would be out to dinner or watching a game with friends. I would be able to escape by leaving a message.

"Hi, Gary," I said sheepishly.

"I've been hoping you would call." His tone was reprimand-

ing, but only slightly, his mind logically figuring that since he
was the one leaving, I deserved a grace period.

"So, I was thinking that we should probably figure out a time
for me to come up, to get my stuff." There wasn't much, just the
few boxes that I had packed up before the drive to Jersey. During
early discussions about our settlement, I had told him that all I
wanted was money. Not things, bought together during happier
times, not mementos or furniture. Just nice, clean, amnesic money,
so there wasn't much room for incendiary debate or argument.
When I was at my most hurt, I had threatened to contest the
divorce, lashing out wildly behind the protective cover of e-mail,
bluffing that I was having second thoughts, that I wouldn't sign
the agreement. That was when Gary backed off, stopped pushing, and allowed me to adjust to the fact that he no longer considered me his wife. He treated me like a troublesome client rather
than the woman with whom he once swore to spend the rest of
his life.

He cleared his throat, a nervous tic that plagued him in
the courtroom, where it was his only sign of weakness. "Well,
actually . . . I can just have everything sent to your parents. And
you don't need to be physically present at the final hearing, so . . ."

"No," I said, my shock turning to indignation at his pre-
sumptuousness. "No." He thought that our marriage could be
packed up, disposed of neatly and efficiently. "I'd like to be there,
Gary. I think it's important."

"I just thought it might be easier this way."

"Yes, I'm sure you did," I said, thinking that this was *supposed* to be hard. It was supposed to be painful and tragic and
difficult.

"That's fine, Ellen," he said, quickly seeking to placate me and prevent more months of limbo. "We can do it however you'd like."

"I would like to see your mother and Daniel when I'm there, to say good-bye to them." I hoped he felt a sting of guilt, as he hadn't sent so much as an e-mail to my parents, who I know thought of him like a son.

We ended the conversation like the diplomats of nations with opposed interests, each cordially saying good-bye, claiming that great progress had been made, when really all that was agreed upon was that things could not continue as they had been. I fell asleep that night wondering who, besides Gary, was sleeping in my sweet little cape.

.   .   .

It was seven in the morning when my mother walked into my room without a knock and sat down on my bed. "Ellen, honey. We're going to the eight-thirty service this morning."

I lifted my head and looked foggily around the room. "What?" I asked. I was disoriented from the abrupt awakening.

"Ellen, you agreed to go to church, and your father and I think it's very important that we go this morning."

"No, yeah . . . I know. I just . . . Don't you usually go to the ten-thirty service?"

"We're going to the early service today," said my mother tersely, standing up. "You need to get ready, honey."

I realized then that the Arnolds must attend the later service.

The mood on the way to church was somber. My parents barely spoke and my mother stared distractedly out the window.

"We need to stop at the store on the way home," she muttered. "Luke's coming for dinner." I felt a rush of relief. Telling Luke everything would be cathartic, and only he would fully understand what had taken place between my parents and Kat. Even Jill, who knew everything about my family, couldn't possibly fathom the ramifications of that relationship, which had lurched back fourteen years to when the bitterness started.

As we turned onto the main drag, Christ Church stood gracefully occupying a long, verdant stretch of the road. It was a large white building with a series of satellite structures, including the Arnolds' enormous wing, all protecting a private and well-tended cemetery. Mercedes and BMWs flipped on their turn signals at the church's driveway, idling to allow older couples—the women in quilted Burberry jackets and Hermès scarves, the men in sport coats—to make their way across the lot. The sanctuary was very traditional, with rows of pews and stained-glass windows, though it was light and bright and lacked the medieval feel of some churches. I took this Sunday's program from a slim, gray-haired man who looked slightly younger than my father, and whose face might have graced corporate newsletters with titles like *Q4 Earnings Exceed Analysts' Predictions.* They greeted each other by name in quiet, church voices before we proceeded down the aisle to take a seat in the front left side of the church. My mother closed her eyes and began what I can only describe as meditating, though she would bristle at that description. "I'm getting in the spirit," she'd say. "Leaving the flesh and getting my eyes on Jesus." *Not* meditating. Meditating was like a false idol, an empty, dangerous substitute for what she was doing.

A few couples came over to offer hushed greetings to my parents before the processional started and the pastor came quickly toward the pulpit in his traditional black robe. Upon seeing who, from the church's handful of ministers, would be giving today's sermon, my mother elbowed me in the ribs. "It's John Blanchard today; you'll like him."

Christ Church was Presbyterian, but despite my long indoctrination, I had no idea how most of Christianity's sects differed.
The Catholics, of course, were another breed, and I always envied
their approach to religion. Their faith seemed more cultural,
more of a generational obligation, whereas born-again Christians
didn't have that excuse. To identify yourself as born-again seemed
much more significant than identifying yourself as Catholic.
To say you were Catholic was like saying you were Irish or Italian. Certain associations and assumptions were made, but they
generally weren't held against you. To say you were born-again
summoned images of tent revivals and televangelists, tanned,
manicured men offering salvation and grace from their large,
well-lit stages. You were born Catholic, but you chose to be born-
again.

So what, then, was I?

I always tuned out the first part of church, the rote rituals
and hymns and tedious announcements. The minister then
moved on to the prayer concerns, prayers requested in advance
by members of the congregation. We bowed our heads and closed
our eyes and collectively petitioned God to help an eight-year-
old boy named Thomas find a suitable kidney donor, and to grant
sixty-six-year-old Martha more time on this earth despite her
battle with MS. Our lips mouthed their names, but really, we
were praying for ourselves, praying for amnesty. We prayed that
tragedy and trials faced by others would pass over us, that we
wouldn't get what we deserved.

For the sermon, Pastor Blanchard was teaching on John 8, a
well-known story in which a woman who had committed adultery was brought before Jesus by the Pharisees. Adultery was
punishable by stoning under the law, and the Pharisees, who
sought to discredit Jesus, challenged him to judge her.

"The Pharisees thought that they had him," said Pastor Blanchard. He was a soft-spoken man whose eyes seemed filled with awe as he spoke of Christ. "They knew that if Jesus didn't join them in condemning this woman to death by stoning, he could be accused of disobeying Mosaic law. But Jesus"—he allowed a glowing smile to form on his lips—"Jesus just bent down and began to write with his finger in the dirt." He paused and let the image form in our minds, then looked at his parishioners conspiratorially. "Wouldn't you love to know what he was writing?" The congregation responded with a subdued chuckle. "Such a humble act that preceded one of the most brilliant lines in the Bible.

"When Jesus stood, he looked at the gathered crowd. And he said, 'He that is without sin among you, let him first cast a stone at her.'" He scanned the pews, slowly and silently looking over the believers. "And who, among any of us, is sinless? Who among us is fit to cast stones?" Again he paused, letting his question weave its way through the pews in a moment of prompted self-reflection. "The crowd was so convicted by their own sin that, one by one, they departed. Because the only one, the *only one* who was fit to judge that woman was Jesus. But when he was finally alone with her he asked her, 'Hath no man condemned thee?' to which the woman replied, 'No man, Lord.'" He quoted directly from John 8:11, and his voice took on greater resonance, drawn from someplace visceral and deep. "And Jesus said unto her, 'Neither do I condemn thee: go, and sin no more.'"

When the service was over, my mother looked soothed and calmed. "That was a wonderful message." We stood to make our way out of the narrow pews. "I hope he delivers that same sermon to the ten o'clock service," she said, clearly hoping the Arnolds were reminded of and inspired by Jesus's grace. "I swear, some preachers forget that all they need to do is stick to the gospel of Christ. They come up with these convoluted messages that they think will make them *relevant*." She sounded like a sixteen-year-old mocking her parents for trying to be *cool*. "Jesus will *always* be relevant." I imagined her turning her gaze upward and giving the Lord a big high five.

. . .

After church, my father shut himself away in his office, his reading glasses propped on the tip of his nose and stacks of file folders splayed out in front of him. My mother slipped away to another church service, as she was often known to do. Most people put in their obligatory hour on Sunday morning and called it a day, but my mother scurried off to one of several other churches at which she would show up intermittently, looking for another fix. I had never gone with her, but from what I understood, these were the types of churches where she could cut loose, where she didn't have to tone it down. She could close her eyes and reach her hands above her head and shout *amen*. These were churches that popped up in school auditoriums or town recreational centers, nomadic churches that had no brick-and-mortar home, just a flock of believers. It was exactly the type of thing that sent me running. I could imagine the bug-eyed loons who would show up there. They were the same ones who stood on street corners, shaking Bibles and speaking in tongues.

When Luke arrived at my parents' around lunchtime, we immediately cracked open midday beers and I began my debrief at the kitchen table. I gave him a condensed, diluted version of what had happened with my parents and Kat. When I finished, we both agreed: Kat was clearly out of line. But Luke was able to see the humor camouflaged within the disaster.

"Oh my God," he said, laughing. "Here Mom was majorly kissing some Arnold ass, and in comes Kat, chugging wine and talking about sucking dicks."

I winced. "It was pretty painful."

"I'll bet Edward Arnold got a total hard-on."

"Gross . . ."

"I'll bet he broke out the gimp mask that night and had Lynn wear a strap-on."

"Stop it," I said, biting away a laugh. "I'm serious."

Luke switched gears, his mind moving back toward our sister. "Have you talked to Kat?"

I shook my head. "I left her a message yesterday but she hasn't called me back."

"Maybe I'll stop by and see her on my way back to the city."

Hearing the low rumble of the garage door opening, I shushed him. Mom was home.

We heard her keys clink as she dropped them in the glass bowl on the console table in the mudroom. "Hey, y'all," she said, sounding peacefully blissed-out. "Ellen, that was a *wonderful* service. You have to come with me sometime." Luke stood to greet her and she kissed his cheek. "Luke, I wish I could get you to come, too, but I know you never would." She always made these suggestions as if it was a foregone conclusion that Luke would refuse, like he had a handicap and Christianity didn't have a wheelchair ramp.

"What church was it?" I asked, more in the spirit of small talk than out of any real interest.

"Prince of Peace," she replied.

Oh, that's just perfect, I thought, shooting Luke an amused look. All her hobby churches always had some high-flying, evangelical name. *Prince of Peace, King of Kings, Lord of Lords.*

"I'm telling you," she said, yanking open the fridge and pulling out a seltzer, "this church was *really* cool."

I shared an eye roll with Luke. "Yeah, it sounds it." This was my mother's common ploy, trying to convince us that Christianity was "cool."

"Oh stop, Ellen," scolded my mother. "They have this *dynamic* young minister who is just amazing. So many preachers get it all wrong, even John Blanchard sometimes. He focuses on works, works, works, everything that we are *supposed* to be doing to get to heaven, instead of letting the gospel speak for itself." This was the side effect of her church hopping: the comparing and contrasting that we all had to endure as old favorites were knocked down a peg or two by new discoveries. "But this minister was something else." She took a long sip of her drink and let out a small, closed-mouth burp. "I'm telling you, Ellen, that's the type of man I would like to see you end up with."

"You can stop right there, Mom," I said as I conjured an image of this "dynamic young minister"—a description lifted straight from one of her Christian magazines. He probably had nineties alt-rocker chin-length hair and belted out Creed songs on his acoustic guitar. Or better yet, he was some frosted-tipped, spiky-haired Ken doll in a black blazer over a fitted printed T-shirt who stared at his reflection in the stained glass as he sipped a Starbucks chai latte from the pulpit. "I'm not going to play Tammy Faye to anyone's Jim Bakker."

"Come on," joked Luke, "you could be like Rick Warren's wife. I hear she has a Birkin."

While I imagined myself doomed to organizing spaghetti suppers and church bake sales, my mother went on. "Ellen, you need to start looking for a man of God. I'm not saying that it has to be a minister, just someone who walks with Christ. They'll understand about your . . . situation."

"My situation?" I asked assertively, unclear as to which, of my several situations, she might be referring.

"Honey, you know what I'm talking about," she muttered as she nervously eyed Luke. She hated talking about female issues in front of her son, thinking that the mention of anything anatomical would plunge him further into the depths of gayness. So clearly, it wasn't my looming divorce that she thought only a God-fearing man would accept; it was my infertility.

"Listen, Mom, I'm not looking for another husband."

"Well, of course not right now, but . . ." I gave her a look that warned her to go no further. "All right, *fine*. I'm just saying."

. . .

My father emerged from his lair for dinner, looking harried and stressed. Church hadn't had the same effect on him as it had had on my mother. For most of the meal he was silent, staring straight ahead and chewing determinedly, making only the most perfunctory conversation.

"Luke," he said, addressing his only son as if he were a soldier under his command, "how's work going?"

Luke shrugged and reached for another piece of garlic bread. "All right, I guess."

There wasn't much else to say. Luke ran the production department of a well-known men's magazine. It paid relatively well for publishing and had some nice perks but wasn't a particularly challenging job and had next to no room for growth.

My father took another bite and set his jaw to work. He longed to have the type of son who followed the market and had a five-year plan, but though Luke had many strengths, ambition was not among them. He did volunteer work with the homeless, he brought his elderly neighbor soup, and he rooted for the underdogs on *American Idol*, but he just didn't care about success, at least as it was traditionally defined.

"What about you, Ellen?" my father asked. "How is your job search going?"

Being as my job search had just started, it really hadn't gone anywhere. "Uh, well . . ." I smoothed the napkin in my lap. "I have been looking online, but there isn't much out there in my field right now." Seeing the look on his face, I quickly added, "But I am going to a temp agency tomorrow." And I immediately decided that I would. My father looked slightly appeased, though I was sure that later on, when Luke had gone and I was out of sight, he would tally his children's professional lives. A production director with no plans for advancement, an unemployed ex–account manager, and a hairdresser. He shouldn't have bothered to send us to private school.

CHAPTER SEVEN

The building that housed McPharrell Staffing was intended to be generic, with shiny reflective windows that looked out onto the several other identical structures that shared its industrial park address. In the cheerless lobby, I studied a wall-mounted directory to find the appropriate floor, skipping over the accountants and optometrists and insurance agencies before making my way down a bland hallway and into the low-budget-looking office with faded back issues of *Good Housekeeping* and *National Geographic*.

Though the waiting area was empty, the woman at the front desk seemed put out that I didn't have an appointment. "I'm not sure anyone will be able to see you," she said as she tapped an extension into the phone with her long, fake, French-manicured nails. "Hi, Dana. Can you see an applicant? . . . No, no appointment . . . I know, I know . . . Fine." She hung up and looked at me, flicking at her dark, wispy bangs. "Dana can see you, but it's going to be about five minutes since you weren't on the schedule."

"That's fine," I said cheerily, taking a seat. I watched the receptionist stare at her computer screen, clicking her mouse at regular intervals, her keyboard clattering. Whether or not her task was work related, she was performing it quite diligently.

Ten minutes later Dana came out, a small woman with masses of black curls and a thick application of makeup.

"Dana Sacco," she said, extending her hand. She had a thick Jersey accent and a voice that combined a whine and a growl. "Come on back." She walked briskly, her black suit making the telltale *swish* sound of synthetic fabric as she moved. She swung open the door to her office, which was small and littered with personal effects, pictures of sunbaked friends, a sorority paddle, and a Yankees mouse pad. "Have a seat," she said, pointing to a blue office chair with itchy-looking, pilled fabric. That this was supposed to be the best temp agency in the area was forcing me to recalibrate my expectations.

"So," she said, leaning back and appraising me carefully. "Do you have a résumé?"

I handed her a freshly printed copy and in my most chipper interview voice launched into the audio version, reciting my work experience and indicating that I had recently been laid off. "I would love to find another agency position," I said, "but I'm open to anything."

She laughed with a snort. "Well, that's good. Because there definitely aren't any agency jobs around right now." She leaned forward and inspected my résumé. "There aren't any jobs around right now *period.*"

"Really?" I asked nervously, picturing myself in a fast-food uniform. I'd always told myself that I wasn't above any work, but I didn't think my ego could take wearing a visor right now.

She looked at me in a way that made me think she almost relished knocking me down a peg or two. "Honey, you know how many people are coming in here after getting laid off from good jobs? I've got vice presidents working as admins."

I uncrossed and recrossed my legs, my foot bouncing spastically, without rhythm. "So there is nothing for me?"

She pursed her lips in thought, then drummed her nails loudly on the desk. "There might be one option." Turning to her computer, she pulled up a listing for the position she had in mind. "Yeah, see," she said, pointing at her screen. "We've got a picky one here. A lawyer. His assistant left a few weeks ago and we've sent over four girls for trial periods, but none of them has worked out."

"A lawyer?" I asked, suddenly hit by a painful pang. I apparently sounded less than enthused, because Dana gave me a look. I was clearly in no position to be choosy.

She gave me another appraising inspection. "He might like you, though."

"Why is he rejecting all the other candidates?"

"You know," she said dismissively, "he wants the right fit for his office." She reached for my résumé. "I'll fax this over to him. I'll let you know if I hear anything."

"And if this doesn't work out, are there any other options that I might be able to pursue?"

She shook her head as if to say *sorry, sister*. "I'll keep your name on file."

. . .

Four hours later, my cell phone rang. It was Dana. "Good news," she said in a flat tone that didn't seem to register any news, good or bad. "Mr. Kent would like to meet you tomorrow morning."

Dana gave me his address and instructed me not to be late. "Nine a.m. sharp," she said. "Wear a suit and bring a clean copy of your résumé." Her phone gave a telltale dead silence of a call waiting. "Oh, I gotta take this. Let me know how it goes." Then she hung up.

CHAPTER EIGHT

"Pleased to meet you," said the smooth, well-groomed man standing behind the enormous wood desk. "I'm Philip Kent." He gave my hand a shake that I imagined would be much more robust if I were a man. Philip Kent. It was a name that I could see on campaign lawn signs: classic, powerful, easy to pronounce.

"Ellen Carlisle," I said. "Thank you for taking the time to meet me."

"So," he said. "Why don't I start by telling you a bit about this position?"

Philip Kent was an attractive man in his late thirties with an appealing smile and a tall, thin frame. He had thick, floppy, Hugh Grant hair, though his features were less quirky than Hugh's and more traditionally handsome. I could tell from his desk, which was scattered with sterling silver picture frames, that he was a family man. They were all turned away from me, but I imagined the posed Christmas portraits next to the candid beach shots, where sandy, smiling children peered around the legs of a beautiful wife.

"I'm sure Dana mentioned that we've had trouble filling this position," he said, almost apologetically.

"She did indicate that there were a few other candidates that didn't work out."

"I'm not sure how to say this in a way that won't sound terrible," he said, searching for the right tone and words, "but polish and discretion are very important to me in an assistant. In some cases, you may be speaking with my clients more often than I do. And you will be privy to sensitive information."

"Well, I was in account management for several years, where I was often trusted with confidential client information," I said confidently. "And the nature of that work also requires that you are detail oriented and organized." I was in interview mode, which meant that I was pulling out all the stops. I sat up straight, smiled, and spoke with crisp enunciation. I didn't have the luxury of being picky.

He asked me a few more questions about my work in Boston, my schooling. "I see you went to Horton," he said, glancing at my résumé with an inscrutable smile. "I was a Delbarton boy. I'm sure we have several mutual acquaintances."

I smiled and agreed.

"Well, now that you know all about my unrealistic expectations and ridiculously high standards"—he gave a self-conscious smile—"are you still interested in the position?" He seemed more candid and prudent than unnecessarily picky.

"Absolutely," I said with a polite laugh. "I hope I meet your expectations."

He straightened a pen on his desk, placing it parallel with the edge of his notepad. "Oh, I'm sure you will."

I was to start the next day and would be trained by Brenda, his partner's assistant, who had been absorbing the excess workload. "Brenda will be delighted to have you on board. I think she's had it with me."

. . .

Dana Sacco congratulated me. "I thought you might be right up Kent's alley," she said in a way that I found slightly disconcerting, though I ignored it. The trial period was to last two weeks, at which point I might be offered a permanent position, and the pay was better than I had hoped. However, I wasn't ignorant of the fact that I was now utterly on my own. With Gary, I had always assumed that at some point I would no longer work; consequently I never directed my ambition toward my career, focusing it instead on the increasingly problematic task of starting a family. Without a husband, I had to make my own way, and I knew that I didn't want to work for Philip Kent forever.

"It's just a bridge," I told Luke.

"To what?" he asked.

"Exactly." To what? I had no idea.

Nevertheless, I felt optimistic about the job; it was a step forward. I would answer his phone and schedule his meetings and proof his letters, all the while riding out the recession and doing what all the books called "renewing my sense of self."

"Oh, praise the Lord," said my mother when I told her that I had found a job. "That's answered prayer!"

And I thought that maybe it was. I felt the strongest I had in months. *Maybe I really can do this*, I told myself. *Maybe I can start over.* It was a sentiment that stayed with me all through the evening, as my parents congratulated me, as I left another message for Kat, and it continued the next day on my way into the office that bore the Kent name. It stayed with me through my cup of coffee, the introductions and handshakes, and my training with Brenda, right until the moment when I stepped behind Philip's desk to grab a stack of file folders and got a glimpse of the beautiful wife in the framed photos. It was my high school nemesis, Parker Collins.

Philip saw me staring. "Do you know my wife, Parker?" he asked. "She went to Horton as well."

"Yes," I said. I tried to summon a smile to mask my shock as my face burned. "She and I were in the same class." And, thanks to a cruel alphabetic coincidence, always seated right next to each other in assembly. Parker Collins and Ellen Carlisle, even then a juxtaposition.

"I thought she might have been," he said amicably. "Well, she comes in often, so I am sure you will have a chance to catch up." And with that, he disappeared for the rest of the day.

I was left to acquaint myself with the office, so I sat at my desk and stared blankly into my computer screen, all the while thinking of Parker. She had the life I was supposed to have: married to a handsome lawyer, with three beautiful children and a house in the suburbs. She attended parent-teacher conferences and scheduled doctor appointments. She planned dinner parties and booked their vacations. A few times a year, Philip would send her away for spa weekends. "Poor Parks really needs a break," he would tell his friends. I knew her life. I knew it inside and out because it was the life I had imagined, the life that had made me keep *trying*, the life that I now tried desperately to dismiss as dated and bourgeois.

My desk was outside Philip's office. It was slightly smaller and had less prime real estate than Brenda's, which I was glad about. Brenda was older, probably in her mid-fifties, and had an apple-shaped figure and dark brown hair that she pulled back into a tiny ponytail. Though her face showed her age, I was sure she was once considered quite a beauty. She didn't wear a wedding ring but displayed a series of old, faded school photos of two children, a boy and a girl, at her workstation. There were no pictures of a husband, and there was something about the quiet way she ate her salad at her desk during lunch that made me think she was on her own, too. She was used to meals by herself.

I asked about lunch protocol, if I could step out of the office. She graciously told me that lunch was usually half an hour and suggested a deli a block away, where I ordered a cup of corn chowder and ate at a small table with my back to the window. I hadn't expected a typical new-hire all-office lunch for a temp and was relieved to find out that I was right.

After I finished my soup, I sat back in my chair, recalling the photos of Parker. She looked much the same as she had in high school, with long, straight blond hair that she had highlighted every four weeks, a slightly upturned nose that gave even her most neutral expression an air of arrogance, and a petite frame that boasted D cups.

Unless Parker was an entirely different person than she had been in high school, I knew that she would come sniffing around the office the minute she found out that I was in her husband's, and by extension her, employ. And what could I do? I wasn't going to quit. I could only hope that Parker would be too busy chasing three kids around to stop by much. But Parker had beaten me, again. I was a thirty-one-year-old divorcée with no kids and a dead-end temp job, and soon she would know it. As I listened to the street traffic outside, the rushing cars and occasional horns, for the first time I questioned whether home was really the best place to run.

On the way back to my parents' that night, I left a message for Kat. My voice was tired and short when I said, "I really hope you call me back this time. I need to talk to you. I found a temp job . . . It's working for Parker Collins's husband . . . I'm *not joking*."

Jill, of course, answered right away. "Oh my God, how *was* it?"

"Philip Kent," I said. "I'm working for Philip Kent." I had never told Jill the name of the man I had interviewed with, saying only that it was some lawyer.

"Noooo!!!" gasped Jill. Of course she knew he was Parker's husband, but in all of our conversations, his name had never come up. I had known that Parker was married to a wealthy, successful man; Jill may have even mentioned that he was a lawyer. But that was it. "Oh my God, what are you going to do?"

"What do you mean, what am I going to do?" I said, slightly antagonistically, feeling, for the first time, spiteful of Jill's easy life. She had the luxury of not working, of being taken care of. She spent her mornings at the gym and her afternoons at the mall.

"I mean, are you going to quit?"

"Jill, I know that you don't concern yourself with such things, but the economy sucks. There is double-digit unemployment and people are losing their homes." I knew I was being overly dramatic and more than a little mean-spirited, but I was angry and Jill happened to be at the other end of the phone. "So no, I am not going to quit. I am going to keep this job and work for Parker Fucking Collins's husband."

Jill indulged me in my rant and neither defended herself nor retaliated. "All right. Well, I just hope you don't have to see *Mrs. Kent* too often." I was sure that Parker did go by Parker Kent now, but in my mind, all the legends from my Horton days would eternally carry their maiden names. Parker Collins, Elizabeth Holland, and Gretchen Daimler: they were the triumvirate.

I remembered the first time Jill and I were invited to hang out with them. It was a slumber party at Gretchen's house during our sophomore year. Parker convinced us all to take off our bras and shirts so we could see who had the biggest boobs, even though she was clearly the winner, shirt or no shirt.

"It's not a big deal, Jill," said Parker dismissively when Jill, always painfully self-conscious about her body, expressed reticence. "We're all girls. Why are you being so weird about it? I'm beginning to think your boobs are, like, deformed," she said with a giggle. She instructed Jill to go first, then me; Parker had a way of dictating orders so that they were followed without question. After Jill and I were standing topless in Gretchen's well-lit Laura Ashley bathroom, looking at Parker and Gretchen expectantly, Parker gave her cruel, sugarcoated laugh. "Oh my God, stop staring at us! You guys are, like, lesbians!" She moved behind her sidekick, as if trying to get away from us. "Gretchen, can you have them sleep in the guest room?" Jill shifted uncomfortably and crossed her arms over her chest. I reached for my shirt.

But Jill and I always went back for more. Parker had that kind of pull, that kind of power. And Jill and I were desperate to be accepted by the popular, well-bred Parker Collins. It continued that way until senior year, when Jamie Lawrence asked me to the homecoming dance. Parker had high school's version of a serious boyfriend and had no claim on Jamie, other than the fact that he was decidedly in her league, a male member of Horton's elite. That was when Parker went from my sometimes friend to quite the opposite; she was with Jamie by the time we graduated in June. They both ended up going to the same just-shy-of-Ivy-League college and, from what I understood, dated throughout their freshman year.

"Did you hear about *Mr. Collins*?" asked Jill, and I knew that Mr. Collins meant Parker's father, who was the CEO of a major investment bank in New York.

"No—what about him?" I asked, immediately sucked back into the Parker drama, almost as if she were a vortex that became more powerful with geographic proximity.

"He retired from Fishman Bach last year and totally cashed out everything, went entirely liquid." Jill spoke with the authority of a seasoned financier. Presenting herself as an unequivocal expert on topics she knew next to nothing about was one of her many charms. "Now the word on the street is that the firm is in serious financial trouble and might totally fold."

"Of course. No Collins would ever go down with the ship."

There was a moment of dead silence on the line before Jill said, with genuine sympathy, "Shit, Ellen. I can't believe you have to work for Philip Kent."

I apologized to Jill for being so short and got off the phone, promising to call her tomorrow. "It's just been kind of a heinous day."

. . .

When I walked into the house, I expected to find my mother fluttering around the kitchen, getting dinner ready. "I made your favorite, honey, Aunt Kathy's shrimp étouffée," she'd say. "To celebrate your new job." But the kitchen was empty, clean, and silent when I arrived.

"Mom?" I called as I made my way into the living room. Though her car was in the garage, there was no sign of her. "Mom!" I shouted louder and more frantically, suddenly picturing those television commercials with elderly women lying immobilized for hours from an injury or a stroke. My mother was only in her early sixties, but she was so fragile-looking, so thin.

I barged into my parents' bedroom, which was at the far end of the first floor.

"Ellen!" said my mother, startled. She was sitting in the wingback chair looking out the window.

"I was calling you!" I scolded. "Didn't you hear me?"

"Sorry, honey," she said distractedly, offering no explanation. "How was work?"

I pictured Brenda alone at her desk, eating a salad, and shook my head. "This is just all really, really hard." There was a catch in my voice.

This was my mother's cue to leap up and hug me, to tell me how brave I was and how proud I made her. But she just sat there and looked back toward the window. "The enemy is really attacking this family," she said, her blue eyes looking sad and empty.

I gave a humorless, mocking laugh. It was archaic, blaming the devil. She was like a starving, ignorant medieval peasant, believing the failing crops were the work of a witch.

"We wrestle not against flesh and blood, but against principalities and powers in high places," she said, paraphrasing a passage from Ephesians. My mother truly believed that the events of the world, large and small, personal and shared, could all be directly or indirectly attributed to the epic, ongoing struggle between good and evil.

"Mom, the devil didn't make Gary leave me. Gary made Gary leave me," I said bitterly, always trying to inject logic and reason.

"Your poor father," she mumbled, shaking her head, almost as if talking to herself.

"Dad?" I asked, alerted to a new concern. "What's happened to Dad?"

She snapped her head up and met my eyes, like a skilled actress who can jump instantly back into character. "Oh," she said with a sigh, "he just has a lot on his plate with Channing Crossing."

CHAPTER NINE

When my first couple of weeks passed without any sign of Parker, I began to think I had overreacted. That I had, for even a millisecond, viewed the fact that Philip Kent was her husband as grounds to give up a paycheck seemed absurd. When I saw him, Philip was professional and amicable, though more often than not he was out of the office at meetings or lunches. Since Brenda was seated just a dozen or so feet away from me, happy to answer questions and fill in any blanks left by Philip, I expected that he was very pleased with my performance so far.

On the Wednesday of my second week, Philip announced that he would like to "formalize my employment" a few days before my trial period officially ended. "I have no doubts about your ability. I'll contact Dana at McPharrell," he said with a smirk. "She'll be so pleased to be rid of me."

That Saturday night, Jill and I made plans to meet Luke in the city to celebrate. Kat, who had eventually returned my calls, made a weak excuse as to why she wouldn't be able to join us, a more modern version of "I'm washing my hair." She had made no mention of what had happened with the Arnolds and offered no explanation for the cold shoulder, but I knew better than to push my luck and question her. While I might have to endure a period of distance, I would eventually get back into her good graces. My parents were another matter entirely. Their lines of communication could remain closed indefinitely. Again.

The situation with Kat was weighing heavily on my mother. "I have so much to pray about," she said as she pulled a silk scarf around her neck on her way to her Thursday evening prayer meeting. "Do you want me to pray for anything for you?" she asked, pausing at the open door. She could have been asking if I needed anything from the store.

"The usual," I replied.

．　．　．

Luke called me Saturday morning. "I'm bringing Mitch tonight," he said. "I want you to meet him." Luke had only ever introduced us to a boyfriend once before and was always a little evasive about his relationships, so I knew that Mitch was important.

Jill picked me up and we drove into Manhattan, pulling into a lot near the restaurant and paying a small fortune to have her car squeezed into a spot so tight that a piece of paper could barely have fit between the cars. We were meeting at a sushi place that Luke swore was the best in New York. "It's just starting to get hot," he said ruefully. New Yorkers are always so territorial about their restaurants.

"I thought San-Mi was supposed to have the best sushi."

"No, San-Mi is kind of over," said Luke sympathetically. It was the way you'd tell a ninety-year-old with dementia that Carter was no longer president. "Once tourists from Cleveland hear that they might see Howard Stern there, you may as well be eating at Epcot."

Luke and Mitch were seated at the bar of the narrow, dim restaurant when we arrived, Luke drinking white wine and Mitch sipping sake. Mitch smiled warmly and followed Luke over to greet us. We went through the round of hugs and handshakes, then took our seats. Mitch seemed shy in a sweet, goofy way, and had the sort of subterranean appearance of someone who spent a lot of time in front of a computer. Together, he and Luke looked like a perfect, unlikely fit—Luke with his penchant for kitschy, touristy souvenir T-shirts that stretched over his unbuff abs, and Mitch with his milky skin that had never seen a Hamptons summer. Serving as the master of ceremonies, Luke led the conversation in directions that would foster interpersonal connections.

"Mitch, I told you that Ellen used to do a lot of writing." He turned to me to explain the relevance. "Elle, Mitch is an editor." Mitch worked for an iconic metro monthly that enjoyed readership beyond its city limits.

"Well," I started awkwardly, "I wouldn't say that's true exactly. I mean, I was an English major and did some writing in college."

"And she was the editor of the student newspaper at Northeastern," added Luke proudly. I shot him a look, as his hard sell of my meager experience made it seem that much more amateurish and childlike. Mitch was gracious, though, telling me he'd love to read anything I'd written.

When it came time to order, Mitch's and Luke's selections were adventurous and bold, as they skipped the rolls and headed straight for sashimi. Jill and I had more pedestrian tastes, Jill unabashedly so. While I pretended to be comfortable with the esoteric menu, Jill asked the waiter if they had anything cooked.

"Like shrimp? Or scallops?" But it wasn't the sort of place that had volcano rolls, so we made do with tuna maki and miso soup.

"If I get a parasite," whispered Jill after the waiter had departed, "I'm going to be seriously pissed."

"But what if you get one of those worms that makes you lose, like, thirty pounds?" teased Luke, fully aware of Jill's obsession with her weight.

"Shut up," she retorted, rolling her eyes as if Luke were her brother. But as she looked consideringly at the sushi bar, I knew she was weighing the relative pros and cons of having a tapeworm set up camp in her intestine.

When the miso soup arrived with shrimp heads floating it, Jill and I squealed like schoolgirls, thoroughly embarrassing Mitch and Luke in their temple of authenticity. This restaurant was exactly the type of place where the initiated came to avoid the likes of Jill and me, with our McSushi palates.

"Stop it, you two," scolded Luke with restrained amusement, "or I'm sending you back to Jersey without your supper."

But Luke was right about the food. We ate around the shrimp heads, and when our rolls came, even we confessed how superb they were.

"So," said Luke tentatively, in a tone that signified a turn toward the serious, "any trips to Boston planned?" He dipped an almost translucent rectangle of pale pink fish into his tiny pool of soy.

"Yeah," I said, "in a couple of weeks." Jill and Luke exchanged glances and the mood of the table sobered appreciably. I hadn't told them that Gary had called with a date for the final hearing. The Tuesday before Thanksgiving. I imagined all the paperwork, so carefully complete, with the lines needing my signature so considerately pointed out with neon flags.

"Really?" asked Jill quietly.

"That's good, Ellen," said Luke confidently. "You're ready."

"Am I?" I asked, unconvinced.

"Yes, you are. I was worried for a while," he confessed, "but you're ready now."

I simply refilled my soy moat and avoided their empathetic expressions.

. . .

On the way home, I slumped back in Jill's leather passenger seat as the city began to disappear behind us. Jill was a shockingly fast driver, whipping from lane to lane and weaving between cars like she was in a video game. She had already been to traffic school once, despite the fact that she had something of a sixth sense for the police and usually spotted them in plenty of time to slow down.

Why she ever drove in the right-hand lane I didn't know, though I suspected she enjoyed bearing down on the cars in front of her, then zooming by them with the kind of exaggerated velocity that was supposed to shame them for obeying the speed limit. I watched her go through the routine again and again, as she sped past luxury cars, nondescript sedans, and finally a somehow familiar dark blue Subaru wagon.

I gasped when I saw it and whipped around and stared at the rear window to get another look.

"What?" asked Jill. "What's wrong?"

From the bright glow of the tall sentinel lights of the highway, I could just make out the lines of his face before his turn signal went on and he veered off to the exit behind us.

"That was Mark," I said with certainty. "That was him." I was at once elated that I had found him, bereft that he was gone again, and confused as to why I should feel this heart-pounding longing. My initial attraction could be explained by the whole white-knight phenomenon, but I shouldn't still be thinking about him. The only man I should still be thinking about was Gary, and finding the strength to stand in the same room with him in front of a judge.

Jill furrowed her brow, taking her eyes off the road to look at me. "Who's Mark?"

CHAPTER TEN

I glanced over at the alarm clock, which read 8:22. Clearly we weren't going to the eight-thirty service today. Pushing the covers off, I got up to get dressed for church. It was all becoming so routine, just as it always had been. Every Sunday we used to pile into my mother's minivan and drive to Grace Bible Church. This was before my parents made the switch to Christ Church, when we thought everyone's mother spoke in tongues.

Later, when we were old enough to ask the questions that we had been afraid to consider as children, my mother would remind us of our roots. "I remember when you came off the bus after the preteen retreat and told me that you'd been saved," she said. "Jesus lives in you, Ellen." Like the prodigal son, we may wander, she thought, but we'd always return to Christ.

My father looked up from his paper when I walked into the kitchen. "Morning, Ellie," he said. There was a weariness in his voice, and I wondered how long it had been there. "How is work

going?" I hadn't seen much of Dad since I started at Kent &
Wagner.

"Oh, it's okay," I said, grabbing a mug out of the cabinet. "It's
a paycheck, ya know?"

My mother approached the kitchen and, as usual, I could
hear her before I could see her. "Roger, where is the . . . ," she
called, stopping when she saw me. "Oh, hey, honey."

"Hi, Mom."

My mother turned her attention back to my father. "Where
is the checkbook?" she asked, lacking her usual Sunday morning
enthusiasm.

"Why?" he asked, almost defiantly. Since they had written a
fairly large check to the church every week for as long as I could
remember, even I knew the answer.

My mother said nothing and simply planted her hand firmly
on her hip and tilted her head, her face becoming stern.

"It's in my top left desk drawer," he answered.

She turned on her heels to go fetch it. When she returned, she
poured a cup of coffee and sat down at the counter, while my
father stayed at the table.

"So I guess we're going to the ten-thirty service today?" I
asked, thinking of Lynn and Edward Arnold, who would no
doubt be seated front and center.

"Yes," my mother replied firmly. "Then I'm going over to
Prince of Peace again. Ellen, why don't you come with me?" She
said it as if the thought had suddenly occurred to her, when I was
sure she had been planning this pitch all morning.

I groaned. "One church, Mom. I said I'd go with you guys to
one church a week."

"Well, maybe next week we can go to Prince of Peace instead.

Now, *that* is a cool church. I would just love for you to hear that minister."

"Mom, please stop trying to sell me on that kook."

"Ellen Louise Carlisle," she said, slapping the table. "How dare you assume that he is a kook? I'm telling you, you kids pretend to be so *open-minded*, and here you are judging a man you've never even met."

I instantly regretted what I had started. The blatant hypocrisy that, as she put it, "politically correct liberals" had toward Christianity was one of her favorite soapbox rants. "They want to accept everyone and everything except Christian values," she would say. "I'm telling you, it's like the time of Herod all over again."

"All right, all right. I get it. Don't judge the minister," I said, employing the same inflection used for *don't shoot the messenger*. Without looking up from his paper, my father gave a quiet chuckle, but my mother didn't get it.

She furrowed her brow. "I don't catch on. What's so funny?"

. . .

I could tell my parents were ill at ease when we walked into church, and my mother's pale blue eyes darted around the building. She was looking for the Arnolds. We took our seats in a pew that was just a bit farther back than usual. My mother flipped through the program to see that the head pastor, her least favorite, would be speaking today. "Shit," she whispered. "It's Thomas Cope." I chuckled silently at my mother, the preacher's daughter, resorting to profanity over who would be leading the service.

My mother kept her gaze on the aisles, waiting for the Arnolds to make an appearance. When they finally did arrive, my parents gave them a small wave, which they returned, before they took their front-and-center seats, which almost seemed to be reserved for them. After the dreaded first encounter was over, my parents' stress level seemed to diminish palpably.

When the service began I could see that Thomas Cope was something more of a showman than John Blanchard, using grander gestures and more high-flying language. Aside from the delivery and variance in content, however, the services were largely interchangeable from week to week, the wildcard always being whether Communion was being offered. I followed the rest of the church as we stood and sang "Blessed Assurance" and then read responsively Psalm 150. When the prayer concerns began, I flipped through the church bulletin in my lap, almost tuning out the booming voice calling for the faithful to "come together in the spirit."

Together, we silently asked the Lord to protect twenty-six-year-old Michael, who was leaving for a tour in Afghanistan: "Lord, shelter him in your secret place, Lord. Protect him and his fellow soldiers as they stand against darkness, and let no weapon formed against them prosper!" As the minister spoke, the words seemed to gain speed and strength like a growing wave. There were murmurs of agreement throughout the church. Reverend Cope stopped and patted his brow, as if allowing time for the prayer to reach heaven, and when he began again, his tone had softened. "And Lord, we hold up to you this morning Ellen"— my head lifted ever so slightly, like an antelope alerted to a lurking lion—"who at thirty-one is struggling with infertility and divorce." I froze, feeling the blood rush to my face as my stomach dropped. I looked at my mother, whose eyes remained squeezed stubbornly shut, and then at my father, who looked as confused as I did. Reverend Cope paused dramatically before continuing.

"We ask you to fill her heart with love and her womb with light, healing both, by your stripes, Lord."

"Amen," my mother whispered.

I was frantic, furious. I grabbed a felt-tipped pen and a sheet of "Hello, my name is . . ." name tags, which were always kept in slots with the hymnals for visitors. *WHAT THE FUCK??!!* I wrote on one of them, before sliding it forcefully to my mother. She glanced at it quickly, then pursed her lips and shot me her most menacing look, warning me not to make a scene. This was a common tactic when one of us was angry with her, to see our rage and raise it.

I crossed my legs away from her and slid toward the end of the pew, turning as much of my back to her as possible while still officially facing forward. I wanted to walk out, to get up and leave and refuse to ever come back. But I knew such a scene would only confirm to my parents' less well-informed friends that the prayer request *was*, in fact, for Ellen Carlisle. Seething and humiliated, I scripted the monologue I planned to deliver in the car on the way home. How could she possibly think it was appropriate to air that here?

Throughout the rest of the service, I made sure that my body language was speaking for me. Reverend Cope said the Lord's Prayer, and then the offertory began. "And this morning, as you are called upon to tithe," he said, addressing the congregation, "I ask you to consider the church's need for an expanded youth center, to better serve our young members who are just beginning their walk with Christ." I quietly snorted and rolled my eyes. This would be my last visit to Christ Church. *That* I guaranteed.

I heard my mother as she rustled around in her purse in search of the checkbook, which she gave to my father. When the usher arrived at our aisle with the collection plate, which was to be passed down the pew from parishioner to parishioner, I handed it roughly to my mother without looking at her. Seconds later, I felt the cold metal rim tap my arm. I glanced down at its contents before returning it to the usher. Although my parents' check was folded in half, I could see that it was in the amount of one thousand dollars. "You give out of your own need," my mother used to say. "The more of a sacrifice, the less you can spare it, the more pleased the Lord is."

As the ushers made their way from row to row, the rest of the parishioners placed their checks in the red velvet–lined brass tray. Lynn and Edward Arnold had exchanged affectionate glances as Ed placed in his check, which almost seemed to land with a thud. I looked subtly behind me, to see just how full the church had been for my mother's little prayer request. *Fucking full,* I thought to myself as I glanced from face to face.

And then I saw them.

Philip Kent was closing a leather-bound checkbook case and putting one of his Montblanc pens back in his inner jacket pocket. Parker Collins was staring straight ahead, with picture-perfect posture and an almost indiscernible smile on her face.

CHAPTER ELEVEN

The moment the service ended and the congregation began to mill about, I grabbed my coat. "I am getting out of here," I hissed. Keeping my eyes focused on the exit, I marched down the aisle, excusing myself as I sidestepped and squeezed between bodies. It was a relief to feel the blast of cold air as I pushed open the heavy wooden door and walked out into the clear November day.

After making my way across the parking lot, I leaned against my father's black Mercedes, which was becoming conspicuously dated by the standards of my parents' circle, and kept my eyes on the church's front door, ready to bolt at the first sign of Parker. Tapping my foot like a metronome, I counted the seconds and became increasingly furious that my parents had the *audacity* to linger. Kat would never just *sit* here like this, waiting for them as they clasped hands and double-kissed friends and acquaintances.

The congregants had started to make their way outside,

forming cozy little groups as they stood chatting on the side-walk. When I saw my mother's silver bob emerge from the church, I gestured wildly for her to hurry up. She ignored me and rested her hand on the back of a chubby gray-haired woman with a body like a penguin. The penguin squawked in delighted surprise at the sight of my mother and the two began talking. My father stood with Reverend Cope and another older man who looked like a well-fed, aging Baldwin brother. I did not yet see Parker or Philip and surmised that they must be collecting their children from Sunday school. Seizing my opportunity, I darted into the crowd and interrupted my father.

After greeting Reverend Cope and the Baldwin with a quick hello, I asked my father for his car keys. "I'm not feeling well. I think I need to lie down."

My father played up his parental concern just a bit for the benefit of his audience. "Why, sure, honey," he said, reaching into his pocket with a creased brow. "Would you like me to walk you to the car?"

"No, I'm fine. Just feeling a little nauseated." I scurried back to the car, got in the backseat, and lay down, hoping that I couldn't be spotted by a passing Parker. As I lay there, with my knees hanging off the seat and my head wedged uncomfortably against the door, it occurred to me that this was probably the least elegant and mature way to handle the situation. Rather than hiding like an escaped convict, I should graciously approach Philip and Parker and exchange warm but restrained hellos; I should take whatever subtle barbs Parker might throw my way squarely on the chin and then tell her how nice it was to see her. Though I had no intention of budging from the backseat, at least I was able to identify the best course of action. That had to count for something.

. . .

After a few minutes I heard the passenger door swing open. "Well," started my mother, sounding as upbeat as an Osmond, "you'll never guess who I just saw. Parker Collins!"

"Are you kidding me?!" Still lying down, I smacked the leather seat back. "After what you just did, you are going to come out here and tell me that you saw *Parker Collins*." Parker's name came out in a mocking version of my mother's singsongy southern chirp.

"Well, first of all, yes, it was lovely to see Parker." Her tone was reprimanding and superior. "And as a matter of fact, I had a rather nice chat with her and her husband. She said that Lynn Arnold recommended this church and they've been coming for a few weeks now."

"What?!" I gasped. "You talked to them?"

"Yes, I most certainly did. My goodness, Ellen," she said, clearly ashamed of my behavior as I cowered in the backseat. "That man is your *employer*. And for your information, I told him how grateful you were to have that job."

I covered my face, picturing Parker's poised little smile as she listened to my mother go on and on about sad, childless, unemployed Ellen, and what an act of mercy it was for Philip to hire me.

"And I have no idea why you are so upset. Parker used to be one of your good friends." On this I couldn't entirely fault her. She never knew what happened with Parker, never knew that we weren't just friends who drifted apart.

My father opened the driver's side door and peered into the car while my mother and I initiated a brief and tacit cease-fire. It was clear that he had delayed joining the melee for as long as possible and decided to take preemptive action on the part of my mother, unaware that we hadn't even gotten to the bit about my loveless heart and lightless womb. "Ellen," he began sternly, "your mother can't be blamed for Thomas Cope's interpretation of her prayer request."

"Interpretation? How many ways are there to interpret that?" I said, lurching into an upright position. "He pretty much nailed all the bullet points, wouldn't you say? And do you realize that Parker Collins is the *last* person on the planet I wanted to know that? You completely violated my privacy."

Confused by the reference to someone named Parker, my father, who had never been much involved with our social lives, started the car.

"Ellen, you need to shed your pride," scolded my mother.

"You need to cut all the religious shit! I don't want to hear about how pride cometh before the fall. You *humiliated* me!"

"I will not apologize for requesting prayer for you. The Lord *answers* prayer." She sounded more desperate than assured. "Where two or three are gathered in his name," she began, referring to Matthew 18:20. But I cut her off, feeling my hot, red face tighten as I was hit with the full force of my aching sadness. I thought of the words that had come silently, the quiet pleas that had found their way to my lips, all those nights when I lay awake wondering if I was going to get pregnant, then whether Gary would come back.

"You think I haven't prayed!?" I demanded. "You think I haven't gotten down on my knees and *begged* God to give me a child?" I furiously swatted away the tears. "You think I didn't pray that my husband wouldn't *leave me*?" The sobs escaped from my chest and I could no longer speak. I collapsed weeping in the backseat, oblivious to everything but my grief.

. . .

The next morning, I woke up feeling that specific numbness that comes after all your pretenses are stolen. When you feel naked and beaten and lifeless. Shaking me wouldn't have been enough to elicit a response. So in many ways, it was the perfect day for my first encounter with Parker.

It was just before lunch that I heard her unmistakable voice coming from the reception area on the floor below, echoing up to the mezzanine, where the partners had their offices. She was calling after her children, whose wild footsteps clamored across the marble floor toward the floating staircase. "Careful, Austin!" she yelled, and I could picture one of the towheaded children from the pictures on Philip's desk leaping up two steps at a time. "Remember what happened when you slipped!"

A tall blond boy appeared first, dressed in a striped button-down and a pair of jeans. He looked to be about five years old and was followed by Parker. She held the hand of a little girl while balancing a toddler boy on her hip. From her seated position in church, I hadn't noticed that she was pregnant.

"Ellen Carlisle!" she crooned upon seeing me, flashing me a perfect, bright white smile. She was wearing tan riding-style pants, tall, expensive-looking boots, and an olive cable-knit cashmere sweater that was stretched over her rounded stomach. Her straight blond bangs grazed her eyebrows and her long hair was pulled back into a smart ponytail. The overall look was frustratingly chic.

"Parker Collins," I said. I intended it to come off as a cheery greeting, but instead it sounded like we were about to take twenty paces and draw our guns.

"Kent now," she said with a smile. "When Philip told me that you were working here, I just *couldn't* believe it." There was an angle to her head and a narrowness in her eyes that suggested she wasn't marveling simply at the coincidence, but rather at the state of my life. I felt vindicated in the fact that this was, after all, the same old Parker. I could indulge in my decades-old grudge without remorse.

Instead of taking the bait and explaining how I had found myself working for her husband, I focused on her children, getting up from my desk and squatting to talk to them.

"Hi!" I said to the oldest boy. "What's your name?"

"Austin," he said quietly as he tried to kick scuff marks onto the shiny wood floor with his shoe.

"And this is Avery," said Parker, gesturing to the pretty little girl with the curly blond hair and her father's intelligent eyes. She looked at me carefully, as if trying to discern something unknowable.

"I'm three and a half," reported Avery proudly, holding up three fingers on one hand. "I don't have half a finger so I can only hold up three."

"That's right." I laughed. "That's very smart."

The toddler made a series of noises that sounded like a demand to be put down, before wriggling out of Parker's arms. "And that is Alden," she said as he ran over to a potted ficus and began pulling the leaves off. "He's my handful."

"And you have another one on the way!" I exclaimed like a good little Girl Scout, pointing toward her belly.

Parker gave her smooth, taut belly a few strokes. "Yes, in three months we'll either have Abbott or Aubrey."

"All As."

"And their middle names all begin with Cs, of course." I

looked at her blankly, prompting her to elaborate. "So their initials can be ACK."

"Why ACK?"

There was a confused little twitch on her face. "They're the call letters for Nantucket," she said, as if she felt just a little sorry for me that I didn't know this. "It's where Philip and I met. His family has a house there, too."

"Oh, right . . . ," I said. Just when I thought her children's names couldn't have gotten more pretentious. I had forgotten about her summers on Nantucket. Parker always made a very big deal about who would be invited to spend a week with her there. She used it as leverage throughout the school year; it was her trump card when her usual manipulations weren't working.

"We can't both have the same dress," she said when we were together at the mall and I spotted a little summer shift that I liked. Parker decided that she liked it, too. "Because what if, like, we both want to wear it in Nantucket this summer? We can't match. That would be stupid."

I never did end up going with Parker to Nantucket, but Jill did. She came home three days early after calling her mother and asking to switch her flight. "You don't just decide you want to leave when someone has invited you on vacation," scolded Mrs. Larkin. She had plans for Jill, and being part of Parker's inner circle was one of them. "The Collinses were kind enough to invite you and you are going to insult them like this?" Though Mrs. Larkin put up a fight, wanting the Collinses to view her as nurturing and maternal, she finally agreed. "I don't think she's feeling too well," Mrs. Larkin said sympathetically when arranging for Jill's departure with Mrs. Collins.

"So," began Parker, "was that you I saw yesterday at Christ Church?"

Of course it was me, I thought. "Yeah, my mom mentioned that she saw you. I wasn't feeling well, so I kind of got out of there after the service."

"Oh, I don't blame you," said Parker, a little too knowingly. "With everything you've been through."

Brenda then rounded the corner from the ladies' room and let out a long, trilling, "Hiiiiii!" when she saw the Kent clan. I couldn't blame Brenda, as Parker played the role of the boss's wife beautifully. Brenda simply went along with it. After briefly acknowledging Brenda, who began talking to Avery and Austin, Parker turned her excruciating focus back to me.

"Well, I thought Reverend Cope's prayer was absolutely beautiful," she said, adopting a pensive air as she continued. "It's just so strange that you had such trouble when Kat was able to—" She gave a small, shy little breath, as if she'd really prefer not to discuss such matters. "Well, you know . . . so easily." Shaking her head with armchair sympathy, she looked like she was contemplating a sad story she had heard on the news about a tragic family who lived in some faraway, dusty place and spoke another language.

I put my hand on my desk to steady myself. I was absolutely floored, unable to react or even to move. A ticker tape of protests scrolled through my mind, but I couldn't verbalize one of them. I just stared at her and she back at me, with a smile that to the casual observer may have looked kind. For her to so blithely reference the event about which none of us ever spoke . . .

After a moment or two of silence, she turned to Brenda, her task complete. "Is Philip in his office?"

Brenda's eyes darted from me back to Parker. "Uh, yup," she replied, fiddling with her earring. "He should be in there—right, Ellen?"

Parker did not wait for my answer, as she followed Austin's charge into Philip's office. "Daddy!" he cried as he swung open the door. As I sat back down at my desk, I heard their exchange.

"Kiddo!" replied Philip, and I imagined Austin leaping into his lap. "I wasn't expecting you guys!"

"We thought we'd surprise you," said Parker indulgently, and I heard her and Philip exchange a kiss. "Want to take us to lunch?"

"I want a cheeseburger, Daddy," came Avery's sweet little voice. "Can I have a cheeseburger, please?"

"Sure, Aves," he said. "I'll meet you guys down by the car, okay? I just have to finish up a few things."

"Okay, kids. We need to give Daddy a couple minutes!" Parker began to shoo her brood out of Philip's office.

"Yes!" shouted Austin, doing what looked like a kung fu move as he exited. "Cheeseburgers!"

"Ellen, it was so nice to see you. I'll have to stop in when I have more time to catch up," said Parker as she breezed past my desk, wiggling her fingers in a wave as I watched her walk away.

I was still mute.

Philip came out of his office a minute later. He stood there awkwardly for a moment before rapping lightly on my desk with his fingertips, not to get my attention, which he had, but to buy himself time as he worked something over in his head. "Ellen, I can't have *anyone* coming into my office unannounced. Not even my family."

"Oh, I'm sorry," I stammered, taken aback by the reprimand.

"I could have been on a sensitive call or in the middle of something . . . delicate. I just need to make sure that you can act as my gatekeeper."

"Of course. I'm so sorry." I felt my face flush.

"No harm done. Just good practice for next time, all right?"

"Yes. Absolutely."

He rapped on my desk again, once, as if to signify that our meeting was adjourned. "Good. So, I should be back in an hour or so, then." And he disappeared down the hall.

"I'm so sorry," whispered Brenda. "I know he hates when people barge in, but I didn't think Parker would just . . ." Her look indicated that she was apologizing for more than Philip's scolding.

"It's all right," I said quickly, not looking up from my desk.

. . .

When I walked in the house that evening, my mother was lying on the couch in the living room, looking worn.

"Oh, hey, honey," she said weakly.

"Are you all right?"

"Oh yeah, I'm just tired. I don't feel like cooking tonight so your father's picking up some subs from Martelli's. I told him to get one with just turkey," she said, knowing I didn't eat the mortadella that my father usually got.

She patted the couch next to her, gesturing for me to sit down, and asked me the obligatory questions about my day.

"Parker came in," I said ominously.

"Oh, how nice!" exclaimed my mother, not picking up on my tone.

Unable to hide my bitterness, I let out a humorless laugh. "Oh, was it nice, Mom?" I asked sarcastically. "Was it nice to hear Parker marvel at how ironic it is that I can't get pregnant when Kat *seems to so easily*?" I widened my eyes with Parker's mock innocence and rested my pointer finger on my cheek.

My mother inhaled sharply and closed her eyes. It had been a long time since everything that had happened with Kat was the subject of gossip, and I'm sure she thought that it was all safely behind her now. But her still-unresolved issues with Kat, and now Parker's comment, had seemed to thoroughly unstitch the wound and I watched the doubt and regret begin to seep out.

But, hurt and angry and looking for a target, I continued. "Yeah, I was thinking that maybe we could invite her and Lynn over for a prayer meeting. Maybe we could bust out the BeDazzler and make some American flag T-shirts. I'm sure Sarah Palin would *love* one. Then we could all hold hands and ask God to heal my defective uterus. It would be nice, wouldn't it?" I waited for a reaction, wanting this to escalate to a fight, wanting to say to her what I couldn't say to Parker. My mother just kept her eyes shut.

. . .

The following Monday, when Philip asked me to arrange to have lunch brought in for a meeting later that week, I reminded him of my upcoming personal days, which he had already agreed to.

"I can have the food delivered, but I'll be out of the office that day. I could ask someone to help set things up, though."

"You're going to be out?" asked Philip, seeming to have forgotten our conversation.

"Yes, I have to attend to some personal matters. In Boston." I hoped that my formal phrasing would communicate the gravity of the situation. "I mentioned it last week." Though I'm sure it wouldn't have come to it, I was not about to forgo attending the final hearing. I needed to see Gary again.

"Oh, that's right. Of course," he said quickly, his memory

jogged. "Yes, if you could ask Brenda to set everything up—you know, cups, silverware, that sort of thing—that would be very helpful."

I agreed and left his office, closing the door behind me. Brenda was seated at her desk. "I heard you with Philip. I can absolutely help out," she said, practically raising her fist in solidarity. Brenda knew *exactly* why I was going to Boston. That day, for the first time since I'd been there, she asked me if I'd like to get lunch together.

. . .

As we sat in the little deli on the corner, Brenda dabbed the corners of her mouth in a very ladylike fashion. She had the look of someone who was on the verge of a confession, so I wasn't surprised when it awkwardly began. "I just wanted to let you know that if you need anything over these next few weeks, please just ask." I nodded, knowing where she was going but not sure how much she knew. "I went through a very difficult divorce a few years ago. And I know . . . how hard it is."

I picked a tiny piece of rye bread off my sandwich and put it into my mouth. "Thanks, Brenda. I appreciate that."

She leaned back in her chair and look at me squarely. "He left me for another woman." It was her way of telling me that she knew why Gary was leaving me, too, her way of putting us back on an equal footing. Parker had surely whispered what had happened, feigning concern. "And you know about Ellen?" she would have asked while I was out to lunch or in the printer room, her arms crossed and forehead creased. Brenda would have said that she didn't and Parker would have sighed. "Poor thing is getting divorced. Her husband wants children and they've been trying for *years*."

I soon learned that Brenda and her husband had lived quite comfortably in a nice middle-class neighborhood. They had raised two children who were grown and on their own, and they were beginning the years in which they had the financial and personal freedom to go out to nice dinners, to take weekend trips to the ocean, and to buy new furniture. "I didn't see it coming," she said. "You never do, do you? And, of course, she is much younger."

Now her children had a stepmother, whom they called Denise, and Brenda no longer had the luxury of two incomes. She was the antithesis of the stereotypical wealthy divorcée who lazed around in silk robes entertaining pool boys while big, fat alimony checks kept rolling in. Brenda sat alone in her house, which seemed too big and too full of memories, while her husband and Denise had set themselves up in an Upper West Side apartment in Manhattan. "I just want my kids to always have their house," she said when I asked her if she ever thought of going somewhere new, starting fresh without history constantly imposing itself upon her. "Kids always need to be able to come home." So Brenda's ex-husband got to create an exciting new life, while Brenda was left to serve as the caretaker to the past.

. . .

"Kat, I really think I need to do this by myself," I said unconvincingly. Kat was insisting that she come with me to Boston for the final hearing.

She made no excuses as to why she thought she needed to be there, hid behind no pretext other than the fact that she thought I would need her. "You know you're going to wish I was there. Why are you being such a masochist?"

"Kat . . ."

"Just let me come. I already took the time off."

However much I wanted to be on my own when I saw Gary, I knew this was an olive branch from Kat. "But that is such a busy week for you!" I said. The days leading up to a holiday were always busy for Kat, as the salon was packed with women who wanted to be dyed and smoothed and trimmed for the inevitable holiday photos.

"Lisa is covering for the appointments I couldn't rebook. Wednesday is just going to be back-to-back blow outs anyway. You'll be sparing me."

I imagined how it would feel to be alone in my hotel after the hearing, sitting by myself on the paisley polyester bedspread, a bowl of room service minestrone getting cold as I replayed the end of my marriage. "Okay," I said. "But I want to be *alone* at the courthouse."

"Fine. I'll go shopping or something," said Kat dismissively.

I paused for only a moment. "Kat?"

"What?"

"Thanks."

. . .

The days leading up to Boston went much too fast. The hearing had been months in the making, and now it seemed that time had accelerated. I stayed up until almost midnight every night, trying to delay the ticking off of yet another day.

It was late in the afternoon the Friday before I left, and Philip called me from his cell phone on his way into the city, where he was meeting Parker for dinner. He had been out of the office in meetings all day, and I had seen him for only a second in the morning. "Listen, I forgot that Parker asked me to have you get in touch with her." In the background, I heard him pay the toll at the Lincoln Tunnel. I knew that their dinner reservations weren't until eight p.m., and I briefly wondered why he was heading in so early. "She's been planning this holiday party for some clients and key business associates, but she's gotten too busy with all the bustle at this time of year and says that she really needs your help."

"Oh, of course," I said, somewhat unsure of how to respond. It wasn't lost on me that Parker had requested *that I contact her*, which I took as a reminder of my subservient position. "I'm out all of next week, though. I have my trip to Boston and then we're closed for Thanksgiving."

He exhaled his displeasure. "That's right."

"Would it be too late if I got in touch the following Monday?" I couldn't imagine the party was very far off, which meant that either Parker hadn't yet done a thing and needed someone to lay it on, or she had already attended to every detail and had some other motivation for seeking my help. I was sure it was the latter.

"Just drop her an e-mail today and let her know your schedule. Maybe she can send you some information on what still needs to be done."

As Philip recommended, I quickly sent a polite but vague e-mail, hoping that Parker wouldn't receive it until I had turned on my out-of-office alert. At 4:57 p.m., my phone rang.

"Ellen, it's Parker. I just got your e-mail and wanted to catch you before you left. Do you have a few minutes?"

I pulled out a notebook and a pen and took a deep breath. "Sure."

CHAPTER TWELVE

Kat turned off the radio, which was practically inaudible over the pounding rain. I was concentrating on driving and had slowed to forty miles an hour, as had the cars around me.

"Shit," I said, leaning forward toward the windshield. "I can't see a thing." I was being led by the rear lights of the cars in front of me. When they braked, I braked.

"Maybe you should pull over," Kat suggested. "We can wait until this downpour is over."

The tractor-trailers around me had done just that, but I hesitated. "No, let's just get there." I strained my eyes to read the exit sign on the side of the road. It was only five o'clock in the evening, but it looked like the dead of night. "I hate daylight saving time."

We crept up I-95 for a bit, until the heaviest of the rain lifted as suddenly as it had come, brightening the sky a bit before the official sunset. As soon as I saw the big, rambling Boston Globe building, I knew I was back. We passed all the old familiar landmarks, and I eyed them suspiciously. It was as if they had all taken Gary's side, like mutual friends who had made their allegiance known.

"What's with that mural?" asked Kat disapprovingly as we passed the building covered on one side with an airbrushed-looking under-the-sea scene.

"I don't know. It's just always been there."

"It looks like a giant coffee mug."

I looked at my sister. If Boston belonged to Gary, at least I had Kat. "I'm really glad you're here, Kat," I said, realizing the truth of it.

She reached over and squeezed my leg. "Me, too." Kat wasn't one for emoting, so she quickly turned our moment together to the practical. "It's nice to get away from work for a few days."

"Yeah, tell me about it," I said ominously.

"What?" asked Kat. "Working for Parker Collins's husband isn't a dream come true?"

"He's actually fine," I conceded. "He's never there. I just hate having to deal with Parker."

"Well, you shouldn't have to *deal* with her. It's not like she works there. She's just the boss's wife."

"Yeah, and she *relishes* that role, let me tell you. She's been planning this holiday party thing, but now she's claiming that she's *swamped* and needs me to help her."

"Like, a personal party?"

"No, no," I said quickly. "It's for Philip's clients, associates, that kind of thing. His last assistant had started it before she left." I found myself almost trying to legitimize my involvement, not wanting to seem like a pushover.

"All right, so what does she need help with?"

"She called me on Friday and gave me a to-do list. Let's just say that I hope I can find a company in New Jersey that will rent a Gorham silver service for eighty. Apparently, silver plate or stainless will not do."

"So she'll be a pain in your ass until the party's over. Then I bet you won't have to deal with her for months." Kat was doing her best to put the situation in perspective for me.

"I don't know, Kat. She came in the other day and said some stuff . . ." Realizing that I didn't want to go down that path, I quickly tried to backtrack. "Whatever. You're right. I just need to suck it up for a month."

But Kat's antennae were up. "What did she say?" she demanded, her well-manicured brows forming hard angles above her eyes.

Knowing it would be useless to try to keep it from Kat now, I told her everything. I told her about the prayer request and my fight with my parents and what Parker had said.

Kat listened silently, her lips thinned and tight. "She is such a bitch," she spat.

I was salivating at the opportunity to trash Parker. "And you should have seen what a nightmare her kids were, too. I am sure the oldest is going to need to have his Cheerios sprinkled with Ritalin."

Kat gave me a look. "Not Parker," she said. "Mom. Parker is just a miserable witch who has been competing with you since the day you met. But Mom is supposed to be your *mother*. And she totally disregarded your feelings and your privacy. She doesn't give a shit about anything except her *religion*." Her words were thick with bitterness that had been steeping for fourteen years, steeping since the day everything changed for her. "It's *always* been that way."

Regretting what I had started, I weakly defended Mom.

"Kat, I don't think she knew how much it would upset me. She just didn't put herself in my shoes."

But Kat had been unleashed. "She *never* puts herself in anyone else's shoes. Never." Her voice was hard and her every muscle seemed contracted. "Do you think she put herself in my shoes? Do you think she was thinking about how my life might be impacted when everything went down?"

Kat never talked about what had happened. Only a handful of times since she had gotten back from Aunt Kathy's had she ever mentioned it. And now, just like then, I didn't know how to react.

I kept silent as Kat went on. "I was sixteen, pregnant, and scared, and all she could talk to me about was sin and accountability and 'reaping what I had sown.' " Kat's breath was uneven, and she fought, as she had always fought, to remain in control. "She made me *have a baby*, Ellen, so that she didn't have to challenge her faith. So that she didn't have to have a daughter who had had an *abortion*." It was a word that no one in my family ever said out loud, a word that no one spoke with the stark gravity that Kat had just given it. Not since that night when Kat came home.

Jill had been spending the night with me. We were supposed to be studying for our finals, but since it was our senior year, we had spent most of the afternoon lying on my bed and flipping through catalogues looking at bikinis and trying to decide which would be best for our respective body types. We talked about college and the summer and who we were going to be come September. It was just before five when my mother came into my room, wringing her hands. She looked as though it was taking all of her strength to keep her building hysteria just below the surface.

"Jill, honey, I think you better go home," she said. Jill and I exchanged looks, both sensing that we should keep our mouths shut, that we should duck and cover. "We have a family matter to discuss."

"Sure, Mrs. Carlisle," Jill said tentatively.

I walked Jill out to her car, then cautiously approached my mother, fearing that she had found out about Kat. She was at the kitchen sink. "Mom, what's up?" I asked nervously, but with enough attitude that she wouldn't suspect me of being complicit.

"Your father and I need to talk to your sister," she said, bracing herself against the counter. And with that I went upstairs.

From my bedroom window, I saw Kat's car drive up. She had been at an away lacrosse game. I had no chance to warn her about what was waiting, so I stayed as still as I could and prayed that I was wrong. This was before my parents had moved to their new house with its cathedral ceilings and open floor plan, and our home then was a center-hall colonial in an established neighborhood. Its multitude of smaller rooms rambled over its nice, large lot, making it difficult to hear conversations taking place on different floors or at other ends of the house. But I heard everything that night. It was as if the world around us had stilled and there were no distractions, no rustlings of life to drown out the confrontation. I heard my mother's shrieks and sobs, I heard my father's quiet monotone, and I heard Kat wailing her protests. I sat in front of my full-length mirror and watched my face as I listened.

My mother's voice shook the house when she yelled, *"You are going to have this baby!"*

She had found out. From just a phone number written on a Post-it note in Kat's room and tucked carefully into the bottom of her underwear drawer. My mother had figured out the rest.

I heard Kat's feet fly up the stairs and into my room. Kat and

I spent the rest of the night sitting on the roof outside my window while my mother was on the phone with Aunt Kathy, making plans. Kat would leave at the end of the summer. She would stay with Aunt Kathy until she had the baby, which would be put up for adoption. As those first tense weeks passed, the story we would all learn to tell began to take form. Kat was taking the first half of the year off from high school, to go stay with family in Southern California. She would be attending school there and helping our aunt, who was ill.

By the time Kat left, we all had it down. "Cancer," we would say. "Breast cancer," which we discovered invited no further conversation. And Kat learned the story, too. Her face was emotionless and empty as she recited her lines. But she never—no matter how hard my parents pressed, no matter what they threatened or took away—told them who the father was. She never told anyone. Not even me. Everything else, Kat went along with. She was like a rag doll that summer: lifeless and static, at the mercy of whoever was holding her.

But the truth of her pregnancy eventually came out. And all of our careful constructs were revealed. "Did you tell Jill?" my mother demanded. But I hadn't. I always could keep a secret, and it wasn't until the rumors were weaving their way around us that I confided in my best friend. The only other person outside the family who knew what had happened was the boy. He was the only possible source of the gossip.

The talk had started long before Kat came home. I was in college and far away from it all, but I felt my mother's panic every time she would call me, wild and frantic, over a comment that was made or a remark she had overheard. "Do you think they know?" she would ask.

I would always tell her that no one knew. "How could they?" I said quickly, before making an excuse to get off the phone.

When Kat finally did come home, on January 3, two weeks after she had given birth to and then given away a seven-pound, six-ounce baby girl, she was fundamentally changed. Her wildness, once always coupled with a carefree spirit, with youth and innocence, was now hard and defiant. Having that child was the last thing she ever, *ever* let anyone make her do.

Kat never did return to Horton, never did finish high school. She took some odd jobs until she turned eighteen, and then she left, heading first back to California. But over the course of three years, she was slowly pulled, as if by gravitational force, back to New Jersey, moving first to Colorado, then to North Carolina. I had just graduated from Northeastern and was living here in Boston when she went home. I remember sitting in my bedroom, looking out onto the stretch of road that we were now flying down, when she called with the news that she was going back.

"Isn't that your old apartment?" asked Kat, breaking the silence.

CHAPTER THIRTEEN

Before going to the hotel, we drove by my old house, the sweet little cape with the oak tree in the front yard. After the final hearing, Gary and I were going to go through the house before heading to see Daniel, where Gary's mother, Beverly, would meet us. Although from what I understood there would be some red tape around filing the divorce judgment, I knew that as far as we were both concerned, we would no longer be married as soon as we signed those papers in front of the judge.

"I still can't believe you didn't get a lawyer for all of this," said Kat as we slowed to a crawl, looking into the dark windows of my house. I hadn't expected Gary to be there, but some residual jealousy stirred all the same when I thought about where else he might be.

"It just would have been an unnecessary expense," I said. "Gary made sure that everything was weighted in my favor; *that* I assure you."

I was almost bitter that he got to feel noble about his

generosity. I imagined him furrowing his brow as he said somberly to the friends that were close enough to ask about the settlement, "I just wanted to be more than fair to Ellen."

"I can't believe you didn't want to keep this place. You could have stayed here in Boston," said Kat as she looked around the neighborhood, a suburban utopia. "You should have made Gary find a new place to live."

"I could never have afforded it on my own. Honestly, I really don't know how Gary's going to do it." But in truth, I knew exactly how Gary was going to do it—with someone.

.   .   .

I couldn't sleep that night at the hotel. The pillows on the beds were thick and hard and the sheets smelled like industrial-strength laundry detergent. I rolled from one side of my double bed to the other, trying to find rest on my stomach, then my side, finally flopping onto my back when I had given up. I had wanted to get a good night's sleep; I had wanted to look refreshed and rested when I saw Gary.

Kat, who was sleeping in a duplicate double bed across from me, rolled over to face me.

"Can't sleep?" she asked.

"Not really."

"Are you nervous?"

I stared at the ceiling. "No. I'm not nervous. I think I just want to get it over with." I had been so insistent that I needed to see Gary again, to see Daniel and Beverly and the house. Now I almost wished that I had followed Gary's advice and let this all play out remotely.

"I think you are doing the right thing, being here and everything," said Kat, seeming to read my mind.

"It's been three months since I saw him." Lying in the dark, I pictured his face, and the way it used to soften when he was amused with me. "Ellen," he would say, during the first couple of months we started trying, "we're going to have a baby; it just takes a little bit. Don't worry so much." And then he would wrap his thick, strong arms around me and I would take a deep breath and he would kiss the top of my head. *He's right,* I thought as I relaxed into him. *Of course he is right.* His arms seemed to be able to hold the weight of the world. It's hard not to believe someone with arms like that.

. . .

As I dressed the next morning, the black pants suit that I had planned on wearing didn't seem right. It was the suit that I had picked out with Jill for my interview with Kent & Wagner.

"Does it look too severe?" I called from the bathroom, where I stood twisting in front of the mirror. Kat was lying on the bed drinking a cup of Starbucks that she had just retrieved from the hotel lobby. Her face was freshly washed and smelled like lavender.

"It only looks severe because you have your hair pulled back like a nun. Wear it down," she said as she considered other edits to my look, "and put on a statement necklace."

"I didn't bring a statement necklace!" I said, panic-stricken, sticking my head out of the bathroom.

"Relax," said Kat as she reached down into her handbag next to her and pulled out a gorgeous costume necklace that she had purchased at Barney's, a twisted tangle of gray pearls and smoky crystals.

"Oh my God, thank you, Kat!" I gushed as I rushed to retrieve it.

She eyed me as I fastened it, then turned to appraise the

revision in the mirror. "What shoes were you going to wear?" she asked.

"My black pointy-toed flats." I always wore flats, a throwback to being the tallest girl in the class, beginning in elementary school.

"Wear those instead," she said, pointing to her beautiful black ankle boots.

"Should I do a dramatic eye?"

"No . . . ," she said, as if she had already thought it through. "I think we might already be pushing the limits for a nine a.m. court appearance."

. . .

The courthouse was a foreboding brick building with squeaky tile floors and archaic letter-board signs that provided information about departments and locations. It looked perfectly content to sit stoically as the wind attempted to batter it, whipping about the few stray leaves that had managed to hang on this long. With my head down, I marched forward with a confident determination that I didn't feel. It just seemed to be the way that one should approach such a structure: with purpose. I nestled my face down into my thick scarf and stepped quickly up the stairs, Kat's shoes making a muted clacking noise as I went.

"Ellen." He said my name with quiet recognition, stepping out from the portico.

I jumped, more surprised than I should have been at the sound of Gary's voice. I'd thought that he might try to meet me outside. It was part of why I had arrived thirty minutes early, to deny him his last act of chivalry.

"Hi, Gary." He was wearing his gray wool overcoat and was holding his leather briefcase.

"It's good to see you, Ellen." Resting his hand lightly on my elbow, he leaned forward and gently kissed my cheek. As his clean-shaven face brushed against mine, I could feel how cold it was. He must have been waiting for some time. "I know that it can be . . . intimidating in there, so I thought that we could walk in together."

My hair blew across my face, and I pulled a hand from my pocket and tucked it back behind my ear. "I would have been fine."

"I know," he said softly, trying to smile. "You look great."

My face did not change, but I averted my eyes. "Thank you," I said coldly.

An older man with a salt-and-pepper beard and a thick, lined sweatshirt walked past us into the building. As he opened the door, a gush of heat rushed out. "Well, we may as well get out of the cold," said Gary, reaching for the door with a glove-clad hand. I paused, looking at him as he held it open. He was the archetypal ideal husband. He was the man that an advertising agency would cast to sit on the deck of an oceanfront summer home to sell financial services. He'd stare triumphantly at the horizon as the camera panned out to show a wife collecting shells on the beach and two children sailing toy boats in the water. *We can get you here sooner than you think,* would come a deep and steady-sounding voice. Then the background would drop to black and a staid-looking logo would flash on the screen.

"After you," Gary said, gesturing me into the warmth of the courthouse.

. . .

I held my cell phone against my cheek, hoping that no cops were around as I sped up to the on-ramp of the Mass Pike, the heat in my car blasting on high. "It's done."

Kat took a deep breath. "So . . . how are you?"

"I'm fine."

Kat paused. "You don't sound fine."

"The only thing that isn't *fine* is that I'm *fine*."

"Uhh . . . okay."

"I mean, I just got divorced. I shouldn't feel *fine*, but I do. We went to the house; I saw Beverly and Daniel. And I'm *fine*."

All day, I had expected it to kick in—I was waiting for the agonizing sense of loss to rip through my core—but instead, it felt like I was just going through the motions to formalize something that already was. Ironically, it was how I'd felt on our wedding day. All those months of planning and anticipation for an event that didn't seem to fundamentally change what we were to each other. It seemed as if we were married before we were married and divorced before we were divorced.

"So it really wasn't hard to see Daniel and Beverly?"

"No. I mean it was all hard, I guess." I pictured Daniel's face as he gestured toward a large flat box wrapped with paper that looked like it had been hanging around the home since last Christmas. "Daniel made me a collage with magazine clippings of the Celtics," I said with a fond, bittersweet chuckle. "And Beverly cried when she hugged me good-bye."

"What about Gary?"

I thought of how Gary had walked me to my car. I hit my turn signal and changed lanes. "Gary said all the right things," I said bitterly.

"Ellen, I would love to still be part of your life," he had said. "In any way that you'll have me."

It felt like my chance to stomp and scream and tell him that I'd have him as my husband or nothing. It was my chance to tap into some of the anger to which I felt I was entitled. *Would your girlfriend like that? Our being friends?* But I could summon none of it. "I don't know, Gary," was all I could manage. "Let's just see how things go."

He took my hand, and again, I knew that I should pull it back, scold him for daring to touch me. "Thank you, Ellen," he said.

"For what?"

"For coming here for this. I am so glad you did." He looked at me sheepishly. "I didn't know how good it would be to see you."

. . .

When I got back to the hotel, Kat was waiting in our room with an open bottle of wine. She gave me a long, silent hug, then handed me a glass. "I made reservations for dinner." I knew what she was thinking, that I should celebrate being newly single, but she had the sense not to say it.

"All right," I said reluctantly, kicking off Kat's shoes. I had no energy for an argument. "But I want to get to bed early. I didn't sleep well last night."

"Then let's hurry. Wet your hair in the tub. I'll blow it out."

I plopped down on the bed. "Can't I just go like this?"

I knew I was ruining the girls'-night-out vibe that Kat was trying to create for me, but I wasn't in a cupcakes-and-cosmos sort of mood.

. . .

We arrived early for our reservation and took seats at the bar. A handsome young bartender immediately approached us. "What can I get for you ladies?" He had an English accent and an appealing little dent in his nose that kept him from being too pretty.

Kat flipped open the drink menu. "I'll have a glass of the

Malbec," she said with a flirtatious smile. Then she leaned back in her stool and recrossed her legs. She sure could turn it on when she wanted to.

"And for you, miss?"

I looked at the elegantly lit bottles behind him. The bar was small and dim and warm. "Just a Maker's Mark, with a couple of ice cubes, please."

He smiled approvingly. "All right, then," he said, giving me a wink as he went off to fetch us our drinks.

"He's cute," whispered Kat conspiratorially.

"Kat, don't."

"Don't what?"

I looked down at my left hand. I hadn't worn my ring since I left Boston, and I pictured how my hand used to look, with a simple but beautiful two-carat round diamond set in a classic platinum band. I remembered how proud of it Gary was, telling me that princess cuts were trendy, but this style would last. "It's an heirloom, Ellen," he had said.

"I'm not up for the single-girl thing. Not tonight, Kat."

"Oh, really?" she asked with playful defiance.

"Yeah, oh really."

"What if it was that guy Mark back there, pouring you a glass of bourbon?"

At the mention of his name, I felt a stirring that I knew I wasn't supposed to be feeling.

CHAPTER FOURTEEN

My mother pulled a loaf of cubed French bread from the freezer and bit the bag open with her teeth. "I'm keeping things simple this year," she said as she dumped its contents onto a baking sheet and poured on a full cup of melted butter. "Just a turkey, my oyster stuffing, mashed potatoes, and a salad."

"Sounds great, Mom," I said reflexively, taking a sip of my peppermint tea, then scrunching my feet up onto the barstool. It was only eight o'clock in the evening, but I was already thinking about bed.

"I mean it. No one ever eats the candied yams or green bean casserole, so I'm not making them."

"I think that's smart."

She opened the door to the top oven and slid in the baking sheet. "Christmas, too. Things are going to be different this year. Your father and I aren't doing big gifts for y'all. You don't need all that anymore."

I nodded in agreement and she seemed disappointed that I didn't put up any selfish protests.

She turned to the kitchen sink to wash her hands. With her back to me, she asked, "So, I guess your sister isn't coming tomorrow?"

"No . . . I don't think she is."

"I still can't understand why she thinks that *she's* the one who's got the right to be mad."

I didn't answer, having learned not to try to position myself as moderator between my parents and Kat. Instead, I tried to redirect her. "So, Luke will be here in the morning?"

"Yes," said Mom, drying her hands on a dishrag hanging on the oven door. "His train will be here around noon, and then he's going to stay until Saturday."

Luke usually came out to New Jersey for only one night at a time, so his extended stay was something of an event. What my parents didn't know was that Mitch was going to his father's house in Boca Raton for Thanksgiving, so Luke would have been alone all weekend. "That'll be nice," I said. "To have Luke here."

My mother propped one hand on her hip and looked at me directly. "So, what's Kat doing, then? Did you ask her?" The overhead lights above the island harshly lit her face, casting dramatic shadows over her bags and wrinkles. She looked older than I had ever seen her look.

"She was invited to spend Thanksgiving with a friend, Mom." I was shorter than I had intended to be.

"I can't imagine what friend would be more important than family."

"I don't know, Mom. I didn't really get a chance to ask her. I was too busy getting divorced." I knew I was being something of a martyr, but I did not feel that I had received an adequate level of sympathy for my ordeal.

"Well, excuse me, Ellen! Seeing as you spent the past two nights with her, I thought it may have come up."

"All right, Mom. I just am kind of tired and drained and don't really feel like getting in the middle of it."

"Stop being so dramatic, Ellen. No one is putting you in the middle of anything. For your information, I just found out Aunt Kathy will be coming for Christmas, and I was hoping that maybe Kat would at least grace us with her presence then."

"Aunt Kathy's coming?" We all loved Aunt Kathy. Even Kat.

"Yes, she's going to be here for Christmas and she's staying until the second. She'll be here for Eugene White."

"Oh, right," I said, remembering the Arnolds had arranged for him to speak at our church. "So, when is that happening?"

"The twenty-seventh. Lynn and Ed were really hoping to have him come before Christmas, but I think this'll be nice. They postponed their holiday party so that they could have it that night, too." Her pointer finger shot suddenly into the air, as if she had some urgent information to convey. "As a matter of fact, Lynn specifically asked me to invite you." Anticipating my resistance, she quickly added, "It would be very rude if you didn't go."

"Oh, come on," I begged.

"Ellen, this is a very big deal to your father and me. For Lynn to ask us after everything that happened during that terrible dinner . . ."

"Fine," I said, shaking my head. "I'll go."

She headed to the pantry and came out with a five-pound bag of russet potatoes.

"And don't forget about the Donaldsons on Friday."

"What?" I couldn't so much as place the Donaldsons, much less recall an invitation to their house. "Who are the Donaldsons?"

"Ellen! I told you about this weeks ago. They are a very nice couple from our church and they have a party the day after Thanksgiving every year. You met them three Sundays ago."

I vaguely recalled meeting a large woman who was built like Julia Child. She had a horsey face and ashy blond Princess Diana hair.

"So it's going to be all churchies there?" I imagined the typical spread laid out for "fellowship" after a church service. "What, are we going to sit around drinking burned coffee from foam cups and eating mini powdered-sugar donuts?" Even the snobbiest churches had much to learn when it came to catering.

"Listen to yourself," said my mother, as if astounded that I had come from her womb. "As a matter of fact, it's going to be a very nice party. The Donaldsons live up in Chester; their property is just stunning." She emptied the bag of potatoes into a colander. They landed with dull thuds. "They breed these beautiful horses called Friesians. Glenn hooks them up to a wagon and gives hayrides. And Ann makes her delicious homemade eggnog."

"Eggnog with rum in it?"

My mother rolled her eyes and bent down to rummage in a cabinet under the island. "Yes, Ellen. With rum in it."

"Is Luke going?"

My mother hesitated. "Luke wasn't invited."

I gave her a look. She was always so on edge when Luke came to church with us, always staying right next to him, steering him through the crowd after the service and jumping in if she thought the conversation might head in the direction of the personal. *So, do you have a girlfriend?* It was her worst fear to hear those words come naively from a member of the congregation. I imagined that the Donaldsons' party would be much the same.

"But we're not just going to leave Luke sitting at home alone, right? I mean, it sounds like this thing is pretty casual, so it's not like one extra person would be a big deal."

My mother stuck the colander in the sink and flipped the water on high. "If Luke would like to join us, then of course he can," she conceded.

. . .

On Thanksgiving Day, I knew that we all felt Kat's absence. It was like those first early years after everything happened, when she was out west and never came home, not even for holidays. My mother stayed in the kitchen, listening to worship music and trying to coax herself into the Thanksgiving spirit. She denied all offers of help. "Y'all just stay out of the kitchen. I can certainly fix a dinner for four people by myself." So, Luke and I sat in the family room while my father watched football. He tried to engage us in the sport, explaining the plays and inserting his commentary, but our remedial comprehension and inane questions seemed only to silence him, so Luke and I ended up flipping through catalogues and dressing ourselves for the lives we didn't have.

"Luke, if you lived in Maine, you could totally pull off these flannel-lined L.L.Bean jeans."

"Let me see," he said, reaching for the catalogue. He glanced quickly at it before handing it back. "No," he said dismissively, "the cut is funny."

"The cut is supposed to be funny. They're supposed to be kind of uncool. It's the whole so-uncool-it's-cool thing."

My father exhaled loudly and pointed to the television screen without shifting his gaze from the action. "See that quarterback?

Grew up in one of the most violent areas of Los Angeles. He was shot in the arm when he was five years old. Then he went on to be the star player at Virginia Tech." Having begun his career working construction, my father was always impressed by a bootstrap success story. So Luke and I emitted the appropriate *oohs* and *aahs* and then went back to our stack of shiny catalogues. And my father went back to wishing Gary was seated next to him, sipping beer from a chilled glass and enjoying the bowl of smoked almonds on the coffee table.

After we were called for dinner and had taken our places around the overwhelmingly large table, my father said grace. We all bowed our heads as he thanked the Lord for our blessings. "Thank you, Lord, on this day and every day, for all that you have given to this family. We are humbled by your continued blessings and continued mercy, and we give the glory to you forever, Lord. Amen."

My mother mumbled her own prayer to herself in tandem, unintelligible except for the periodic *Jesus*. Then platters were passed and plates were filled. Luke made several attempts to jump-start the conversation, with what would normally be hilarious stories about his department's motley crew of temps, but even my laughter sounded forced.

Luke and I, subconsciously adapting to our parents' mood, began eating in subdued silence. My mother had an obligatory piece of turkey but sat quietly for most of the meal, staring at her plate. My father piled on the dark meat and doused it generously with gravy. "I don't know why you kids prefer the breast. Any chef will tell you that the thigh has more flavor."

I wondered if this was what holidays would be like from now on, without a table full of little children to fuss over, without their turkey to cut and vegetables to coax down. Without anyone to teach about the wishbone. And since Kat and Luke had no plans to start families anytime soon, the void would be indefinite, quite possibly permanent. It was a loss that my parents never spoke of, especially in front of me, but I saw the look my father would get when casually announcing the pregnancy of a friend's daughter or the arrival of a colleague's grandson. I poured myself a big glass of wine from the bottle Luke had brought, hoping that it might lubricate the evening. When I poured a second one, my mother spoke up.

"My goodness, Ellen. It's not even five o'clock." We were eating earlier than usual this year; I think we all wanted to get it over with.

"It's Thanksgiving," I said as I took a sip. I think we were all aware of the irony.

.   .   .

The Donaldsons' house was probably technically an estate, with a beautiful large white home set almost half a mile off the road. The property included a series of stables and pastures, sectioned off into paddocks for their massive, regal-looking black horses. "They were traditionally used in wars," said Ann Donaldson, roughly patting the haunches of a towering male. "There used to be only a handful of breeding stallions left in the world." The animal stomped his hoof and snorted. I took a step back.

"Ellen, would you like to ride Ludolf?" asked Ann.

"Oh, no, thank you," I stammered. "He really is beautiful, though."

"Isn't he?" gushed my mother. "Such a specimen."

Meandering over to get a glass of eggnog, I wished that Luke were here. When my parents had invited him, Luke had declined, saying that he wanted to do some reading. "All right, honey,"

Mom said, putting her hand on his cheek. "You stay here and relax. We'll bring you back something."

Sidestepping a wobbly-looking woman in riding boots, I made my way into the heated atrium, where the bar had been set up. I hadn't expected this to be a catered affair, but there were passed hors d'oeuvres as well as a table filled with various stews and sandwiches. The bartender, like the servers, wore a Black Watch plaid wool scarf draped around the neck of his standard tuxedo uniform.

As he handed me my glass of eggnog, I heard a familiar voice next to me. "Do you have any nonalcoholic eggnog?"

It was Parker, rubbing her tight little pregnant belly.

"Hi, Parker."

"Oh, hiiiiiiii!" she exclaimed, pretending that she hadn't seen me.

I forced a smile. "So you know the Donaldsons?"

"Oh, yes. Ann and my mother have been friends for years." She cast her eyes about. "My parents are here somewhere. I know they would love to see you . . . Oh, there they are!" She pointed in the direction of the patio, where I immediately recognized Mr. and Mrs. Collins. Mrs. Collins was an impeccably dressed blonde who, like a paper doll, had the same dull, aloof expression on her face no matter how her surroundings changed. Mr. Collins was the type of consummate charmer who called waitresses by name, as in, "Sandy, I'll tell you what I could really use: a Gray Goose martini with three olives. In a rocks glass, please."

"Oh, great. I'll have to go say hi."

"So"—she stuck out her lower lip in a comical little pout and reached out to rub my upper arm—"how are you? How did everything go?"

Of course, I knew that she was asking about the divorce hearing. "Oh, you know, fine," I said quickly. "So, how was your Thanksgiving?"

"It was *great*," said Parker, a little too emphatically. "The kids are so cute with the whole Pilgrim thing. They just can't believe that one of their relatives was on the *Mayflower*. Avery kept asking me, 'How many greats ago was he? Was he my great-great-great-great-great-great-great-great-grandfather?'" As she went through the *greats*, she tilted her head from side to side for effect.

"Oh, how cute," I said with mock interest.

"Yeah, you know, I really should try to organize a Thanksgiving celebration for the New Jersey chapter of the Mayflower Society—just something for the kids." She looked like Sally Struthers in a Feed the Children ad. "It's so important for them to know their history, but I am just so swamped at this time of year. I don't know how I could fit in one more thing." Her eyes lit up. "Speaking of, have you had a chance to get to any of the stuff for Philip's party?"

"Oh, no. I haven't been in the office all week."

She made a *yikes* noise. "Gosh, we are really getting down to the wire. I hope the florist can get those green hydrangeas I want."

Just then, my mother sidled up. "Oh, hey, Parker! How are you, sweetie?"

"Patty!" she said, leaning in for a kiss. "So nice to see you."

"Where are those beautiful children of yours?"

Parker gave us a conspiratorial look. "Their daddy took them into New York today. God knows how he is going to manage them in the city on Black Friday, but he insisted. I think they were going to do a little Christmas shopping."

"Oh, how nice!" said my mother, undoubtedly picturing, as I was, Philip leaning over the glass cases at Tiffany's, three beautifully dressed children at his side. "Do you think Mommy would like it?" he'd ask Avery, holding up a diamond drop necklace.

My mother hooked her arm into mine. "Ellen, honey, can you come here for a minute? There is someone I'd like you to meet." She turned to Parker. "Parker, if you'll excuse us for just a second." And I found myself being whisked in the direction of a tall, skinny blond man with an unflattering gum-to-tooth ratio.

"Christopher," she said, presenting me proudly, "this is my daughter Ellen." She smiled and inched me forward. "Ellen, this is Christopher Hapley."

The man named Christopher extended his hand. "It's nice to meet you, Ellen."

"Yeah, you, too."

"Ellen, you may recognize Christopher from church," said my mother. "He plays the guitar with the worship team and has such a gift for music."

"Flattery will get you nowhere, Patty," joked Christopher, who apparently not only looked like a Sunday school teacher, but had the sense of humor of one, too.

"Well," said my mother smiling, "I'll leave you two to get acquainted."

Get acquainted? My eyes followed her as she walked away, my jaw slack with disbelief.

"So," said Christopher, sticking his hands in his pockets and rocking back and forth on his heels. "Patty tells me that you just moved back from Boston."

"Yup. Several months ago now. It's hard to believe it's been that long, but here I am, back in Jersey." I laughed awkwardly.

"Have you always lived here?" I wanted to appear polite but not overly interested. Friendly but not flirtatious.

"Oh, yeah, I even stayed here for college. I went to Rutgers."

"Oh, really?" I asked, making my way down the list of friendly small-talk topics. "What did you study?"

"Chemistry. I work over at Merck. What about you?"

"I'm just working at a law firm right now."

We stood in awkward silence for a moment as I tried to figure out a graceful way to exit the conversation. Christopher was a perfectly nice guy, but my mother's introduction and clear intentions had made it unbearably awkward.

"Hey, I was wondering," said Christopher, clearly nervous, "maybe we could get together sometime?"

"Sure," I said, not overly enthusiastically and glancing toward an inconsequential point in the distance. "Most of my friends don't live around here anymore, so . . ."

He beamed. "Great. I have Patty's number, so I'll give you a call." Whether deliberately or inadvertently, he had not picked up on my friendship cues.

"Oh, right." He must have had occasion to call my mother when organizing the church's Christmas spectacular.

After saying an uncomfortable good-bye to Christopher, I headed straight for the bar, intent on another glass of eggnog, and was intercepted again by Parker, who had been talking to another woman who was about our age. Parker gave her a quick double kiss, then made a beeline in my direction.

"Ellen!"

"Hi, Parker." I was heading for that bar like it was an oasis in the desert and didn't intend to stop walking, but Parker rested her hand on my upper arm, and I halted like a trained show pony.

"So listen. I'm about to run, but I just wanted to let you know . . ." She leaned toward me and lowered her voice, as if to give the appearance of discretion. "Everyone at Lynn's women's group . . . well"—she bit her lower lip and furrowed her brow—"we've all been praying for your parents . . . and their situation."

CHAPTER FIFTEEN

I spent the rest of the party avoiding any and all conversation as Parker's comment metastasized in my mind. Working out all its possible meanings, all the things Parker might know that I didn't, I concentrated on the fact that my mother requested prayer for even the smallest matters.

As we assembled to make our exit and thank our hosts, my father gave Mr. Donaldson a hearty handshake. "Thanks again, Glenn. We'll see you Sunday."

Mr. Donaldson, a nebbishy man with bug eyes and a toothy grin, seemed to wince a bit at my father's grip, which was always firm to the point of being painful. "You bet," he said. He was the type of ostracized nerd who had gotten the last laugh when he finally cashed in on his intellect after joining the entrepreneurial world, where brains almost always beat out brawn.

My mother clasped hands with Ann and echoed our thanks. "You'll have to give me the name of the caterers, Ann."

We walked through a courtyard and out a large metal gate to

the parking area, where the guests' cars were lined along the perimeter of a long gravel driveway.

"That was a nice party," said my father. It just seemed like the thing to say, like remarking that a baby was cute or a sunny day beautiful.

My mother looked at him as if he had just emitted a particularly offensive odor. "I thought the food was *terrible*. I think she used Class Act Catering, and I can tell you that everything they served was from Costco, right down to the clam chowder." My mother never missed an opportunity to point out any area where her taste surpassed that of the blue bloods.

I slid into the backseat of the car. My mother flipped down the sun visor and briefly checked her makeup in the mirror. Her lips were still lined to perfection and lacquered in shiny magenta lipstick. "How was your chat with Christopher?" She said his name like he was a well-known Casanova. "Isn't he a dear man?"

"Yeah, Mom. He was really nice. But in the future, I wish you wouldn't play love doctor, okay?" It was a toothless reprimand, the sort given by an exhausted single mother after working a double shift.

"Well," she huffed, "I don't see what is so wrong with introducing you to eligible young men. I happen to think Christopher would be perfect for you." She spoke with matter-of-fact impertinence, and her blue eyes looked at me sternly in the rearview mirror, daring me to react.

She was gunning for a confrontation, and I rose to the occasion. "What would make him perfect for me? Anything besides the fact that he's single?" I couldn't help but feel undervalued, like an old spinster daughter from a Jane Austen book, the one whose parents were desperate to marry her off.

"Well, for your information, you two may have more in

common than you think." She settled back into her seat, nestling in as if trying to get comfortable. "His doctors told him he may have trouble conceiving. He only has one testicle."

I was astounded by the personal details that managed to make their way around our church on the wings of prayer requests. "Are you serious? So you thought we would be a match made in infertile heaven?" I crossed my arms, waiting for her defense, which didn't come. "And now you've put me in a position to have to reject this guy."

My father now joined in. "Why would you reject him right out of the gate? You should at least give him a shot."

"Why should I go out with him if I know he's not my type? I'll just be leading him on."

My mother sat up straight, looking hard into the rearview mirror. "Because you can't live with us forever, Ellen!" It came out with more force than she intended, and my father looked at her from the corner of his eye.

"What your mother means is that you can stay as long as you need to, of course, but . . ."

My mother finished for him. "But you need to start getting your own life again." We locked eyes for a moment before I looked away. I didn't say another word for the rest of the car ride, my own hurt indignation trumping my concern over Parker's comment about my parents' situation, which withered in the shadow of the fact that I had worn out my welcome in their home. *I'll find my own place,* I thought, hoping it would be a dank little basement apartment with barred windows and a rat problem.

. . .

After washing my face and changing into sweatpants, I slid between my cool white sheets and I cried, feeling rudderless and rejected and lost. I was just two months away from turning thirty-two, and everything that I thought I wanted was gone. And so I prayed. I prayed like I did on the first night Gary left. I prayed because it was what I'd always done when no one else was watching. When I didn't need to be strong or smart or independent. When I didn't have any answers. When my beliefs didn't need a definition. I believed in God, but was I a Christian? What did that even mean? "It means you've accepted that Christ is your savior." That was what my mother would say. "It means you know that there is only one path to heaven." But I didn't *know* that. All I knew was that that night, I needed help. I wasn't even sure what I was asking for. I just held myself and prayed.

It was a long night, but when I finally did fall asleep, it was deep and dreamless. "That's the peace that passes all understanding," my mother would have said, meaning that it's a peace that can be bestowed only by God.

I walked hesitantly downstairs the next morning, aware of both the late hour and the volume of my footsteps, like a houseguest who is unaccustomed to the rhythm and flow of the household. My mother was waiting in the kitchen. She got up from her stool and rushed over to me the moment she saw me. "Ellen, I'm so sorry about yesterday, honey."

"Don't worry about it, Mom."

"I just have been so scared that you are going to get stalled out here." She gripped my upper arms like she was going to shake me. "You have too much potential for that."

I took an uncertain breath and looked at the floor.

"Oh, Ellen!" My mother reached her arms around my neck and pulled me into a hug. "Please forgive me for what I said."

"No, you were right, Mom. I need to find a place of my own."

I thought of Brenda, tied to her house and her past. "I need to figure some stuff out."

She craned her neck to kiss my forehead. "You take your time, honey. Just take your time."

"I mean, I can start paying rent, too, Mom."

My mother planted her hand firmly on her hip, looking more than a little offended. "What are you talking about?" she asked, her southern accent sounding especially melodic.

"It's only right. I've been living here for months now. I should pitch in." It wasn't too much of a leap to assume that Parker's reference to my parents' "situation" must refer to their finances and the burden of Channing Crossing.

"Well, your father won't hear of you paying rent, and please don't mention it to him. It would kill him to think that you thought you needed to do that."

"But, Mom, if things are tight—"

"What's gotten into you?" she asked as she swept some errant crumbs off the countertop and into her open palm.

"Parker just mentioned something at the Donaldsons'." I hesitated, wanting to spare my mother any discomfort. "Something about how she and Lynn Arnold were praying for your *situation*. I just assumed it had something to do with Channing Crossing."

"Ellen," she scolded, "for months I've been praying that this damn economy was going to turn around and that real estate would pick back up again. We all have." She dumped the loose crumbs into the sink and flipped on the faucet. "Stop being so dramatic."

I felt somewhat relieved of my worry. If their situation were really grave, they certainly wouldn't turn down my offer. I walked over to the coffeemaker and poured a cup. "So, what are you and Dad doing today?"

"Your father has some errands he wants to run, but I am going over to volunteer at a family center that Prince of Peace is involved with."

"What are you going to do there?"

"Well, the center helps single mothers. They do a kind of drop-off thing for the kids on Saturdays, so some of us will watch them and the rest will do some cleaning." She sounded less than enthusiastic about both chores. "But I'm really hoping that I get a chance to pray with these mothers. I guess some of them are refugees." This center was probably expecting a practical, roll-up-your-sleeves type of volunteer, and instead they were going to get my mother. She'd arrive loaded for bear with the 700 Club's hotline on her speed dial and my father's laptop in hand, at the ready for her e-mails with "Urgent Prayer Request!" in the subject line.

"Where is it?"

"It's over in Irvington," she said, her forehead creased like an accordion. Irvington was code for "black community."

"Do you even know how to get there?" I asked, slightly amused.

"A bunch of us are meeting over at Prince of Peace and then carpooling." Her face lit up with an idea that I instinctively knew involved me. "Hey, why don't you come, Ellen?"

My body language spoke for me. "I don't think so, Mom . . ."

"Oh, please! That wonderful minister may be there!"

"I actually have some errands I need to run myself," I said, borrowing my father's excuse.

She was prepared to continue her pitch when Luke padded softly into the room. He was fully dressed but his face was still puffy with sleep. "Can someone drive me to the train station?" he asked.

. . .

I pulled up to my favorite bookstore and found a spot right out front. It was a three-story building with low ceilings, creaky wood floors, and a little café in the back. You always paid a few dollars more for books here, but it was the upcharge for the ambiance. The place had the feel of someone's personal library, with lumpy armchairs and lamps scattered about. After dropping Luke off at the train station, I headed there. It wasn't a scheduled stop, but a whim. A book and a latte seemed like a good idea on a cold, damp Saturday.

They served their coffee in big, mismatched mugs, and I curled my fingers around mine as I crept through the store. The eccentric old owner sat perched on the edge of his stool in front of the register, giving me a yellow-toothed smile as I walked by. Right about now, my mother was probably in the back of a conversion van with eight other well-meaning Christians, feeling every bump and jolt as it sped down the highway, on their way to save some souls. I felt a pang of guilt for not going with her, using my overblown excuse of errands. It wouldn't have killed me to give them a few hours. I could have colored with some kids or scrubbed some floors. So in lieu of real charity I decided to buy a few books to donate to the center and I headed up to the third floor, where the children's books were kept.

A little out of breath by the time I reached the top of the second flight of steep stairs, I paused for a second and looked around the room. The walls were papered with bright, mismatched patterns, and the space had a large carpeted area underneath an enormous tree that sprawled protectively over and around the shelves of books. It looked like it had been fashioned from lumberyard scraps, with felt leaves filling out its magical canopy. Ornaments and lights hung from the branches, making it look like something right out of a storybook. But it was later that I would notice all those details, because in the middle of it all, sitting awkwardly on a too-small stool in the shape of a fairy-tale mushroom, was Mark. He had a copy of *Goodnight Moon* open in front of him, and he pushed his glasses up on his nose before turning the page. He paused, as if giving a memory its due, then closed the book and added it to a stack on his right. He reached his arms out in front of him and arched his back in a lazy Saturday kind of stretch. That was when our eyes met.

CHAPTER SIXTEEN

My heart lurched from my chest, and my lips lifted into an utterly reflexive smile. I let out a breath that came out like a laugh. What I was feeling felt closest to relief, the kind of relief that you might feel upon hearing the jury deliver a not-guilty verdict for a crime of which you were innocent. He smiled softly and genuinely, and I knew, by the look in his eyes, that he recognized me. It was almost as if he was expecting me.

With one hand in his back pocket, he stood and pointed around him. "A family I know just had a baby," he said, by way of an explanation. "I was looking for a gift."

"So you weren't just catching up on your literature?"

He looked down and let out a quiet but heartfelt laugh. "So, how are you?" he asked, his head cocked just a bit to one side.

"I'm good," I said, remembering the state I was in that night. "Much better than the last time you saw me." I then blushed, realizing that I had assumed too much, that he might be trying to place me, vaguely recognizing my face and flipping through his mental files to remember exactly who I was. "I don't know if you remember, but I'm Ellen; I was at—"

"I remember you, Ellen," he interrupted.

I felt that soaring feeling when he said my name. "Hey, you know, I never really did get to properly thank you for everything you did that night. So even though coffee doesn't begin to cut it, could I buy you a cup?" I asked hopefully, pointing in the general direction of the café.

He smiled and gestured toward the stairs. "After you." He was wearing a thin, fitted plaid shirt that looked like it was vintage, a pair of jeans, and Converse sneakers. His hair was a bit longer than I remembered and I thought the extra length looked good on him. His walk was slow, confident, but still totally unaffected.

As we made our way down the stairs, I was aware of every footstep, every creak and groan of the steep wooden steps. "These stairs are more like a ladder," he joked, as he ducked to avoid bumping his head on the low ceiling.

When we got down to the little café, a plump older woman in purple glasses who looked like a retired elementary school art teacher gave us a warm smile. I assumed that she was the owner's wife and probably responsible for the children's space upstairs. "What can I get you two?"

"I'd like another latte, please," I said, holding up my mug for her to refill.

She looked at Mark. "Just a cup of French roast," he said. He had a boyish smile that was unconditionally charming.

"Any room for milk?"

"No. Thanks."

We took a seat at a small table for two next to a window that had a view of the alley and the next building. Mark took a sip of his coffee while the steaming wand screeched in the background.

"I wish you had at least gotten a mocha," I joked. "I owe you much more than a cup of black coffee."

He leaned back in his seat and looked at me warmly. "You don't owe me anything. I'm just glad everything turned out the way it did."

"Me, too," I said, unable to look him in the eye. "I just want you to know that that wasn't something I normally do. I don't usually go to parking garages with men I don't know."

"I didn't think you did," he said, subtly shaking his head.

"And so, do you just roam around at night, looking for damsels in distress?" I instantly regretted the question, the phrasing.

He chuckled and rubbed his five o'clock shadow. "No, I uh . . . saw you in the bar," he admitted. I looked at him expectantly, waiting for him to elaborate. His face turned serious when he went on. "And there was something about that guy that I didn't like."

"Well, thank you. And your instincts."

The plump older woman bustled out from behind the counter and set my latte down in front of me. My mug had a Far Side comic on it and Mark smiled as he read it.

"Do you live around here?" I asked. I had found him. And now I wanted to find out as much as I could about him.

"Not far, over in Maplewood."

He didn't ask where I lived. He thought he already knew.

"Did you grow up there?"

"No." He chuckled. "Pretty far from there, actually. I grew up in Africa."

"Africa. Wow."

"My parents were Peace Corps hippies in the sixties. Then they just kind of stayed. They still live there with my little sister."

"Where in Africa?"

"South Africa now. But we traveled around a lot growing up. We spent a lot of time in Ethiopia."

I was genuinely interested and pressed him for more information. "And what brought you to the States?"

"School," he said. "I went to college and grad school here."

I was quickly becoming irrevocably intimidated when he turned the tables. "What about you? Are you originally from New Jersey?"

"Yup," I said, my tone a telling indicator that I didn't expect him to find this impressive.

"And did you go to college?"

I nodded, noting that he made no assumption that I had any kind of postsecondary education, a hallmark of a broad worldview. It was the antithesis of the Horton crowd, who took for granted that everyone went to college, and it was only a question whether it was Ivy League. "I went to Northeastern, in Boston. I just moved back from Boston, actually."

"Oh, really?" he asked. "What brought you back to New Jersey?"

For a split second, I considered telling him everything. Telling him about Gary and his leaving and why. There was just something about him that inspired trust. I wanted to believe that I could tell him and that he would still sit across the table from me, offering no pity or judgment. But common sense prevailed. "It's a long story."

He didn't push it and instead asked me about growing up here. In turn, we talked about growing up in Africa. "I miss it," he said. "I still have a lot of friends there, so I try to go back twice a year."

I studied the fine crow's-feet at the sides of his eyes and pictured him squinting against the brutal African sun.

"Have you ever been?" he asked.

"No," I answered. The truth was that I'd never really had the desire to go. "It seems like an amazing place, but so . . . tragic, too."

"It is. It's both. It's amazing and tragic."

He asked me about my family, and I asked about his. We talked through our first cup of coffee and then he bought us each a second. Finally, I saw him glance surreptitiously at his watch.

"I don't want to keep you, Mark."

He shook his head. "It's fine."

"No, really, if you have somewhere to be . . ."

He looked reluctant to move. "Well, maybe we could pick this up another time?" He looked at me with eyes that seemed to see everything. "Say, over dinner?"

I couldn't help but beam. "That would be great," I responded, not hesitating for a moment.

He pulled out his cell phone and I gave him my number; then we stood and brought our mugs over to the counter.

"So maybe Friday night?"

"That's perfect."

He inched closer to me, closer than he needed to. "Maybe you can tell me that long story." We were inches apart and I felt the electricity of his presence. "I like long stories."

. . .

I walked giddily back up to the children's floor, smiling and replaying every chord of our conversation. His stack of books still sat next to the mushroom stool, and I picked them up, shuffling through the titles and smiling at his choices. I bought several, including the copy of *Goodnight Moon*.

Sitting in the driver's seat of my car, I shifted into drive and realized that I didn't know where I was going. Still spinning from seeing Mark, I didn't want to go home; I was too happy. So I called Jill.

"Yes, come over!" she practically shouted into her phone. "I've been dying to see you."

I pulled up to Jill's house, which was on a cul-de-sac in the sort of development where people had gates at the beginning of their paver-stone driveways lined with kidney-bean beds of bonsai-like shrubs. Along with garden statuary, black leather recliners, and the mispronunciation of the word *bruschetta*, it was the type of infraction that Kat would categorize as what made Jersey Jersey.

Jill's house was an enormous Tudor-style home that was actually one of the more restrained properties in her neighborhood. I rang the doorbell and Jill's husband, Greg, heaved open the huge, heavy wooden front door.

"Carlisle!" he barked as he pulled me into a bear hug. Greg Wadinowski could accurately be described as a sweetheart, but he looked like a Russian mobster, an impression that was aided by the long, sinister-looking scar down the side of his face. *A knife fight*, you might think, but the menacing effect was due to a clumsy trip at the construction site of a new convenience store.

I reached up and rubbed the top of his head, which I couldn't help but do every time I saw him. He had admirably begun shaving it at the first signs of baldness, so the only hairs on his shiny Mr. Clean dome were from his very prominent eyebrows. He had a thick neck, and his body, which used to be described as stocky, now looked like it was beginning to stretch the confines of his skin; he wasn't fat so much as stuffed. He was wearing a hooded Giants sweatshirt and smelled distinctly of salami sub. If he weren't a very, *very* wealthy man, Mrs. Larkin would never have approved.

"Jill's up in the bathroom. She just went makeup shopping," he said with playful exasperation. Jill's favorite thing to buy had always been makeup. She'd come home clutching her bag and head straight upstairs to begin experimentations in shading and application.

"Oh, I'm in for it, then," I said, knowing that Jill would insist on at least doing my eyes, which at the time had only a bit of shadow smeared onto the lid and some mascara.

Greg patted my back, like I was a buddy he was tagging into a game. Greg adored Jill, and he indulged her shamelessly. He was the type of husband who told her she was beautiful every day, who ordered dessert just so she could have a bite, and who truly believed he was the luckiest man in the world. So what if he came to the dinner table in his boxers?

I knocked once before opening the door to Jill's bathroom. She was perched before the double vanity, inches away from the mirror, carefully lining her lips. She squealed when she saw me and jumped down to give me a hug.

"Elle!" she said, squeezing me hard around the neck. "It is so good to see you!"

"You, too," I said, a bit taken aback by the greeting, which even for Jill was what you might call enthusiastic.

"Oh my God, there is so *much* that we need to talk about. Should we go downstairs and get a cup of tea or something?"

"Tea?" I had never known Jill to drink tea outside the sedative atmosphere of a spa.

She hooked her arm through mine and began leading me out of the bathroom, down the stairs, and into the kitchen, where she quickly closed off the pocket doors leading to their den. Greg was watching a game on their enormous flat-screen and the volume was almost deafening. I took a seat at her massive wooden pedestal table with an ornately carved base. Jill was a big fan of ornamentation.

"So, Thanksgiving was good?" she asked as she pulled a bakery box off the counter.

"Yeah, it was fine. How about yours?"

"*Great*," she answered enthusiastically. "I loved having everything here." This was the first year that Jill had hosted Thanksgiving, which was a big deal in the Wadinowski clan.

"How many people did you end up having?"

Jill placed a tray laden with icing-heavy baked goods down in front of me. "Forty-one." She licked a flake of icing off her finger. She was trying to sound casual about it, but I knew how proud she was that she had pulled it off.

"Whoa, Jill!" I said, thinking of our quiet group of four. "Forty-one people? Did you do all the cooking?"

"Uh-huh," she said, smiling, then clarified, "Well, Theresa helped." Theresa was Greg's mother, a heavy-bottomed Polish matriarch who was fiercely protective of her family. Her wardrobe consisted entirely of velour sweat suits and big designer sunglasses, which she often wore nested into her spiky burgundy hair. She was known as a shrewd woman and an excellent judge of character, who simply sucked in her cheeks, pursed her lips, and turned her head if she didn't like you. It took Jill years to be accepted into the fold, but preparing a Thanksgiving dinner together was a sure sign that she was now viewed as a daughter.

Jill picked up a cheese Danish and took a hearty bite. "Want one?" she asked.

I had never known Jill to casually eat a pastry. I was surprised enough to see them in the house, but the fact that she was actually consuming one, just helping herself to all those refined carbs and that saturated fat, was astonishing. The only time a

Danish ever met her lips was during an all-out feeding frenzy, one that she would punish herself brutally for later with carrot sticks and an elliptical trainer. But this seemed entirely different, as she was simply sitting back and guiltlessly enjoying her snack.

"Sure," I said, choosing a chocolate croissant.

"So tell me, what did you do today?" she asked. She was giddy but trying to hide it, like a fourth grader who just got passed a note from the cutest guy in class. It was very close to how I was feeling.

"Well . . . ," I said, letting myself glow, knowing Jill would never tell me that it was too soon, or even mention the word *rebound*. "I ran into Mark."

It took Jill a moment to process his name, but when she did, her reaction appropriately reflected the magnitude of the situation. "Oh my God, this is *major*!" Her eyes were wide and her voice was a stage whisper. "Where did you see him?"

"At Back Door Books." Grinning, I picked off a corner of the croissant. "We're going out on Friday."

Jill hit the table hard with her open palm. "Shut up!" She looked around the room as if considering a vast to-do list. "We have got to figure out what you're going to wear. Where are you going? Are you going into New York? I'll bet he's a first-date-in-the-city type."

I shrugged. "I have no idea. He's going to call to figure out all that."

This was apparently news that called for further refreshments, so Jill announced that she was making us lattes. "But I only have decaf espresso, okay?"

"Yeah, that's perfect," I said, buzzing from the three I had just polished off at the bookstore.

As she pulled a gallon jug of milk from the fridge, I immediately noticed the telltale red label. It was whole milk. This was too much. "All right, Jill, what gives?" I asked, gesturing toward the milk.

"What?" she asked, pretending to play dumb, though I could see her trying to suppress a smile.

"Jill . . . whole milk?"

"Greg drinks it. I'm out of skim." While this was surely the truth, it was only part of it.

"Come on, Jill."

"All right," she said, bustling toward me. She sat down and inched her chair close. "I promised Greg that I wouldn't tell anyone else until I was at least six weeks, but since his family already knows . . ."

All she had to say was "six weeks." My eyes filled with the sort of happy tears that I hadn't experienced in what felt like years. "Oh, Jill," I sputtered as we locked into a hug. "You're going to be a mom."

"Can you believe it?"

I gripped her shoulders as I began my barrage of questions. "How far along are you?"

"Like, not far along at all. I found out on Wednesday. We were going to keep it quiet, but then Greg told his mom and you know how it goes." Her hands moved together in a rolling motion.

"When are you due?"

"According to those online due-date calculator things, July twenty-sixth."

I felt a brief and fleeting sense of melancholy. I knew those due-date calculators well. I had lived by them when Gary and I were together. *If it happens this month, we'll have a baby in October!*

This brief moment of silence for the past was not lost on Jill. "Elle, is this too . . . hard to talk about right now?"

I put my hand gently on her belly. "Are you kidding? I am so, *so* happy for you." And I was. My joy for Jill was unadulterated. I have often asked myself if my answer could have been so absolute if I had walked into that bookstore that morning and left with nothing more than a couple of paperbacks, novels on love and loss; if I had never climbed up to that third floor. The answer is that I don't know. I would have been happy for Jill, but I would have also, on a more tangible level, been sad for myself.

"So," I said, "how are you feeling?"

"Hungry," replied Jill. She leaned back in her chair and let out a heady, intoxicated giggle. "I am going to get *so* fat." And she picked up the last bit of her Danish and ate it with the wide-eyed look of a child who had just done something naughty and loved it. Jill, who had been on a diet since she was eight, whose mother used to send her to slumber parties with preportioned, shelf-stable Slim-Fast shakes, finally had an excuse to eat without remorse.

CHAPTER SEVENTEEN

It was ten o'clock on Monday morning. My cell phone was placed prominently on my desk, just to the right of my keyboard, stubbornly, deafeningly silent. I was entering the obsessive phase in my wondering when Mark was going to call about Friday. I looked at the phone every few seconds, willing it to ring, all the while trying to temper my expectations and prepare myself for the worst. *He was just looking for an easy out,* I told myself. *Don't expect to hear from him again, ever.* It was a strategy that I had begun to employ late in the days of trying to have a child, beating down my hopes so that on the off chance I got my wish, I would be that much more elated.

When a phone did ring, cruelly, it was my work line.

"All right," began Parker, after the requisite pleasantries, "where are we with the party?"

We weren't anywhere with the party.

"I plan to get to work on it today."

Parker barely let me finish. "I would say the florist is the first priority. Then the guest gifts." I could hear her kids going wild in the back of her car. "Then we need to finalize the head count, of course. And confirm that with Maramar." Maramar was where the party was being held. It was the rarely used estate of a Moroccan prince that had since been converted to a restaurant, or so the story went. "I mean, this party is in, like, two weeks."

"Yup," I said, pressing hard with my pen into a stack of Post-it notes while trying to sound pleasantly professional. "I'm on it."

I hung up the phone and looked over at Brenda. "The Christmas party?" she asked sympathetically.

"What else," I confirmed wearily.

"At least Parker is helping. She is such a doll." Brenda was careful never to say anything about Parker that might be construed as less than worshipful.

I felt an almost irresistible compulsion to bang my head repeatedly on my desk. What else did my job entail besides attending to the needs of Philip and, by extension, Parker Kent? Besides ordering green hydrangeas and buying expensive gifts for business associates? My lack of purpose had never bothered me in the agency environment, but that was when I had other plans for my life. Now I felt as if I'd missed the boat on a meaningful career. As if the smart, hungry girls had put in the long hours and paid their dues while I was preparing for something that was never to be. And now I was doomed to scheduling meetings and making phone calls and eating my lunch alone.

And that was what I did that morning. Exactly that. As Brenda and I sat at our desks and picked at our lunches—each of us had brought salads with leftover turkey packed at home in

Tupperware containers—we made the typical small talk about Thanksgiving. "The kids both came," said Brenda, glowing. "It was just wonderful to have them home." Her daughter-in-law was expecting what was to be her first grandchild. "I just wish they lived closer," she said, explaining that they had moved to Chicago from New York three years ago for her son's, Jake's, career. "He has a great job in marketing for Pepsi." She stared wistfully into her salad as she poked around for a bite that was to her liking. Since Brenda was tethered to her house, she'd have to make do with their twice-yearly visits. "I'll go on the weekends whenever I can, though," she said, as she stabbed a grape tomato with her fork, probably knowing that that wouldn't end up being very often. "Jake has tons of frequent-flier miles from all his travel, so he says that he'll fly me out." It was as if she was selling a product that she didn't quite believe in.

It was a very quiet day at Kent & Wagner, though Philip was in the office. He had spent the majority of his morning on his line with the door closed. I was in the midst of tackling Parker's to-do list when a call came through to me. "Hello, I am trying to reach Philip," came an elegant, breathy woman's voice. "Is he available?"

"I'm afraid he's on another call right now. Would you like to leave a voice mail, or is there something I can help you with?"

"Look, could you let him know that Audrina called and I won't be able to meet him later? Something's come up."

I reached for a pen. "May I have your phone number, Audrina?" As I said her name, I felt Brenda take notice. She did nothing overt. She didn't slow her typing or look over, but she was aware.

Audrina sounded somewhat put out. "He has my number," she said, effectively declining to offer it. "And can you let him know that I tried to leave a message on his cell, but something is wrong with his phone and his voice mail never came on. It just rang *endlessly*."

"Oh," I said, surprised because Philip's phone was his lifeline. "Absolutely."

She said a quick, perfunctory good-bye before hanging up.

I immediately checked Philip's schedule to clear the appointment, but he had no meeting scheduled with an Audrina. It was the rare day when essentially all his meetings were internal, though there was a nebulous chunk of time blocked off beginning at 3:30, which read simply "@WHOB."

When I saw that Philip was off the phone, I gently knocked on his door.

"Philip?" I said, before tentatively walking in. He had several files open in front of him, to which he was returning papers and documents. "An Audrina called just a few minutes ago. She indicated that she wouldn't be able to meet later."

He remained utterly composed and continued straightening his desk. "Oh, right," he said casually. "Thanks, Ellen."

"I tried to clear the meeting from your schedule, but was unclear as to which appointment it was . . ."

"That won't be necessary, Ellen. Thank you, though."

It was a dismissal and so I left. As I sat down at my desk, I again noticed Brenda staring deliberately into her computer screen, her lips pursed just a bit more than usual, a crease in her brow suggesting that she was either concentrating on the task at hand or thinking about something that she'd rather not.

As I closed out of Philip's schedule, I replayed my conversation with Audrina, the familiarity in her voice, the vague details.

It wasn't difficult to imagine that he was having an affair.

Philip was handsome, was charming when he wanted to be,

and had the sort of schedule and lifestyle that made it easy to hide such things. And though I knew that chances were there was a perfectly reasonable explanation for the call, a legitimate meeting or round of drinks with an old friend, something in my gut told me that it was more than that. I couldn't deny that my curiosity was piqued, and not out of sympathy for Parker. It was the sort of schadenfreude that you feel when you hear the first rumblings about a celebrity's drug abuse or troubled relationship, a kind of theoretical conjecture that they might, after all, be human. I wasn't proud that I took some degree of pleasure in the fact that Parker's life may not be perfect, but I also wasn't as ashamed as I should have been. It was all suspicions and assumptions, after all. But the reason for Brenda's affinity for all things Parker had become much more clear. Brenda knew what it was like to be on the other side of an affair. A few days later, when Kat mentioned that she was meeting a girlfriend for a drink at the W Hoboken, Philip's mysterious schedule entry, @WHOB, flashed in my mind.

. . .

It was seven o'clock that evening when my phone finally did ring. I was sitting on the couch with my parents, eating turkey vegetable soup in front of the TV. "Come on, y'all," my mother had said. "Let's eat in the family room tonight. My show's on." Almost every show on TV was my mother's show, but tonight she happened to be referring to a reality series about a family of little people. "I don't know why we can't call them midgets anymore," she murmured, shaking her head in that melancholy way I'd seen seniors do when recalling the good old days. "Everything has to be so *politically correct*, I swear."

I had turned my phone to vibrate, in the likely event that the volume on the TV would render a normal ring inaudible. When I felt the telltale buzzing in my back pocket, my heart leapt, and I pulled out the phone to see a local number that I didn't recognize. I felt like a girl whose boyfriend suddenly pulled out a small velvet box and dropped to one knee. *This must be it!*

"Hello?" I said. Hurrying out of the room, I saw my mother nudge my father to give him a look that was both satisfied and curious.

"Hi, Ellen?" said a man's voice that was too unsure, too nervous to be Mark's. "This is Christopher Hapley. We met the other day at the Donaldsons'?"

"Oh, right," I said, trying to hide my disappointment. "Hi, Christopher."

"I hope you don't mind that your mother gave me your number."

I heard the volume on the TV go down just a couple of levels.

"Of course not."

"So, how are you?"

"Fine," I answered, knowing exactly why he was calling.

"Did you have a nice weekend?"

"I did; how about you?"

"Yeah, it was good," he said, his voice reaching an unnaturally high pitch. He coughed once, quickly, before he went on. "So, I, uh, know we had talked about getting together sometime, so I was wondering if you'd like to maybe see a movie on Friday?"

I closed my eyes and leaned against the wall, wincing as I spoke. "Actually, I'm afraid I have plans this Friday."

"Oh, okay," he said, clearly discouraged but not defeated. "Well, what works for you, then?"

I didn't know what was best, to rip the Band-Aid off now or slowly, in tiny increments, as he called again and again and I just happened to always have plans. "Actually, Christopher, I'm not sure if my mom told you, but I just went through a divorce."

"Uh, yeah," he said uncomfortably. "Yeah, she did, uh . . . mention that."

"And so I just think I should be honest and let you know that I'd love to go out as friends, but I'm really not ready to date yet." It was a lie, but in my mind a harmless one.

"Oh, sure," he said weakly. "I understand. Yeah, maybe we could catch a movie together another time." Now he just wanted to get off the phone.

"Sounds good."

"So I'm sure I'll see you around."

"Definitely. See you around."

"Bye, then."

I felt terrible.

"So who was that?" asked my mother as I walked back into the family room, anticipating just such a question.

"You know exactly who that was," I said coldly, my tone indicative of the outcome of our conversation. "Why would you presume that you could give him my cell phone number?"

She shifted her body on the couch so that she could face me with squared shoulders. "Well," she said, her eyes wide with defiance, "after our conversation in the car, I didn't think you'd have any issue with it."

"You mean the conversation in which you told me he had one nut and that I had to move out? That conversation?"

My father's head was lowered. He was listening but avoiding heading for the trenches just yet. My mother charged onward, working herself into a lather that rivaled my own. "I swear, I think the only reason you won't go out with him is because he is a Christian."

"Bingo!"

"Ellen Louise Carlisle!" gasped my mother.

"Listen, one person forwarding me those 'One Hundred Blessings' e-mails is plenty." Only that day I'd received one, a chain e-mail that you were supposed to forward to ten people within ten minutes, at which point God would be compelled to bless you one hundred times over the next forty-eight hours.

"Don't you mock the Lord!" she shouted.

"That's not who I'm mocking."

"That's enough," commanded my father, always intolerant of us kids crossing the line with my mother from good-natured ribbing to something less kind.

I turned on my heels and walked upstairs.

. . .

When Wednesday came and I still hadn't heard from Mark, I called Kat. But before I launched into a description of our encounter, we had a few other matters to catch up on.

"Have you talked to Jill?" I asked casually. Jill wasn't supposed to be telling anyone about her pregnancy yet, but I knew her too well to think that she'd managed to keep it much of a secret.

"I know! Can you believe it?" I loved hearing that kind of joy in Kat's voice. "I can't wait to find out what she's having."

I realized that I had neglected to ask Jill if she was going to find out the gender. "So she's finding out?"

"Are you kidding? It's Jill. Of course she is," answered Kat. "I hate it when people don't find out."

"I always said that I wouldn't find out."

"Oh my God, are you serious? If I ever have a baby, I'm going to find out *immediately*."

It was the first time I had ever heard Kat talk about having children. As I debated about what to say next, how to follow up on what was a difficult topic for Kat, I lost my opportunity.

"So, Luke said that Thanksgiving was just a *gas*," she said sarcastically.

"It wasn't great. I think everyone missed you."

Kat made a scoffing noise.

"You know Aunt Kathy's coming for Christmas."

"Luke mentioned that, too."

"You've got to see Aunt Kathy while she's here. I mean, I know you're pissed at Mom and Dad, but what did they *really* do, Kat?" We all hated calling Kat on the carpet—we all feared her anger—so I took a deep breath before adding, "You were the one who was out of line that night."

"Ellen," she said bitterly, "you just need to stay out of this. There is *a lot* that you don't know."

I took this to be a proverbial statement about not having experienced what she'd experienced, about never having walked in her shoes. We stayed on the phone in silence for a moment.

"Kat, just tell me that you'll come see Aunt Kathy. It would be so sad if you missed her."

"Fine. Whatever," she said. "Let's just change the subject."

As luck would have it, I had another subject at the ready. I told Kat about Mark.

"So call him," said Kat.

"I didn't get his number," I said meekly. I could see Kat rolling her eyes. She was always the one to take the number, always the one to call, always the one to have the power.

"Well, then you're fucked."

"Why do you think he hasn't called?"

"Maybe he dropped his phone in the toilet. Maybe he has been busy. Maybe he's playing hard to get."

"No," I said. "He's not the game type."

"I don't know what to tell you, Elle."

. . .

When Thursday night passed without a call, I knew that I wouldn't hear from him. It felt like a sucker punch, another disappointment, another hand-wringing period of waiting followed by the inevitable letdown. It was trying to have a child. It was waiting for Gary to come back.

"What's gotten into you, Ellen?" my mother had asked over dinner. It was just the two of us, as my father was working late. Our fight, like all of our fights, hadn't lasted long. My mother hated to be at odds with her children, and since the Kat situation hadn't rectified itself, I was granted leniency.

"I guess I'm just down."

She looked into the distance and muttered something to herself, thinking the solution to my problems was no farther than church. When I went up to my room that night, there was a book lying on my bed with the title *Joy of the Spirit*. I tossed it under the bedside table.

. . .

I was in my car on my way to work on Friday morning, talking to Luke, who was walking to the subway, when a call waiting came in. Since the only people who called me this early—who called me period—were my family and Jill, I answered without checking the caller ID.

"Hello," I said plainly.

"Ellen." I recognized his voice immediately. "It's Mark."

"Mark?" His name came out like a riddle.

"I'm so sorry that I haven't called." His voice was strong but sincere. "But I would still love to take you out to dinner tonight. If you're free."

And all the contingency plans I had made in case he did call went right out the window. I wasn't going to pretend I was busy or tell him that I was seeing someone. I forgot about all the cautions I had repeated, all the warnings about another broken heart. At that moment, I didn't want vindication. All I wanted was to be next to him. "Yeah," I said, feeling a thawing sensation in my body. "That would be great."

There was a smile in his voice when he spoke again. "Do you like Cuban food?"

CHAPTER EIGHTEEN

As he pulled out my chair, the metal legs screeched against the industrial tile floor. The restaurant, which was located at the end of a strip mall in a blue-collar, largely Hispanic town in New Jersey, didn't seem like a typical choice for a first date, but the lighting was dim, the food smelled good, and the music made you feel like all was well with the world. The other tables were filled with families and older couples, mostly Hispanic. I was totally and unconditionally charmed.

Mark sat down across from me, wearing a thin thermal-knit long-sleeve navy blue shirt and a pair of jeans. He smelled good in the way that some men just do, without the aid of aftershave or cologne. He wasn't wearing his glasses tonight but was still unquestionably handsome. He looked around the room, as if trying to view it from my perspective, then smiled shyly. "I know it doesn't look like much, but the food is amazing."

"No, it's great," I assured him. "I'm excited to try it."

As if on cue, a busty, heavily made-up woman with olive skin and curly, almost black hair came to the table with two menus.

"*Hola, Marcos. Me alegro de verte,*" she said, smiling warmly, a large gap between her two front teeth. She set a menu down in front of each of us and appraised me like a mother.

"*Hola, Armena,*" said Mark, rolling his *r* perfectly, sounding as comfortable in Spanish as he did in English. "*¿Cómo estás?*"

"*Buena,*" she answered, before nodding toward me. "*Ella es bonita, Marcos.*"

"*Si, Armena.*" Mark smiled shyly. "*Ya lo sé.*"

"*Bien,*" she said, walking slowly away.

"Sorry," he said, turning back to me.

"What did she say?" I asked.

He lowered his head and leaned toward me. "She said"—he glanced at the waitress, who was staring back at us—"that you are very pretty."

I looked down at my menu and blushed. I had worn a ruffly sleeveless silk chemise and tight black jeans with black boots, which I had rushed home to get on my lunch break. My sweater was hanging on the back of my chair.

Mark had offered to pick me up at home, which as far as he knew was Kat's home. "Actually, I have to work late," I had said, "so maybe we could just meet at the restaurant?" But we settled on Mark picking me up at work. I had changed and primped in the women's room after most everyone had left for the night, the office all but empty and silent as I applied my shimmery gray eye shadow and slicked my lips in a barely there pale pink gloss.

"So what is good here?" I asked, always embarrassed by compliments.

Mark looked reluctantly away from me and at the menu. "Their *ropa vieja* is amazing."

I read the description. "Sold," I said. Though this cuisine originated on a warm Caribbean island, it sounded perfect for a cold December night.

Mark ordered for us after introducing me to the waitress. "He is a good man," she said in heavily accented English, patting Mark on the shoulder.

The restaurant was BYOB, so Mark pulled a bottle of red wine from his beat-up army surplus messenger bag. I immediately recognized the brand; it was a respectable twelve-dollar bottle available most everywhere. I remembered my first date with Gary, how impressed I had been when he ordered a shockingly expensive bottle of cult Cabernet. It seemed like a hundred years ago.

Armena opened the bottle and brought us two tumblers, into which Mark poured the wine. There was no pretentious swirling or sniffing, no bombastic presentation of the cork as there had been with Gary. Mark simply held up his glass. "*Salud,*" he said as our tumblers clinked.

"Where did you learn Spanish?" I asked.

He ran his fingers through his hair and looked like he was trying to remember where along the timeline of his life he had happened to pick up the language. "I lived in Honduras for a few years between college and graduate school."

Again I felt a little intimidated by his adventurous résumé. "What were you doing there?"

"I went down to do some volunteering, building houses and schools, that kind of thing." He spoke as if it were the most natural, commonplace thing in the world. "But then I ended up teaching English after a while."

"How long did you stay?"

"Three years. Then I came back to the States." He took a sip of his wine. "What do you do for that law firm?"

"I'm the assistant to one of the partners. It's just a temporary thing until the economy picks up," I said dismissively. He didn't lie and tell me it sounded interesting, didn't patronize me by pretending to be impressed. He just nodded as if processing the information. "What do you *want* to do?"

"Well, I used to work at an advertising agency in Boston."

"And you want to get back into that?"

"Not really," I said with an embarrassed laugh. "I think I'm figuring all of that out right now." I thought of Luke reminding me of how much I used to like to write.

"What about you?" I asked, realizing that I hadn't yet asked him about his work. "What do you do?"

"Oh . . ." He shifted in his chair, as if surprised I'd turned the focus back to him. "I work for a nonprofit."

"Really? What sort?"

"Well, we are sort of a catchall. But our main focus is poverty, I would say."

"What is it called?"

He paused to take a sip of wine. "The Need Alliance."

It wasn't long before Armena brought our appetizers. We ate with our hands, and Mark watched me, chuckling as I struggled to tame my unruly empanada.

Our entrees came and I drank more wine than I intended to. Soon I had that warm, content feeling in my stomach, and the inhibitions in which I had wrapped myself were starting to fray. But the conversation flowed easily and happily, and I often caught myself staring at the handsome, interesting man across from me, feeling—for the first time in a very long time—lucky.

He cut one of the last bites from his roasted pork loin. We had been talking about college; he had gone to Columbia for graduate school. "Don't you owe me a long story?" he said.

I tilted my head and sighed, remembering everything that had brought me here, to this tiny little Cuban restaurant with the laminate table and neon OPEN sign, thinking that maybe there *was* something to all those clichéd condolences that are intended to give perspective and hope. *Things happen for a reason.* "It's not really a happy story," I said with a bittersweet smile.

Mark rotated his tumbler of wine with his fingertips. With his sleeves pushed up, I saw that the prominent veins on his hands wove their way up to his arms and ran over his taut, long muscles like twine. "I didn't think it would be."

"Why do you say that?" I asked, intrigued by his intuition.

"Long stories never are." He sat back in his chair and looked at me intently. He was effortlessly seductive.

I didn't debate what to say or coyly put off the truth. The facts came out easily and painlessly. "I lived in Boston with my husband," I said plainly. "Well, my ex-husband now," I added quickly. "He left, and so I ended up moving back home to Jersey."

"I'm sorry," he said.

"It's okay." And it was. I realized that it really wasn't such a long story after all. "Now I have a question for you," I said, feeling emboldened by the liberating honesty. "Why did you wait until today to call me?"

He looked a little sad. "It's a long story," he said ironically, trying to smile.

Just then, as if by divine intervention, he was let off the hook as an old man stood and took his wife by the hand. They began dancing with slow, small steps. He had one hand around her waist; the other they clasped, she fitting into his chest perfectly as they danced like they must have danced a thousand times before.

Armena came to clear our plates and nodded her head toward the dancing couple, saying something in Spanish to Mark. "She said that every time they hear this song, they dance," he explained. Conversations paused at tables all around the restaurant as patrons gazed at the old couple with admiration and fondness. The song ended and they sat, with as little ceremony as they had stood. There were a few claps. Mark looked at me and smiled.

. . .

Mark's car idled in front of mine in the parking lot by my office. "Why don't you let me drive you home?" he suggested.

"No, I really am fine." The wine buzz that I had had over dinner had faded, though I didn't want to get out of his car just yet.

"Are you sure?" he asked.

"I'm sure."

He pulled into a spot near mine and got out to open my door, extending his hand to help me out. I lowered my chin into the neck of my coat to ward off the cold.

"I had a great time tonight," I said, as I stood with one hand on my driver's side door handle.

Mark didn't say a word. Instead he leaned slowly in and slid his hand onto my lower back, planting a whisper of a kiss on my lips. I never imagined such a gentle kiss could feel so explosive.

"I'll call you," he said as our lips parted, his mouth still inches from mine.

CHAPTER NINETEEN

I was lying on Kat's bed, staring at the huge glass lantern that hung from the ceiling. It was romantic, I decided, to have something like that above your bed. When I got a place of my own, I'd get one just like it.

"So you like him," said Kat. It wasn't a question, but a statement of fact. She sat up in bed and regarded me carefully, waiting for my reaction. Though she hadn't been thrilled when I'd let myself in early Saturday morning, I had plied her with bagels with cream cheese and smoked salmon, which I'd picked up on the way there.

I rolled over and faced her. "Yeah. I like him."

"But he had no explanation for why he didn't call until the morning of the night you guys were supposed to go out?"

"He just said it was a long story."

This was not an excuse that would typically fly with Kat, but he had earned merit points for the unusual and unpretentious choice of locale for our date.

"So when are you going to see him again?"

"He just said that he'd call."

"He has three days. Tops. If it goes longer than three days, then he has some weird baggage . . . like a wife and kids."

I knew that Kat was just trying to reacquaint me with the rules of the road for dating, but I was too dangerously blissful to pay any attention. "I can't wait for you to meet him," I said.

Kat gave me a look of warning. "Just . . . be careful, Elle. It's been a while for you, and this is the first guy since Gary." She paused, choosing her words carefully. "Just don't fall too hard too fast."

I knew that this was going to become common advice, echoed by Luke and then Jill. But the truth was that it was already too late for cautions and warnings. Even *before* last night, it would have been too late. "Don't worry, Kat," was all I said.

"Does this mean you are over the whole Gary thing?" Coming from anyone else, this comment would have sounded flip and insulting, but Kat wasn't trying to minimize my divorce. We were just treading in uncomfortable waters for her; she hated self-help-y language. *Does this mean that you've begun to heal from the breakup of your marriage?* It was something Kat would simply never say.

"I don't know if you 'get over' things like that. I think you just kind of learn to live with it." I thought for a moment about how easy it seemed to be for Gary to leave, about what, exactly, it was that I had mourned. "But I don't think any of it would have happened if Gary and I had been meant for each other. I mean, by definition it couldn't have."

Kat's silence said everything. I knew that she was thinking about how convenient this epiphany was, what a cozy little coincidence that it came to me on the heels of meeting someone new. I would have thought the same thing.

. . .

Mark did call. He called that same day, when I was elbow deep in dirty clothes in my parents' laundry room. I had been neglecting my laundry for a couple of weeks, and today suddenly felt like the perfect day to tackle it. Not only did I rigorously sort my clothing according to color and fabric type, but I pretreated stains and meticulously folded a load that had been left in the dryer. That's what a great date can do; it can be like a shot in the arm. I closed the door to the washer and pulled my cell phone from the pocket of my sweatpants.

"Hey," said Mark, his voice deep and slow. "You made it home okay last night?"

It sounded like he was in the car. "Yeah," I said, tucking my hair behind my ear. "Totally fine."

"What are you up to this week?"

I grinned like a teenager. "Just work, really."

"I would love to see you." I pictured him driving, gripping the wheel hard as he spoke. "Tonight I have some work that I need to do and tomorrow I have plans, but what about Monday after work?"

"Monday sounds good."

"Do you want me to pick you up at work again? Or do you want to go home first?"

"Why don't we meet at work? It's just easier." I resolved to come clean about where I really lived, whom I really lived with.

"I'll pick you up at five thirty, so we can grab dinner before the show."

"Show?"

I knew he was smiling. "You'll see."

. . .

The message at church the next day was on acceptance, and the soft-spoken, humble John Blanchard stood before the congregation, telling the story of the woman at the well, in which Jesus and his disciples passed through Samaria and stopped at a well to draw water. The disciples continued on to a small village to buy food, leaving Jesus alone. "It was noon, the hottest time of the day, when she came, to find Jesus resting there." Reverend Blanchard held his Bible in both hands in front of him, with gentle reverence. "All the other women had gone in the morning, but this woman—this woman was an outcast among outcasts." The Samaritans, he had explained, were despised by the Jews, but the woman at the well was the object of particular ostracism, having committed adultery. "But Jesus spoke to her. He spoke to her, he drank from her cup, and he offered her the living water, which is life everlasting." His voice grew in power, reaching a crescendo as he spoke of eternal life. "He did these things because Christ doesn't care about our reputation. He doesn't care about our sins or our past. Pauper or prince, leper or king, he offers us all his magnificent grace."

When the service ended, I walked out with my parents. Stopping when they stopped, I greeted the Arnolds, said hello to Christopher Hapley, and waved at Parker, who was there alone this morning.

"What did you think?" I heard my mother ask my father as we made our way to the car.

"It was a good message," he said solemnly.

"I thought it was just okay. It didn't really speak to me today." My mother sounded let down. She liked to leave church feeling as if a divine hand had guided the sermon from the minister directly to her. "You know, I think John Blanchard sometimes gets stuck in a rut."

My father didn't comment; he just marched onward toward the car, his well-coiffed white hair, black overcoat, and serious expression making him look like a somber head of state, the type that knows too much to sleep well at night.

"Next weekend I think I'm just going over to Prince of Peace," said my mother, lowering her voice and offering a friendly wave to a familiar-looking couple engaged in conversation by a potted spruce adorned with a burgundy velvet bow. "I'm telling you, that minister there is alive with the word. You know, when I was over at that family center again yesterday, he and I had a powerful conversation." I was trailing behind them, feeling as I used to as a child, trying to pick up the nuances of their conversation, to read between the lines. "I had a chance to . . . *talk* to him," she said, as if *talk* was a code word of some sort, "and he had such wisdom." My father continued walking, the pace of his steps continuous and steady, like the beating of a heart.

When we got home, my father retired to his office, closing the door behind him. My mother began addressing Christmas cards. "I could really use your help with this," she said, as she pushed her reading glasses up her nose and squinted into her address book. Her penmanship was childlike and illegible, one of the remaining vestiges of being a poor preacher's daughter in the rural South. Unlike the southern belle she often pretended to be, she didn't spend hours a day writing in cursive on monogrammed stationery. "Your handwriting is so much nicer."

I pulled up a chair and picked up one of her fine-tip markers. "Where's the list?" She handed me a sheet of loose-leaf paper with about one hundred names scrawled down it in columns. She had crossed off the cards she had completed so far.

"I'll stuff the envelopes," she said, picking up a gold-trimmed card with a classic oil painting of a trumpeting angel. Inside was printed,

> *For unto us a child is born, unto us a son is given: and the government shall be upon his shoulder: and his name shall be called Wonderful, Counseller, The mighty God, The everlasting Father, The Prince of Peace. —Isaiah 9:6*
> *With love this Christmas,*
> *Roger and Patty Carlisle*

It was a card sent out of tradition, out of obligation, as a sign of life. It would be briefly read, the communication noted; then it would be quickly forgotten, serving only to keep my parents in an ever-extending and expanding circle of acquaintances. The cards they would receive in exchange would feature mannered grandchildren posed in front of trimmed trees with their hands folded neatly in their laps, doting parents and grandparents seated at their sides. Letters would be included with news on Ann and Stephen's move to Paris, where the children would attend the American School. Or James's promotion to vice president at the company that his grandfather had founded.

My mother looked down as she licked an envelope. "Have you talked to your sister?" she asked.

"Yeah," I said cautiously. "Kat and I have talked."

"Is she planning on coming to see Aunt Kathy when she's here?"

"She said she is," I reported, relieved that I wouldn't have to be in the position to either condemn or defend Kat if she hadn't planned on seeing our aunt.

"Well," said my mother, playing the gatekeeper, "I don't know when she thinks she's going to see her. Aunt Kathy has a whole bunch of things she wants to do when she's here. We can't just wait around for when Kat decides to show up."

"I don't think Kat expects you to wait around. I'm sure she'll work around your plans."

"Right," scoffed my mother. "Your sister doesn't care a thing about other people. That's her problem right there." She shook her head, as if reviewing the evidence against Kat. "She's totally self-centered."

"Mom," I groaned. I hadn't wanted to go down the Kat route. "Let's drop it, okay?"

"Fine," she replied indignantly. "I just think that you ought to tell Kat that if she wants to see her aunt, then she should at least call me to make some plans."

. . .

The next day, I sat at my desk, willing the day to pass quickly so that I could see Mark, but the six hours that I still had to put in at the office seemed an impossible, interminable amount of time. So it should have been a given that Parker would call, to effectively halt time with a colonoscopy of a conversation.

"So, everything with the party is all set?" she asked.

I gave her a status update on her tedious, exaggerated little to-do list, the tasks of which I'd mostly accomplished.

"Oh, that's great, because I am so busy that I *literally* don't think I could do one more thing."

I twisted the phone cord around my finger. *I would have*

never been like you, I thought. *If I had your life, I would have been so different.* "Yup, everything is basically done," I said.

"You are such a gem, Ellen," gushed Parker. Coming from anyone else, this remark may have sounded sincere, but Parker's intent was to establish hierarchy, making sure I understood my subservience. As if to prove my theory, she added, "I just wish my housekeeper was as on top of things as you are."

"All right, well, I'm sure I'll talk to you soon," I said, trying to sound cheerful.

Philip walked into the office as I was replacing the receiver. "Was that Parker?" he asked as he hung his coat on the rack near my desk.

"Yup. She was just checking on the Christmas party details."

He forced a smile that almost instantly vanished. "It sounds like you two have managed to become close again."

I smiled and made a small noise that was intended to sound like pleasant agreement, while turning back to my computer. Philip took a few steps and hovered above my desk. Across the way, Brenda shifted in her seat. "I know this is awkward, but since you and Parker are . . . friends, I just want to reiterate the need for discretion. Privacy is very important to me and the firm, and of course I wouldn't want to put Parker in the uncomfortable position of knowing something that she . . . shouldn't."

Instinctively, I knew that this conversation had to do with that strange phone call from the woman with the regal voice. "I understand," I said, feeling uncomfortably complicit. Any voyeuristic enjoyment around my speculations and conjecture was instantly gone, because if it was real—if Philip's affair passed out of the realm of the hypothetical—then Parker would deserve my sympathy. I didn't want that moment to come, when I was compelled to shake my head and avert my eyes, joining with others in their clichéd laments. *What a shame. The poor children.* I didn't want to feel sorry for Parker. I wanted to hate her.

When Philip went back into his office, I looked over at Brenda, who was on her way to the ladies' room. She walked quickly, her ankles wobbling a bit since she was unaccustomed to the heels she was wearing.

"What do you think?" she had asked that morning, turning proudly in front of me, angling her foot so that I could get a good look. "Beth talked me into them." Beth was her daughter.

"They're great," I said. "Very sexy."

I now heard the clack of those heels as they hit the hardwood floor. She brought her curved hand thoughtfully to her mouth as she rounded the corner and disappeared. I wondered if Philip had had the same conversation with her.

CHAPTER TWENTY

Later that day, Helen, the receptionist, rang my line. Helen had been with Kent & Wagner for decades, having been hired by Philip's father when he started the firm. "Ellen, you have a visitor," she growled. Though, from what I understood, she had never smoked a day in her life, her voice sounded like she had a pack-a-day habit.

I immediately panicked. "Oh, okay. I'll be right down." I hadn't expected Mark to come in, thinking he would just call when he arrived.

I grabbed my bag and slid on my coat, logging off my computer before racing toward the stairs. Brenda had left at five p.m. sharp to go to her Pilates class. As I glanced into my bag to make sure that I had remembered my cell, I nearly bumped into Philip, who was leaving one of the associates' offices.

"You heading out, Ellen?" he asked casually.

"Yup," I answered, glancing down the mezzanine to see

Mark sitting on one of the long leather couches. His legs were wide and crossed, and he was leaning back, his arm draped over the seat back. Philip followed my gaze.

"Oh," he said, registering Mark's presence, "have fun."

Mark smiled and stood when he saw me at the top of the steps, which I made my way quickly down. As he gently kissed my cheek, I felt the slight prickle of his stubble. "It's good to see you."

"You, too."

He looked around the office, appearing neither impressed nor unimpressed. "You all set?"

He put his arm protectively around my back and led me outside.

"Where are we going?" I asked, once we were in the car.

"Well, we are going to grab a bite to eat," he began, his eyes on the road. "Then there is a group of Tibetan monks who do this amazing chanting. They are going to be performing at Lane College, so if you're interested, I thought we could go check that out."

"I'd love to," I said earnestly.

"But next time," he said, briefly resting his hand on my knee, "it's your turn to pick what we do."

I smiled, my heart soaring at the promise of a third date.

We pulled up to an Indian restaurant near the college. "It's like a Himalayan theme night," he joked.

Once we were inside, the service was brusque; the waitress seemed to have been abused by one too many college students. She rushed us to a table and dropped two menus in front of us. "I'll be back for your order," she said, before hurrying away. I began to peruse the plastic-covered menu, which, from the dull, matte streaks, looked like it had just been wiped with sanitizer.

"Mutton?" I asked, more to myself than to Mark.

"It's usually sheep, but here they use goat." Seeing the look on my face, he let out a genuine and indulgent laugh. "It can actually be really good." But we kept our order a little more conventional, requesting chicken curry, dal, and a generous basket of naan from our unimpressed waitress.

"Is that all?" she asked, without looking up from her order pad.

"Yes, thank you," answered Mark.

I watched her hurry to the kitchen, then turned to Mark. "So, I have a confession," I said. And for a moment, Mark looked like he was enjoying a private joke.

"Remember that condo where you dropped me off . . . that night?" I could tell that we both avoided any unnecessary reference to the very first night we met.

He nodded, though he looked unsure of where I was going.

Though I had rehearsed what I was going to say a hundred times, had convinced myself that my explanation was reasonable and rational, I was suddenly nervous.

"It was actually my sister's place." I forced myself to maintain eye contact. "I have been living with my parents since my divorce, but her place was so much closer and you had already been so nice, and I just didn't want . . ."

"Shhh . . . ," said Mark, both amused and concerned by my anxiety. "I get it. Don't worry."

"I'm sorry."

"What are you sorry for?" he asked kindly.

I didn't answer.

We finished up our meal and the waitress brought our check, which Mark refused to let me near. Though I appreciated the gesture, I knew that he probably didn't make much at his nonprofit.

"All right, but next time," I said as he handed his credit card to our waitress, "*everything* is my treat."

. . .

We took our seats just before the show started, whispering our *excuse me*'s as we shimmied past the more timely audience members. The lights dimmed slightly as the monks took the stage, dressed in turmeric-colored robes, some carrying long horns. The audience of largely students and professors leaned forward, not from excitement so much as from preparation, the way you might settle in before an important lecture. The monks started their performance with little fanfare; they simply began emitting their deep, vibrating songs while standing below crisscrossing prayer flags that hung in the space above the stage.

"They're saying prayers in their religion," whispered Mark, referring to the chants. He turned to look at my face. I was absorbed. I wouldn't call the sounds beautiful, exactly, but they were unique, exotic. "It's interesting, isn't it?" he asked.

It was.

When the show was over, I thanked Mark. "Where did you hear about them?" I asked, gesturing to the now empty stage.

"I saw a similar group a while back," he said. "I was a religion minor in college, so it was part of one of my courses."

The doors opened and we made our way back outside. It was one of those beautiful clear winter nights when everything seems crisper, sharper, from the crystalline air. "Want to go for a walk?" Mark asked.

It was a nice enough campus, though the buildings were modern, not those quintessential old ivy-covered buildings that came to mind when I thought of universities.

"How has it been, living with your parents?" asked Mark.

"It's been all right. Better than you might expect, actually." As I said it, I realized that it was true. Despite exasperations large and small—maybe in part *due* to exasperations large and small— being in my parents' home had provided the comfort of the familiar. "I'm starting to look for my own place, though."

"Where are you looking?" I knew that Mark lived in his grandparents' house, which had been left to him when his grandmother died a few years ago. His mother was originally from New Jersey and had lived most of her life here before moving to Africa.

"In the general area," I said. "Maybe near Kat's." From Mark's description of his neighborhood, I figured he wasn't more than a fifteen-minute ride from my sister's place.

"So," started Mark, "are you still in contact with your exhusband?" He had made the uncomfortable segue to my divorce.

"We aren't on terrible terms or anything, but I haven't really spoken with him much." I thought for a moment, my hands dug deep into my pockets. "I wouldn't call us friends yet."

Mark hesitated. "If you don't mind my asking, what happened?"

It was the question I had been dreading, but coming from him it somehow seemed neutered. It was as though my fear had magnified it so much that when it was actually asked, I was prepared. Confronting the beast in the flesh was sometimes easier than confronting it in your mind.

I watched my feet as I spoke, avoiding the cracks in the concrete. "Gary really wanted children," I started. It was the first time I had spoken his name to Mark. "But we had a lot of trouble conceiving. We just couldn't." I kept my focus on the ground. "*I* couldn't."

"And so he left you?" asked Mark, with a deep furrow in his brow.

"I mean, I guess that's the story. But it's probably not that simple." I watched my breath cloud in front of me before continuing. "I think Gary and I seemed right for each other on paper, but something was . . . missing."

It was hard to describe what that something was. Gary and I had loved each other; at least we did when we got married. But I had begun to realize that I loved the idea of Gary more than I loved Gary. And maybe it was the same for him. We each had all the résumé points the other was looking for, but somehow they never exactly added up.

Mark took my hand and pulled us gently to a stop. I expected the standard follow-up questions, on why we didn't adopt, what else we had tried, but he just brought his hand to my chin and studied my face for a moment before he kissed me.

We stood there, our faces flushed with the cold, our noses and cheeks red, our warm breath mixing with the winter air, and just kissed.

Later on, I would remember that night as the night I fell in love with him. It was what everyone and everything had told me not to do, the classic mistake after a divorce or breakup, falling in love with the first guy you meet. *Don't look for your self-worth in another man! You need to reconnect with you!* shouted all the books, shouted reason and logic and good judgment.

But maybe it's fate, I whispered back. Now, of course, I'm certain it was, though for quite different reasons.

. . .

"You're home late," said my mother. I hadn't expected her to be awake, but she was sitting in the living room in her bathrobe, her feet propped up on an ottoman. The only illumination in the room came from the blue glow of the TV, which frenetically cast and then withdrew light from the dark room. The volume was so low that it was almost inaudible. She wasn't watching TV; it was just keeping her company.

"Yeah, I had plans after work." I hadn't thought to let her know; I never did when it was Luke or Kat or Jill that I was with.

"With who?" she asked. She looked tired, too tired to fight.

"A guy I met."

I waited for her reaction. It was her reflex to disapprove, to assume that no man I found would be good enough, smart enough, *Christian* enough. That was the one chink in Gary's armor with my parents—he wasn't a devout Christian. He was brought up Catholic and attended Mass on major holidays, but that was it. And though she would never say it, I'm sure she believed that was why he was capable of leaving, because he was somehow corrupted. And he was corrupted because he was corruptible.

"What did y'all do?" asked my mother.

Though I could have and should have lied, though I knew what I was about to start, I told her the truth. "We went to dinner." I dropped my bag by the couch. "And then we went to watch a group of Buddhist monks perform these chants."

She brought her hands to her face and covered her eyes. "Ellen!" she gasped. "Why would you drink from another well when you have the everlasting spring of the Holy Spirit living in you!"

I felt a surge of what closely resembled satisfaction. That was why I told her, because I knew that she was going to say something like that: a dogmatic, overblown line that made Christianity sound small and petty and insecure.

"Mom, please," I scoffed, "there is nothing wrong with listening to Buddhists chanting. Didn't you hear the sermon yesterday in church? Wasn't it about acceptance and tolerance?"

She was on her feet. "Ellen, that's not what Reverend Blanchard meant and you know it! I just don't know why you would open yourself up to that!"

"Listen, Mom. It's a part of their culture. It was a performance. They weren't signing up new monks or anything."

She propped her hand on her hip. "So, what is this *guy* you're dating, a Buddhist?"

"No, Mom," I said. "He's not a Buddhist. He was a religion minor in college."

She acted like I had just punched her in the stomach and she gripped the side of the chair for support. "Jesus," she muttered, not as an expletive but as the beginning of a prayer.

"Good night, Mom," I said, rolling my eyes. My mother could always be counted on to do what we expected. She was a familiar, exasperating constant.

. . .

"Ellen," called my mother as I rushed out the door for work, "remember you need to come with me to the airport on Friday." Aunt Kathy was flying in from California later that week, and my mother, who hated to park at Newark airport, insisted that I circle the terminal while she went in. "So don't make any plans with that *Buddhist*." That was what Mark was now known as, "the Buddhist." After a few attempts to set her straight, I had thrown in the towel.

"I know, Mom. I got it," I said.

"I mean it, Ellen. I don't want to leave my car there for even a minute. The *Ledger* ran a story just the other day about how Newark leads the nation in car thefts."

"You told me." Aunt Kathy would be staying for three weeks, spending Christmas and New Year's with us while her husband, a retired naval captain, went on a sailing trip down the coast of Central America with his brother. Aunt Kathy's only child, my cousin Libby, was married to a Swede and living in Stockholm.

. . .

Mark and I were having a quick lunch on Wednesday; then we would see each other again Saturday night. I was planning on taking him into New York, where we would meet Luke and Mitch for a drink after, as Luke had suggested, going to the Pierre-Alain Rigauraut exhibition at the MoMA.

"Are you sure that's a good date idea, Luke? I mean, I don't exactly frequent museums."

"So?"

"So it just feels a little fake. A little not me."

"You don't have to pretend to be Peggy Guggenheim. And who cares if the only reason you are going is because Mark will be with you?" His voice took on a dreamy quality. "Relationships should get us outside of our own little worlds."

I smiled. I knew how much Luke loved Mitch. He had been reading more, recommending books to me that Mitch had suggested to him. Mitch was bringing out the best in Luke.

"You're right," I agreed.

At lunch I told Mark about our plans. "I thought we could go into the city," I said, as I tried to eat my Reuben, thinking that it was a poor choice. No man should see you eat a Reuben until after you've slept together. "There is supposed to be a great exhibition at the MoMA; then we could meet my brother and his boyfriend for drinks."

"Oh, the Rigauraut thing."

"Yeah," I said, impressed that he had known about it.

He popped a potato chip in his mouth. "I'm meeting the family, huh?" he teased.

"Is that weird?" I asked self-consciously. I knew that we hadn't been together long, if we were even officially together. "It's just that Luke is great, and Mitch is great, and I think you'd really like them."

"Relax," he said, rubbing my knee. "I'd love to meet your brother. Hey, invite your parents!"

Though he was joking, I gave my usual disclaimer regarding my parents. "All right. I just hope you like talking about Jesus."

"Oh, are they Christians?" he asked. In my experience, people only ever asked this question in one of two ways: with Moonie-like enthusiasm that they'd found some like-minded soul, or with a combination of disbelief and disdain, similar to the way you might ask someone if they'd just farted. But Mark seemed entirely neutral.

"Yeah, you could say that," I said sarcastically.

"Are *you*?" he asked. Shockingly, no one had ever really asked me that before, not in any meaningful way. An assumption was always made one way or the other, depending on the audience. My friends and peers marveled at how I managed to escape indoctrination, while my parents' set—the Arnolds, Donaldsons, and the like—assumed I shared my parents' views. I had never

been called upon to communicate the complex and personal matter of my faith and consequently had no idea how to answer. So I
answered honestly, taking a deep breath first.

"I don't know what I am." Mark looked at me as if he understood entirely. "But my mother calls you *the Buddhist*," I added,
seeking to bring some levity back to the conversation, to move
away from the more weighty side of faith and religion.

"The Buddhist?" He laughed. "Why, because of the monks?"

I nodded. Mark looked at me, shaking his head and quietly
laughing, as if it was funnier than I even knew.

CHAPTER TWENTY-ONE

Aunt Kathy was already waiting by the curbside pickup of Terminal C when we pulled up. The moment she and my mother made eye contact, they screamed like teenagers. My mother swung open the door before I had even come to a complete stop and hopped out of the car to embrace her sister. They stood there, not even speaking, just gripping each other like they couldn't let go.

I rolled down the passenger's side window. "Come on, you two," I called. A police car idled behind us, monitoring the area.

"Ellen, honey," said Aunt Kathy, bustling over to my side of the car and giving me a kiss through the window. "I am so sorry about everything with Gary." I hadn't seen Aunt Kathy since before the divorce.

"Thanks, Aunt Kathy." A gray minivan flew by us and came within inches of Aunt Kathy, whose rear end was nearly in the next lane. "Oh my God!" I said, as air currents from the traffic whipped my hair around my face. "Just get in the car."

Aunt Kathy and my mother sat together in the backseat

while I played chauffeur. They had a routine every time Kathy came to visit, which involved stopping first at White Castle for mini-cheeseburgers, then going to a liquor store to buy a bottle of Absolut Peppar. My mother wasn't much of a drinker, but she and Aunt Kathy always had Bloody Marys whenever they got together. They had been doing it for almost forty years, ever since my father—who had been down in Georgia working on the Holster Dam—got a call from a friend who had a job for him, something to do with real estate development, up in New Jersey.

Aunt Kathy was a little plumper than my mother, with big, country-western blond hair and a new set of breast implants. "Feel 'em," she urged me in a southern accent that had stayed even more pronounced than my mother's, plunging her chest forward. "They feel just like real tits." This was Aunt Kathy's shtick; she played at being the bawdy broad, but underneath she was just as much a prude as my mother. Though she had always been the less inhibited of the two, she was just as devout a Christian.

I looked at Aunt Kathy's protruding bosom in the rearview mirror. "Maybe when I'm not doing eighty down Route 78."

"You're going eighty!" gasped my mother. "Slow down; the police are all over this road and you still have Massachusetts plates. They'd just love to get an out-of-stater."

My mother seemed instantly reinvigorated by Kathy's presence, as did her appetite. "Just go through the drive-through," she ordered when I pulled into the parking lot of White Castle, the fast-food chain whose outlets looked, indeed, like small white castles. "And get maybe eighteen, half without mustard and onion and half with."

"Good Lord, Patty!" said Aunt Kathy, laughing. "I'm not going to eat *nine* cheeseburgers!"

"Well, we'll just bring 'em home," said my mother. "Roger'll eat 'em."

"Mom, leftover White Castle burgers are kind of disgusting."

She crossed her arms, acting like everyone was spoiling her fun. "Fine. Just get twelve."

Like a carpooling parent, I grabbed the huge grease-spotted bag from the drive-up window and passed the order to the back-seat.

"Now, tell me again, when is Eugene White speaking?" asked Aunt Kathy between bites.

"The twenty-seventh," answered my mother.

"I can't wait to hear him again," said Aunt Kathy. "You know I saw him that time when Bill and I were in Sacramento. Must have been about eight years ago now."

"I remember," said my mother, nodding as she blotted her still-chewing mouth with a napkin. "I wonder if he'll be as good as he was back then. I've heard he's changed since he's become so successful."

"Isn't that a shame," said Aunt Kathy, leaning over the nap-kin that was spread across her lap, a diminutive burger in her hands. "You know, I think Warren Allen is another one that's getting a little big for his britches." From overhearing my moth-er's twice-daily phone conversations with Aunt Kathy, I knew that Warren Allen was the minister at the megachurch that Aunt Kathy attended in Orange County. "I heard from the church sec-retary that he's been talking to the Christian Broadcasting Net-work." Kathy and my mother both adopted the same resigned but knowing expression. They had seen it all before, the engulf-ing power of even just a little fame.

My mother and her sister grew up in the Pentecostal tradition, the two daughters of a well-known but poor minister who often traveled to perform faith healings at revivals. "Everybody knew Daddy," my mother used to say about the grandfather that I never knew. "He healed half the state of Georgia." As the story went, as my grandfather's acclaim grew, so did his legalism. "We weren't allowed to wear makeup or cut our hair," my mother had once told me. "He wanted us in skirts." He became stricter and stricter, leaving his congregation for their inability to separate themselves from sin, and eventually alienating his wife, my grandmother. Though they never divorced, they lived separately for the last few years of his life. She moved out to take care of her dying father; after he passed, she remained living with her mother. "All he saw was sin," my mother had said. "It eventually drove him out of his mind." He died alone at the age of fifty-one of a brain aneurism. My mother was twenty-five.

When we arrived back at the house, my father came out to the driveway to help Aunt Kathy with her bags. "Roger, honey." She pulled him into her big, silicone chest. "How you holding up?" she whispered.

My father smiled patiently. Being around both my mother and Aunt Kathy always seemed to exhaust him, and I expected that he would be spending more time than usual in his office. "Fine, Kath. Good to see you," he said, as he picked up one of her two suitcases, which he lifted up and down like it was a barbell. "What do you have in here? Bricks?" My father was a firm believer in tried-and-true jokes, so we all gave him the requisite chuckle.

"Honey, I'm staying for three weeks! Plus, I had to bring y'all Christmas presents."

"Kathy!" scolded my mother, who was older than her sister

by only twelve months. "I told you that we are keeping things simple this Christmas. It's not going to be a big to-do." When my father first began making money, our Christmases mushroomed into enormous, epic events. They threw lavish parties, had family portraits taken, and surrounded our huge, beautifully decorated tree with mountains of presents. But over the past couple of years, the parties had stopped, the gifts became more restrained, and the mood turned increasingly more subdued.

"Oh hush, Patty. I didn't go overboard."

I grabbed Aunt Kathy's other bag while my mother and Aunt Kathy rushed ahead into the house, oblivious of the Sherpas behind them.

"Three weeks, huh?" my father said to me.

"Three weeks."

The Bloody Marys were already in the mix by the time we got inside. Aunt Kathy was playing bartender. "Y'all want one?" she asked.

My father declined, but I accepted. "Sure, thanks."

She pulled a jar of horseradish from the fridge, then bumped the door closed with her hip, as comfortable as if it were her own kitchen. "I like *lots* of horseradish," she said as she twisted off the cap, careful not to nick her long, magenta nails.

While my mother had long attempted to at least blend in with the Yankees among whom she lived, Aunt Kathy was still larger-than-life southern. She was wearing a teal, off-the-shoulder sweater that showcased her new DD cups, and she always, *always* looked like she had just had her makeup done by Mary Kay. Her breasts were huge, her hair was huge, and her personality was huge. My mother was wearing a black cashmere turtleneck that she had owned for years, fitted houndstooth pants, and a black velvet headband. As I regarded both of them, it seemed that though they had almost identical faces, they were from different planets.

"Here," said Aunt Kathy, sliding me a giant glass that was almost overflowing and tapping it with her fingernail. "I guarantee that that's going to be the best Bloody Mary you've ever tasted." Aunt Kathy said this every time she made Bloody Marys.

She took a substantial sip of her own and slapped the counter with her open palm. "That is exactly what I needed after that flight!"

My mother looked utterly delighted, like a child being entertained by the antics of the class clown.

"Ellen," said Aunt Kathy, brushing her bangs, which were nearly immobilized with hair spray, away from her face. "Ready to feel me up yet?" She again leaned forward with her chest, ready for a grope.

I reached forward and gave Aunt Kathy's chest a two-handed squeeze.

"My word, Kathy!" said my mother, pretending to be embarrassed.

"Aren't they natural?" asked Aunt Kathy. "I went to one of those Hollywood doctors. He does all the movie stars' tits."

"Oh, Kathy. That's enough," said my mother, now blushing.

Aunt Kathy rolled her eyes. "Patty, they're just boobs. Good Lord." She gave me a wink. "And Ellen may want a pair of these one day when she meets a new man."

My mother crossed her arms, her thoughts instantly and obviously turning to *the Buddhist*.

Aunt Kathy looked first at my mother and then at me, and let her mouth drop open. "Have you met someone?" She swatted my hand and gave me a grin. "And no one told me?"

"Not really; I mean, I've been on a couple of dates," I said, hiding my smile behind my glass.

"He's a Buddhist," interjected my mother, giving Kathy a look as she took a sip of her drink.

Aunt Kathy reacted like she might if my mother had just announced that he was a drug dealer. Or a pimp. "Oh, Ellen," she said, scrunching her face into a concerned grimace, "you're dating a *Buddhist*?"

"He's not a Buddhist, you guys. He was a religion minor."

Aunt Kathy and my mother exchanged looks. Anyone who spent any time studying any religion other than Christianity was highly suspect and, as my mother would say, "opening themselves up" to false gods.

Though Aunt Kathy changed the subject, my mother's mood seemed to have soured. I finished my drink and excused myself, pulling my cell phone out of my purse on the way up to my room and seeing a text from Mark:

Can't wait to see you tomorrow.

CHAPTER TWENTY-TWO

I squinted at the map I had printed out as I wove my way through the working-class neighborhood in which Mark lived. I had insisted on picking him up, rather than vice versa. My mother was enough to handle without the double trouble of Aunt Kathy being in town; I wasn't ready to put Mark through that just yet.

His house was number 65, a small gray ranch on a quiet but densely packed street. The area was blue-collar, inhabited by working people who mowed their lawns, shopped at supercenters, and ate steak on their birthdays. Most of the houses had Christmas lights wrapped haphazardly around trees and porches; some went the extra mile and had giant inflatable snow globes and glowing Santas. Thankfully, Mark's did not. He did not have so much as a wreath, which my mother and Aunt Kathy would have added to their growing body of evidence against him.

I parked in his driveway and made my way up the poured-concrete path to his front door, pressing the doorbell to hear the classic ding-dong, a sound bite of Americana. A few moments later, Mark was there. He was pulling on a long-sleeve T-shirt as he opened the door. His hair was still wet and he had that damp look about him, as if he'd just showered.

"Hey," he said, placing his hand on my back and kissing me in that ambiguous zone between my mouth and my cheek. "Come on in."

I stepped over the threshold and he shut the door behind me. "Why don't you sit down," he said, gesturing toward a nondescript-looking beige couch. "I'll just be a minute." As he strode off, I took in my surroundings.

The front door opened to the living room, the most dominant feature of which was the wall of built-in shelves devoted entirely to densely packed books. A few pieces of tribal-looking art and nature photography hung from the walls, and a dhurrie rug covered the old oak floors, but the room was notably devoid of ornamentation. There was a decent stereo, but only a very small, very old TV on a worn wooden stool. On the rustic wood coffee table lay a notebook from which folded sheets of paper and the shredded spines of spiral-bound tried to escape. From my vantage point, the kitchen looked dated but serviceable, with white cabinets and a linoleum floor. Instead of a table and chairs, the dining room had a weight bench and racks of free weights. The house was immaculately clean and looked like the sometimes residence of a traveling monk.

I assumed that the hallway down which Mark had disappeared led to the bedrooms, as there was no second story. And as I peered toward the series of doors, Mark emerged from the farthest one.

"I would show you around but there's not much to the place." It was true; the kitchen and dining room were off the living room, so most of the house could be seen from the couch.

"No, it's great," I replied, happy that I hadn't walked into the typical bachelor pad, with black leather couches, an enormous TV, and recent Victoria's Secret catalogues strewn carelessly about.

"You ready?" he asked, pulling on a wool coat that looked like it came from an army surplus store.

I hesitated for a moment, disappointed that he seemed to be rushing us out, but I glanced at the digital clock next to his stereo and saw that we really did need to get going if we were going to have any time at the museum before it closed. "Ready," I answered.

I rarely drove into the city myself; keeping up with the lurching sea of cabs and then finding parking always seemed too daunting. But today I did. Before we entered the Lincoln Tunnel, I said a silent prayer, just as my mother always had. I hated knowing that the weight of the Hudson River hung above us, above all the steel and concrete. "It's just a matter of time," she always used to say, shaking her head at the impending doom of the collapsing tunnel, referencing a terrorist attack when such a thing seemed ridiculously implausible, the stuff of science fiction. I preferred bridges. You might stand a chance with a bridge. You might be able to open a window and slide out into the freezing, filthy water, kicking furiously toward that first, gasping breath. Mark seemed to notice my discomfort and rested his hand on my knee as the car sped into the dark.

With some help from Mark, I found the MoMA and a convenient lot. We walked through the Rigauraut exhibition, holding hands, adopting the hushed voices and careful footsteps of the rest of the visitors. "It's amazing," he commented, looking circumspect, "but so dark." In the main collection, Mark gravitated to the nonrepresentational pieces, the Pollacks, the Rothkos, while I liked the surprise of the familiar differently expressed: the way Picasso treated a woman's body, the way Matisse showed movement. As we went from room to room, I thought about how we must appear, what we must look like: a couple. The kind that goes to museums together, reads together in bed, travels and cooks and writes each other long letters. I squeezed Mark's hand. He looked at me curiously. "I'm just happy that you're next to me," I said. I had missed having someone next to me.

After we had walked much of the museum, I lifted Mark's arm to check his watch. "We have to go," I said, not wanting to leave the quiet calm of the museum and head back into the chaos of the streets.

. . .

Luke and Mitch were already sitting at the trendy hotel bar when we arrived. When they saw us, they gave Mark an immediate but subtle once-over, looking pleasantly surprised.

After I quickly hugged both of them, I introduced Mark.

"It's nice to meet you," said Mark with his characteristic subdued confidence, his effortless warmth. He shook Luke's hand first and then Mitch's.

"Yeah, likewise," said Luke.

Mark immediately launched into friendly banter while we waited for our drinks, asking them about where in the city they lived, mentioning landmarks that they knew.

"There used to be a great record shop right around the corner from there," he said to Mitch, who lived in the East Village.

"Oh right. What's it called . . . ?" Mitch snapped his fingers to summon the name. "Sonic Slip Records?"

"Yes! Sonic Slip!" responded Mark, pointing at Mitch.

"It's still there. The guy who owns it is that old Keith Richards look-alike."

"Does he still wear leather pants?" asked Mark.

"Every day." He and Mitch shared a laugh that Luke and I joined, even though we weren't familiar with the record shop or the owner. The mood just had that convivial glow that made you want to laugh, to agree, to get along.

"How do you know the city so well?" asked Luke.

"I went to school here."

"Where?" asked Mitch.

"Columbia," said Mark matter-of-factly.

The bartender—an attractive, icy blonde with Nordic features—smiled demurely as she handed Mark his beer and my wine. He thanked her politely and turned back to our group, looking at me a bit longer than necessary as he passed me my glass.

The conversation inevitably turned to work, with Mitch complaining about chronically late writers and sloppy work.

"What do you do, Mark?" asked Luke, making sure Mitch didn't go on for too long, showcasing the good, southern manners that our mother had brought us up with.

Mark sank his hand into the back pocket of his jeans, looking like he had just lost his train of thought. "Oh, I, uh, work for a nonprofit," he answered.

"Doing what?" asked Mitch lightly.

"I guess I would be called the executive director," said Mark, seeming almost uncomfortable with his answer, like it just didn't fit right. I wondered if he was happy with the path he had chosen. His work was undoubtedly difficult and sometimes thankless, the type of job that was as challenging as any six-figure position, but without the traditional rewards.

"What's it called, the nonprofit?" asked Mitch.

"The Need Alliance."

"Interesting . . ." Mitch repeated the name.

Mark excused himself to go to the bathroom. When he was out of sight, Luke and Mitch gave their effusive approval.

"Elle, I really like him," said Luke, crossing his arms over his chest, playing the part of the protective older brother.

Mitch agreed. "He seems like a really good guy."

"Yeah, I like the whole do-gooder, nonprofit thing he has going on," said Luke. "Plus it doesn't hurt that he is *gorgeous*."

Mitch gently nudged Luke with his elbow. "Hey, remind me to check out his charity later. It may be a good one for Christmas this year."

Luke made a disgusted throat-clearing noise, then turned to me to explain. "Mitch's family makes charitable donations every year instead of giving each other gifts. Can you believe that?"

"Oh, come on," said Mitch. "Lots of families do that."

"No families we know," said Luke, looking at me for corroboration. "And don't get any ideas about messing with *my* gift. We Carlisles like material goods, things that can be wrapped and, if needed, *exchanged*."

We had one more round of drinks before Mitch and Luke left to go see a movie, and Mark and I went out in search of dinner. "Let's just grab a slice," Mark had suggested, which seemed appealingly low-key after the art exhibition and swank bar. Sitting at the counter of one of the interchangeable, ubiquitous New York–style pizzerias that litter the city, we faced the street and watched the human traffic march purposefully by, with cell phones pressed to their faces and ears plugged with headphones. They walked with deliberate oblivion past the muttering, pacing homeless woman who had begun patrolling the sidewalk next to the door.

She wasn't the innocuous type of homeless person that sits lucid but vacant on the ground, an emptied-out McDonald's soda cup next to her. The type that's easy to ignore and conveniently present when you wish to feel benevolent and magnanimous by tossing a few coins at their feet. As she marched back and forth on the six square feet of sidewalk to which she had laid claim, growl-like utterances escaping from her lips, mental illness seemed to ooze out onto the concrete around her. Limp strands of her unwashed hair escaped from beneath a black knit hat as she stared down the passersby. She wore a purple hooded sweatshirt, the hood of which was pulled from beneath her puffy jacket and bunched around her neck. Her shiny face looked as if it had been smoothed down by the elements, like a stone that was constantly lapped by the sea. She had filthy once-white sneakers on her sockless feet and was rendered nearly androgynous by destitution.

As we finished our meal, I eyed her, hoping she would move on before we left. I saw the men behind the counter glance cautiously at her as well. *Make her leave,* I thought. *Go out there and shoo her away.* But they didn't.

"Ready?" Mark asked after I had tossed the last bit of my crust onto a grease-stained white paper plate.

"Sure," I said. So I wiped my mouth and pushed in my stool and planned to mimic everyone else, to widen my berth and walk by with my gaze focused straight ahead, ignoring the filthy, raving woman a few feet away. But as I opened the door, with Mark's hand on my back, I heard her let out a mad cackle as she pulled down her grimy gray sweatpants and lowered herself into a squat. I was close enough to see the spray hit her legs, close enough to see the urine pool before running back down the sidewalk, her left foot like a boulder in a river.

I felt myself cringe and turned my head.

"Go on," said Mark as he gestured down the block. "I'll catch up in a second."

Without a word, I obeyed, walking quickly and stopping in front of an electronics shop a few storefronts away. It wasn't until I was staring through the glass window into the display, pretending to be interested in DVD and MP3-player pricing, that I surreptitiously peered back toward Mark. The homeless woman was standing with her pants around her ankles in a puddle of her own piss, her face contorting as she growled nonsensically. She was oblivious, lost, as Mark bent down and—taking the waist of her pants—pulled them back up over her body. He said something that I was too far away to hear, but something awoke in her eyes, snapped back into place almost, and she finally saw him. He pulled out his wallet and handed her a few bills, the denomination of which I couldn't see. She took the money and was quiet, looking at him curiously.

Mark jogged up to me. "Sorry," he said, offering no explanation. I forced a smile. I didn't know what to make of what Mark had just done. I was humbled and awed and repulsed. It was kind, to be sure, to cover her up, give her a shred of dignity. But I couldn't help but recoil at the thought of it. He could have chosen to bestow his kindness on one of the dozens of other homeless people we had seen today, including the Hallmark homeless man near the MoMA, the one you could imagine feeding flocks of pigeons in the park and helping lost children. But Mark chose the most vile, repellent one. He chose the one who would have made me run. We walked in silence for a couple of blocks. I found myself glancing at his hands.

"Here's the lot," Mark said. I would have passed right by it. "Do you want me to drive home?" he asked, looking a little concerned.

"Sure," I said, reaching into my purse for my keys. "I think that wine went to my head."

He drove steadily home, as if he was on autopilot. The huge arms of the lights that stood stationed at regular intervals along the highway straddled the lanes, making the road almost as bright as day. As the city faded behind us, any awkwardness disappeared and was replaced by the anticipation of finally being alone with Mark. I didn't care whom he had touched or what, and I played out the sequence of events I was sure were coming. We would get to his house, and then he would invite me in. My breathing became heavy as I looked at him next to me, how he squinted slightly at the road, even with his glasses on. He saw me staring and reached over to rest his hand on my thigh.

When we pulled into his driveway, we came together like magnets, instantly and without restraint. His lips found my neck and my head dropped back as he breathed my name. The car was still running, but I urgently unbuttoned his coat and ran my hand up his warm chest.

"Let's go inside," I whispered.

His lips stopped, his forehead fell against mine, and he took a deep breath. "I can't tonight, Ellen," he said, sounding pained.

A confused, blank, "Oh," was all that I could manage.

He stroked my hair, worked his face into the crook of my neck. "I wish I could. I really do."

"Why can't you?" I asked in a small voice.

"I just . . ." He glanced at the time on my dashboard. "I told a friend that I would meet him at his place at nine thirty tonight." It was nine. "He's kind of going through a rough time. He called when you were at the ATM, and I said that I thought I'd be back in time."

"No, yeah," I said, making no sense. "No problem." I pulled away. "I should be getting home, too." I reached for my door.

"Ellen," he said. It was a plea.

I gave him a brave smile and got out of the car, walked around the front to take my seat on the driver's side.

Mark looked defeated as he opened the door and stood up. "I really *don't* want you to leave, Ellen." Taking a step toward me, he pulled me into him. "You know that, right?"

I ignored his question. "I hope your friend is okay," I said sincerely. And I meant it. I tried to imagine if Jill needed me tonight.

I gently pulled away and took my seat behind the wheel.

"Ellen," he said again.

I closed the door and rolled down the window. "Have a good night. Drive safely."

. . .

I drove quickly home, flooring the car down the windy narrow streets by my parents', letting my mind go to all the dark places that I had been trying to ignore. Before getting out of my car, I checked my cell. I had received two texts on the way but hadn't dared to look at my phone.

I took a deep breath; they were both from Mark. The first read:

Next Friday, my place? I'll make dinner.

The second was:

My friend better be seriously messed up when I get there . . .

I wiped my eyes and couldn't help but let out a relieved, manic laugh. I texted him back:

I'd love to come over Friday. I'm sorry if I left abruptly . . . I just thought you needed to get going.

It wasn't the whole truth, but it was a safe one. And though I felt better after our exchange, reassured by the invitation, I still thought back to that night when we'd walked through the college green. My stomach lurched as I replayed our conversation in my mind. I wished I had settled on a safe truth then, rather than revealing everything. I wished he didn't know that I was broken.

CHAPTER TWENTY-THREE

I nearly slammed into the back door when it didn't open. It was never locked—none of our doors were—and so muscle memory caused me to propel myself forward as soon as I turned the knob, but the dead bolt was latched. I walked around to the front, the grand ceremonial door that was never used except for company. It opened easily and quietly, with no resistance.

The lights were out in the family room. I had seen from outside that there was only the dim flicker of the TV in my parents' room. Not wanting to wake anyone, I came in quietly. I was right outside the kitchen when I heard their hushed voices, my mother's and Aunt Kathy's.

"The Lord has always provided for us before," said my mother. "We just need to keep trusting him."

"Oh, Patty," said Aunt Kathy. "You know I told you that if Bill and I can help at all . . ."

My mother let out a grim, sad laugh. "Don't think that I

218 · SARAH HEALY

don't appreciate it, but this is just so much bigger than that. We are in way over our heads."

"Do the kids know?" asked Kathy.

"No," said my mother hopelessly. I knew exactly the expression she had on her face, that resigned, limp look. "Roger is still hoping that things will work out somehow. But the only way that's going to happen is if the Lord intervenes . . ." She sounded angry, betrayed, as she continued. "You don't know how hard I've been *praying*, Kathy."

"He *tests* us," affirmed Kathy. "He tests us to strengthen us."

"I tried to tell Roger that," said my mother sadly, "but he won't even hear it. I don't know if I've ever seen him so depressed." The heater kicked on, making an almost inaudible rumble from deep in the basement before I felt hot air gush from the vent by my feet. I imagined my mother noticing it, the breath of the house. "Listen, let's drop it. I don't think Roger's even asleep yet. He'd just die if he heard us talking about this."

I waited a solid three minutes before I walked loudly into the room, overcompensating, overplaying. Aunt Kathy and my mother were seated at the counter with two cups of chamomile tea in front of them. My mother's face was washed clean of makeup and she was wearing a red flannel nightshirt. Aunt Kathy still looked freshly made up, with her hair pulled into an updo. She was wearing leopard-print silk pajamas.

"Hey, you guys," I said, placing my keys on the counter with a little less entitlement than usual.

"Ellen!" said my mother, adopting her upbeat mask. "Did you just get home?"

"Yeah. I just came in through the front. The back door was locked."

"Oh, I must have done that, honey," said Aunt Kathy. "It's

just habit for me." No one understood why my parents were so lax about home security, especially Aunt Kathy, who lived in a gated community but still acted like her neighborhood was under siege. "I guess it's just different where we live."

"Kathy and I were talking about tomorrow," said my mother. "We think we're going to go to the eight-thirty service with your father so we can make the eleven o'clock service over at Prince of Peace."

I knew she was telling me so that I could commit to one or the other, and I wasn't about to deny her. "I'll go to the eight-thirty with you guys," I said. "That way I can pick up Luke if he decides to take an early train."

"Oh, is Luke coming?" asked Aunt Kathy.

"Uh-huh," I said. "I met him in the city tonight for a drink"—I was always careful never to mention Mitch—"and he said that he was going to try to come for dinner."

My mother frowned. "But I was just going to have that leftover gumbo that I have frozen." She always liked to make a big deal about Luke coming home, clinging to the notion that if she could present him with the perfect, idyllic home life, he might turn away from his "lifestyle" and decide to start a family of his own. It was as if homosexuality was a disease to which she simply needed to find a cure.

"Luke will be fine with gumbo, Mom. Don't worry," I said.

She wrung her hands. "Well, maybe I'll just get some Gulf shrimp to add to it."

. . .

At church the next morning, I sat between Aunt Kathy and my father. It was the contemporary service, and Christ Church pulled out all the stops, including rock-concert lighting and a video montage of inspirational scenes. A dramatic photo of the silhouette of a cross at sunset, two sets of footprints along the water's edge of a sandy beach: it was the Christian version of motivational office posters.

The first half of the service was devoted to the type of music that to me sounded like the religified version of easy listening. A dozen or so men and women stood on the stage, closing their eyes and swaying. They tapped tambourines against their thighs and spontaneously lifted their hands into the air. It was clearly supposed to appeal to a younger, hipper audience and seemed to fit perfectly into my mother's definition of "cool," so I was surprised that she didn't care for it. "I wish they'd just sing the old hymns," I heard her whisper to Aunt Kathy between songs.

As an overly coiffed blond woman took center stage for a solo, my mother again leaned toward Aunt Kathy. "That's Reverend Cope's wife," she explained. "She leads the worship team." Mrs. Cope didn't seem to be following the humble-preacher's-wife model and instead was decked out in gold jewelry, a fluttery black shirt, and tight boot-cut jeans. Her highlights were freshly done and expensive looking. Though she was in her late forties, she had a youthful, Pilates-toned body. As she sang, a close-up of her face, fraught with dramatic emotion, was projected onto the enormous screens on either side of her. She would periodically turn her head away from the microphone, to offer the cameras a nice profile shot, while she tapped her hand on her thigh to keep the beat. I felt as if I had accidentally found myself in a TV studio audience.

The contemporary service did have one thing going for it: Parker wasn't there. A weekend respite from her presence was much welcome, particularly while I was in the throes of event planning. I had spoken with her several times over the week, to confirm and reconfirm that everything for the party was being taken care of. The flowers were set; the head count was in; personal gifts had been ordered. Parker had me check with the restaurant to see if the waiters would be wearing their standard all black. "So you can coordinate and wear all black, too," she said. "That way the guests will know that you are part of the staff. You know, in case they need anything." I would be attending the party, but only in service to the Kents. On hand to answer questions from the restaurant, hand out gifts as the guests left, and generally oversee the evening, my presence would free up Parker and Philip for schmoozing.

When the collection plate was passed that morning, I watched as my father pulled his checkbook out of the breast pocket of his sport coat. My mother tried to catch his eye, tried to give him a look that I couldn't read, but he resolutely ignored her. He uncapped his pen and wrote out a check. It was for one hundred dollars. He dropped it unfolded, right side up, in the collection plate, then passed it down our aisle. It went first to me, then to Aunt Kathy, then to my mother. Mom looked at the check and pursed her lips.

After the service my mother and Aunt Kathy headed off in my mother's car to Prince of Peace, while my father and I rode back home together.

"Your mother says that Katherine hasn't called her to make plans to see Aunt Kathy yet," said my father. His use of Kat's proper name always indicated his displeasure with her. "You know, she really should make the effort to see her aunt."

"I know," I said, once again finding myself in the role of Kat's spokesperson. "She plans to."

"Aunt Kathy has done a lot for her. She needs to understand the importance of family." His jaw shifted as he stared at the road. "She needs to understand the importance of a lot of things." Had he elaborated, I knew exactly what he would have said. Manners, dignity, propriety—my father put tremendous stock in such things. And Kat had thumbed her nose at them that night with the Arnolds.

I didn't argue with him; I sat there as if I were the one getting the lecture.

When he pulled into the driveway, he didn't shut the car off. "I have some errands to run, kiddo." His tone had softened. "If your mother gets home before I do, tell her I'll be back for dinner."

I eyed him nervously. "Sure, Dad."

He gave the top of my head a sad, paternal pat. "You're a good girl, Ellen."

"Thanks, Dad," I said, wondering what I had done to be labeled "good," the designation sitting uneasily.

I got out of the car and my father pulled away, his car gliding smoothly over the long, blacktop driveway. In a few hours he would be back, carrying a small brown paper bag that he would immediately stow in a never-opened drawer in his desk.

· · ·

Luke ended up taking a later train from the city, so I found myself alone in the house. I was never alone there. In our old house, the rambling center-hall colonial, you could tuck yourself into one of the many small rooms and feel hidden away, but here, in this cavernous space with the vaulted ceilings, the emptiness was amplified. I grabbed my keys, got in my car, and went to Jill's.

Jill had already started the pregnant-person waddle, resting her hand on her lower back and sticking out her nonexistent belly as if she were in her ninth month, not the seventh week.

"How are you feeling?" I asked, knowing that Jill had been dying to tell me.

"Ugh, *so* sick!" She took a sip of herbal tea. "I haven't wanted to touch food. And meat?" She looked like she was about to vomit. "I can't even watch Greg eat it."

"I'll bet he loves that," I said sarcastically. Bacon and eggs, Philly cheesesteaks, and prime rib were the core of Greg's diet.

"No, you wouldn't even believe how sweet he has been about it. He's been going to Whole Foods and getting us salads from their salad bar every night."

I warmed at that endearing image, of thick-necked, bulky Greg lining up with his recyclable container in hand, using the tongs to grab the mixed greens and suspiciously eyeing the dressing assortment, wondering what the hell tamari was.

As if on cue, Greg walked into the room, swaggering toward the fridge to get a beer. "Ellie!" he said as he jerked open the door. "You came to see the little mama?"

I gave Jill a look, unsure whether to acknowledge her pregnancy. Last I had heard, it was still top secret, with Greg not aware that I knew.

Jill rolled her eyes. "He knows you know."

I stood to give Greg a hug. "Congratulations." I wrapped my arms around his thick body. It was like hugging a steer.

Greg snapped up the tab on his Coors Light. "You're next," he said, pointing at me with a sausagelike finger. "Fuck all this infertile business. Those doctors don't know shit. You just need yourself a Polack."

"Greg!" scolded Jill.

Though I felt myself redden, I wasn't offended. Greg meant no harm. And though I never knew how much Jill told Greg about what had happened with Gary and me, I assumed that it was everything. "It's okay," I mouthed to Jill, meaning both Greg's comment and his knowledge.

Greg sat down at the table and readjusted his Mets cap.

"So, how's business, Greg?" I asked.

"Ah, you know." He shrugged. "The shops aren't doing so bad. We got two more opening up over the next couple of months. If I'd have known the freakin' economy was going to shit the bed, I wouldn't have pulled the trigger. But people still need their gas and their Powerball, right?"

"But if the new stores don't do well . . . ," I started hesitantly, "and you've just invested all this money in them . . ."

He let out a muffled, closed-mouth burp. "Then I shut that shit down."

"But won't you owe, to, like, lenders and whatnot?" I was out of my comfort zone here. Financing a house was a far cry from financing a business.

"Oh, the banks get their money."

"But what if you don't have it?" I tried to hide the desperate edge to my voice.

"Like I said, the banks get their money." He narrowed his eyes and leaned back to look at me. "Why? You got some business deal I don't know about, kid?" He was only half kidding.

"No, no, I just . . . I feel bad for all the people who are going through tough times right now," I said, thinking of two people in particular.

He looked off, as if having a moment of silence for all the fortunes lost to the downturn. "Yeah, it's a bitch right now. But you gotta be ready for this kind of shit. Some of those people who lost their shirts just made some bad decisions. That's all there is to it. It's like Darwin and shit."

"Greg," said Jill. She stared at me with restrained concern

before turning to look at her husband. "Could you do me a huge favor? I am starting to feel a little sick. Could you go to the store and get that ginger tea I like?"

"You're out already?"

She nodded. "I had the last bag this morning."

"Jeez." Greg leaned toward Jill's belly. "Quit making your mama sick," he said in his version of a stern voice; then he stood and grabbed his keys off the countertop. "All right. I'll be back."

As soon as Greg was out the door, Jill asked, "Elle, is everything . . . okay?"

"Yeah," I said, pretending to be confused. "Why?"

"You just seem . . ." Though she didn't force the issue, Jill knew me too well to believe my questions were theoretical.

CHAPTER TWENTY-FOUR

It was snowing when Luke got off the train, big fat flakes that lumbered lazily down from the sky. They melted the second they hit the windshield of my car, which had been running while I waited.

"This is crazy," he said, opening the door and gesturing to the winter wonderland around him, a swirl of snow dusting the seat of my car. "It wasn't snowing at all when I left the city."

"We're supposed to get four inches. Maybe you'll have to spend the night," I said hopefully.

"Uh, no," he said definitively. "That is the beauty of public transportation."

As we drove back to the house I caught him up on the latest with our parents, on what I had heard between Mom and Aunt Kathy.

"Elle, don't get so worked up. Hasn't Mom been claiming financial ruin for as long as you can remember?"

It was true. Even in the fattest of days, she used to remind us that the rug could be pulled out from under us at any moment. "We just need to remember to thank the Lord for all we have, because it's him that's providing it. He could take it away like that," she said, snapping her fingers. "Then things would really change around here." My mother never forgot her humble roots, always feeling that at some point the jig would be up and the life in which she found herself would be knocked down, like the obsolete set of a canceled production.

I looked at Luke accusingly. "But *you* were the one who told me you think Mom and Dad are in trouble."

"Ellen, I said that things are tight, and they are. But it's not like Mom and Dad are going to be out on the streets. I mean, it's Mom and Dad."

I thought about that as I drove, cruising slowly down the whitened streets, following the tire tracks of the car ahead of me. *What if you're wrong, Luke?* I thought as I held on tight to the steering wheel. *What if we're all just staying in character?*

Luke, believing that he had adequately squelched my fears, began rambling on about his and Mitch's upcoming weekend in Vermont.

"You and *Mark* should come," he said, elbowing me in the ribs.

The mention of his name managed to coax a smile from my lips. "I don't know if we have hit weekend-trip status yet."

"Why not?" asked Luke. "He's totally into you."

"I don't know if he is *that* into me," I said, thinking about how he had cut things short last night, hesitating before adding, "He hasn't touched me, beyond, like, kissing." It wasn't the revelation I typically made to Luke or Kat, but I was looking for the sort of reassurance that Luke always seemed to provide.

"Are you serious?" he asked, his face scrunched in confusion.

"Yeah. I thought something was going to happen last night, but . . ." I explained the reason Mark had given for his early exit.

"Give the guy the benefit of the doubt," urged Luke. "It's nice that he wanted to help his friend. And how was he supposed to know that you were the type of floozy who gives it up on the second date?"

"It was *not* the second date," I said as I counted the number of times we had been out together and realized that it wasn't much more than that.

"While we're on the subject of *Mark*, can you ask him for the Web address of his nonprofit? Mitch Googled it and couldn't find anything."

. . .

Aunt Kathy and Mom both descended upon Luke the second he walked in the door.

"Oh, Luke!" squealed Aunt Kathy as she rushed toward him.

Luke glanced at Aunt Kathy's chest and then shot me a look as he was enveloped in a flurry of silicone and mohair. She leaned back and patted his cheek, studying his face. "You look *good*, honey," she said with surprise, as if she expected a skeletal frame and oozing sores.

"You, too," replied Luke, as he petted her shoulder. "Love the sweater."

"Luke, you have to fill me in on all the New York hotspots. Your momma and I are going into the city while I'm here, and we need to know where all the *cool* people are hanging out." Aunt Kathy said *cool* in the most uncool of ways, as she launched into a bizarre dance that was all gyrating hips and pumping arms. "I'm gonna get your momma to cut loose." She bumped Mom's hip with her own, sending my mother off balance.

"For heaven's sake, Kathy." Mom was trying to be reproachful but couldn't help but be delighted. "Imagine us old birds at a club."

Aunt Kathy doubled over laughing and Mom couldn't help but join in. Luke and I exchanged warm looks. This was why we loved Aunt Kathy; it was in her presence that we got to see flashes of my mother as a girl.

"How was Prince of Peace?" I asked snarkily, emboldened by the jovial mood and by Luke's presence.

Aunt Kathy leaned dramatically against the counter, like she was saving herself from a weak-kneed tumble. "It was *wonderful*," she breathed. "I wish we had something like it back home."

From the fridge, my mother pulled a huge Tupperware container full of a sloshy brick-colored liquid and peeled off the lid, revealing an unappealing layer of congealed fat that stuck to the plastic. She scraped it back into the container with her finger. "You're going with me next week, Ellen. I don't want to hear another word about it."

"We'll see," I said, having no intention of joining her.

My mother stood at the stove. The gumbo landed in a large stainless-steel pot with an unappetizing splash. She ordered Aunt Kathy and me to peel the shrimp. "They're from the Gulf," she said proudly. "They're not those farm-raised *Chinese* kind." The Chinese were villains in my mother's eyes, bent on poisoning the world with melamine-laced formula and lead-based toys.

When dinner was ready my father emerged from his office and we all quieted down, letting his silence set the tone. Aunt Kathy tried to keep the conversation going with what seemed like unobjectionable talk about old family memories. "Do y'all remember when you kids came to stay with me and Uncle Bill, and Kat ended up sleepwalking to the bathroom and lying down in the tub?" We all muttered that we remembered. "I called the police before I found her! And there she was, fast asleep and talking about going swimming."

My mother pushed the gumbo around in her bowl. "It's too bad your sister couldn't humble herself and come over here tonight." Though she was addressing Luke and me, she looked at neither of us. "It would have been nice to all be together," she said bitterly.

"I talked to Kat on the train ride over here," said Luke tentatively. All eyes were instantly on him. "I think she's planning on coming over sometime this week."

My mother and father exchanged looks, and my mother wiped her mouth with a paper napkin. "It certainly would be nice of her to tell *me* that."

"I'm sure she will," said Luke. "She's just been busy, I think."

My father snorted in amused contempt. *A hairdresser,* he seemed to be thinking. *Busy.*

Dinner wound down after that. Aunt Kathy and my mother drove Luke back to the train station and my father retired to his office. As I headed upstairs, I caught a glimpse of him through a crack in the door. He was staring at the black screen on his computer the way the lobotomized might stare at the floor. I rapped on his door and pushed it partway open.

"Dad?"

His head snapped up. "Hey, Ellie," he said, leaning back in his chair.

"You okay?"

"Sure. I'm okay." He tried to give me a smile. "Why?"

I shifted uncomfortably. "You seem like you have . . . a lot on your mind."

"I do." He nodded thoughtfully, averting his eyes. "But everything will work itself out."

I said good night and hurried to my room, not wanting my father to have to endure the concerned stares of the daughter who once considered him invincible. Who, in many respects, still did.

Closing the door, I lay down on the bed and dialed Mark's number. He picked up on the second ring. "Ellen," he said. His voice was deep and scratchy, the way Gary's used to sound during a trial. He always said it was from having to talk so loudly.

"I just wanted to see how your friend was doing."

"Oh, he's fine," he said quickly before correcting himself. "I mean, he'll *be* fine. Thanks for asking."

"I'm excited to see you on Friday," I said, rolling over onto my side so that my back faced the door. I pictured him sitting in his living room, his thin gray T-shirt stretched over his chest, his bare feet up on the coffee table. The lights would be dim, with just a reading light on above him.

He exhaled, as if thinking the same thing I was, as if imagining our being together. "I wish it could be sooner," he said, and I waited for him to offer either an invitation or an explanation. "I just have a really busy week at work. I have something scheduled every single night." I wondered what he was doing, whether it was the type of thing that a girlfriend could join him for.

"That's okay," I said. "I know you're busy."

"Maybe I can take you to lunch?"

"Sure," I said, trying to hide my disappointment at another G-rated, approved-for-all-audiences, thirty-minute daytime date. At least I would get to see him. At least he would slide his hand onto my lower back and kiss me good-bye. "That would be great."

.   .   .

Before work on Monday, I went to the bank, stood in line, and requested a cashier's check for six thousand dollars. "Made out to Roger Carlisle," I told the teller, spelling his name out slowly. I felt that I owed my parents at least that much for living with them over the past several months. I tucked the check carefully into an envelope in my purse, keeping the bag under my arm as I left.

My mother was at a prayer meeting when I got home that night, and my father was at his usual post in his office. I knocked gently before walking in.

"Dad?"

He was seated at his desk, facing the bay window in front of him. His back was hunched slightly, his shoulders rounding under his blue-and-white windowpane shirt. "Hi, Ellie," he said gently and without turning around.

I held the envelope awkwardly as I hovered behind him. "I just wanted to give you this." It was burl wood, his desk, a beautiful piece that I remembered him and Mom picking out. The surface was so highly polished that it reflected my hand as I laid down the check.

"What's this?" My father still did not look at me.

"It's for room and board for four months."

He stared at the envelope with a defeated, hopeless look, like it was one of the apocalyptic headlines from his financial papers. He made no move to touch it.

"So that's it," I said, to fill the dead, empty air. "And I'm going to get a place of my own after the New Year."

"Have you started looking?"

The question felt like a blow to the gut. "I've started browsing—you know, just seeing what's out there." I couldn't explain my resistance to finding a place of my own. Unlike Kat, I'd never liked living independently. My parents' home had been a sanctuary, a refuge when I left Boston, and moving out would mean that I was truly alone.

"Maybe your sister can ask around her complex, see if anything is available."

"Yeah," I said, backing away. "That's a good idea."

I closed the door as I left. Only then did I hear the envelope being torn open.

. . .

Brenda was aflutter at work all week with talk of her upcoming trip to Chicago and soon-to-be-born grandchild. "Jake says that Nora feels like she could go any day now," she said, sitting on her hands, almost unable to bear the excitement. "I just hope she lasts until I get there."

"When is her due date?"

"Christmas Eve." Brenda was flying out on the twentieth and would stay for ten days, at which point her ex-husband and new wife would go for a visit. "I hope she's not late," she said, her face darkening as she imagined her replacement ingratiating herself, changing diapers and tickling chins with her long red nails. She would be the type of woman who would wear strong perfume to the hospital and dress the baby in uncomfortable, starched clothing.

"Don't worry. I'll bet Nora will go into labor when you're there."

Brenda looked at me gratefully. "That would be wonderful. Just imagine if he was here in time for Christmas."

Brenda had purchased a shocking number of gifts for the baby, legacy items that would serve to mark her territory, to solidify her role as grandmother. There was a rocking horse, a sterling silver cup, a cashmere receiving blanket. Brenda didn't have tons of money, but she was sparing no expense for *the baby*.

"I'm going to give him a Christmas ornament every year. It'll be our tradition." This year, she had found a blown-glass baby bootie with a satin ribbon for hanging. "Have you finished your Christmas shopping?" she asked. This question invariably came from those who started in August, taking the time to find that just-right gift and tucking it away lovingly for months.

"No," I said plainly. "I really haven't started."

"There's still time," said Brenda, meaning that there was no time. She used the exact same tone that I had used when assuring her that she would be present for her grandson's birth.

When I was with Gary, we had always spent Christmas with his family. This would be the first Christmas in five years that I would be with mine. And while I hadn't really taken much time to shop in the past, usually devoting just one solid evening to online ordering, I decided that this year I wanted to find something special for everyone. This year seemed important somehow, seminal.

Gary and I had spoken only twice since the final hearing. Each time, he'd reached out, wanting to foster something close to a friendship. I decided that I would get him a gift, along with gifts for Daniel and his mother—not really as an olive branch, but more as a reminder. I didn't want to be so easily forgotten. And even though I had come a long way toward accepting that Gary and I weren't right for each other, it still hurt that he had realized it first.

And then there was Mark. Mark was much harder. The first occasion for exchanging gifts was always so telling. Gary and I had started dating just before Valentine's Day, and it was when I received two dozen red roses at work that I knew we were officially together. But that wasn't Mark's style. How intimate a gift, how much to spend: these were the things that Kat would know.

. . .

"Ellen, I am *so* busy," scolded Kat. She spoke loudly to be heard over the din of the salon. "Why are you calling me at work anyway?"

"I called you yesterday and you never called me back," I retorted.

"All right, well, what is it?"

There were so many things that I could have said. Yes, I wanted her advice about Mark, but I also missed her; I wanted to hear her voice. Despite our trip to Boston, I felt that there had been a distance between us since that night with the Arnolds. But as I opened my mouth, my intentions stumbled, and I said only, "I was just wondering if you are coming to see Aunt Kathy."

She exhaled. It was a long guttural noise that sounded as if she were clearing her throat. "Are you serious? That's why you're calling?"

"Yeah, I mean, everyone has been wondering where you are."

"I'll come when I can, Ellen," she said.

"You should probably call Mom and let her know."

And with that, Kat hung up.

. . .

Over the next day or two, I didn't see my parents. My mother and Aunt Kathy had gone to Connecticut to visit one of Aunt Kathy's friends from when Uncle Bill was stationed out of Groton; my father was either not home or holed up in his office. Jill was absorbed into Greg's family's holiday preparations. "Theresa is going to show me how she does her stuffed cabbage so I can make it on Christmas Eve." So with few distractions, I began to look in earnest for a new place to live. I was on Craigslist when Parker bounced into the office.

"Don't you look cute!" oozed Brenda when she saw her. Parker was dressed for a day at the mall with lime green driving moccasins, a cashmere trench coat tied above her pregnant belly, and a pair of designer maternity jeans.

She slipped her sunglasses up onto her forehead. "I have had it up to here"—she raised her hand well above her head—"with *Christmas shopping*. I'm telling you, if I see so much as one more twinkling light, I think I might vomit." Brenda giggled, delighted by Parker's practiced, clichéd suburban angst.

"Ellen," she said, turning to me, "is Philip in? I have some papers I need him to sign."

"Um, yup," I said as I brought the phone to my ear. "Let me ring him."

She held up a familiar-looking heavy, white, watermarked envelope with crisp blue type and an elaborate crest. "Can you believe that Austin is starting at Horton already?" she trilled.

Philip answered. I was instructed to send Parker right in. When she came out she again waved the envelope in victory. "One more thing checked off the to-do list! You are so *lucky*, Ellen." She kept walking as she spoke, letting her words trail behind her. "You wouldn't believe how busy these kids keep me!"

Brenda looked at Parker, then at me, with an uneasy, confused expression. She was unfamiliar with the cruel side of Parker.

On her way out, Parker passed Mark, who held the door open for her as she sashayed regally out of the office. His eyes scanned the expansive lobby and made their way up to the mezzanine, looking for me. I didn't wait for Helen to call me and tell me that he had arrived. Instead, I grabbed my things and hurried toward the stairs, bouncing down them with a grin on my face. He met me at their base.

"Hey, you," he said, brushing the hair off my face.

"Hi," I said, inching closer.

"Let's go get you some lunch."

Though it had stayed cold, all signs of the weekend's pristine snow had vanished, transformed into gray slush that gathered at the edges of the street. It was as if Monday was reminding us that all that white was too romantic, too special to linger. As we walked, Mark reached for my hand.

We passed window after window of elaborate displays, all elegantly done in natural tones or tasteful metallics. It wasn't a colored-lights-and-tinsel sort of town. "What are you doing for the holidays?" I asked, not wanting to assume that he celebrated Christmas.

"I usually spend Christmas with some friends, since my family is so far away. This year we're actually going to do some volunteer work."

I squeezed his hand. "*Of course* you are," I teased.

"What do you mean?"

"You are so *good*," I said, turning to see his profile against the backdrop of the shops.

He reddened. "No, Ellen. I'm not."

"Yes, you *are*. You are so kind and honest and *good*."

He pulled us to a stop. "Ellen," he said, turning toward me, words forming on his tongue.

I wrapped my arms around him. I wasn't going to let him deny it. With our bellies pressed against each other, I felt his stomach growl. "Come on," I said, pulling him forward. "You're starving." His feet reluctantly followed.

We sat with our legs intertwined under the table, talking about the holidays and our plans. He told me how he missed his family, how he wanted to plan a trip to Africa soon. "You would love it, Ellen," he said. It wasn't an invitation, but I allowed my mind to meander down that path.

I, in turn, gave Mark the highly edited version of my family turmoil. The years-long feud between Kat and my parents became a little tiff; weeks of silence and resentment became a communication issue. "I think it's taking its toll on my mother. She and my dad have been really stressed-out lately about some other stuff, so this is just the icing on the cake." And again, as whenever I revealed a small personal detail to Mark, I immediately felt as though I could tell him everything and anything. *But there's time,* I reminded myself, remembering my too-early confession about Gary. And about me. *No need to rush it.*

After a quick lunch, Mark walked me back to the office. He tucked us into a small side street next door to my building and leaned against a brick wall. "I'll see you Friday," he said, pulling me close to him. He looked at once proud and mischievous as he added, "*I'm* making dinner."

"You can cook?" I asked, not quite skeptically, as it seemed that Mark could do anything.

"I can make a thing or two."

I leaned up and kissed him.

CHAPTER TWENTY-FIVE

Kat never did call my mother. Instead, she came walking defiantly into the house. It was Thursday evening. Aunt Kathy and my mother had gotten home late the night before from Connecticut. I didn't know where my father was.

I was alone at the kitchen table writing a Christmas card to Daniel when the back door swung open. From the look on Kat's face, she expected—she *hoped*—for an ungracious welcome. Standing in the doorway for a moment, she let the cold, stark night air rush into the house. We looked at each other but said nothing. It seemed like such a simple thing, walking into our parents' house unannounced, but it would be seismic in its repercussions.

Mom came hurrying in from the family room. When she saw that it was Kat, she didn't look surprised, only wearily prepared, like a battle-hardened soldier. She straightened her back, made the effort of taking on a more formal posture. "Katherine," she said. It was a reprimand, an accusation, and a prayer. I knew that she was relieved to see Kat after so long, after so much anticipation, but now it would begin.

"Where's Aunt Kathy?" asked Kat coldly.

Aunt Kathy, following my mother, appeared from around the corner. "Hey, Kat, honey!" she said nervously, in a futile attempt to defuse the situation. "You look as gorgeous as ever." She strode toward Kat with open arms.

Kat gave her a guarded but still somehow warm hug, with her elbows tucked into her sides and hips back. Aunt Kathy hooked her chin over Kat's shoulder. "You girls are so lucky that you got your daddy's height."

Aunt Kathy then leaned back and stuck out her chest, ready to deliver her breast-implant routine, but Kat peered around her and looked straight at my mother. "So what, no cozy little dinner with the Arnolds tonight?"

My mother was instantly ignited. "How *dare* you come into this house and mention their name after the way you acted that night!"

Kat rested the fingertips of her open hand daintily over her heart. "Did I offend your dear friends the Arnolds?" Though the words themselves were innocent, there was menace in her voice.

"Don't you start that, Kat," spat my mother. "You offended everyone. And you *humiliated* your father and me."

"You humiliated yourselves." Kat was brutally calm as she stood, seemingly feet above my mother. "With that fucking display. All the brownnosing and main-course bullshit."

"For your information, Katherine, you single-handedly ruined one of the most important dinners of your father's career." Angry tears had sprouted from Mom's eyes, and she fought to continue. "He was working on a business deal with Edward. A very, *very* important business deal." My mother was always insecure when discussing business matters, since it was then that she was most acutely aware of her poor southern roots and tenth-grade education.

"Of course," scoffed Kat. "A *business deal*." Her arms were crossed casually in front of her. "If the Arnolds didn't have money, you wouldn't give a shit what I said to them."

My mother leaned toward Kat with her hand on her hip, her voice becoming loud and clear. "They were our *guests*, Katherine. And you were deliberately vulgar and *attacked* their son." Looking away, she shook her head as if reliving the evening. "I had to call Lynn the next day and apologize for your behavior."

It was visible and instant, the release of Kat's rage. "You apologized to *the Arnolds*?" She was now inches from my mother's face. "You apologized *for me*?"

"Kat," I whimpered. "Come on." It was a pitiful little plea that went unacknowledged as Kat and my mother stared at each other like old and formidable foes.

"Of course I had to apologize!" said my mother incredulously. "I didn't want the Arnolds to think that we condoned your behavior."

"*Fuck the Arnolds*." Kat's voice shook the house. It shook it in the way it had all those years ago. It shook the air out of it, until everyone and everything was silent and still. Then Kat spoke again, quieter, fighting to regain the advantage of calm. "All you care about is what people think. It's all you've *ever* cared about." And suddenly, she wasn't fierce and brave and strong. She was a wounded, scared teenage girl. She was what she had really been all along.

We all knew the topic that she was circling, the unspoken event that had as much a presence in the room as any of us. Aunt Kathy took me by the arm. "Come on, Ellen," she said as she led us out of the kitchen. Already we were invisible to my mother and Kat. We sat across from each other on the big, overstuffed leather couches in the family room, just out of sight. We could hear everything. We didn't pretend not to be listening.

"When are you going to *stop this*?" pleaded my mother. "When are you going to stop acting like some rebellious teenager? You need to *let go* of the past!"

"*I can't let go!*" screamed Kat. "I can't do what you do and pretend it *never happened!*" I could hear her sob. It was a pained, violent noise. "You made me have a *baby*." More primal cries escaped her chest before she screamed again, "*You made me have a baby!*" It was an agony that served as irrefutable proof of just how changed Kat had been on that day in December. No matter how much we all wanted to deny it, she had become a mother.

"*You had to have that baby!*" wailed my mother back, doubt and regret infusing her once-steadfast resolve. "The Lord made that child . . ."

"*Stop it!* I don't want to *ever* again hear that *Jesus* didn't want me to have an abortion." I closed my eyes, but Kat went on, her words coming fast and hard. "I bought that shit when I was sixteen and stupid, but I have heard *enough*. You were supposed to be protecting me. Not the baby, not your friends, or the church or anyone else. Just *me*."

"*I did it for you!*" My mother's voice sounded raw and cracked, as if every word hurt, as if she had doubled over to get them out. "It was always about you. I made you have that child because I knew you would regret it for the rest of your life if you had an abortion. And I knew it because *I do. I regret it.* And not a day goes by that I don't think about it."

I felt a breath of air fill my mouth and rush into my lungs before I froze. I looked at Aunt Kathy. She met my eyes only briefly, her expression unwillingly corroborating my mother's confession.

There were a few beats of silence, stretched-out seconds where I imagined Kat absorbing, trying to process what my mother had said. Mom didn't wait for Kat to speak. "You are my *child*, Kat," she said, her tone more plaintive. "I wanted to protect you. That's all I ever thought I was doing."

I heard Kat give a cynical snort. "Right," she said sarcastically, struggling to stay on script. "You were protecting me by taking away my *choice*. You had one, and you took away *mine*." In her shock, Kat resorted to what sounded like lines from an after-school special.

"Choice?" my mother asked quietly. "This was 1964. Georgia. We didn't talk about 'choices.'"

And to that, Kat said nothing.

CHAPTER TWENTY-SIX

Aunt Kathy brought her hands, which she held palm to palm, against her lips and closed her eyes. "Oh, Lord," I heard her whisper. Then she took a deep, fortifying breath, and stood. With her arms crossed as if to fight off a chill, she walked purposefully toward the kitchen. I got up and followed a few steps behind. When she reached the doorway she paused, and I looked in over her shoulder. Kat and my mother stood facing each other. The gravity of what had just been said hung between them. My mother glanced toward us. Kat turned to stare out the window.

"Patty, are you all right?" asked Aunt Kathy. She was the only one for whom my mother's revelation did not come as a shock.

Mom looked at Kat, who didn't react, then back at us. She nodded.

"Do you want to be alone?"

Mom shook her head. "It's all right." Looking like she didn't have the energy to support herself for one more second, she slowly pulled out a barstool and sat down, preparing herself for the things she now needed to say. And though Kat continued to stare out the window, our presence seemed to relieve her of her almost pathological need to fight back. She didn't have to retort or retaliate. She could simply listen. And though I would piece the whole story together later, that night Mom gave us the bones of it.

She was seventeen, the daughter of a Pentecostal preacher and more like Kat than anyone knew. When her father was traveling, she snuck out at night and went dancing. "It was a strange time," she said. "This was right when the Vietnam War was about to get started. All the boys in town were joining the army, wanting to go fight. We were all for the war. There were no protestors, no *conscientious objectors*." Her words were detached but somber, as if she was an academic lecturing on a tragic but distant era.

"For years I pretended that I was somehow tricked, that I didn't know what I was doing, but the truth is I knew exactly what I was doing. The boy's name was John and he was leaving for the service. He thought he picked me, but I picked *him*. This was right when Daddy was getting bad, when all he saw was sin. He was so ugly." She shook her head, her eyes seeing things that we couldn't. "I hated it. I hated being his daughter. And so I did what I knew he would never forgive me for doing. Of course I didn't ever want him to find out. I just wanted to hurt him without his knowing it. But I was like a little girl playing with an atom bomb. I had no idea what I was about to unleash."

The only person she told was Aunt Kathy. And then when her period was late, it was Kathy who helped her figure out what to do. "Kathy was volunteering at a hospital. One of the nurses there gave her the name of a doctor, told her what to say. Of course we had no money, nothing but a little savings each. So I sold a brooch, a gold brooch that Daddy's mother had given me before she died. It was beautiful, filigree with a little sapphire set in there."

Kathy drove her to the doctor, two hours away, in a borrowed car. "We told Mother that we were going to see a friend who had just gotten married and moved closer to Atlanta. But I was sure she knew the truth, because when we got back, she just *looked* at me. She told me to wear the brooch to church that Sunday. 'Patty,' she said, 'go get your grandmomma's brooch. I'll shine it.' I pretended to go and look for it, then told her it must have been stolen.

"When Daddy came home from his trip, he was on fire. Ranting and raving about everyone and everything. He and Mother must have talked, because he came into our room that night and ripped me out of bed. He made me get on my knees. It was like he was possessed. He had never been violent before, but Mother had to threaten to slit her wrists to make him stop. That finally snapped him out of it. Then he just put his belt back on like nothing had happened, and walked out of the house. My back was so raw I couldn't lie down on it for weeks. I don't know what exactly Mother told him. Sometimes I think all she said was that I lost his momma's brooch.

"That was the beginning of the end for Mother and Daddy. The next year is when she left. And Daddy was never the same." She paused, as if trying to find her way back to the point. "I should have done right by my mistake but I didn't. I wasn't brave enough."

Later I would ask her how, after all that, she could still be, still *want* to be a Christian. She looked at me, both frustrated and patient. "Because God is real, Ellen. Jesus is real. No matter how Daddy, or Thomas Cope, or anyone tries to pervert it, that's the truth. It's not about what you've done or how much you can give. It's about the Lord's grace."

When my mother had finished, it felt like a hurricane had just ripped through the room; everything was leveled, but the worst was over. I tried to hug Kat; her stiff, hard body yielded only slightly. Then Aunt Kathy and I left Kat and my mother alone again in the kitchen; they had things to say that were between just them. And had my mother thought to ask her, in those vulnerable, honest moments, Kat may have even told her. But as it turned out, after that night Kat was the only one left with a secret: the father.

CHAPTER TWENTY-SEVEN

From the doorstep I could hear the music inside, rhythmic, pulsating beats that seemed to have their origins anywhere and everywhere but here, in this ho-hum little New Jersey neighborhood. I pressed the bell and heard the clatter of pots and pans inside, and the music dropped a few decibels. Moments later Mark appeared, wearing a plain white T-shirt and jeans. He opened the door to his cozy, eclectic little home and gave me a long, still kiss.

"It's good to see you," he whispered.

"It's good to see you, too."

He took my hand. "Come on in," he said as he led me inside.

The lights were low, except in the kitchen, which was illuminated by harsh fluorescents that seemed all wrong. They were the utilitarian lights of pot roast and mashed potatoes, not whatever was generating the warm, exotic smells that had filled the house. On the stove sat a clay, cone-shaped pot with arabesque markings on the outside.

"What are you making?" I asked, tempted to lift the lid.

"Lamb tagine," he said, his thumb pointed at the pot. "My mother used to make it, but I'm sure I'm going to massacre it."

"It smells amazing."

His smile was shy. "Can I get you a glass of wine?"

"Sure. Please." He uncorked a bottle on the coffee table.

"Cheers," I said as the bowls of our glasses met.

I took a sip and let the pleasant burn roll down into my stomach.

"Make yourself at home," he said. "I just have a couple more things to do and then dinner is pretty much on autopilot."

"Do you need some help?"

He shook his head. "You just relax. I got this tonight." He headed back into the kitchen and began intently reading the instructions on a box of couscous.

Meandering over to his bookshelves with my glass in hand, I began to study the endless rows of spines. There were books on the economies of developing nations, on poverty; there were biographies of Gandhi and Mandela; there was a Bible, a Koran, books on Buddhism and Taoism; there were rows from the literary canon, books that most people had heard of but never bothered to read.

"Not much of a reader, huh?" I asked sarcastically.

"It's kind of my vice."

Then I noticed an academic-looking book tucked away toward the bottom. I pulled it off the shelf and flipped through the pages. It was on microloans. The author was Mark Oberson.

"Did you write this?" I asked, astonished.

Mark glanced quickly in my direction, then turned back to the stove. "Yeah, it, uh, was my dissertation."

My jaw hung open. "That's amazing, Mark."

He tossed a spoon into the sink, which landed with a clatter, then came quickly back into the room. "Not really. It was just a small academic press. I think they sold three of them." He gestured to the copy in my hand. "One of them is right there."

"I'm officially intimidated," I said.

"*Please* don't be."

He took my hand and led me over to the couch. We sat and he pulled my legs over his lap.

"Did you know that you wanted to do nonprofit work when you were in grad school?" I asked.

"Not exactly," he said. "I knew that I wanted to do something . . . positive, but I thought it would be more from inside the system, working in academia or something like that." His head rested on the back of the couch as he studied the ceiling. "But I got impatient."

"So how did you get involved with the Need Alliance?"

One side of his face tightened a bit. "Through the grapevine."

As he spoke, I noticed a small, framed photo on the table next to the lamp. It was Mark standing between an older couple and a black woman, who looked a little younger than me, with high, full cheeks.

"That's my family," he said, following my eyes. "My sister Ebele is adopted."

I studied the faces of his family. "You look like your dad," I said. His parents were old hippies. His father had a bushy beard and Mark's knowing, wise brown eyes. His mother had long gray hair that was parted down the middle and pulled back into a ponytail. They stood flanking their children with beaming smiles, looking proud and healthy and carefree.

"Yeah, I think I'm starting to look like the old guy." He smiled fondly at the picture. "That photo was taken the last time I was home."

"Do you still think of Africa as home?"

He considered it for a moment. "Not really, I guess. I've been in the States for a long time." He paused before adding, "I definitely don't plan on moving back."

I nestled in closer to him, more relieved than I expected.

He shifted to face me and put his hands on either side of my head, looking almost troubled. "You are so beautiful, Ellen."

I felt something rise from my heart into my throat, almost choking me with emotion. Shifting onto my knees, I slowly drew one leg over him. He sank back on the couch and looked up at me. Straddling his lap, I felt my heart race. He let out a long, slow breath. I kept my eyes focused on his as I took his hand and brought it to my lips, feeling its rough texture, feeling him beneath me. He ran his hands down my body, between my breasts, over my stomach, until both palms came to rest on my hips. I leaned down and kissed him, my hair falling on either side of our faces like a curtain. His body lifted into mine; I pressed down on him. Our exhalations were mingling, twisting, our kisses becoming more urgent. It felt inevitable, unstoppable, as our feelings built. And then a dull, anemic-sounding kitchen timer rang with nagging insistence from the other room.

His lips paused but did not leave mine. "Dinner's ready," he said into my mouth.

I pulled back reluctantly. "Dinner, huh?"

He straightened himself up. "I better . . ."

"Yeah," I said, swinging my leg off him, unreasonably, illogically disappointed. "Let me help you."

252 · SARAH HEALY

. . .

Since Mark's dining room was occupied by a weight bench, we brought the spread into his living room and ate sitting on the floor around his coffee table.

"Oh my God," I said, covering my still-full mouth with my hand as I chewed my first bite of the lamb. "This is delicious. I can't believe you made this." There were almonds and raisins and tender hunks of lamb that pulled apart in succulent shreds. It tasted like an incantation of the exotic, the sensual, and conjured up colors, warm and dense and saturated. I sopped up some of the sauce with a piece of a flat, naan-like bread.

"I can't believe the lamb was actually edible," he said, smiling, his modesty ever present. "The last time I made it, the meat was like rubber bands."

I let my fork skate over my plate, scooping up another bite of lamb, some couscous. "Your mom cooks like this?" I asked.

"Sometimes. But she used to make American food, too. Whenever I go home, she always gives me a shopping list from the States, things that she misses."

Nodding, I thought about the flavors and tastes that were home to me, the foods I would miss if I found myself a world away. It wasn't about a food being good or bad, just familiar, nostalgic. "Like what?" I asked.

"Like grated Parmesan cheese. Bottled ranch dressing. Nilla Wafers."

"Oh, I hate Nilla Wafers," I said, laughing. "They remind me of Sunday school."

"You hate Nilla Wafers?" he asked in disbelief, pretending to take it as a personal affront.

"I can't even look at the box."

"Well, so much for dessert," he joked.

I blushed even before I spoke. "I have something else in mind for dessert." Realizing that I had just resorted to the most clichéd of seductions, I looked shyly down at my plate. Now, of course, I wish I had forced myself to look at Mark. I wish I had seen his reaction.

All through the meal, as we were loosened by the wine, the food, the conversation, our bodies kept finding their way back to each other. Mark's palm would rest on my thigh; I would brush my foot against his. Each time, I felt the charge that I had always heard about. *It's like sparks,* I had heard women say, never really knowing what they meant. Now I understood. And in my bones I knew that tonight was going to be important.

After the meal, we lingered around the table, leaning back on our hands and extending our legs. It was a delicious interlude before what we both knew was coming next, an anticipation that would make everything that much more pleasurable.

Finally Mark reluctantly gathered his body up and stood. I followed suit, picking up the plates and silverware that were scattered over the table.

"I'll do the dishes," I offered as I set the pile down into the sink and turned on the water. Standing in front of the sink in the bright white kitchen was a shock to my senses. I blinked my eyes to adjust, feeling like I had been abruptly jolted from a blissful sleep.

From behind me, Mark set down a few more dishes, then reached and turned off the water. "I'll get them later," he said as he brought his hand around my lower stomach and pulled me into him.

And that was it. I turned and our lips met furiously. His hands ran up my shirt over my bare back, leaving a trail of heat. I let my fingers snake through his thick hair.

"Let's go to your room," I whispered.

Without a word, he swept his arm beneath my legs and I was being carried. He set me down on a soft, white bed in a sparse room. He was instantly on top of me and I felt his weight melting into my body. I pulled off my shirt. He sat up and looked at me, running his fingertips over my breasts, breathing my name. The moon looked almost full and was huge outside the bedroom window, flooding the room with light through the rice-paper shades. And then he was on me again, his hands sliding underneath my back and unhooking my bra. I lifted his shirt over his head and gasped as I let myself feel his warm skin on mine, chest to chest. I felt desperate to have him inside me; I needed to feel that again. I needed to feel that from him. I worked open the button of his jeans, and he hesitated only for a second before slipping them off. His body was amazing, the way it looked, the way it fit into mine.

"I want to be with you," I whispered as I unzipped my own pants, hooking my thumbs along the waist and pushing them off my hips.

His body instantly tensed and he rolled to his side, looking at me with a silent plea. Our eyes remained locked as I tried to slide off my panties, a final dare. His hand met mine, holding it in place. "Ellen," he said with a new gravity in his voice.

"What is it?" I asked, trying to hide the panic in my voice, feeling the physical sensation of all my suppressed fears being freed.

He broke our gaze and reached for my hand. "I just . . . can't let this go too far."

I took a sharp, painful breath and held it, nodding with pursed lips and reaching for my clothes.

"Ellen, please," he said, trying to hold me in place. "Just sit. I need to explain. I should have explained a long time ago."

I wriggled free. With my back to him, I stood and pulled up my jeans. "You really don't need to explain." *I've known this was coming all along,* I thought. He didn't need to verbalize it. I knew why he didn't want me. He was too good a man to sleep with me when he knew we had no future. I fumbled awkwardly for my bra, trying to cover my body.

He was buttoning his pants. "I *do* need to explain. Please, Ellen."

Don't say the words, I thought. *Just don't say it out loud.* I wanted to get out of the room without having to endure hearing him tell me the same things that Gary had.

He blocked the door with his arm. *"Ellen,"* he pleaded, trying to meet my eyes. "Just *listen* to me. I don't understand why you won't listen. There are just some things you need to know."

Unable to look at him, I squeezed my eyes shut to keep the tears at bay. "I have to go," I said as I pushed past him.

He followed me down the hall.

Slipping into my shoes, I grabbed my bag and coat in a bundle and held them in front of me. Mark stood next to the front door. I gripped the brass knob. He extended his hand across the door to keep it shut. "Don't leave, Ellen."

"I'm so sorry, Mark," I said, then yanked the door open. I knew that I should stay and hear him out, but I just couldn't bear it.

As I hurried down the walkway to my car, I heard his fist slam into the wall, once, twice, and then a third time. Only once the car was started in reverse did I let myself look up at him. He was sitting in the doorway, shirtless in the December cold, with his head in his hands.

CHAPTER TWENTY-EIGHT

He called me three times on the way home. With my phone lying in the passenger seat, I watched his name light up on the screen through the dark. I was right, I had always been right, and I felt the hollow, aching satisfaction of knowing it. Everyone had set me up with their empty encouragement and false hopes, their talk-show platitudes about love and grace and understanding. But I knew what would happen.

Though it was only half past nine, my parents' house was dark when I pulled up, with even the exterior lights turned off. It looked uninhabited compared to the neighbors', whose front doors still glowed with welcome. My footsteps echoed uncomfortably on the stone floor in the kitchen, so I walked with deliberate force through the house and up the stairs, making my presence known. But no one stirred.

I lay in bed, unable to sleep, for what felt like hours. Letting myself relive those few blissful moments with Mark, I remembered the sensation of his bare chest against mine. It couldn't hurt, I decided, as I allowed my hand to slip down my stomach, mimicking his. Only then did I sleep.

By the time I woke up, the house was empty again. I must have missed the morning clatter of Aunt Kathy and my mother as they prepared for the day, and of my father reading the paper at the kitchen table while eating his standard Saturday morning fare of a bagel, yogurt, and a cup of coffee. There was not a dish in the sink, the TV was off, and mail wasn't scattered over the kitchen counter. Everything was static, still, and quiet.

Finally dialing into my voice mail, I listened to Mark's message. Though he had called a total of five times, he had left only one voice mail. "Ellen, it's Mark." He sounded exhausted. "Please call me. I want to try to explain things." And I could almost hear him say it; I could almost hear him telling me that I was great, really great. And that he hoped we could be friends, or even more. He just wanted me to know where he stood before things got too serious, before I got too attached.

. . .

"You realize that you could be totally wrong," said Jill as she sat cross-legged opposite me on her huge velvet sectional.

I shook my head. "I'm not wrong."

"I think you should call him back."

"Okay, Jill, let's just say that you're right," I began, playing the devil's advocate, "and that there is some other reason why he didn't want to be with me. It doesn't even really matter, because after I flew out of his house like there was an air raid, I might have set off some psycho alarms, don't you think?" *That chick is nuts.* Ted's words echoed in my head. That was what he had said that night in the parking garage.

"I don't know why you assume that *you* are the issue. Maybe it's something about him."

"Like what?"

"Maybe he has his own issues, Elle."

I recalled Kat's warning about how long he had to call me after our first date. *He has three days. Tops. If it goes longer than three days, then he has some weird baggage ... like a wife and kids.*

Jill read the expression on my face. "What?" she asked.

"I don't know. His place is pretty spartan. It doesn't even really look like he lives there. There isn't a dining room table or anything. It's like ..."

Jill's eyebrows lifted. "Like maybe his wife has it?"

No, I thought. I couldn't fathom that Mark—*Mark*—would have such a secret. This had to be about me. I shook my head. "It doesn't matter. We're done."

Jill somberly considered this for a moment. "All right, if that's how you feel, you've got nothing to lose anyway, so why not hear what he has to say?"

I imagined Mark's handsome, guilt-ridden face as he struggled to tell me the truth. "I just don't want to hear another man tell me that he doesn't want to be with me. Not yet," I said, shaking my head. "I just don't want to know the reason why."

Jill looked away and I waited for her to contradict me, to offer me salvation. After a few seconds of silence I changed the subject. "I have to go with my parents to this party at the Arnolds'."

"Why do *you* have to go?"

I worked my foot underneath one of Jill's throw pillows.

"Lynn invited me and so my mother begged me to accept. After the fiasco with Kat that night, my Mom's being overly gracious."

"Well, we'll stalk the caterers with the passed hors d'oeuvres and shoot Parker dirty looks."

"Wait—*you're* going to be there?"

"I told you that."

"No, you didn't," I said, marveling at Jill's ability to omit critical information. I knew that she knew the Arnolds—*everyone* knew the Arnolds—but I had no idea she was going to be at the party.

She pulled her hair back into a ponytail, her shirt lifting enough to reveal the navy blue band at the waist of her designer maternity jeans. "Oh. Well, Greg's father invested in Ed's company way early on and they've known each other for years. Greg always goes, so this year I'm being roped into it."

"Thank God," I said, smiling genuinely for the first time all day. "That evening just got so much more bearable."

. . .

On my way home from Jill's, Luke called my cell phone.

"Fa-la-la-la-la," he said. I could hear the cacophony of holiday shoppers in the background. "Guess where I am?"

"I don't know, Luke. Where?" I wasn't in the mood for games.

"Buying your Christmas present," he said, sounding chipper and spirited. "We need to know your shoe size." *We.* He and Mitch were now so totally together that all sentences were phrased in the first-person plural.

"Luke, you don't need to get me anything." It was my standard line, but I meant it this year.

"Oh, whatever. You're always skulking around in those flats. You need some come-hither heels. Consider it a gift for Mark."

"Luke . . . ," I started, but he wasn't listening. I could hear Mitch murmuring in the background and Luke's muffled voice.

"Mitch wanted me to ask you if you ever found out the Web address for Mark's thing."

I knew that the "thing" Luke was referring to was Mark's nonprofit, but it didn't matter anymore. "Actually, no. And I don't think I will."

"What do you mean?" asked Luke cautiously, finally reading my foul mood.

"It's just . . . not going to work out between us."

"What happened?" he asked, aghast.

"Look, I don't really feel like going into it. I'll talk to you later, okay?"

"Okay . . . ," said Luke reluctantly.

. . .

There were suitcases set out by the back door when I got home. Aunt Kathy was putting on her coat as she and my mother stood facing each other, both looking forlorn and anxious. Their emotions, whether good or bad, were always mirrored in each other's expressions.

"What's going on?" I asked.

"Aunt Kathy's going home," said my mother, putting on a brave face.

"Why?" I asked, shocked.

Aunt Kathy looked at me tenderly. "Y'all have a lot going on right now, honey. I think it would be best if it was just your family."

"What do you mean? You're our family." I glanced from her

to my mother, expecting her to voice a similar protest, but she couldn't meet my eye. "What are you going to do for Christmas?" Libby was in Stockholm and Uncle Bill was somewhere off the coast of Central America.

"I'll be fine," said Aunt Kathy in the overexaggerated, syrupy southern accent that she and my mother always used when trying to be convincing. "Lord, I can't wait to have a few days to putter around my house by myself."

From behind me, I heard my father's distinct, heavy footsteps.

"Are we ready?" he asked.

"Wait—you're leaving *right* now?" I asked.

"Daddy and I are going to take Kathy to the airport. We'll be back in about an hour," said my mother.

My father picked up two of Aunt Kathy's bags, then stood a few feet back while my aunt and I said good-bye. It was as if he didn't want to get too close to anyone, as if he had some virulent and contagious virus. Once so indomitable, he now seemed almost meek.

"You have a wonderful Christmas, honey," said Aunt Kathy, gripping my shoulders.

"You, too," I said, bewildered and stunned. "I just can't believe you're going."

"Say good-bye to your brother and sister for me." And with that, the three of them disappeared.

There were dishes in the sink. I began obsessively washing them. Not just giving them a rinse and sticking them in the dishwasher, but cleaning and drying by hand. When that was done, I wiped down the already clean counters and vacuumed the floor before moving on to the living room. It was the first time I really noticed that there was no tree. It was a week before Christmas and there was no tree. There were no stockings and no nativity. There were no amaryllis bulging from their fleshy bulbs, ready to bloom. The lack of ornamentation immediately seemed like a flashing, foreboding symbol, a red flag that I had missed. Aunt Kathy knew everything there was to know about my mother, and, by extension, my parents. There was nothing I could imagine being beyond the pale of their relationship.

I got in the car and drove to one of the roadside Christmas tree stands that popped up around that time of year. As I stood looking at the trees, constrained by netting and leaning up against the A-frame display, I pictured my parents' living room, with its huge cathedral ceiling and massive stone fireplace.

"What size you looking for?" asked a gruff man with a red beard shot with white.

"I don't know exactly. Something big, though."

"The biggest we got left is about twelve feet."

"Perfect," I said, wanting a tree to fill the space, to totally overwhelm and consume it.

He tied it to the roof of my car and I drove awkwardly but urgently toward home, wanting to get the tree set up before my parents returned. I would find the decorations in the basement. The tree stand was there, too. Everything was going to look *perfect*, I thought as my hands shook.

But my father's car was already in the garage when I arrived.

"Where's Dad?" I asked my mother. She was sitting in the living room, leaning forward with her elbows resting on her knees. Music was playing in the background, a modern recording of "Jehovah Jireh." It meant "God the Provider."

"Your father's not feeling well. He's lying down."

"I bought a Christmas tree. I can't get it in by myself."

My mother took a deep breath. "Ellen, sit down."

"What's going on, Mom?" I asked, dreading her answer, realizing that no matter how old I got, my parents would always be my parents. I would always feel helpless and vulnerable in the face of their problems.

"Your father and I have declared bankruptcy."

"Oh, Mom," I whispered. By the look on her face, I could tell she was not done.

"We are figuring out what assets the bank is going to get. We are hoping to keep the house."

"What?" I didn't have the foresight to hide my shock or fear. "You might lose *the house*?"

She covered her eyes with her hand and I saw her mouth quiver. "Your poor father," she said. "He's worked so hard his whole life, and to be left with *nothing* is just . . ." *Beyond words.* His was the story you heard about on the news. The greedy developer who rode the real estate bubble to riches until it burst and he finally got what was coming to him. He was the villain, the fool, and the problem.

"What's going to happen?" I asked, echoing the question that had probably been ringing in my mother's ears for months.

"Nothing is definite. Your father's been talking to the lawyers. They don't usually go after your residence, but—" She swatted at the air, and I realized that my mother's understanding of the situation was most likely minimal. "I guess we have a lot of equity in this place." She laughed sadly. "Lord, you'd think that was a *good* thing."

"Oh, Mom," I said, putting my hand on hers. As I was trying to formulate the right words, ask the right questions, my mother turned to me with sudden urgency.

"Ellen, you just have to promise me—please don't let on to your father that you know. He doesn't want *anyone* to know yet."

"Mom, it's nothing to be ashamed of," I said, but even as I spoke, I knew it wasn't exactly true. Wasn't failure—particularly financial failure—what men like my father were *told* to be ashamed of?

"Promise me, Ellen." Her words were more emphatic, more desperate.

I nodded reluctantly. "Do you have a plan?" I asked quietly.

"I just have to pray." Her head began to nod steadily. "We just have to all keeping praying."

I was filled with a sudden and violent fury. I had expected her answer to involve payment plans, budgets, mentions of funds that were protected, untouchable—but prayer? *It doesn't work,* I screamed in my head, wanting to shake her. *It doesn't fucking work.* But I said nothing. My mother read the look on my face.

"What else can I do, Ellen?" she asked, fresh tears streaming down her cheeks. "Please, tell me, what else can I possibly do?"

CHAPTER TWENTY-NINE

The car bucked violently as we went over an enormous pothole in the parking lot of Prince of Peace Church. It was located in one of the better areas of what was typically considered a not-very-nice town.

"Shoot," said my mother, cringing as her car bottomed out. "I didn't see that."

She was distracted, eager to get to church, to thank Jesus for "the word" he had given her last night.

"I sent out a prayer request and you wouldn't *believe* how many people I had praying for us." That night, she said, she had awakened suddenly, almost as if shaken. "I had a feeling of supernatural peace. That's when it came to my lips, 'prosperity and abundance.'" She shook her head fondly, as if at the reliability and loyalty of a very old friend. "That's the Lord. God the Provider." In my mother's mind, it was prophetic, a message from the divine that everything was going to be just fine.

She pulled the car into a distant spot in the crowded lot and we walked together up to the building. The church was housed in a smallish, seventies-looking structure with brown vertical siding and chalet-style stained-glass windows. The sign, which was beginning to fade and chip, read, PRINCE OF PEACE CHURCH. ALL ARE WELCOME, and featured a dove, an olive branch, and a cross. Though Christmas was less than a week away, the only seasonal adornments were two anemic-looking evergreen wreaths that hung on each of the double-entry doors. They looked like the kind sold on roadsides by mute, disabled veterans, with their twist-on red polyester ribbons and plastic gold bells.

"I see they don't have the same decorator as Christ Church," I said with grim sarcasm. Christ Church, with its hand-carved walnut nativity scene and elegantly adorned Alberta spruces, subscribed to the belief that the gospel goes down easier when tarted up a bit. But Prince of Peace was cut from a different cloth: the itchy kind. Once inside, I imagined that I would be surrounded by pale-faced women with big gums. Their long hair would be parted down the middle and pulled back into a utilitarian ponytail. Their seven children, who had never watched TV or eaten Froot Loops, would peer out from behind their legs with wide, frightened eyes and ill-fitting clothing. The men would heartily shake one another's hands and greet their neighbors with the prefix *brother* or *sister*. "Brother Paul!" they would say. "I missed you at the retreat last weekend!"

Ignoring me, my mother kept a few steps ahead, anxious to get inside. "They do the most adorable children's sermon here, too," she said as she hurried up the concrete walk. "The minister really knows how to speak to the little ones, to talk about the Lord in a way that they understand."

"Yeah," I said. "I'll bet all the homeschoolers love it."

"Stop it," said my mother sharply. "I don't want to hear any negativity."

I hadn't intended to be so snarky. I had only come this morning to support her. "Please come, Ellen," she had said. "Your father just doesn't want to go to church today." But on the drive in, as I heard more about how the Lord was going to make everything okay, how she just needed to trust absolutely, to pray harder, to believe more, I had found the venom building in my throat. "All this financial business is really just an opportunity to cleave to the Lord," she said as I stared out the window at the rented duplexes and electronics repair shops that littered this run-down town.

We entered the sanctuary just before the service was to begin, and I noted with a combination of disappointment and relief that, for the most part, the other congregants were ordinary-looking people. There were, as promised, several refugees, and the socioeconomic status was decidedly more mixed than at Christ Church, but this wasn't the tent revival I had expected.

With nearly all the seats filled, we took our places in an uncomfortably upright pew toward the back. In her quiet, church voice, my mother began to give me the necessary background, as if the service was the sequel to a movie I had never seen. "This church was nearly dead until a few years ago, when the old pastor passed away and they got this new one. Now it's growing like crazy."

I nodded without interest and began thumbing through the program, trying to gauge how long a service I was in for. If Communion was being offered, I would be here for at least an hour, maybe more.

It was only a minute or two before the large band positioned behind the pulpit sprang into action, the cue, I assumed, for everyone to crane their necks and watch the minister make his way down the aisle. I kept my gaze on the "upcoming events" section of the thin, xeroxed sheets of paper. It seemed that the church would be organizing several trips, volunteer service opportunities to places like El Salvador and Kenya.

"Here he comes," my mother said, elbowing me in the ribs. I looked up lazily, following the eyes of the crowd.

At first, I didn't understand it, why Mark was there, striding purposefully down the aisle.

"He was raised in Africa. His parents were missionaries," my mother whispered. "Isn't he handsome?" I couldn't respond, couldn't move. I was frozen. My mind was screaming, but my body was immobile.

I wanted it to be a mistake, a look-alike, a misunderstanding. Maybe he was just making an announcement, a pitch for volunteers for his nonprofit. But though he was still dressed like Mark, still had on jeans and a plain brown sweater, he was carrying a Bible and stepped assuredly up onto the stage, as if he had been doing it for years.

As it turns out, he had.

CHAPTER THIRTY

"You know, he's spending his Christmas with the inmates up in Rahway at the state prison. That's a true man of God," said my mother, nodding in agreement with herself. "I get the feeling he's a little more liberal than I usually like, but what can you do . . ." She trailed off, oblivious to my shock.

Once in position, Mark ran his fingers through his hair, then looked up calmly at the congregation. "Good morning," he said in his strong but soft voice. "Thank you for joining us in fellowship this morning."

I flipped wildly to the front of the program. Under the church's logo in small type was "Pastor Mark Oberson." My cheeks burned instantly and I shrank back into my seat as my breath sped up unnaturally. I flipped the program over, as if to hide his name, and there on the back was a small logo for a church-run organization whose mission was alleviating poverty in the community. It was called the Need Alliance.

"Ellen, what's the matter with you?" demanded my mother.

I couldn't answer; I could only recall the things I had said and done just two nights ago, reframing them in this shocking new context. *I want to be with you,* I had whispered as I undressed myself. I once had a friend in college who took a job as a dancer at a high-end strip club. A women's studies major, she spun her lucrative employment as liberating, a sort of feminism 2.0, until one night, a few minutes into her routine, she saw her uncle in the audience, looking stunned and excruciatingly uncomfortable as the German businessman whom he was entertaining stared at her appreciatively. I instantly had greater empathy for both of them.

It was all I could do to keep from running from the building right then and there, but I knew that I had to get out with as little notice as possible. Hunching so deeply that my face was practically on my knees, I looked through the program while my mother cast me sidelong glances. I would bide my time, then slip out calmly, as if just going to the restroom. Mark would never see me, never know I had been there.

I kept my eyes down as he spoke, his words becoming just sounds, unintelligible and meaningless as I concentrated on breathing, in and out. "Ellen, for goodness' sake, *sit up,*" ordered my mother. We were called to stand and the music began again. I dared to sneak a glance up at the stage. Mark was watching the band, singing with the rest of the congregation, his head nodding rhythmically.

When the music ended, he opened his Bible and turned the pages carefully. Pushing his glasses up on his nose, he began to speak: "Romans 8:28 says, 'And we know that all things work together for good to them that love God, to them who are the called according to his purpose.'" It was one of my mother's favorite scriptures, and she'd often say, "Even what seem like problems can become blessings in the Lord's hands." When Mark was finished, he looked up at the congregation, then closed his eyes. "Let us pray."

It was a beautiful prayer, my mother would later tell me, but I couldn't recall a word of it. As soon as it ended, there was another song; then Mark invited us to greet one another. As my mother quietly shook hands with our neighbors, I reached into her purse and pulled out her keys.

"Where are you going?" she hissed as I slid smoothly from the pew.

"I'll be in the car," I whispered, a desperate edge to my voice.

My hands were on the metal door push when I heard my name echo over the church's PA system, drowning out the murmured exchanges of welcome among the congregants. "Ellen." It wasn't a question; there was no uncertainty in his voice. Frozen, I glanced back at the pulpit. He was staring at me, looking confused and pained and shocked.

Our eyes met for only a moment. Then, pushing the door open just wide enough to slip through, I escaped into the foyer and pressed the door shut again behind me. I flew through the second set of doors and outside, immune to the cold as it hit my burning face. Overwhelmed and stunned, I swatted unwelcome tears from my eyes. I didn't know why they were coming. As I began to walk purposefully toward the car, my heart jumped as I heard the doors lurch open behind me. "Ellen!" he called. "Wait!" My pace quickened and I felt my stomach make panicked flips. His hand caught my arm and suddenly he was in front of me.

"Ellen, please," he said, trying to catch my eyes.

For a second, when our eyes locked, I wanted to collapse against him. But that feeling was almost immediately overtaken by a deep sense of indignation and betrayal, which neither began nor ended with Mark.

"So *the Need Alliance*, huh?" I asked caustically.

"Just walk with me?"

I clutched the collar of my coat closed. "I don't want to walk," I said flatly.

"All right. I'll say what I need to say right here." He tried to take my hand, but I pulled it back. "I'm sorry I lied to you, Ellen. There were so many times when I wanted to tell you."

"Why didn't you?"

"Because of this." He gestured to the space between us. "Because with every day that passed that I didn't tell you, it became harder."

"Why did you lie in the first place?" I asked, pretending that it was his dishonesty that caused my repulsion, forgetting my own initial omissions.

"Ellen, women either *won't* date me because of my work or they *only* want to date me because of my work." He laughed humorlessly. "Neither really works." I looked to see the members of the church beginning to peer from around the side of the building, taking cautious, wary steps toward us. "I really care about you. I didn't want you to find out like this. I hoped it wouldn't matter, but I can tell that it does." He looked at me, waiting for me to contradict him. I couldn't.

My mother emerged from the church, followed by several congregants looking protectively at "Pastor Mark" and suspiciously at me. Walking gingerly toward us, Mom looked back at the group and offered a nervous, apologetic smile.

"Hi, Pastor Mark," she said as she reached us, her sugar-sweet southern accent kicking in. "I don't know if you remember me, Patty Carlisle; I went with y'all to the family center a few times?"

Mark forced a smile. "Hello. How are you?"

She looked back and forth between us. "Is everything all right?"

"Mom, can you give us a minute?"

"Do y'all know each other?" she asked hopefully.

"Mom . . ."

I pulled Mark farther away. "Listen. This is clearly not the place to discuss this. Let's talk later."

He nodded. "I'll pick you up," he said. "What time?"

"No . . . ," I said quickly. "Let's just meet somewhere."

CHAPTER THIRTY-ONE

"Well, I think it's wonderful that your boyfriend is a minister," clucked my mother as she merged onto Route 78. "I don't understand what you are so worked up about, why we had to leave church, for goodness' sake."

"He's *not* my boyfriend. We went out a few times, during which he never told me the truth about what he did." I found myself quickly trying to unweave the fabric of what Mark and I had become, pulling at the loose threads and frayed edges of our relationship, not knowing where to stop, not knowing whether to unravel it completely.

"He didn't exactly lie," rationalized my mother defiantly. "Churches are nonprofit organizations."

I couldn't even summon a response.

"He's a good man, Ellen. He had every option in the world and he dedicated his life to Christ." To hear Mark put in those hokey, idiomatic terms made me want to plug my ears and scream, but my mother went on. "If you had just *stayed* to hear his sermon, you would have seen what he's all about. I've never heard another minister preach so beautifully on God's love."

"Look, Mom, I'm sure he is a wonderful, talented preacher and a good, kind man." My intonation indicated that there was a large and burdensome *but . . .*

My mother turned to me, her pool blue eyes looking so much like Kat's. "So what's the problem?"

I contemplated the answer to that question all afternoon, right up until the moment I walked into the little café at Back Door Books. Mark was at the table where we had sat just a few weeks ago. He had a glass of water in front of him.

"No coffee?" I asked as I hung my coat over the back of the chair.

"I was waiting for you."

Walking up to the counter, he ordered a black coffee for himself and a latte for me.

"Here," I said, trying to hand him a five-dollar bill to cover the tab.

He looked down at the folded money in my hand like it was a particularly mean-spirited joke. "It's okay, Ellen. I've got this."

We took our seats back at the table and Mark stared into his coffee cup.

"I'm really sorry that things turned into such a scene today at church," I said awkwardly, the words not feeling right in my mouth. "Did everyone . . . understand?"

"It was fine," he said, his words so quick and reassuring that I was sure it *wasn't* fine, that it was uncomfortable and difficult. "I'm just sorry you had to find out that way." His being a minister seemed shameful and secret, and I shifted in my chair as I remembered him up behind that pulpit. As if reading my body language, he continued. "But I am not ashamed of what I do, Ellen. I should have told you in the beginning, but I didn't and I've been trying to figure out how to make you understand why. And I think the best way is to ask you this: if you knew I was a minister, would you have acted differently around me?"

Yes.

His eyes searched mine. "Would you have been able to get to know me, the way you did?"

No.

I'm sure he knew my answers, as the questions were for my benefit, not his. He went on. "But I should have accepted that. I should never have misled you. I was weak and I regret that."

It was here that I was supposed to say that I understood, that I knew what it was like to fear divulging the truth. Instead I said, "Is this why . . . the other night . . . ?"

"Yeah," he said sadly, quietly. "I let it all get out of hand."

My voice lowered to a near whisper. "Have you ever been . . . with a woman?" He looked disappointed that this was my first line of questioning, that my insecurities had elbowed their way to the front of the line.

"I wasn't always a minister, Ellen," he said simply, and I recalled the way he had touched me that night.

"What made you want to join the church?" I had to force myself to say the sentence fluidly, naturally. As my mother had put it, Mark had *every option in the world.* And I probably would have been thrilled with his choosing any one of them over this one.

He sat back in his chair and, with crossed arms, studied the edge of the table. "I was working on my doctorate. My focus was on economic solutions to poverty in the developing world. My parents were missionaries and they saw God as the only way to improve people's lives. They thought that if you had Jesus, everything else would fall into place and God would take care of all your needs. I fought against that idea; I wanted to develop the policies that would accomplish all that. It was when I was writing my thesis that I had a sort of epiphany, I guess it was—about me, about who I was.

"My father had come to visit me in New York. He had me go with him to a shelter run by an old friend of his for runaway teens. Some of these kids had fled the most appalling circumstances. We spent the night just talking with them, hearing their stories, listening. They were so grateful to have someone listen. It was God that was working through my father that night, allowing these kids who felt like no one cared for them to feel his love." He was now looking me in the eye, speaking with a kind of restrained passion that I was sure he brought to his sermons. Though I maintained eye contact, I uncomfortably judged the proximity of the other patrons, whether they were within earshot, whether they could hear Mark sounding like this, sounding like a Christian.

"I don't know; I guess I realized then that if my thesis, this thing I was pouring hundreds of hours into, did as much for one person as my father did for dozens on that night, I'd be lucky. I wanted to help people in a tangible, one-on-one way. I wanted God to work through *me*."

But, I thought. *But.* My objections were nothing I could verbalize. "Is this something you think you'll do forever?"

He paused for a moment. "I don't have any plans to leave the ministry right now. Not with God doing such amazing things at Prince of Peace."

Instantly, the life we would have if we stayed together played out in my mind. In rapid succession I pictured myself in Mark's house, surrounded by his books, my legs stretched over his lap. I pictured trips to Africa. I pictured adoption. But when I started to panic, when the picture became too vivid, was when I saw myself sitting in the front row of Prince of Peace Church. It was then that I again felt the urge to run for the door. Because the problem wasn't that I was afraid I didn't fit there, but that I *did*, that I had been drawn blindly to an inevitability. That I was destined to sit wringing my hands and waiting for a deaf God to solve my problems. That religion would define me. That I would become my mother. That I already had.

I met his eyes. "I admire you," I said, my voice heavy with caveats. "But, Mark . . ."

He leaned closer, his forearms resting on the table. I thought about what a compelling policy maker he would have been. "I understand it's a lot to digest," he said patiently. "And I know that my choices have implications for whomever I am with, both good and bad. But I really care about you, Ellen." He laid his warm hand on top of mine.

"Mark," I said, not knowing how to say what came next. We sat in silence for a second before I continued. "I care about you, too. I just . . ." I couldn't stop thinking of my grandmother, the preacher's wife.

He only nodded, expecting as much. He slid his hand slowly away and gripped the handle of his coffee mug.

And suddenly I wanted desperately to get away. "I better get going," I said, my chair screeching against the tile floor as I pushed it back to stand.

"Ellen?"

I looked him in his eyes.

"Take care of yourself."

My heart ached. He was altruistic and good, too good for me, to the very end.

. . .

My mother was waiting for me in the kitchen when I got home. "How was your date with Mark?"

"You mean *the Buddhist*?" I asked sarcastically as I sloughed off my jacket. I irrationally felt as though our breakup was her fault. It was her fault for having a Jesus fish on her car when she picked me up at school and sending me to Christian camp. It was her fault for telling me to "rest with the Lamb" and that I should cast my burdens at the "foot of the cross." *She* did this. *She* made this happen. It was so much easier for me to resist what my mother believed than to divine my own faith. It was so much easier to blame.

She gave me a look.

"Listen, Mom, I don't think it's going to work out with us," I said, wanting to cushion the blow. Mark was a dream come true, an answer to her prayers. She was like an old Italian mother coaxing her firstborn son into the priesthood in order to get a backstage pass into heaven.

"Don't write him off, Ellen," she commanded. "Give him a chance. You only just started dating."

"I know."

"And I can't understand how you would view his being a minister as some kind of *flaw*."

"All right, Mom," I said, as I tried to escape the kitchen, feeling suffocated, as if the neck of my sweater was too tight. "We'll just see how things go."

"Hold on a second. I need to talk to you." Sidestepping the island, she scurried up next to me. "Have you told your brother and sister anything about what I told you about Daddy and me?" she asked, her voice a whisper.

Having already assured her that I wouldn't discuss things with Kat and Luke, I was thrown by her need for additional assurance. "No," I said, my voice softening as I was reminded of the reality of her situation. "I haven't told them."

My mother nodded in relief. "Your father wants to tell everyone all at once," she said, her red sweater looking too bright, too festive for her pale, gray face.

I knew how Luke and Kat would react. Like me, they would cling to an ignorant, desperate optimism. This was when we still had the luxury of believing that it wasn't quite real, that it was going to be a close call and cautionary tale. *Do you remember when Mom and Dad almost lost the house?*

"When?" I asked, wondering at what time, besides Christmas, we would all be together again.

"I don't know, Ellen," said my mother impatiently before taking a deep but unsatisfying breath. "Your father has it all worked out."

. . .

I tried not to think about Mark the rest of the day, but my mind veered in his direction, again and again.

"Why couldn't he *really* be a Buddhist?" I asked Kat, my cell phone pressed surreptitiously to my ear as I drove into work the next morning. "I could get on board with Buddhism." It was after I said it that I realized I was only half kidding.

"Why? So you can trade one ideology that probably isn't true for another that probably isn't true?" asked Kat harshly, hyperintolerant, as ever, of hypocrisy. "So you can hang out with Richard Gere and wear prayer beads and talk about being an *old soul*?"

Better than hanging out with Mel Gibson. "Relax, Kat. I was just joking."

"I don't think you were."

Screw you, Kat. I didn't want to be challenged. "Whatever. Listen, I'm at work. I gotta go," I said as I slowed for a traffic light a few miles from the office.

. . .

I wasn't deep into the day before I had to field several calls from Parker, who was obsessing over that evening's party. "I want to make sure you are there at least an hour before the guests arrive."

"That's no problem," I said in the same chipper yet professional tone I had taken to using almost exclusively with Parker. "I'll leave right from here."

Philip sauntered out of his office as I was hanging up.

"Is Parker driving you nuts?" he asked apologetically, adjusting the collar of his overcoat.

"Oh, no." I laughed unconvincingly. "She just wants everything to be perfect. I understand."

Philip sat on the edge of my desk, an uncharacteristically familiar gesture that I attributed to the somewhat more relaxed vibe that permeated all offices during the week before Christmas. "She gets so worked up about this kind of thing. Frankly, I can't wait until it's over."

My only response was a smile, in hopes that Philip would move along. I wasn't interested in engaging in personal banter with Parker's husband, even if he was my boss. But Philip didn't take the hint.

"So, do you have any plans for Christmas?"

"Uh, yeah," I said lightly. "I'll be spending it with my parents."

"They're friends with the Arnolds, right?"

His body language was so informal that I straightened up and stiffened in compensation. "I suppose you could say that."

"I think Parker has us going to their Christmas party." He arched his back in a little stretch. "She's been going to some women's group at Lynn's house and can't say enough about her. I must hear Lynn's name"—he paused to make an accurate estimate—"six times a day."

"Oh, that's great," I said. My tone was perfunctory.

Philip rolled his eyes. Unlike Greg, who was adoringly amused by Jill's idiosyncrasies, Philip seemed to merely tolerate Parker's. "Yeah, well"—he drummed his fingers over my desk—"if Parker calls, I have a meeting in the city. I'll be home in time to go to the party together."

As Philip walked away, I stared at his back, noticing that he didn't have his briefcase with him.

. . .

I stood just inside the doorway to Maramar, where I had been for at least an hour, ready to escort guests to the large and lavishly decorated private dining room that the Kents had reserved.

"Make sure they don't set up the raw bar until the very last minute," ordered Parker into her cell phone. "I would *die* if someone ate a room-temperature oyster."

"I'll tell them," I said, just as I had told the florist to pluck any spotted petals from the cerise rose and green hydrangea bouquets, as I had told the waitstaff to be sure that the wine was served from decanters, "but with bottles displayed so that the label shows."

I heard the clatter of Parker's stiletto heels before I saw her.

She marched through the door, which Philip held open for her, and immediately searched for me, disappointed, I could tell, that I was exactly where I was supposed to be.

"How is everything going?" she asked as Philip took her coat. "Does the room look good?"

"It looks beautiful," I said, though Parker would not be satisfied until she saw it herself.

"Does it feel tight with the banquet-style tables?" She took a discreet but distinctly appraising glance at me. I was wearing a black turtleneck and black pencil skirt with black, kitten-heel boots. I didn't have on an apron, but I was, as requested, wearing the all-black attire of the rest of the staff.

"No, it's great," I said. "That was a good call." Parker, on the other hand, was dressed to be noticed, with a strapless fuchsia satin cocktail dress that was tight over her chest but belled out into a tulip skirt that accommodated her enormous belly. She had on sexy heels that added at least five inches to her frame and her hair was pulled into a chignon with her bangs grazing her brow.

"Philip, honey," she said, as she rested her fingers on his upper arm, her voice an octave higher than when she was speaking to me, "let's go back there. People should be getting here soon." I could see that she was taking to heart Lynn Arnold's lessons on how to be a "fine Christian wife." Philip probably got back rubs, blow jobs, and beer in frosty mugs brought to him on wooden trays with a little bowl of smoked scallops.

The guests began to arrive soon after, and I greeted them cordially. *Good evening. Are you here for the Kent party? Right this way.* I knew how to hold my hands behind my back and smile; Horton had trained me for that. And I wasn't surprised when they looked through me when asking the whereabouts of the restroom, or when they followed silently without a pleasant word. I was, after all, the help.

When the Arnolds arrived, and Lynn saw me, her face instantly lifted into a practiced smile, the kind she could probably hold for hours at a time during a ribbon-cutting ceremony.

"So nice to see you, Ellen," she said, stopping just a few inches too far away for her greeting to be considered sincere.

"Good to see you, too," I said.

"So, I hope you are still coming to our party next week."

"I wouldn't miss it." The immobility of her smile indicated that she wished I would. Her distance suggested that she was fully aware of the severity of my parents' financial troubles. To the Arnolds, losing your money was worse than having a divorced daughter. It was worse than having a pregnant teenager or a gay son.

As the party reached critical mass, the chatter in the room became a laughter-punctuated buzz. I stood on the sidelines, rendered redundant, as I knew I would be, by the very capable staff of the well-respected restaurant. I was there because Parker was in the position to tell me that I had to be. So I stood in the corner and watched as Parker sought to be the perfect hostess, twirling between conversations and giving face time to everyone in the room. She rested her hand on her swollen belly and nursed her glass of San Pellegrino, every so often directing Philip this way or that. The evening, it seemed, was orchestrated to show Philip exactly how valuable she was, how lucky he was to have her. All powerful men need their Jackies.

As the cocktail hour ended, I approached Philip and Parker to let them know that the guests could be invited to take their seats. They were talking with the Arnolds and Parker's parents.

"We need to get you into the attorney general's office, Philip," said Edward Arnold as he snatched a duck spring roll off a passing tray.

Philip took a sip of his wine. "I'm not nearly altruistic enough to go into public service," he said, to his audience's riotous delight. It wasn't funny so much as true.

"That's the problem. No one in his right mind would take that job," said Parker's father. "That's why our government is run by idiots." Lynn stood by with her hands crossed in front of her, listening to the men, while Parker's mother looked vacantly off in the distance, like a socialite of old, anesthetized by privilege. Privilege and something darker.

The meal was beautifully prepared and expertly served. Philip gave a lovely toast, thanking his wife for putting the evening together and his friends and colleagues for attending. I didn't know if anyone noticed that his speech was beginning to slur.

After dessert, the guests began to trickle out and Philip took his post at the bar with a few other men around his age, some of whom I would learn he had known since he was a boy. They had gone to school together, played on the same hockey teams, gone on ski trips, and spent time at one another's summer homes. Parker looked like she was beginning to flag, taking a seat on a stool and glancing at the clock every few minutes. When the Arnolds came to say thank you and good night, Edward commented on it.

"Parker, you look like you're ready to put your feet up."

Philip glanced toward his wife. "Yeah, you look bushed, Park," he said reluctantly. "I guess I ought to be getting you home."

"We can bring her home," offered Edward. "No need to leave your party."

Parker straightened up and immediately began to attempt to assuage their concerns. "Oh, I'm fine, really. I just needed to sit for a minute."

"Honey," said Philip, resting his hand on her belly, "you really should get some rest. Why don't you let Lynn and Edward get you home, hmm?" Something about his affection seemed opportunistic.

Parker looked nervously over her shoulder, searching the room. I didn't know what she was looking for until her eyes found me. "No, Philip," she said, turning back to her husband, steel beginning to form in her voice. "I really am fine."

Lynn rested her hand on Parker's shoulder. "Your husband thinks you should get some rest, Parker. For the baby's sake." And that was all Lynn had to say. Lynn, from whom Parker was supposed to be learning how to be an obedient Christian wife. She wouldn't dare defy Lynn.

Gathering up her things, Parker said a few good-byes, then walked over to the corner in which I was standing. She looked at me with an expression I didn't recognize. "You really don't need to stay any longer, Ellen." There was an edge to her voice.

"Okay. I'll check with the manager that everything is all set. Then I'll head out."

.   .   .

After tracking down the manager, I returned to find the room nearly empty. Philip was still at the bar, his tie now loosened, his hand curled around a crystal tumbler. I heard him give an unrestrained barroom laugh as he sat turned toward the man to his right.

"Pardon me, Philip?" I said from a few feet away.

He swiveled on his stool. "Ellen!" he exclaimed, seeming pleasantly surprised. "I'd like you to meet a few of my friends."

He gave the man closest to him a slap on the back, a get-a-load-of-this backhand, and I instantly had three sets of male eyes on me, looking me up and down.

"This is Ellen . . . my assistant." There was an uncomfortable subtext to the way in which he said my title.

One of his companions whispered something to the other before both began snickering.

"I just wanted to let you know that I was heading home. Everything is all set."

He turned to his friends. "See how competent she is?" He set his drink down and stood up. "I'll tell you what. I'll walk you to your car." Pointing to his friends, he added, "I've seen some unsavory types hanging around here."

"No, really, that's not necessary, Philip."

"Nonsense," he said, resting his hand on my back. "Where's your coat?"

I glanced at the two men, one of whom nudged the other, both looking expectant and entertained.

"Really, Philip," I said, trying to outpace him. "Stay with your friends."

He ignored me and guided me toward the coat check, where I pulled on my black overcoat. He awkwardly, drunkenly tried to help me with it. "It's okay," I said. "I got it."

I tried to leave him at the front door, to say good night, but he insisted on seeing me outside. "Don't be so stubborn, Ellen. I'm just being a gentleman."

Is that what you're being? He held the door open and I walked out.

"So," he said, his breath turning to crystalline frost under the lights of the parking lot, "you're going right home?"

It was ten o'clock at night. "Yup," I said, hitting the unlock button on my keys.

"Maybe we could go get a drink somewhere," he said, his hand once again on my back.

I looked at him sharply. "Philip . . . ," I warned.

We were at my car and I reached for the handle. Philip's hand pushed the door shut. My heart jumped into my throat. Here I was again, in a dark parking lot. But this time there was no Mark.

CHAPTER THIRTY-TWO

Philip tugged playfully on the belt of my coat, letting it slide through his hand. I swatted him away. "What are you doing?" I demanded.

He laughed and leaned against the door to my car, cocking his head to the side with a suggestive smile. "Come on," he said, nodding toward his Land Rover. "Let's go get a drink." At that moment I realized that the look I had seen on Parker's face was fear. She knew what her husband was. She knew everything. She had watched it, helplessly, time and time again. Every barb she had sent in my direction, every deliberate reminder of my servitude, was a preemptive retaliation for this, for this inevitable night. She kept me on a short leash to keep an eye on me. Dana Sacco's voice echoed in my head: *I thought you might be right up Kent's alley.* She said it like a shrewd, ruthless madam.

"I'm going home, Philip. You should, too." His eyes struggled slightly to focus. "Actually, you should call a cab."

"You're so serious, Ellen." He inched closer, taking my chin in his hand. "How can we get you to loosen up?"

With that I pulled hard on the door, causing him to take a step back to balance himself. Getting in, I slammed the door shut, locked it, and cracked the window. "Don't drive, Philip. I'm calling you a taxi." I didn't bother trying to hide my disgust.

With his fists on his hips, he breathed a superior, haughty-sounding laugh, then looked off toward the restaurant. I put the car into reverse and backed out, watching him in the rearview mirror as he walked back inside. His friends would be surprised to see him, but he would appease them with a disparaging comment or two about me. *Good thing she files better than she fucks.* Then they would have another drink before moving on. Maybe he would go home, taking the cab that I was now instructing to head to the restaurant. Or maybe he would head to another venue, arriving at his house close to dawn and crawling into bed without explanation, not bothering to hide the receipt for the bottles of champagne, not bothering to shower, to rinse the women from his body. For Philip, to whom everything came so easily, our little exchange wouldn't even really be remembered in the morning. He simply didn't care enough about me, or about Parker for that matter, to be affected.

. . .

I almost didn't go to work the next day. I wanted to call in sick, knew that I would be justified in doing so, but for some reason I couldn't. In some perverse way I was curious about how Philip would behave in front of me. And since I knew I would have to either face Philip again or quit, I decided that ripping the Band-Aid off might be the best tactic.

Philip arrived only fifteen minutes or so later than usual and greeted me with the same rote politeness that he always had.

"Good morning, Ellen," he said, his tone professional and courteous.

"Good morning. I see you made it home safely last night."

I was being deliberately pointed, but Philip looked perplexed. "Yes, thank you." It was as if nothing had happened.

It wasn't until later in the day, when he called me into his office, that there was any indication that he remembered the previous night.

"Ellen," he said, sticking his head out of his office, "can I see you for a moment?"

My stomach churned as all my false bravado dissolved. "Sure," I said nervously. "I'll be right in." The fact was that I didn't want to verbally acknowledge anything about our exchange. I was happier pretending that Philip now feared me for what I knew.

He was sitting at his desk, leaning back in his chair with his arms crossed. He regarded me for a few seconds before he spoke. "How do you think the party went?"

"I think it went well," I said, a little too enthusiastically. "Everyone seemed to have a good time."

He nodded. "Parker seemed happy, which is all I really care about."

Sure you do. "That's great."

He opened his desk drawer abruptly and pulled out a crisp white envelope. "This is for you," he said, holding it out in my direction. I took a few tentative steps toward him and reached for it slowly, as if afraid to make any sudden moves. "I know that your help in planning last night went a bit above and beyond your duties at the firm. So consider this a gesture of gratitude, for your hard work."

"Thank you."

"Thank Parker. It was her idea," he said, turning back to his computer.

· · ·

I didn't open the envelope until I got home that evening. It was their family Christmas card, a trifold on heavy card stock with multiple photos on each panel. All the shots were professionally taken, beautiful pictures of the kids, of Philip and Parker. There were photos of the family together, pictures of just the boys, of just the girls. But as a collection it seemed to shout, to plead, *Look at us! Aren't we happy? Isn't everything perfect?* It struck me as desperate and sad, though I wondered if it would have had the same impact just a few days ago. Inside it read: *Happy Holidays, with Love, the Kent Family, Philip, Parker, Austin, Avery, Alden, and Number Four.* Though what I noticed before the message, before the members of their family were listed for emphasis, were five crisp one-hundred-dollar bills. It wasn't much, by Parker's standards, just the value of a few of the dozens of bottles of wine that they had ripped through last night, but it was five hundred dollars more than I had expected. I stuffed the money back into the card and stowed it deep within my purse.

· · ·

"I can't *believe* he came on to you," said Jill. Pulling my cell phone from my ear, I turned down the volume.

"I don't know if I would say he *came on* to me."

"Oh, please."

"Some people might define it as inappropriate flirting." I wasn't trying to defend Philip; I just couldn't take the pleasure in his behavior that Jill did. Not anymore.

"Okay, fine," said Jill, rolling her eyes, I'm sure, at my hairsplitting. "I can't believe he *flirted inappropriately* with you."

"Jill, let's not talk about it anymore." I almost wished I hadn't told her.

But Jill went on, unable to tear herself away from what she saw as irrefutable evidence of karma. "So Philip Kent is a slut," she mused.

"You have to *promise* that you won't tell anyone."

"Who am I going to tell? Parker?"

"I know, I know. I just don't want this to get back to her."

"Believe me, if she gave you five hundred dollars, she already knows."

"No . . . ," I said, praying that Jill wasn't right. "That was just because I helped out with the party."

"So you think Parker did that out of the kindness of her heart?" asked Jill sarcastically. Jill and I both knew that Parker's generosity always, *always* had strings attached.

"I'm just dreading seeing them at the Arnolds'." I envisioned myself with a stiff, fake smile, an unwanted guest trying to fade into the background. "I'm dreading the Arnolds', period."

. . .

After work that evening I headed to the UPS Store and waited in line with the rest of the procrastinators. Christmas was three days away and I hadn't sent Gary and his family their gifts. They were simple, small things, but I had put thought into each one, hoping to inject a sense of melancholy into their celebrations. I suppose my generosity came with strings, too. For his mother, I had bought a set of tea towels with depictions of Florentine monuments, to remind her, I hoped, of the trip to Italy we had given her for her sixtieth birthday. I bought Daniel a fleece-lined cable-knit wool hat because I knew how he hated the way hats scratched his ears. For Gary, I had intended to give him just a cookbook, as

I had always done the cooking when we were together. But at the last minute I added the bookmark that had been intended for Mark. It was hammered sterling silver with a suede tassel, made by hand in Mexico. I felt a pang as I passed the box over the counter, thinking more of Mark than of Gary or anyone else.

. . .

"Where were you?" asked my mother when I got home. She was cleaning up some dishes, just two bowls. She and my father had had leftover spaghetti for dinner.

"I had to get some gifts sent out."

My mother nodded, the warm water running over her hands. "Gary?" she asked.

"Yeah. And Daniel and Beverly."

She set the bowls on the dish rack. "How are things with Mark?"

"Things . . . didn't really . . . work out between us."

She had turned off the water, but her eyes did not leave the sink. She stared into it like it was a dried-up well. "Because he's a minister?"

"No," I said defensively, not wanting to have to admit the truth to my mother. "That's not the only reason."

"So, you've *just decided* that you don't want to see him anymore?"

I was supposed to correct her, but I couldn't.

"Well," she said sadly, "to leave a good man because he's a minister seems almost more foolish than leaving a woman you love because she can't give you a child." Without looking at me, she dried her hands on a dishrag and began to walk out of the room. "There's some leftover spaghetti in the fridge," she said as she disappeared into the dark family room.

CHAPTER THIRTY-THREE

As the arrival of Christmas began to be measurable in hours instead of days, I felt as though I was being pulled forward against my will by some insistent gravitational force. With every day that passed, my panic built. Though I didn't quite understand why, the thought of being alone with my parents for even a moment during that holiday seemed excruciating, so I began a campaign to get Luke and Kat to come on Christmas Eve instead of arriving sometime in the late morning on Christmas Day.

"Please just spend the night, Kat. *Please.*"

"I don't get why all of a sudden you want to have a slumber party. Why can't I sleep at my own house? I'll be there for presents and all that."

The fact that Kat was coming for Christmas at all was a major, epic step. A sign that while she and my mother had a long way to go, they had established a newfound understanding on which to build.

"I just really think we all need to be together," I said. The truth was that I hoped that if we could reassemble our family, we might be able to harness some small amount of joy to help soften the blow of the announcement that I was sure was imminent.

"Is Luke coming?"

"I haven't asked him yet, but I'm sure he will."

"If Luke comes, then maybe."

. . .

In the end, I couldn't convince Kat or Luke to come out a day early. Christmas Eve was much as I had imagined, with my parents and me on autopilot, going through the motions as we tried to replicate holidays past. My father read from the Bible and we held hands during grace and thanked the Lord for our blessings. My mother put out stockings, and the tree I had bought was decorated, though my mother hadn't bothered to twine lights through the branches. "They're such a hassle to get off." My mother began to open the Christmas cards that had accumulated in a basket on the counter. One at a time, she ripped them open without pleasure, as if they were bills, snorting quietly at each card that had a generic "Seasons Greetings" message rather than a specific reference to Christmas. "People love to pretend that Christmas is about something other than Jesus." Every so often she would pass one to my father, who would briefly acknowledge it before passing it back. Christmas music played loudly through the house until my father turned it down. "I'm sorry, girls. I have a terrible headache," he explained.

Come seven o'clock, we were all in front of the television, watching a Christmas special we'd seen dozens of times, the lines of which we could recite from memory. My father quietly nursed a drink, and my mother stared off into space until she announced at eight that she was tired and going to bed.

. . .

Kat and Luke both showed up early on Christmas Day. They came together, Luke having taken the train and Kat having picked him up at the station.

"Merry Christmas," said Luke as he opened the front door and peeked his head inside.

"Merry Christmas!" called my mother, rushing to greet him. She was doing her very best to be enthusiastic.

Kat followed him in, then shut the door behind her. "Hey, you guys," she said, setting down a shopping bag full of wrapped gifts. "Merry Christmas."

I heard my father click off the TV in the family room and walk into the foyer. "How was the train ride, Luke?" he asked. He and Kat had yet to reconcile on any level and they both stiffened slightly in each other's presence.

"Oh, fine," answered Luke. "Very festive. The conductor was wearing a Santa hat."

"It definitely doesn't feel like Christmas out there," said Kat, taking off her light jacket. It was unseasonably warm, forecast to be in the low sixties.

"Isn't it awful?" asked my mother with a worried expression. I knew that she was considering the possibility that the warm day was some sort of sign, a portent of doom. "And on Christmas of all days."

"I don't mind it." Luke shrugged. My mother eyed him skeptically, as if his tolerance of this springlike Christmas was yet another indication of his compromised morality.

"Well, your mother made a delicious-looking quiche," said Dad, the cue for us to begin to make our way into the kitchen for breakfast.

As we passed through the family room, I saw Kat eye the tree and the modest display of gifts underneath. She knew the very least about my parents' *situation*. "Is there coffee ready?" she asked.

Gathering around the table, Luke began to instinctively fill the palpable void with chatter, talking incessantly and nonlinearly. Every so often, one of us would throw him a conversational bone.

"I hear the whole East Coast is like this today," he said, gesturing outside to the sunny, balmy weather.

Kat nodded. "A friend of mine went up to Vermont for a ski trip and she said only a few trails are open."

"Oh, where did she go?" asked Luke, eager to latch onto a thread.

"Stowe."

"Oh, we just got back from Stowe. We loved it!"

Luke was aware of his slip immediately, and Kat and I instinctively tensed.

My mother zeroed in on that pertinent little pronoun. "Who'd you go with?" she asked, her fork frozen in midair and balancing a bite of quiche.

"Just a friend," answered Luke dismissively. Seeking to segue gracefully out of this line of conversation, he began to exhibit an unusual amount of interest in Kat's friend. "So is this a friend from work? How long has she been at the salon? Is she a stylist or an aesthetician?" That sort of thing.

. . .

Throughout the day, I expected my father to clear his throat and tell us in his chairman-of-the-board voice that we needed to have a "family discussion." That was always what he called them.

"Kids," he would say, "your mother and I have something to tell you." Then they would hold hands and use words like *bankruptcy* and *assets* and *collateral*. This was how it happened in my head. But he never said those words. In fact, he barely spoke at all.

When it was time for Luke and Kat to go, after the presents, after several dead, painful hours, then dinner, he walked them to the front door. *Maybe now,* I thought, both dreading the sound of my father having to admit his failure and desperate to get it over with. But instead he hugged them both, pulling Kat in first, then reaching out to Luke. Gripping the backs of their heads with his hands, he lowered his chin to his chest so it looked as though they were huddling against something fierce and cruel. My father never hugged us like this. It was a pat on the back or a tousling of the hair, but never this. And after the awkward, distant day, it was entirely unexpected. Kat and Luke were frozen, and when he let go, it was clear that they knew something was wrong. But instead of asking if everything was okay, instead of our familial pack instinct kicking in, we all scattered. Luke and Kat hurried out the door; I went upstairs. Only my mother stood next to Dad, with her arms crossed, her thin body radiating worry. "Roger," I heard her say as I reached the top of the stairs, "what's going on?"

Later, I would find out that my mother already knew that they were losing the house. She knew it was definite when she had told me that it was only a possibility. The plan was for my father to tell us all officially on Christmas. Terrible timing, but it couldn't be helped. In retrospect, it would have been freeing. It would have begun to loosen the suffocating hold of the many secrets that hung in the air unspoken. But my father couldn't do it, he told her now. Wouldn't do it. He wasn't going to let it happen.

I imagine my mother's heart splitting at that moment, cracking from the pressure. "Honey," she said tenderly, "it's happened. We just need to put ourselves in God's hands." But my father, we would come to learn, had a different interpretation of what that meant.

. . .

I sat on the edge of my bed—I don't know for how long—with my cell in my hands. I could call him to say Merry Christmas, just to hear his voice. And when my phone rang I felt my heart soar, only to plummet when I realized that it wasn't Mark's ring but, once again, Gary's.

"Merry Christmas," he said softly. It was late, but Gary's family always ate a late supper on Christmas.

"Merry Christmas."

"How was your day?"

"It was good," I said automatically, though unconvincingly. "How was yours? Did you go to your mom's?"

"Actually, I had Christmas here at the house this year." He sounded almost ashamed. I didn't speak. "I really just wanted to call and thank you for your gifts. I know that Daniel and my mom are going to reach out to you as well."

I wasn't in the mood for formalities. "Oh, you're welcome," I said quickly. "I hope you like them."

"Yeah . . . that bookmark is something else." *Something else* was the way Gary always described things that he didn't really like but felt that he should. *Oh, that concert was something else. Did you see that painting? It was something else.*

I let out a tired, sad laugh.

"Listen, I'm really sorry that I didn't send anything . . . I didn't know that we were exchanging gifts . . . But I have something for you . . . that I'll send . . ."

I interrupted him. "Gary, you don't need to get me anything."

"No, no. I mean I have something, but I didn't know if we were going to do that, so I didn't send it."

He was always so phobic about faux pas. I just wanted to get off the phone. "Okay, well, I am beat, so tell everyone Merry Christmas for me."

"Ellen," he said, "there is just one other thing that I wanted to tell you."

"Okay," I said expectantly, wanting him to get on with it. *There is a problem with the divorce; he needs me to come back up. There is something else I need to sign, a tax document.*

"I'm engaged." He said it frankly, without any pauses or signs of ambivalence. Just like when he had told me that he wanted a divorce.

"You're engaged." I had to say the words out loud to understand their meaning.

"Yes, just today. I wanted you to know. I thought I should tell you."

I held my head in my hands. "Congratulations."

Her name was Natalie. She was an occupational therapist who worked with some of the men and women in Daniel's home. I had met her before. She was pretty, blond, with a good nose and white teeth, and came from somewhere in Florida. She also had a three-year-old daughter from a previous marriage. *Well done, Gary,* I thought. Not only would she be an even better advocate for Daniel, but she had a proven breeding record. He didn't just replace me; he upgraded.

CHAPTER THIRTY-FOUR

My mother stood in the kitchen, next to her mink stroller jacket, which was slung over a chair. She wore a full face of makeup, with bright red lips and what Kat always called her Miss Piggy blush, two big smears of pink on the apples of her cheeks. It sounds clownish, but actually, she looked lovely. Her silver bob was smoothed away from her face. She wore an ivory beaded cocktail shell and black silk pants.

"Your father isn't coming tonight," she said, tugging anxiously on a pair of cashmere-lined gloves.

"Okay," I said simply, not asking for an explanation.

She wearily hoisted the heavy fur onto her body. "Well, we should get going. I don't want to be too late." Despite everything, my mother still viewed the Arnolds as their Great White Hope. Edward was connected, and whether because of or despite my mother's business naïveté, she viewed connections as the most valuable of all commodities. "Madeline Palmer told me that Lynn and Edward were invited to a special dinner at the governor's next month." She had said that to my father on the way to church that morning. It was a reminder, a not-so-subtle hint that the Arnolds could still play a role in fulfilling God's promise of prosperity and abundance.

. . .

My mother flipped on her signal, then slowed to a stop to let a sports car whiz by before turning into the Arnolds', the entrance of which was flanked by stately brick posts. They lived in a beautiful area not far from the Donaldsons, with twisting streets peppered with horse farms and the bramble-covered remnants of old stone walls. "So Eugene White is supposed to be here?" I asked, craning my neck and squinting to get a better look at the house, front lit with floodlights.

"Mmmm," said my mother, giving a single nod. She was concentrating on navigating up the long, narrow drive, weaving and winding past mature trees that formed a canopy overhead.

Slowing in response to the series of brake lights in front of us, we saw a handful of uniformed valets collecting keys and dispensing claim tickets. "This is some do," I said, watching the silhouettes of the passengers in the handful of cars in front of us. I was surprised, though I shouldn't have been, by the formality of it all.

My mother checked her face in the mirror. "Lynn was worried that no one would come since it's after Christmas," she murmured. I glanced over my shoulder. Clearly, that wasn't an issue. Dozens of cars were already parked in a large field on the Arnolds' property, with a steady stream following behind us.

Abandoning the warm quiet of the car, I opened my door as my mother spoke with the valet, slipping him a few bills before he replaced her in the driver's seat.

"You tip after," I muttered as we made our way up the wide stone steps.

"Hmm?" asked my mother, distracted.

"You tip valets when you get your car back. Not when you drop it off." Her generosity seemed more like a bribe, or at least an entrance fee, an attempt to prove that we belonged here.

At the door, we were stopped by a security guard with a walkie-talkie.

"Isn't this a little much?" I muttered to my mother as the guard searched his clipboard for our names.

"They need to have security for Eugene White," she said. On any other day, her comment would have come off as defensive, but tonight she seemed too drained.

Though I was sure the security had more to do with the Arnolds' showboating than with Eugene White's need for protection, the temptation to criticize the celebrity pastor was too great. "Yeah," I said as we were waved through the door, "I am sure he doesn't want someone running off with his big fat speaker's fee."

My mother stopped and looked at me. "He doesn't accept a speaker's fee, Ellen. All his speaking engagements are pro bono."

"Come on," I said skeptically. "The Arnolds didn't have to pay anything to get him to come to Christ Church?"

"Of course not. He's not some charlatan."

My eyes narrowed at this unwelcome information. I preferred to imagine him sitting in a beachfront house opening seven-digit royalty checks from his book sales, while his flock filled the collection plates with offerings that they couldn't afford, every week praying that by this act of faith God would provide a way, some way, forward. That by some miracle, they'd be able to pay for their daughter's college or their mother's surgery. That they'd be able to keep their house.

As my mother stared at me, waiting for my response, Lynn Arnold approached.

"Patty!" she exclaimed, grasping my mother's hands. "I am so glad you could make it." Lynn was a consummate hostess, and having been prepared for my mother's attendance, she was able to hide the obvious discomfort she had exhibited with me at the Kents'. "And where is your handsome husband?"

"He wanted so much to be here," gushed my mother in an exaggerated version of her accent. I was always impressed by her ability to turn it on. "But his back was acting up."

Lynn, not really caring about the reason behind my father's absence, gave a sympathetic little clucking noise and turned her attention to me. "And Ellen! You look lovely!"

"Thank you, Lynn." I glanced around at my surroundings, which could only be described as opulent. "You have a beautiful home."

She swatted the air. *Oh, this old thing?* "Well, you ladies enjoy yourselves. There are some nibbles set up by the bar," she said, flopping her hand toward the French doors and the large living room beyond. Then she glided off. She had higher-rent guests to attend to.

My mother soon fell in with a group of churchies. I stood on the sidelines as they recounted in excruciating detail the highlights of Eugene White's sermon that morning. She began to relax, tension visibly slipping from her shoulders as she discussed a topic with which she was well versed and comfortable. It was the sort of physical transformation you saw with salesmen in airport bars, as they drained their vodkas and settled into the comfortable void of transit. They knew what lay on either side of their trip, but there, they were untouchable.

Glancing frequently around the room in search of Jill, I

noticed that Philip and Parker had regrettably beaten her there. Philip hovered by Parker's side, periodically rubbing her back and kissing the top of her head. *He's overcompensating*, Kat would say. *Anytime you see a public display of affection in a married couple, you know that they sleep in separate beds.* Since Parker was obviously and enormously pregnant, it seemed the separate beds theory may not have been accurate, but all the affection did seem to be staged.

Being a card-carrying member of Lynn's women's group, Parker was happy to play Lynn's understudy, directing people to bathrooms, answering questions about the floral arrangements, that sort of thing. And though I had given Philip and Parker an uncomfortable wave when we accidently made the eye contact we were both seeking to avoid, I hadn't yet said a formal hello when Jill and Greg finally did arrive.

I was watching Parker and Philip out of the corner of my eye, pretending to be engaged in my mother's conversation, when I heard Greg's gruff South Jersey bark behind me. "Carlisle," he said. Before I turned around I knew exactly the look that would be on his face, a half smile with a mischievous glint in his eyes. "How are ya, kid?"

"Hi, Greg," I said, taking in his Armani suit. "You clean up nice."

His lips puffed in a tough-guy smile. "You know how we do."

I kissed him on the cheek before giving Jill a discreet pat on the belly. "You're totally starting to show!" I whispered.

"I know!" she beamed. "My doctor says I'm measuring, like, two weeks ahead."

"See, your baby's already *advanced*." Though Jill rolled her eyes, I knew that she was no different from any other parent, beginning to benchmark her child against *average* in utero.

. . .

Jill, Greg, and I gradually gravitated away from the churchies and toward the enormous table of hors d'oeuvres. Greg cut right to the chase and stuffed slice after slice of prosciutto into his mouth, not even pretending to be interested in the accompanying crostini or fig jam. While he busied himself with decimating the antipasti, Jill tilted her head subtly toward Parker and Philip.

"Did you?" she mouthed, her way of asking if I had made contact with the Kents yet.

I shook my head. "Just a wave."

Jill picked up a shard of Parmigiano from a sizable wedge and took a small nibble. "She keeps looking over here."

"I should probably go and say hello," I said grudgingly. "Get it over with."

But Parker beat me to the punch. Greg was at the bar, getting me a glass of wine and himself a martini, when she sauntered up, leaving Philip talking to two men, one of whom I recognized from his and Parker's party almost a week ago.

"Hiiiii," she crowed, zeroing in on Jill first. "I haven't seen you in *ages*! You look *fabulous*."

Jill shot me a look before she responded coolly, but politely, "Hi, Parker. Good to see you."

"I didn't know you knew Lynn and Ed."

"I don't, really." She gestured toward Greg, who was standing in front of the bar, picking his teeth with a cocktail toothpick. "But my husband's family has known them for years."

"Oh, *right*, you married Greg Wadinowski." Parker kept on her plastic smile while giving Greg an appraising look; then her eyes returned to Jill. "Well, Lynn is *great*. You should totally talk to her about joining her women's group."

"What women's group?" asked Jill, with only a hint of mocking detectable in her voice.

Parker's face became earnest and almost philosophical. "It's just a chance for married women to get together. There are all different ages, so the older women kind of mentor the younger women."

Though my presence had yet to be acknowledged by Parker, I knew that the qualifier "married women" was for my benefit. Exclusion was always Parker's weapon of choice. As I stood there, I marveled at how little Parker had changed since high school. In my silence, I wondered if I had.

"Sounds great," said Jill, in a way that indicated Lynn's group had little or no appeal for her.

Parker then turned toward me, as if she had only just been alerted to my presence and was almost taken aback. "Ellen, it's so funny to see you out of context." She splayed her open palm over her heart. "I guess I'm just used to seeing you at the office."

I laughed politely as I took my glass of wine from Greg, who had slipped up next to Jill.

"Parker, this is my husband, Greg," said Jill flatly.

Parker immediately extended her hand. "It's so nice to meet you. I've known your wife for *years*."

Greg, the toothpick still in his mouth, shook Parker's hand. "Yeah. Good to meet ya."

With the formalities out of the way, Parker again focused on me. "So, Ellen," she began, "Philip says that you are seeing someone." She glanced around the room with wide, innocent eyes. "Is he here?"

I imagined how this detail would have come up, if Philip would have offered it to Parker as some sort of insurance policy.

"No, actually we aren't together anymore." I did my best to sound brave and confident, reminding myself that it was *my* choice.

Parker's face scrunched up in sympathy, her lips forming a little pout. "It must be *so hard*," she said, "to be single and in your"—her voice lowered to a near whisper—"situation."

Jill tilted her head and looked hard at Parker. "What do you mean *in her situation*?"

I shot Jill a warning look, begging her not to escalate anything with Parker. But Jill had been waiting for years to show Parker that she now had the backbone that neither of us ever had before. For reasons I didn't yet understand, her resentment of Parker, of Parker's family and everything they represented, was bigger than even she knew.

Parker was the only one who should have realized how deep Jill's animosity ran. She should have seen the steel in her eyes. But instead of backing down, of minimizing her comment, she gave Jill a knowing look, one that pretended to beg for discretion, and gave Jill exactly what she was waiting for.

"I just think it would be *devastating* to face infertility," she breathed, looking from Jill to me, and extending her hand to rub the top of my arm, her own pregnant belly mockingly swollen. "It must be so hard to start to date again."

"Ellen has no trouble attracting men." I heard the innuendo in Jill's voice and looked at her again, begging her not to do it.

"I didn't mean to imply *that*," oozed Parker. "I just think that most men aren't enlightened enough to get past that sort of thing. Even my Philip has said that starting a family was hugely important ..."

"Yes, *your Philip* is quite the family man," interrupted Jill, with a caustic smirk.

"Jill . . . ," warned Greg, sensing the danger of the ground on which she was treading.

Parker's face spasmed as she tried to remain calm and in control. "I'm sorry, Jill—what?" She enunciated every syllable, the threat in her voice making it clear that the question was not to be answered. She had intended to intimidate Jill, but Parker no longer knew the woman who was standing in front of her, the woman who had been emboldened by unconditional love.

Jill raised her chin. "Let's just say that Philip sure can be enlightened when he wants to be."

"What are you implying?" hissed Parker. Greg wrapped his arm protectively around Jill.

"Like I said, Ellen has no trouble attracting men."

With that, Parker's face twisted free of its mask, and every muscle that had struggled to contain her hate, her humiliation, was now free. "What?" she demanded louder than was comfortable, her lower jaw jutting out aggressively. There was no answer but silence. "*What?*" she repeated, even louder this time.

Philip, now alerted to the exchange, came walking quickly up. "Parker, sweetheart, what's going on?" Though his words suggested his concern was for Parker, his eyes darted nervously around the room, taking stock of who was watching, of who was present.

But Parker was now focused on me, her eyes boring into mine with unadulterated fury. "What is your fat fucking friend talking about, hmm? What did you tell her?"

Greg was trying to lead Jill away, but she shrugged him off. "She didn't have to tell me anything, Parker. *Everyone* knows." It was a cruel thing to say, and probably untrue, but Jill wasn't concerned about fighting fair.

Parker whipped around, shaking with rage as she looked at

Jill, who up until now had been frightening in her calm. Only a hint of emotion crept into Jill's voice as she asked, slowly and with clear purpose, "Married a guy just like dear old Dad, didn't you, Parks?"

I took a reflexive step back, realizing immediately that something deep and poisonous had been unearthed. Greg said Jill's name emphatically and took her hand. "Come on. Let's go," he said.

But Parker couldn't be so easily contained. "Fuck you," she spat, her eyes filling with acid tears as she looked at Jill, then at me. "Fuck you both."

Murmurs erupted from the handful of couples around us as discreet glances were cast over shoulders. "Parker . . . ," scolded Philip through gritted teeth, as he firmly took her upper arm.

I stepped between Parker and Jill, resting my hand on Jill's back to help Greg guide her out of the room.

"Stay away from my husband," I heard Parker say, though I didn't turn around.

Once in the foyer, Greg immediately took charge. "I'll take Jill to the car. You go tell your mother that I'm driving you home."

I nodded gratefully, then headed back to the living room, peeking through the door to confirm that Parker and Philip were gone.

Mom was still chatting obliviously, part of a large group on the opposite end of the enormous room. As I slid quickly through the crowd, past the absorbed conversations and engaged discussions, I realized that what had gone on between Jill, Parker, and myself was in actuality a quiet implosion, registering only with those directly around us.

I tapped my mother's shoulder. "Mom."

She turned around, her face pure light. "Oh, hey, honey!" The group parted slightly to make room for me, and my mother gestured to the tall man in front of her. He had gentle eyes and dark brown hair that was graying at the temples. It was Eugene White. I recognized him from church that morning. "Pastor White, this is my daughter Ellen."

He reached out to shake my hand, grasping it between both of his. "Hello, Ellen," he said. "It's nice to meet you."

The moment he touched my hand, I felt tears spring to my eyes. "You were overwhelmed by the spirit," my mother would say. But I think that in Eugene White's quiet confidence, in his strong but gentle nature, he reminded me of someone. Someone I missed. "You as well," I managed before I turned back to my mother and he was reabsorbed into the fold.

"Are you all right?" asked Mom, scrutinizing my reddened eyes.

"Yeah, I'm fine," I said dismissively. "But I'm actually going to head out. Jill and Greg are going to take me home."

"Well, all right, honey," she said.

. . .

I flew through the front door and down the stone steps to the driveway, where Greg and Jill were waiting in Greg's idling tank-like Mercedes.

I got in and fell against the backseat. None of us said a word for several minutes. Then it was Jill who spoke first.

"I'm sorry, Ellen."

I paused. "What happened, Jill?" Jill knew that I didn't mean tonight.

Her head rested against the cold glass window. "Remember when I went to Parker's house in Nantucket?"

Of course I did.

They had been out on one of Parker's family's boats and were going to go water-skiing on the sound. "I had never been before, so I was nervous," said Jill. "And Mr. Collins was being so nice." Parker's father wasn't supposed to have been there that week; he was supposed to have gone back to New Jersey after the weekend, but he had stayed. "It was Mr. Collins, Parker and her two brothers, and her mother. Her brothers were both in the water, and I was going to go next."

"Go grab a wet suit, Jill," said Mr. Collins, pointing to a locker from his post behind the wheel. He was younger then, but his blond hair was still nearly white. He had those muscular calves you sometimes see on active middle-aged men and his chest hair peeked out from the neck of his navy blue polo.

Jill began digging through the thick black skins, trying to look like she knew what she was doing. She didn't want the Collinses to know that she had never worn a wet suit. She didn't want the Collinses to know that her summers weren't full of clambakes and yachts and madras.

"I don't think we have one that'll fit," said Parker. "Stephen and Chris both have the larges." Jill felt herself redden, self-conscious enough already in the new bikini her mother had bought her for the trip.

Mr. Collins ignored Parker and hurried to help Jill, who heard the squeak of his boat shoes on the deck behind her. "Let me help you, sweetie," he said.

He pulled out a short suit and held it up, then unzipped it and bent down, holding the neck open for Jill. "Just step right in," he said.

Mr. Collins's back was to his family, and over his bent form, Jill looked at Parker, who was eyeing her intently, as tense as a cat ready to spring. Parker's mother was staring deliberately out to sea, her blue eyes vacant and fixed on the line where ocean met sky.

Jill placed one foot, then the next, tentatively in the leg holes, and Mr. Collins jerked hard on the wet suit, pulling it up over Jill's thick thighs. Jill grabbed a railing to steady herself. Holding the waist of the suit, Mr. Collins tugged it again and again, until it stretched over the lower half of her body. Then, as if checking for fit, he cupped his hand between Jill's legs, holding it there for a moment, then slowly moving it back and forth. "Good," he said, giving Jill a wink.

"It was like it was nothing," said Jill. She stared helplessly at Parker, who just looked coldly back at her, watching their every move.

Mr. Collins then guided each arm into the suit with quick, efficient, no-nonsense motions. His eyes were on his work as, one at a time, he ran his fingers inside her bikini top and over her bare breast, pulling the fabric back into place like he was just making a minor adjustment before finally hauling up the zipper.

"And do you believe that I actually got in the water and tried to water-ski?" asked Jill. She didn't know what else to do. No one else reacted, so neither did she. But the next day, after lying awake in her bed all night, petrified that he would come in, she called her mother and told her that she wanted to go home. She never told anyone what had happened.

"What do you even call it, what he did?" asked Jill when she had finished. Had he molested her? Had he sexually assaulted her? What was it that he had done, in full view of his wife and daughter? What?

Jill didn't see Parker for the rest of the summer. Though Jill wasn't aware of it for weeks, by the time school had started, Parker had already begun her campaign against her. I could see it now, the way Parker's mind had worked. *Who would believe that my father would touch that fat pig?* So the Jillie Jelly picture was circulated as a cruel, childish way to discredit anything that Jill might say. Jill had become a pariah so that she couldn't become a victim.

Greg took deep, angry breaths while Jill told the story, and he was still unable to speak as he pulled up to my parents' house. I imagined that he, like Jill, was incapable of feeling what I unexpectedly now felt: deep and unqualified sympathy for Parker. Parker, who watched her father touch her friend, watched her mother ignore it. Parker, who endured God knew what herself. Parker, who was desperately trying to become a fine Christian wife, thinking that maybe, *maybe*, if she was good enough, Philip wouldn't stray.

From the backseat, I wrapped my arms around Jill's neck. "I'll call you, okay?"

"Ellen, I really am sorry. I know I screwed things up for you."

I shook my head. "Don't worry."

I took my time walking up to the house, opting to go around to the back and taking slow steps as I assessed the damage of the evening. There was no way I could continue working for Philip; that was clear. But that should have been clear days ago. I thought about Parker and Philip, and what, if anything, this meant for them. I suspected nothing. They were probably on their way home right now, riding in silence. Once at the house, Parker would go right to bed while Philip sat in his office, slowly draining a bottle of liquor. The next morning Philip would make pancakes for the kids while Parker slept late, and that would be that. Swept right under the rug.

As I walked in the house, I thought that the worst was over.

CHAPTER THIRTY-FIVE

I don't know what made me knock on his office door. And I don't know what made me open it when there was no answer. My father had left his desk lamp on, but on countless nights before I had walked past the dim light escaping from the gap above the floor without a second thought. Tonight, though, I turned the knob.

At first I couldn't move; I was frozen for three interminable heartbeats with blood roaring through my ears as my mind worked furiously to scroll through the possible explanations for why my father was lying facedown on the floor: heart attack . . . stroke . . . aneurism. Then I saw the vomit and I knew. I ran to him and knelt down. "Dad!" I said loudly, with my face next to his. He didn't move. There wasn't even a rise and fall of his chest.

I know that I grabbed the phone; I know I dialed 911. But those memories are vague and cloudy. What I do remember, what I can still replay in my head with absolute clarity, is picking up my father's hand, closing my eyes, and praying. Stripped of everything else, every pretense, every shred of pride, I had nothing left in me but my desire for my father to live. With my eyes closed, all I heard were my whispered pleas to God, and my breath. I don't know how long it was before the paramedics got there, but when they came rushing in I told them what had happened.

"My father's tried to kill himself." It came out so matter-of-fact.

I didn't know what he had taken, but I knew what he had done. Only later did we find the bottle of vodka, along with an empty bottle of tranquilizers, placed neatly in the wastebasket under his desk beneath a stack of papers. On his chair was a note written on his monogrammed stationery. It had the name of his insurance company, where he had a sizable life policy that he had purchased decades ago, a policy that didn't have a suicide clause.

I rode in the back of the ambulance, still holding my father's hand and still praying as the paramedics moved about, communicating with each other in a brisk, austere language all their own. At the hospital I called my family. I found a secluded corner of the waiting room and turned against the wall. I called my mother at least a dozen times, but her phone was in the pocket of her mink coat, vibrating mutely in the catacomb of the Arnolds' foyer closet. Luke answered right away, sounding tipsy and relaxed. *Get Kat and come to Allen Memorial. It's Dad.*

I weighed the phone in my hand for a few moments, pretending to debate doing what I had wanted to do all along. Then I called Mark. I was always going to call Mark. I called him because I knew he would come; I called him because I never should have left him. And tragedy has a way of delivering a brand of clarity all its own.

"Ellen?" he said tentatively.

When I heard his voice, feeling rushed back into my numb heart. I couldn't formulate words over my tears.

"Ellen, what's wrong?"

"It's my dad," I wept. The veins in my neck felt like they were strangling me.

"Where are you?" he asked, urgent but calm.

I told him.

"I'll be right there."

Though I never intended to admit it, waiting for Mark to arrive was more excruciating than waiting for the ambulance. As the automatic doors of the hospital silently parted, he rushed through. Our eyes met and he came to me. With vomit still on the knees of my black panty hose, I fell into him. His body yielded slightly but was tense.

At first, he was gentle but clinical, asking questions. "What did he take? Have the doctors been out yet? Where is your mother? Should I go and get her?"

I clung to his jacket like a child. "No, please don't go. Please."

He was next to me when I told my mother. She had gotten all the way home before she checked her phone. She had seen the state of my father's office and the note on his chair and she knew. "He'll be okay, Mom," I whimpered. "I promise he'll be okay."

My mother arrived before Luke and Kat. Perhaps it was the shock, but when she saw Mark, it was as though she had expected him to be there. Like he belonged there, next to me. Luke was the same way, nodding in acknowledgment before asking about Dad. Only Kat, whom Mark had never met, recoiled a bit when she saw him, her tear-streaked face suspicious and wary. But as we all sat together on the immobilized blue pleather chairs, waiting for news, even Kat let her guard down.

It was the middle of the night when a tired-looking doctor in blue scrubs came out and told us that my father would live. "He will be unconscious for a while still," said the doctor, seeming a bit put out by the wastefulness of it all, the needlessness of this entirely preventable event. There are blessedly few moments like that in life, when you see someone you love teetering on the stark line that separates life from death, light from dark. And when I found out that my father had landed in the light, it was as if the hand that had been twisting my chest suddenly released its grip, and I could breathe.

After relief flooded our bodies, after we thanked, thanked, thanked the doctor, after we wrapped our arms around one another in shared gratitude, it became quiet. Mom and Luke both stepped aside to make phone calls—Mom to Aunt Kathy and Luke to Mitch. Mark excused himself. I collapsed into a chair. Kat, who had stayed on the fringes of the group, pushed away from the wall against which she had been leaning and walked toward me. She took the seat next to me and rested her elbows on her knees, the look on her face ancient and sad. Her full lips were cracked and peeling, with a hairline strip of dried blood forming in one of the ridges. She had been uncharacteristically silent as we held our vigil, even when she learned that my mother and I had been at the Arnolds' party when it happened.

"It was Christian Arnold," was all she said. And there, under the buzz of the fluorescent lights, in a waiting room surrounded by strangers whose loved ones were hidden behind those steel doors, I finally understood. I understood the anger that had surfaced in Kat that night when she walked into my parents' house to see the Arnolds at their table. We had all betrayed her without even knowing it.

I breathed a sound of recognition. *Christian Arnold,* I repeated to myself. I had long ago stopped wondering who the father was. I sometimes even doubted that Kat herself was sure. But while Kat was wild, she hadn't run rampant. Though she neither confirmed nor denied it, I had heard hushed conversations between my parents about the overnight trip that Kat had taken with the boys' and girls' varsity lacrosse teams, and its coincidental, suspicious timing with her pregnancy. Christian played lacrosse. I believe that he went on to be captain, the spring that Kat officially dropped out of school.

"I never told anyone," she said. "Only him."

"Oh, Kat." I took her hand. And she let me. Then she rested her head on my shoulder and closed her wet eyes.

. . .

When my father regained consciousness, Mark waited while my mother, Luke, Kat, and I went in to see him. I imagined that we would cautiously surround his bed, whispering our greetings like lullabies. *We love you, Dad. We are so glad you're okay.* But as soon as my mother saw him, her jaw clenched and her hands formed tiny fists and she rushed his bed, beating at his legs like they were snakes under the blanket. Her admonishments were strung between sobs. "How dare you? How could you? How could you try to leave me?" She wept and wailed and pounded at him until he caught her hands and their foreheads met and they cried, their tears mixing.

Kat knelt by the foot of his bed, weeping in the silent, muffled way that Kat sometimes did. My father's hand reached down and tried to find the top of her head. "I'm so sorry, Kat, my little girl. I'm so sorry." His words came out in sorrowful sputters, and I knew that his apology extended far beyond the events that had brought us all here.

Luke wrapped his arm around me and inched me closer to

the bed, and my mother reached up and grabbed his hand. "Hold hands," my mother commanded softly, her voice shaky. Kat clasped my father's hand; Luke and Kat held mine. My mother closed her eyes and began a prayer of thanks.

When she had finished, I kissed my father on the cheek and looked at my mother, who nodded. She knew what I had to do. And so without a word I left the room and went back to find Mark. He was sitting with his eyes closed, his feet propped up on the chair across from him. His breath was the slow and steady sort that comes on the brink of sleep. I sat next to him, then reached over to pick up his hand, cradling it in both of mine. He took a jagged, startled breath and opened his eyes.

"Mark," I said, staring at the dry, red patches over his knuckles. "I'm so sorry."

He looked at me but did not speak.

Seeing the wariness in his eyes brought on fresh tears. "Please?" I pleaded. "Please forgive me?"

"I'm not going to give up the ministry, Ellen."

I pulled myself onto his lap and wrapped my arms around his neck. "I don't want you to," I said, my damp face hiding in his neck. "I don't want you to change."

And then his hands slowly found their place on my back.

CHAPTER THIRTY-SIX

It is seven months later and I'm sitting next to my mother, four rows away from the pulpit at Prince of Peace Church. Mitch and Luke are on my other side. Mark is speaking this morning on grace, on the idea that God's love is without conditions. Sometimes I still notice the curious stares from the other congregants. *That's the pastor's girlfriend. I hear she's not even a Christian.* But it's not enough to make me run, not even close.

My father was kept in the hospital for several days after that night. We all stayed, taking shifts to ensure he would rarely be alone. And it was during that time, when we were so grateful to have one another, so grateful to be a part of our family—our flawed, imperfect family—that my mother first met Mitch.

Mitch had come because he loved Luke. It was really that simple, that plain. He didn't intend to infringe on what he assumed was a private, delicate time, and so he met Luke at a small table in the hospital cafeteria. He and Mitch were still there when my mother returned earlier than expected from one of her brief, infrequent dashes home to shower and change clothes. She was headed for the elevator when she saw them, sitting with their heads inclined, holding hands discreetly under the table. She faltered for a second; then, feeling her stare, Luke turned his head and met her eyes.

I don't know what Luke expected her to do, but it certainly wasn't to walk calmly to their table and shake Mitch's hand. "I'm Patty Carlisle," she said. "You must be Mitch." No one knows how she knew his name. Maybe one of us had slipped and said it. Maybe she had known it all along. Either way, Luke hadn't expected her to say it with such warmth. "The Lord prepared my heart." That's what my mother says when asked about that moment. "He used me to demonstrate his grace." I tend to think it was one of those rare, pure instances when we don't put qualifications on love. When we need it so desperately, so urgently, that we accept it when it's offered. So maybe my mother and I are really saying the same thing.

It didn't happen instantly, Mitch becoming part of our family. It happened slowly, gradually, in a series of increasingly frequent meetings, some more tense than others. It's still happening. And there is still far to go. But it's better. And I'll take better.

Less than a month after my father was released from the hospital, my parents had to leave their home. We all helped them pack and move their things—Kat, Luke, Mitch, Mark, and I—into a rented two-bedroom condo in Kat's complex. My mother stared at the house as they pulled away, quoting softly from the Book of Matthew, " 'Lay not up for yourselves treasures upon earth, where moth and rust corrupt . . . But lay up for yourselves treasures in heaven . . . For where your treasure is, there will your heart be also.' " My father rested his hand on her knee as they drove off.

We have found many small mercies in their situation. My father, having taken a desk job with the commercial construction company of an old associate, has a steady but relatively small paycheck. And though much of what would be considered their "wealth" was lost, their IRAs remained intact. My father still hopes to rebuild his business, but he knows it will be a long road, maybe too long a road at his age. He keeps himself busy, though, and is with Kat this morning, looking at possible spaces for a new salon she's hoping to open. My mother, having found that a forty-year gap in employment is problematic in today's job market, has taken a more active role in managing my parents' finances and continues to volunteer at the family center, where I sometimes join her.

I never returned to Kent & Wagner. After a few days, I called and left a message for Philip. It was brief and to the point. I didn't hear back from him. I sent an e-mail to Brenda in which I apologized for leaving so suddenly, and congratulated her on becoming a grandmother. We exchanged a few more e-mails, the last of which indicated that she had given her notice at Kent & Wagner and was moving to Chicago. "I can be a secretary anywhere," she wrote. "But I can only be a grandmother there."

Jill is due in a matter of days with a baby boy that they are naming Gregory Jr., after his father. She has asked me to be his godmother. "And when you and Mark get married, Greg Jr. can be your ring bearer," she suggested, pushing, as always, for us to "make it official."

Later, I'll go to work at the Italian restaurant where I waitress several nights a week. It's not a career, but it helps supplement my gig as an intern at the magazine where Mitch works. "They are going to offer you something permanent soon, Elle," promised Mitch, who got me the position. But I don't mind paying my dues, even if it means being the oldest intern in the history of the publication. I live simply, in a studio apartment near Mark, and use the money from my divorce settlement to get me by until I have an actual salary.

Soon Mark's sermon will end, and he'll step away from the pulpit, looking at me as he makes his way down the center aisle. He'll spend a while greeting the congregation, patiently listening, nodding his head and offering comfort, hope, and kindness. I'll stare at him as he gets pulled from conversation to conversation, and I'll see him sneak glances at me as I talk with my mother, Luke, and Mitch.

My mother will leave first—there is a new church that she has heard wonderful things about, and she is just dying to visit it. Mitch and Luke will then walk to Luke's car, holding hands, two people who love each other.

I'll wait for Mark.

And though I still don't know what I am, or how to define my beliefs, I know, beyond a shadow of a doubt, that I am blessed.

Photo by Shem Roose

Sarah Healy lives in Vermont with her husband and three sons.

Can I Get an Amen?

. . .

SARAH HEALY

A CONVERSATION WITH
SARAH HEALY

Spoiler Alert: The Conversation with Sarah Healy and Questions for Discussion that follow tell more about what happens in the book than you might want to know until after you read it.

Q. Can I Get an Amen? *is your first novel. How did you take up writing, and why were you inspired to write this book in particular?*

A. I never expected to be a writer. That I have managed to become one comes as the most pleasant kind of shock. I was in my late twenties and had just had my first child when I realized that it was what I wanted to do, and so I quietly set to work. My exposure to writing in college was limited to mandatory, requirement-filling English classes, to which I am ashamed to say I put in only a cursory effort. So I had a lot of catching up to do. For five years I wrote constantly, without really trying to get anything published. I began with nonfiction essays— personal pieces on my life and family—as an attempt to try to teach myself the craft. The idea to write about a Christian family was born out of one of those essays. And I actually think attempting nonfiction first was a great way to get started, as writing is essentially telling the truth, even in fiction. Every story has its truth; you need to discover it and then tell it.

Q. How long did it take you to write the novel?

A. I remember sitting at my kitchen table on a sunny day in late July and typing the first sentence. Then the next. The story that had been in my mind became fully shaped in the execution of that first chapter. From that point on, I worked as feverishly as my children and job would allow. Each night, I went up to my room, sat on my bed, and wrote about a thousand words. That was my goal: at least a thousand words a night, at least six nights a week. That level of discipline might sound excessive, but being pregnant with my third child, I had something of a deadline in mind. And I did let myself slow down a bit toward the end. The first draft was finished in about four months. While I suppose the pace was rigorous, I wouldn't have done it any other way. By working so constantly, I never had to get my head back into the plot or the characters; there wasn't any ponderous, "Now, where was I . . . ?" I always knew exactly where I was; I always remembered the tone of a scene.

Q. I suspect that many readers will see something of themselves in your protagonist, Ellen Carlisle. Is she you?

A. The unsatisfying but honest answer is: not really. I have imposed a number of my opinions, frustrations, and fears on poor Ellen. But she is very much a unique character in my mind, distinct from myself. She also rises to the occasion more than I think I could, given her circumstances; I would indulge in a bit more self-pity. I would have drowned my sorrows in spinach dip.

Q. Few writers of contemporary women's fiction have tackled religion in a thoughtful but entertaining way, as you do here. Why do you think that is? Why did you want to write about it?

A. To be honest, I didn't *want* to write about it. And I certainly didn't want to tackle it. I think this was one of those cases where your subject chooses you; I found myself writing about Christianity in spite of myself. And once I realized that I was in some way compelled to pursue this topic, I knew that I wouldn't be doing it justice by just sticking my toe in, so it ended up taking center stage in my first novel. Now, that's not to say that I thought it was a good idea. For the duration of my work on *Can I Get an Amen?* I couldn't imagine that anyone would actually want to read it. But I've come to believe that it's the subjects that make you a little nervous, those that make you shift in your chair and glance over your shoulder, that prove the most fertile.

Q. I had a strong reaction to the scene in which Ellen is sitting in church and hears her mother's prayer request for the healing of her infertility and divorce. Did something in particular inspire that memorable scene?

A. Perhaps this says something about my sense of humor, but I actually think that is one of the funnier scenes in the book. Of course, it turns into one of the saddest, but that may be why I find it so resonant. Sadness lends humor poignancy; it gives it more than a single note. And while I can't recall a personal experience exactly analogous to the request made for Ellen, I'm sure my mother's prayer group knows much more about my personal life than she lets on.

Q. Family lies at the heart of Can I Get an Amen? *Can you tell us something about your own family? Did you grow up in New Jersey?*

A. I did grow up in New Jersey, in a big, close-knit family with born-again Christian parents. And as soon as I was old enough to be embarrassed about anything, I was embarrassed about religion. I'm sure part of that was simply pubescent angst, searching for a source of humiliation like a heat-seeking missile. And, like all thirteen-year-olds, I viewed my parents as inexcusably bizarre.

(Although, let's be honest, I think I had a better case than most . . .) However, what was once embarrassing has become endearing. And I would never be able to write *anything* without the unflinching support of my family.

Q. Often writers say that they couldn't find the kind of book that they wanted to read, so they decided to write it themselves. Is that true for you? What do you like to read?

A. There are so many amazing writers out there that I find plenty of books that I want to read. That being said, I haven't come across many that deal with religion—and, really, Christianity specifically—in a way that doesn't seem loaded. Books involving Christianity tend to have the agenda of recruitment and conversion—or just the opposite. In *Can I Get An Amen?* I wanted religion to serve as a medium for a story full of compelling, sympathetic characters. And I love characters—that's the common denominator in everything that I enjoy reading: great, quirky, flawed, familiar characters.

Q. What are you working on now? What do you hope to explore in your writing over the long term?

A. I am at work on my second novel, which again deals with family and love. And again, it is set in New Jersey. Though I live in Vermont now, I'm still a Jersey girl at heart.

QUESTIONS
FOR DISCUSSION

1. Have you ever played with a Ouija board? Attended church school of some kind? Are you willing to fess up and share your experiences?

2. What was your general reaction to the novel? What did you like and not like about it?

3. Which characters did you especially enjoy? Did they all ring true for you?

4. Did you have any sympathy for Ellen's husband, Gary, who divorces her because she can't have a child? What would you do in a similar situation? Do you think men and women tend to approach infertility in very different ways?

5. What do you think of the way Sarah Healy explores faith? Did the novel make you think about how faith can both bring families together and tear them apart? Did you find the depiction of religion respectful?

6. Would you say that you currently practice more or less religion than you were brought up with? What role has religion played in your own family?

7. Ellen's mother, Patty, accuses her of being closed-minded about religion. In what ways might that be true? In what ways might the same criticism be lobbed back at Patty?

8. Ellen realizes that no one has ever asked her what religious beliefs she holds. People in church assume they know and everyone else steers clear of the subject. Has that been your experience? Why don't we talk about our religious beliefs? Do we lose something by failing to?

9. Though Ellen seems ambivalent about Christianity, she always seems to turn to prayer during her most desperate times. Is it out of habit? Or do you think it signifies a deeper belief than she wants to admit?

10. It's ironic that Ellen's mother, Patty, makes Ellen's divorce and infertility public through a prayer request, yet Ellen's parents won't tell even their own children about their imminent bankruptcy. What do you think is going on in Patty's and Roger's minds to make such inconsistency possible? Have you ever found yourself in a similar situation, with someone accusing you of one thing while being guilty of it themselves?

11. In the novel, Sarah Healy gently bursts what some might consider religious fantasies—for example, the idea that "being Christian" and attending church will somehow protect us from bad things happening, and that the material goods we buy are "blessings" from God. Without getting into specific religious beliefs, can you think of other current religious fictions?

12. Abortion is another highly sensitive subject that is rarely explored in contemporary women's fiction. Do you think Patty was right in insisting that Kat give birth and then give her child up for adoption? Compare the "choice" Kat had in the mid-1990s to the choice that Patty had in the 1960s. Do you think our

society has made any progress in finding common ground regarding this controversial issue?

13. Parker Kent is the villain of the novel, but Ellen has some sympathy for her at the end. Discuss the price that Parker pays to keep her marriage intact. What do you think Parker knew and didn't know about her father's behavior toward Jill during that visit to Nantucket? Do you think Parker's complicity back then influenced the kind of marriage she ended up having?

14. Have you ever dated a minister, or been a minister looking for dates? What particular challenges do ministers face in their love lives? Discuss some of the reasons why the love interest in women's fiction is so rarely a minister. And, by the way, what did you think of Mark?

15. Unconditional love, both human and divine, is a theme in this book. Do you think it's possible to love unconditionally?

16. Did you find the end of the novel satisfying? If the book continued, what do you think would happen to the characters? What would you like to see happen to them?

17. In the last line of the novel, Ellen states that she still doesn't know what she is, or how to define her beliefs. Can you sympathize with her uncertainty?

Keep an eye out for Sarah Healy's next novel,

GOD SAVE THE QUEEN

Available in paperback and e-book
in the summer of 2013

Jenna Parsons grew up on Royal Court, but her life
is no fairy tale. Her eccentric twin brother is missing.
Her mother, a former beauty queen, is afraid of being
alone. And Jenna herself has a daughter, a house in the
suburbs, and a live-in boyfriend—but no ring on her
finger. She's not expecting a happily-ever-after ending,
but is a normal, ordinary life too much to expect? Or
is it in the broken places where the richest treasures lie?